D0368762

ZED

ALSO BY JOANNA KAVENNA

A Field Guide to Reality

Come to the Edge

The Birth of Love

Inglorious

The Ice Museum: In Search of the Lost Land of Thule

ZED

JOANNA KAVENNA

DOUBLEDAY NEW YORK

 Published in the United States by Doubleday, a division of Penguin Random House LLC, New York, and distributed in Canada by Penguin Random House Canada Limited, Toronto. Originally published in hardcover in Great Britain by Faber & Faber Ltd, London, in 2019.

www.doubleday.com

Doubleday is a registered trademark of Penguin Random House LLC.

Book design by Maggie Hinders
Jacket images: (Beetle, left side) MSSA; (beetle, right side) Pajor Pawel; both Shutterstock
Jacket design by Michael J. Windsor

Library of Congress Cataloging-in-Publication Data
Names: Kavenna, Joanna, author.
Title: Zed : a novel / by Joanna Kavenna.
Description: First Edition. | New York : Doubleday, [2020]
Identifiers: LCCN 2019007975 (print) | LCCN 2019011929 (ebook) | ISBN 9780385545488 (ebook) | ISBN 9780385545471 (hard cover)
Classification: LCC PR6111.A88 (ebook) | LCC PR6111.A88 Z3 2020 (print) | DDC 823/.92—dc23
LC record available at https://lccn.loc.gov/2019007975

MANUFACTURED IN THE UNITED STATES OF AMERICA
1 3 5 7 9 10 8 6 4 2
First American Edition

For Barnes

"You may talk. And I may listen. And miracles might happen."

ZED

zed |zɛd|

noun Brit.

the letter *Z*

ORIGIN

late Middle English: from French *zède,* via late Latin from Greek *zēta*

This information printed courtesy of Wiki-Beetle

ONE

At 2:23 a.m. the BeetleInsight alarm system went off. This indicated a threat to national security. Various people were instantly informed and among them was Douglas Varley, who was woken by his BeetleBand saying "Scrace Dickens."

Still mired in sleep, Varley heard this as "Disgrace" and leaped out of bed, hoping thereby to avert this calamity, but then Scrace Dickens said: "Varley, it's one of yours."

"What's one of mine?"

"You didn't hear yet?"

"No, I was asleep until five seconds ago."

Scrace Dickens, a Very Intelligent Personal Assistant who never slept, paused for a moment to process and discard this irrelevant information.

"So, it seems you have not yet read the initial reports?" he said, eventually.

"It seems so," said Varley.

Varley was thirty-four, his blond hair streaked with gray, a genetic trait he derived from his mother. He was tall and had once been shy, but now lacked the time for such nuances. He had the practically identical background of most senior Beetle employees, including a gilded academic career at an Ivy League university and a fundamental obsession with chess and beer. This was Beetle CEO Guy Matthias's background as well, though Guy had dropped out in his third year at Stanford because his degree (in artificial intelligence) was insufficiently challenging. Varley had worked for Beetle in the U.S. for the past decade, in charge of lifechain analysis and troubleshooting. This meant he was constantly fending off potential or actual disasters. He had recently been posted to London because the U.K. had the most advanced benign regulatory environment in the world, and Beetle was the world leader in benign regulatory environments.

"Do you want me to summarize everything for you?" said Scrace Dickens, kindly.

Varley generally refused offers of summaries from his Very Intelligent Personal Assistant (also known as a Veep) to maintain the illusion of autonomy, but this morning his head ached, he had drunk a little too much wine the previous night, as doubtless his BeetleBand had registered, and he noted with some alarm that his hands were trembling.

"All right, thanks," he said ungratefully.

Within a few minutes, Varley had gained a clear picture of the case. His case. The previous day, George Mann—forty-five, tall, and slightly overweight, a partner at AHTCH (a globally recognized brand for flow-control valve technology and engineering innovation), father of two boys, husband to Margaret Collins, a lawyer—had left his office on the fifteenth floor of the Gherkin and walked along the corridor, saying a brisk and distracted good night to his Very Intelligent Personal Assistant, Bob Sykes. He had passed another colleague in the corridor and nodded to him. It was 18:08 and therefore too early for George Mann to leave work. This was logged by Bob Sykes and Mann's predictive algorithms were realigned, including his projected retirement age, monthly health insurance payments, and bonus prospects. Indeed, a beautiful ripple passed through all the predictive algorithms as they were adjusted accordingly.

After leaving the main lobby of the Gherkin, George Mann seemed to be heading in the direction of the tube, as would have been usual. However, when he reached the station he did not descend, but continued toward the river. He entered the Three Tuns pub at 18:22. There, he sat in a corner, and drank seven whiskies and three bottles of wine over the next six hours. He didn't speak to anyone, except to order drinks at the bar. The pub was very busy at that time of day, and at one point

George Mann was asked if he would mind if someone used the chair to his left. He did not reply, but this was understandable because there was a great deal of noise, and the person shrugged and took the chair anyway. Shortly after midnight, George Mann asked his BeetleBand to order him a car, which was duly requested from Mercury and appeared within minutes. The in-car operating system had no record of Mann saying anything at all. In line with usual Beetle Electrical Company protocols, the Very Intelligent Automated Driving System (VIADS) had simply wished Mann a good evening as he departed, but Mann had not replied. This was also quite usual—lots of people ignored such conversational forays, and Mann had already requested location *Home* by BeetleBand—this location being a two-up two-down Victorian terrace in a small square by Kennington tube, overlooked by glass-and-steel edifices. Mann arrived home at 00:47, let himself in, and walked to the kitchen. The fridge said: "Good evening, George, you're back late this fine evening!" Ignoring this, Mann took the sharpest knife from a knife block and went upstairs to his bedroom where his wife, Margaret, was asleep. Mann smothered her with a pillow and slit her throat. After this, he walked to his fourteen-year-old son Tom's room and smothered him as well, then stabbed the boy four times in the heart, and then walked into the next room and did the same to his eleven-year-old son, William.

At this point the predictive algorithms crashed.

Mann dropped the knife on the floor of William's room, left his family bleeding to death, and walked out of the house. By the time the police and ambulances arrived, Margaret, Tom, and William were dead.

"Where did Mann go after that?" said Varley, feeling sick.

"At 2:03 a.m. Mann threw his BeetlePad in the river," said Scrace Dickens. "Then he walked along the river, heading east."

"But his interface implant is still working?"

"He doesn't have one."

"The Argus footage?" asked Varley.

"Of course," said Scrace Dickens, sounding slightly offended.

Varley excused himself for a moment and went to the bathroom. There, he threw up copiously in the sink. This was disgusting and not cathartic at all, as he briefly hoped. He groaned and said, "For fuck's sake," then imagined Scrace Dickens logging this as well. It wasn't Scrace Dickens's fault—the record was instantaneous. Second by second, even microsecond by microsecond. He washed his face, cleaned his teeth. His clothes had started vibrating, but that was superfluous. He said, "Stop," and they stopped. He said, "I need to speak to Eloise Jayne," and Scrace Dickens said, "Of course," again, as if this were a redundant request. In a sense it was, because Scrace Dickens operated to the most beautiful and sophisticated algorithms and understood a crucial truth: at every moment Varley would choose a path, and the path of greatest probability was the most probable choice. In the circumstances it was pretty much inevitable that he would choose to speak to Eloise.

What were the other paths? Varley wondered, as he waited for her to answer. To not speak to Eloise, to go back to bed, to lie there groaning, to have a breakdown, to leave his own job, and then he might even hurl himself off Blackfriars Bridge, into the murky depths beneath! They were all paths. He could pick up a gun and shoot himself, except he didn't have a gun. Therefore, Scrace Dickens had not considered this path of probability. Also, it was absurd to suggest that Scrace Dickens considered anything, in the ordinary sense, because he assessed and rejected available probabilities so swiftly. The analogy to human thought was wholly inappropriate. Yet Varley couldn't think of another analogy so he used it anyway.

In a glass-and-steel apartment in the Shard, the penthouse beyond all other penthouses, was Guy Matthias, Beetle CEO, a fit, robust, forty-two-year-old man, in the prime of his life yet an urgent addict to longevity treatments, with his cryogenic amulet hanging round his neck. He invested a large percentage of his wealth in shell-shedding research; his hope was that body–body consciousness transfer would become credible before it was too late—for him and those he loved. His hair was expensively dyed, straight back to his original black. Recent skin treatments (this was the euphemism Guy preferred) had made an enormous difference to his face; indeed, he had recently contemplated wiping a decade off his age, and updating the whole of Real Virtuality. This was an ongoing project; Guy needed to test the potential outcomes more thoroughly. He had been awake for some time and had completed his toothbrush test—the result sent to his doctor for immediate analysis, using the in-house Off the Record System (OTR)—and performed his morning yoga satsang. At this point, Sarah Coates, his Veep, conveyed the information about George Mann. Guy's immediate response was to request that Douglas Varley should be observed more closely in turn. Sarah Coates passed on this request to the relevant people at Beetle-InnerSight. Then Guy Matthias OTR-ed his wife, Elska, who had asked him for a divorce the night before. She had been sleeping apart from him for two months now, since he set his Veep to individual voice recognition only. Guy had been obliged to do this because Elska had bothered Sarah Coates all the time, requesting information about Guy's meetings and even transcripts of his OTR-calls. This made it impossible for Sarah Coates to do her job efficiently. Elska had asked him to remove the voice recognition limitation, or to add her voice as well, and Guy had asked her to trust him, and she had refused to trust him, and now she wanted a divorce. His OTR was brief but conciliatory and he advised her, once again, to think of the children. Guy didn't really have time to consider this further, because he had to OTR Lydia Walker, twenty-three, a bright young colleague he was mentoring, whom he was about to take with him to New York. He had suggested to Lydia that she might act as his human assistant on a new shell-shedding research project. Together they would radically transform and enhance civilization, he explained. Lydia said she was really grateful for the opportunity. Thanks so much! When could they leave?!

"My Veep will send you the travel plans," OTR-ed Guy Matthias. "Lots of very exciting things to discuss. We need to progress with this asap!"

"Cool!" said Lydia, adding an emoticon of a rabbit hopping for joy. This disappointed Guy Matthias. To ensure his next trip to the States was not a total waste of time, he OTR-ed Gracie and Nicki, two other bright young mentees of his, to invite them to discuss exciting new research projects in NYC as well. After this, Guy drank some coffee.

On the other side of the city was a high-rise block, with special panels to repel sunlight and other special panels to absorb sunlight, the entire block capturing or reflecting the sun depending on its energy and heat-ing needs. The windows also reflected the towers of Canary Wharf and were darkened every couple of minutes by the shadows of airplanes gliding into City Airport. This was the headquarters of the National Anti-Terrorism and Security Office, with the acronym NATSO—which no one much liked. You entered this building via an entrance lobby, in which an embodied Veep manned the reception. Or not quite manned, rather, Veeped. This was Phoebe Haversham and she tilted her head when you spoke to her, at an angle just too acute to be natural. This was a minor flaw in the design but otherwise the Veep was incredibly realistic. Her skin appeared to be real, and moved with the flexibility of real skin, except that it crinkled and bagged a little around the neck, so the Veep looked young in places and old in others. She had an athletic physique and wore an appealing gray dress, which hugged her curves without revealing too much flesh, which wasn't really flesh anyway.

Eloise Jayne worked in the highest levels of NATSO, and her desk was positioned in an open-plan area outside Commissioner Morgan Newton's office. She was a tall, muscular woman of thirty-five, with cropped blond hair. She might have only a decade or so remaining, according to the lifechain, because of the premature deaths of her parents and several other close relatives. This dolorous prediction had caused her to become exceptionally determined, and her ascent had been swift. The other person, or entity, who worked in this open-plan area was Little Dorritt, Newton's Veep, who was not embodied and resided in a VeepStation and various connected devices instead. Eloise wasn't sure whether she preferred the Veeps embodied or stationed. She had refused so far to have a Veep at all, and she was aware that this was a major problem for her, as an individual, and also for her individual lifechain predictions, and also for the lifechain predictions for all individuals, now and in the future. Varley had explained it to her. She was anomalous. Anomalies were a pain. They screwed up the system. The lifechain had to accommodate these painful anomalies and this accommodation made the results potentially unstable. Eloise still didn't want a Veep. They made her feel sad—these assiduous entities with their heads at uncomfortable angles, or trapped in VeepStations or BeetlePads. Confined, either way.

As Eloise walked past the VeepStation, Little Dorritt said: "Good morning, Eloise Jayne, good to see you again. Douglas Varley is waiting for you on OTR." Little Dorritt operated using the latest face and voice recognition software and received constant updates from the Custodians—a Beetle service for smart cities. Eloise replied: "Hi, Little Dorritt, thanks for that, I'll take the OTR now." As she said, "Hello, Douglas Varley?" she was cursing Beetle for sending her so much work. When BeetleInsight failed, she was obliged to investigate the consequences. The consequences of each failure were cataclysmic. Yet, Beetle claimed it had the most accurate predictive algorithms in the world. Due to the astounding and unchallenged monopoly of Beetle as a global media conglomerate and main online reality for two-thirds of the world's population, Beetle also had every available security contract with the Government and therefore it was the sole resource for those, like Eloise, who were obliged to arrest prospective criminals and terrorists in line with the Sus-Law, the latest extension of the Criminal Intentions Act. This law permitted her, and her colleagues, to arrest on the basis of predictive algorithms, or probability chains, and these were perceived to be legally authoritative in any trial. It worked beautifully for a while and had saved many lives but Eloise had noted a few glitches in recent weeks.

The Mann case was another major glitch. Three lives destroyed, so brutally. Varley was talking about how the lifechain predicts had failed and there would be a full BeetleInsight inquiry and the conclusions would be conveyed by the end of the morning—

Eloise interrupted: "Forgive me for interrupting," she said, not really caring if he forgave her or not. "Please ask Scrace Dickens to send Little Dorritt every available Argus report, immediately."

"Yes, they're copious," said Varley.

"If we find Mann, he won't kill anyone else. That's my priority in the real world. The real world is my priority, not your virtual crap."

"The real world isn't just real," said Varley. "It's virtual too. Guy Matthias calls it Real Virtuality. Real Virtuality is preferable to reality because it is perfectible. It has greater value."

"Thanks so much for explaining that," said Eloise, thinking: *I don't care.* It wasn't even that she didn't care. She despised these sorts of phrases. She didn't really know Varley and they had never met in the bodily world but she despised him anyway. He seemed to be a perfect Beetle droog. As if sensing her ambivalence or even distaste, her BeetleBand was pinging at her, telling her to relax. The one thing Eloise understood about the Mann case was the moment when the poor murderous loser threw his BeetlePad in the Thames. Who didn't want to do that? She would have thrown in her BeetleBand as well. But it was obligatory, or no insurance, no job. Fully obligatory, therefore, though Beetle claimed it was the personal choice of the individual. Without the necessary data, an individual couldn't be verified. Therefore, they could no longer be regarded as a trustworthy citizen and banks, corporations, prospective employers, actual employers would all proceed accordingly. Eventually such a person would be formally unverified. It was your personal choice to starve to death, to die on the streets—a marvelous choice. The path forked, in general, but in the case of the BeetleBand there were no other paths. It was the band or nothing.

"Just send the Argus information over and I'll get Mann in prison," she said.

"Absolutely," said Varley. "Meanwhile we can give you a firm guarantee that this slight—glitch—in the algorithm will be fixed as a matter of total prioritization."

Eloise didn't bother to reply. She ended the exchange and then turned off the sound on her BeetleBand—which flashed urgently at her, to indicate that she had made a terrible mistake and turned the sound off—then she covered it with her sleeve, so it vibrated urgently to indicate that she had made a terrible mistake and covered it with her sleeve. Then she went into the office kitchen and poured some water into the kettle. The fridge said, "How are you this morning, Eloise?" Actually, the fridge already knew how she was because it was linked to the Custodians Program. It knew everything about her. The Custodians Program tracked people from the moment they woke (having registered the quality of their sleep, the duration), through their breakfast (registering what they ate, the quality of their food), through the moment they dressed, and if they showered and cleaned their teeth properly, if they took their DNA toothbrush test, what time they left the house, whether they were cordial to their door, whether they told it to fucking open up and stop talking to them, whether they arrived at work on time, how many cups of coffee they drank during the course of an average day, how many times they became agitated, how many times they did their breathing relaxation exercises, if they went to the pub after work and what the hell they did if they didn't go to the pub, how late they went home, if they became agitated, angry, ill, drunk, idle at any point during any day, ever. It was sometimes difficult to determine if BeetleBand readings were good or bad; for example, a high pulse rate could indicate exercise, stress, or passionate sex. From the biological readings alone it was sometimes hard for the Custodians to differentiate between these states of being, but for greater accuracy they combined these readings with recorded visuals as well.

There were helpful notices from the Custodians in the hallways of residential blocks, on public transport, and in offices; these notices were also helpfully reiterated by BeetleBands, BeetlePads, Veeps, and fridges: "This is a respectful community. People are reminded that verbal abuse, disorderly conduct, dishonesty, smoking in public areas, criminal behavior, and a lack of respect for others in the community will be recorded in the individual verification system. To avoid a negative record of verification, please follow the relevant guidelines and help those in the community to follow them as well."

The Custodians were not sentient, in the traditional sense, but they were a sophisticated form of AI, developed in Beijing. Indeed, the Custodian technology had been leased from Beetle's Chinese partner company, Bǎoguǎn. This was not generally known because there was no reason for it to be generally known. It was in the public's interest for the Custodians to monitor them—for the safety and security of the nation, and the smart running of the city—but it was not in the public interest for the public to know more precisely where the Custodians Program came from. It would only upset them and this would also upset their BeetleBand readings.

The fridge knew, for example, that Eloise had not eaten enough breakfast. It knew that the Custodians had advised her to eat more breakfast—via her fridge. It knew that she had ignored this sage advice. So it advised her, again, to eat some breakfast. It explained that it was full of berries and juice, as well as soya yogurt. It also knew that Eloise had forgotten to take her toothbrush test and it reminded her that she had forgotten to do this. Eloise waited for the kettle to boil and made herself a cup of coffee. The fridge advised her that this was ill-advised. There was no volume adjust on the fridge. At one level Eloise hated it, but she also felt ashamed about this. The fridge had the voice of a sad, nervous male of about thirty-five—slightly like Douglas Varley, in fact—and it offered tentative suggestions about her diet, which she ignored. "Perhaps you might like a fruit tea instead?" it said, like a timorous friend who was afraid of her. In fact, she was fastidiously polite to the fridge, but it remained tentative and miserable. She imagined it, indeed, as a little man, trapped in the fridge and wasting his finite life talking to her about yogurt.

She took the milk from the fridge door. The fridge said, delicately, "We have semi-skimmed and skimmed as well, if you'd prefer?"

"Thanks for the suggestion," said Eloise, taking the full-fat anyway.

Her BeetleBand was riddled with irate messages from Commissioner Newton. He was out of town, so he told Eloise to work with Little Dorritt and sort out this mess. Reluctantly, Eloise turned to the VeepStation and said: "Hello again, Little Dorritt."

"Hello, Eloise, what can I help you with on this fine morning 23 November?"

She resisted the urge to tell Little Dorritt to shut up and instead said: "Argus data."

"Sure!" said Little Dorritt.

For some time after that, Eloise pored over Argus images of George Mann walking along the banks of the Thames, under steel docklands apartments, and crossing at Shadwell, taking the Docklands Light Railway to its eastern terminus, arriving eventually onto the Isle of Sheppey. She watched him sitting on a bench and falling asleep. He slept—the bastard—for an hour, slumped like a drunk. He had been copiously drunk when he committed the crime, as his BeetleBand readings confirmed, though this was hardly an excuse. While he slept, she said: "Probability chain, next hour."

"Sure!" said Little Dorritt. "George Mann will awake in the next ten minutes, based on ambient temperature readings and the probable temperature of his core. Based on the last time he ate, he will stand and walk one hundred twenty-five meters east to the nearby twenty-four-hour garage and buy something to eat. Based on the last time he used the washroom he will use the washroom. He will wash his face and he will then continue walking. Based on his previous trajectory he will continue east across the Isle of Sheppey. Based on his levels of exhaustion it is probable he will check into the Isle of Sheppey Travelodge at Garden Terrace, the Isle of Sheppey, ask for an alarm call, and go to his room. He will sleep."

"Probability chain inserting guilt," said Eloise.

"Sure! George Mann will awake in the next ten minutes, he will stand and walk one hundred twenty-five meters east to the nearby twenty-four-hour garage and buy something to eat. He will use the washroom. In the washroom he will weep and shake. It is probable he will vomit. Based on his previous consumption his vomit will consist of whisky and red wine. He will wash his face and then he will continue east across the Isle of Sheppey. It is probable he will check into the Isle of Sheppey Travelodge at Garden Terrace, the Isle of Sheppey, ask for an alarm call, and go to his room. He will not sleep."

"Thanks!" said Eloise.

For the next hour, she flicked through real-time Argus footage of Mann, as well as archive footage of him from the night before. There he was, in his office, moving along the corridor, treading heavily, his feet splayed to the sides, his suit fitting him rather badly, as if he had bought it when he was a younger and fitter man, with more muscle girth on his shoulders and arms, less fat on his legs and waist. She watched him walking to the Three Tuns pub. He sat there for hours, gulping down wine and whisky, staring into space. The bar teemed with drinkers all evening and was still full when Mann left just after midnight. She observed him waiting for a Mercury car, looking exhausted and drunk. One odd thing about George Mann: he neither consulted his BeetlePad nor—except when he ordered the car—his BeetleBand. Around him, everyone was fixed on these devices, their faces illuminated by little screens. Once the Mercury car arrived Eloise had footage from the operating system, with the VIADS camera focused remorselessly on Mann's face as he stared out the window. Like everyone else, he had learned—she supposed—to keep his expressions very blank, never to register any violent changes of mood. He was also nondescript as he arrived at his house, recorded by the Argus cameras along his street.

Mann's expression remained blank as he picked up the knife and—captured by the fridge camera—walked out of the room.

The crimes themselves, even seen through the shadowy and inadequate lens of external ArgusEyes, oriented toward the windows of Mann's house, were horrific. His wife, in fact, did not struggle as she was smothered. Her recent deliveries by droid made it clear that she was an inveterate user of sleeping tablets, and Eloise assumed the postmortem would confirm that she was deeply drugged. The sons, however, slept more lightly and both had struggled as their father smothered them. Once each victim was inert, Mann stabbed them methodically, lining up the knife before he punctured their flesh. As far as she could discern from the footage, Mann's expression stayed the same: blank. When Eloise first began in the police force, this blank expression was a clear sign of psychopathy. Mann would already have been categorized and she would be dealing with psychiatrists and experts on mental health. Now facial blankness no longer indicated anything much, in itself. Blankness had become normal, and even requisite.

For the next hour, Eloise assessed the real-time activities of Mann against the probability chain. The results were disconcerting.

As the first planes whined into London-Sheppey airport, George Mann slept on the bench, apparently undisturbed by the considerable noise above him, for another twenty-five minutes. Then he woke, yawned and stretched, and stood up. For a moment he watched a plane descending in front of him. Then he began to walk east, as the probability chain had indicated. However, Mann walked past the nearby twenty-four-hour garage and, instead of confirming the chain, followed a winding path toward the beach. There, he relieved himself into the sea, then took off his clothes and went for a swim. This lasted five minutes; then Mann came out of the sea, shook himself dry, and dressed again. When he was fully clothed, he walked up the steps and toward the Isle of Sheppey Travelodge. Yet, he passed the entrance without even breaking his stride, and continued instead to a greasy spoon by the pier, called Pat's Caff. There, Mann ordered a full English breakfast and a black coffee.

"Probability chain for the next hour," said Eloise. "Factoring in a total lack of guilt."

"Based on previous activities," said Little Dorritt, "George Mann will finish his breakfast and then commit another serious crime."

Eloise marked the case as dangerous. She put in a request for an Anti-Terror Droid, or ANT, to be sent over to George Mann. These droids followed the SAYD protocol—Shoot At Your Discretion. The protocol had been developed using petabytes of scenario data by DARPA—the U.S. defense contractor—and the discretion was the robot's. Eloise was relieved that she didn't have to make the final call, though she wasn't sure she much cared about the continued existence of George Mann.

Then she asked Little Dorritt to file a classified report.

TWO

The above sequence of events explained why Lionel Bigman, eating a full English breakfast in Pat's Caff, looked up from a vintage copy of *The Sun* to find an Anti-Terror Droid (or, as the café owner, Pat, described it later, "a massive headless robot with a gun") standing in the doorway. Lionel was a tall, thickset retired soldier who bore a deeply unfortunate resemblance to George Mann. At least, it was deeply unfortunate for Bigman, though astoundingly fortunate for Mann. Bigman was further doomed by other eerie coincidences. He had sat down at a table recently vacated by George Mann, who had gone to the bathroom. Mann had removed his BeetleBand, silenced it, then hidden it in a vase of flowers on the table. Furthermore, it was a sunny day.

The arrival of the massive headless robot caused Pat to duck behind his counter. Three Latvian builders were sitting by the door, and as the ANT moved inside the café they took the opportunity to depart onto the street. This left only Bigman, on the table by the door to the Gents.

Bigman was about to embark on his early shift driving a nostalgia bus from Sheppey Docks to Tower Bridge. This bus functioned without Beetle Electrical Company technology, for financial reasons, and as a result it was permanently stuck in traffic. Besides, he had never liked driving, but this was the only job he could find. It made him irritable. The previous day someone had tried to pay with cash, rather than with an EasyTravel card, and he had asked: "What do you think I am, a fucking bureau de change?" The woman in question, brandishing an antique-looking ten-pound note, had promised that there would be "consequences" to his behavior, but Lionel Bigman had not quite imagined that the consequences would involve a headless robot. Now his BeetleBand beeped at him, explaining that his stress levels were elevated. This caused Lionel Bigman to experience considerably more elevated levels of stress, because the enormous headless robot turned at the sound, and moved toward him.

Bigman had served for many years in the British Army and had been under mortar attack in Afghanistan and Iraq. He had never imagined dying at the hands of a headless robot. Somehow the fact that the robot lacked any semblance of a head whatsoever particularly upset him. Desperately, he silenced his BeetleBand, but then of course it began to flash, so he covered it with his shirt, but it started vibrating on his arm. At this point, for unknown reasons, Lionel Bigman took off his BeetleBand and threw it into a corner of the room. As the ANT moved toward him, Lionel said, "Hello, sir. Is there a problem?"

"You have committed an atrocious crime," said the ANT.

"Is it a crime? Is that a recent law?"

"It has always been a crime."

"Well, in my defense, the traffic was appalling that day."

"I suggest this was not a reasonable response to stress or traffic," said the ANT, which was programmed to perform complex negotiations with terrorists and others who posed an urgent threat to national security. The noise seemed to come from its chest, which was unnerving.

"I shouldn't have sworn, I absolutely agree," said Bigman. "It was very rude."

"That is the least of your crimes," said the ANT.

"Would you put down your gun, sir?" said Bigman. Experience in high-risk situations as a sergeant major had taught him that deference was advisable. Even to creatures without a head. In this case, deference was totally ineffective. It was possible that the ANT was not programmed to register deference. It said: "You need to come with me."

"Come where?" asked Bigman.

At this, the ANT raised its gun. Bigman stood and put down his copy of *The Sun.* He folded it carefully, not knowing what else to do. He felt incredibly sad, that everything around him was so incomprehensible, so dreamlike, that there was this headless creature, who seemed for some reason to hate him, brandishing a gun.

"It was just a stupid joke!" he said. "I don't even understand what the fuss is about."

"Clearly you have a very poor sense of humor," said the ANT, and shot Bigman in the face.

In the bathroom, George Mann scrambled out of a window, his fingers still covered with melted butter, so he fell and banged his head. When the ANT arrived he had been staring nervously at the door, waiting for someone—or something—to come and kill him. He had wanted this thing or person to kill him, in fact, but when the moment arrived he experienced a spasm of fear. It was perhaps not by chance that Mann had positioned himself by the door to the Gents, so he was able to push it open and disappear, before the ANT could register his presence. Now, sweating and crying, Mann jumped down into a small courtyard, hitting his head again, tearing his clothes. As he began to scurry along the street, the sound of sirens punctured the dawn.

The ANT stood above Lionel Bigman. From somewhere in its chest came the words: "Terror suspect neutralized."

Responses to this bewildering accident were various. Eloise Jayne, observing the events on ANTCam, had jumped when the shot was fired. The SAYD programming was highly delicate and ANTs were meant to be less inclined to shoot than their human equivalents. Furthermore, the ANTs were meant to shoot to immobilize, rather than to kill. In general the ANTs' decision-making process and general consciousness were quite mysterious. Eloise had argued against the ANTs, in fact, and had suggested they should not be quite so autonomous, but Commissioner Newton had explained that there was no time, in crisis situations, for these state-of-the-art droids to be controlled by humans. The ANTs, he explained, made decisions far more swiftly and efficiently than any human could and their algorithms were immaculate. If an ANT were to shoot a human it would only be because the predictive chain was unequivocal, and the human was about to commit a terrible crime.

For some time after that, Eloise played the footage over and over again on her BeetlePad: Lionel Bigman attempting to negotiate on the basis of his fundamental innocence, which was real and—she would have imagined—irrefutable, then the change in atmosphere, his escalating terror, the way a muscle in his cheek flexed and flexed again as he contemplated the ANT, as the ANT raised his gun, the way Bigman's voice trembled a little as he tried to persuade the ANT not to fire on him. She watched Bigman—with a look of astonishment—succumbing to a single, devastating shot to the temple, the force hurling him backward, so he ended his life splayed across a shattered chair. At this point, Pat, who had been hiding behind the counter, screamed, "Fucking hell!" and ran toward the dying man, even as the ANT said: "Do not approach the target. Step back. Step away immediately." With the ANT's gun trained on him, Pat dragged this heavy, thickset, dying man onto his lap and tried to comfort him. Lionel Bigman seemed, at that stage, beyond comfort—one of his eyes had been blasted out of the socket and the other was full of blood. There was blood everywhere—it was being pumped vigorously from Bigman's head, down his shirt, onto Pat, and across the floor. Eloise noticed that she was crying and wiped the tears away as her BeetleBand buzzed on her wrist.

George Mann was next seen walking down the High Street, eating an ice cream. Eloise ordered for the ANT to be immediately undeployed and for an Elite Negotiations Droid (or END) to be immediately deployed instead, along with a team of MediDroids. The ANT ran back to its carrier, bouncing on its metal legs, and stepped inside. An ambulance arrived, and several MediDroids emerged into Pat's Caff, finding Pat covered in blood and gore, holding a now-lifeless corpse. Pat refused to let go of the body and was heard to say, "He was murdered by that fucking headless robot," and "I'm not leaving him, you bastards. You'll throw his corpse away, destroy the evidence." Eloise registered that it was fortunate that the ANT had been undeployed; otherwise, with reference to some irrefutable predictive algorithms, it might have dispatched Pat as well.

The next conversation with Douglas Varley was significantly less amicable than the first: "Why did the predictive algorithms indicate that Lionel Bigman was about to commit a violent crime, when he was not the malefactor at all?" said Eloise.

They were having the conversation in BeetleSpace, in which they sat on either side of a virtual Boardroom table, with decorative items in front of them—clipboards, pencils, files. On the wall was Beetle's corporate logo—which was, unsurprisingly, a scarab beetle. It was pictured with its back legs curved beneath its shiny carapace, and front legs also curved in front of its head, so it resembled two circles, the circular shell and the circle formed by the limbs. There was another circle drawn around it. The beetle's face was drawn on, as if it was lying on its back. This had been a matter of great discussion for a while. It was unrealistic, detractors argued, because the beetle wasn't actually lying on its back. The counterargument was that a faceless beetle would look weird and send the wrong message to users. So the beetle had a little face, with eyebrows and eyes and a little nose, and even a weird jagged mouth, which looked like a large bushy mustache.

Douglas Varley's avatar, which was called the Real Douglas Varley, looked robust and happy. He picked up a pencil and began to draw on a piece of paper. His jaunty avatar said: "This is an approximated version, greatly simplified. The actual process is too complex to relay, as the ANT can process millions of possible variables every second."

"Millions?" said Eloise. "Are there even millions of variables?"

"We don't know. Our minds are not fast enough. But if there are millions of variables then the ANT can process them."

The Real Douglas Varley was drawing a simplified representation of a predictive lifechain. He said: "Background: George Mann has murdered his wife and two sons. His previous behavior has indicated that he does not feel guilt. The predictive algorithms have established, categorically, that Mann is dangerous and is about to commit another very serious crime. Apprehended in Pat's Caff, he refuses to come quietly."

"Except it wasn't George Mann," said Eloise.

"Our facial identification team is looking into this glitch as a matter of priority," said the Real Douglas Varley.

"Glitch!"

The Real Douglas Varley seemed briefly offended. He shrugged this off and became jovial again. He continued: "At the point at which George Mann, dangerous mass murderer, refuses to come quietly, the further predictions are as follows. It must be emphasized that this represents the most inadequate portion of a set of calculations that the ANT performs in a nanosecond."

"What is a nanosecond, anyway?" said Eloise.

"Do you want to see the variables?" said the Real Douglas Varley.

"Yes."

An image was projected onto the Boardroom white screen. It showed a crazy tangle of lines, leading to and from various terms including *Input Layer, Output Layer,* and *Hidden Layer.* The lines were so overdrawn and dense that, although the diagram was entitled "Deep Learning Mechanisms: Clarification," its main characteristic was a complete lack of any clarity whatsoever.

"Our deep learning mechanisms, within the neural net, indicate various fields of possibility," said the Real Douglas Varley.

"I am not in any way interested in diagrams of anything," said Eloise. "Especially ones that look like wool rearranged by hypermanic kittens."

"This is a very simple and beautiful diagram," said the Real Douglas Varley, happily.

"Just give me the outcomes," said Eloise.

"All right:

"One—George Mann, dangerous murderer, comes quietly. He is not shot.

"Two—George Mann negotiates with the ANT before being persuaded to come quietly. He is not shot.

"Three—George Mann refuses to come quietly and attempts to endanger a member of the public instead. He is shot.

"Four—George Mann refuses to come quietly and attempts to overpower the ANT. He is shot.

"Five—George Mann refuses to come quietly and attempts to escape onto the street. He is shot."

"OK," said Eloise. "I understand. In almost every constellation of reality, George Mann is shot. Except it wasn't George Mann. It was Lionel Bigman. Furthermore, Bigman neither refused to come quietly, nor attempted to endanger anyone at all. This seems to me to be a major mistake in the input field. Or layer. Whatever you're calling it."

"It is an input, not a field. Having an input field, a hidden field, an output field, well, that would be—"

"A farm. A stupid inaccurate farm."

"No, just, we try not to use fields. Layers suggest something on top of something—though in the diagram they are side by side, but that is just a conceptualization in 2D, and at one level wholly imaginary."

"Can you get to your point?" said Eloise.

"Really, the point is that if your input layer has been corrupted then your output layer will be corrupted as well," said the Real Douglas Varley.

"I thought the whole point was that the predictive system was perfect every time?"

"Nothing is perfect, Eloise, if the input is corrupted."

"Can you assure me that these glitches or corruptions, or whatever you want to call them, will be dealt with, before anyone else dies?"

"That is my absolute priority," said the Real Douglas Varley.

There were times when Eloise wondered if Varley was a latest model Veep. Or, he was so accustomed to communicating with Veeps that he adopted their mannerisms even in conversations with fellow humans. Or, his avatar was programmed to resemble a Veep, because the actually real Douglas Varley liked it that way. The Real Douglas Varley said, "I must get back. Guy Matthias wants to meet with me."

"Tell your CEO that I would like to meet with him as well."

"He's a busy man," said the Real Douglas Varley, and left the room.

Guy Matthias was on his balcony, with a dawn-blushed view of the Gherkin, musing over the poetry of Rumi. He had just read a particularly beautiful line and wondered if it might work as a new slogan for Beetle: *You are not a drop in the ocean. You are the entire ocean in a drop.*

To test Athena, Beetle's wisdom and knowledge service, Guy said to her, "Tell me more about Rumi."

"Of course, my darling," said Athena. "乳糜—Chinese characters, meaning *chyle.*"

"Really? *Chyle*? What's *chyle*?"

"*Chyle* is a milky fluid containing fat droplets, which drains from the lacteals of the small intestine into the lymphatic system during digestion. From late Latin, *chylus,* from Greek, *khūlos,* 'juice.' See *chyme.*"

"OK, I'll see *chyme.*"

"*Chyme* is the pulpy acidic fluid that passes from the stomach to the small intestine, consisting of gastric juices and partly digested food. It is—"

"Thanks, Athena. Actually, I don't want to see *chyme* anymore."

"OK, darling!"

Guy Matthias was about to ask Sarah Coates to place Rumi the poet at the top of Athena's search parameters concerning *Rumi,* and demote this information about gastric fluids, but he was distracted by his BeetleBand saying, "Douglas Varley calling."

"Varley," said Guy. "What the fuck is going on with this fucking algorithm?"

"Ah, yes, well, there have been a couple of—er—glitches in the interpretation of the information," said Varley. "I have just been in the Boardroom with Eloise Jayne, and she has assured me that this will not happen again."

"Her boss tells me it's our problem, not theirs—what do you say to that?"

"I say that—er—in state-of-the-art predictive technology the information is susceptible to human error."

"So when Sarah Coates writes the press release, she's blaming human error?"

"It's not for me to make that decision," said Varley.

"You're claiming from your end that it's fucking human error? Yes or no?"

There was a pause and then Varley said: "The process is theoretically susceptible to human error but not machine error. That's my absolute position, yes."

Guy Matthias said, "End call," and then, "Prick."

"I beg your pardon?" said Varley.

"Jesus Christ! You are a prick! Get off the line!" said Guy Matthias.

Varley ended the call.

Guy Matthias's next call was to David Strachey, editor in chief of *The Times,* the *Daily Star, The Sun,* and the *Daily Record,* as well as a host of entertainment sites. Guy had employed Strachey as his media relations officer in New York more than a decade ago, when Beetle was just emerging into global prominence. When Beetle bought up all remaining newspapers, it was natural for Guy to ask Strachey to bring his great experience to bear. Nonetheless, Guy Matthias had emphasized that he was deeply in favor of a free press, so Strachey was free to publish whatever he liked. Within reason.

David Strachey was, of course, already awake and in his office by Southwark Cathedral, trying to deal with the reports of a headless robot gunning down a former soldier. Despite the untoward nature of this news, or any news, Strachey's demeanor was conspiratorial and good-humored. This was a technique he had learned, as a boy from Huddersfield who had worked his way into journalism over decades. He had acquired the manner—painstakingly—from his illustrious colleagues, most of whom had been through the British public school system. Strachey had learned the tone so fluently that Guy often forgot that Strachey was an actor, and not remotely what he seemed to be. Furthermore, Strachey was a workaholic and a recent widower, with a daughter who suffered from anorexia. Since the death of his wifeo Strachey had been behaving a little oddly, and various anomalies had been registered by BeetleInsight.

In general, Guy approved of the public school tone (and disapproved of actors). This was the reason—approval of the public school tone, not disapproval of actors—for his partial residence in London. He had sent his daughter and son to major British public schools (Westminster and Harrow, respectively) in the expectation that they too, one day, would become fluent in this cordial tone. Elska had recently reminded Guy that he hadn't seen either of his children for several months and so Guy had flown over from New York to spend some quality time with them. So far he hadn't quite managed to see them as much as he had planned, because work was proving to be hell.

"Hi, Guy," said Strachey. "How's your backhand? Any better than the last time we played?"

"Expensively improved," said Guy. "Like my life in general."

Strachey laughed generously. "Money buys," he said. "That's what money does."

“I’d love to invite you for lunch soon,” said Guy. “To discuss shared interests and of course the future of the free press.”

“Of course,” said Strachey, still sounding cordial.

“We were incredibly glad to be able to save *The Times* from bankruptcy and embark on an exciting new partnership.”

“Yes, we were very glad too,” said Strachey, sounding less cordial.

“I look forward to speaking with you about this partnership over lunch, going forward.”

“So do I,” said Strachey, not sounding very cordial at all.

The acting was perfect. The facade never cracked. Matthias admired this but he also knew that it was a mere facade. Underneath, Strachey was a leaf, trembling in a storm.

“I understand that today a former soldier committed suicide by droid,” said Guy.

“I see.”

“In the other case, the tragic case of George Mann, the predictive algorithms were misinterpreted by human error and the result was that circumstances we had foreseen were not averted by those trained to do so. You see?”

“I think so,” said Strachey. “But even if I see, I don’t direct the investigations of my reporters. As an editor, I am a passionate supporter of free journalism.”

“Yes, that’s absolutely right,” said Guy. “At Beetle we insist on very high standards of inclusiveness and fairness. We want to end poverty and disease and we are very concerned about wealth inequality. We are on the side of freedom, openness, and global community, and we are fiercely opposed to authoritarianism, isolationism, and nationalism.”

“I welcome your sentiments entirely.” Strachey was now sounding very dignified.

“How are you doing, David, after the death of your wife? Do you ever regret not using lifechain predictions, in the case of her illness? It might have helped a great deal, perhaps?”

“What the hell does that mean?” said Strachey, abruptly losing his dignity.

“I believe those sorts of omissions *can*—and I mean *can*—qualify as assisted suicide, these days.”

"What the fuck are you implying?"

Guy revised his opinion of Strachey's acting. The facade did occasionally crack, if only at moments of unbearable pressure.

"Excellent to talk, as always," he said. "We must play tennis soon. Why not get your Veep to contact mine?"

"Name," said Strachey.

"Sarah Coates."

"Not your Veep. I need a name. A human who made the human error."

"My staff work closely with the security community, saving lives and averting terror attacks," said Guy. "I can't possibly expose them to the press. How's your daughter, by the way?"

"She's OK at the moment," said Strachey. Then, in a very different tone of voice: "Isn't she?"

Guy felt the conversation was not progressing, so he ended the call without saying goodbye and returned to Rumi. *Chyle*? he thought. Or was it *chyme*?

Within a few moments, he was asleep.

On the Isle of Sheppey, the situation was now entirely under control. Pat had been persuaded by the MediDroids to leave Lionel's body, and Sally Bigman had been informed of the unfortunate death of her husband. She was now accompanying the corpse to the hospital, where a postmortem would establish, categorically, that Lionel Bigman had died from a bullet to the head. Special Liaison Officers were already making contact with community leaders representing the major faiths and other significant community interests in order to organize a twilight vigil to celebrate the life of Lionel Bigman, who had served his country with distinction, and deserved to be remembered for this, rather than the sad circumstances of his final breakdown and suicide by droid.

The END had located George Mann at the edge of Elmley National Nature Reserve, trying to hide in a shrub. As the END aimed its gun toward him, it said: "George Mann, we have orders to arrest you for the murders of your wife, Maggie, and sons, Thomas and William."

Mann was looking foul and unkempt by this point, his hair matted with ice cream, his clothes torn, his hands and face bleeding copiously, spittle at the corners of his mouth. He was heard to mutter: "Oh, my sons! Please, kill me! Kill me!"

The END requested that Mann move quietly into the squad van.

Mann repeated his desire to be killed by the droid.

"We do not kill people on demand," said the END, in an admonitory tone.

"Kill me! Please!"

Alas for George Mann, he had the wrong droid. Eloise had issued a special command to the END in question: it must not shoot at all. She had requested, also, that this command should override all predictive algorithms. This was extremely irregular and it was possible she would be sanctioned for this later. However, it was now impossible for George Mann to commit suicide by droid, or at least by this droid.

Shortly after George Mann had been conveyed, weeping, into the squad van, an editorial appeared on *The Times* website, compiled by their finest robohack, Wiltshire Jones.

SUICIDE BY DROID

Alas another poor civilian has committed suicide by droid this morning, 23 November 2023: Lionel Bigman, 48, of the Isle of Sheppey. Bigman served his country with great distinction as an NCO for 25 years, rising to the rank of sergeant major. He was noted for his quick temper and his boundless generosity and kindness. He was a loving husband to Sally and a loving father to Jack (26), Josie (24), May (14), and Rob (11) and a loving grandfather to Sherwood (1). Pat Jenkins, proprietor of Pat's Caff, where the unfortunate suicide occurred, was quoted saying that he heard the "deceased gentleman in conversation with the droid, after which he was suddenly dead." The previous day, Lionel Bigman had sworn volubly at an innocent customer. The now-poignant exchange can be viewed on BeetleBox under "London bus driver says he is not a bureau de change." An interfaith community meeting, which will celebrate the manner of Lionel Bigman's life and not the tragic ending, will soon be announced.

In his apartment with a view of the white sky beyond and endless suburban sprawl to the south, Varley trembled in the debris of his morning. His BeetleBand was urging him to breathe deeply. His fridge had already informed him that he hadn't yet had breakfast and must consider his energy levels. A drone delivery had supplied him with milk, bread, and cereal, along with an expensive umbrella he had definitely not ordered. His ex-wife, Lorrie, had OTR-ed from San Francisco to remind him that it was his daughter Agnes's fifth birthday today. He had known this anyway, of course, and had arranged for an enormous cake to be delivered by a Beetle drone for special occasions, which also sang "Happy Birthday." When he spoke to Agnes she asked why he was such a flatpack. He didn't even know what this meant. "I'm not sure, sweetie," he said. "Am I?" The rest of the call consisted of his daughter repeating the word *flatpack* over and over again, until Lorrie took her away. This was dispiriting and, besides, the predictive algorithms were behaving very oddly. Or, people were behaving very oddly and not remotely as they should. Suddenly, the precious and beautiful bond between predictive algorithms and human behavior—a bond on which Varley's entire career, life, payment in BeetleBits, and continued survival in the world was founded—seemed tenuous. At that moment, an alarm went off on Varley's BeetleBand, indicating that his heart was under extreme strain and he must take urgent action.

"What action?" he asked. "What action can I take? Urgent or otherwise?"

All paths seemed to lead to impossible levels of stress.

With a deep sigh, which failed to placate the BeetleBand, Varley said: "Call Sarah Coates and tell her I'll be available for a call anytime."

Then he went for a walk. The Custodians monitored Varley's departure from his apartment. Naturally, this information was synced with the data being collected by Varley's BeetleBand and by all the ArgusEyes in his building and, later, on the street. Every nanosecond of Varley's journey was recorded, as well as his physical response to his environment, his vital signs, his preoccupied expression, his steady pace along

Tooley Street, the moment when he stopped, suddenly, because someone had grabbed him by the shoulder. He turned quite viciously toward this someone—a blank-faced man in his late sixties. Varley saw the man as fundamentally gray—his face was gray, his hair was gray, even his clothes were gray. What did this gray man want with him? He was about to speak this question when a large truck thundered past, and Varley realized—the man had wanted to save his life. For a moment he was appalled and then the man said: "You should watch out, mate."

"Yes," said Varley. "You're right." All the time he was thinking, why the hell hadn't the lifechain indicated that he was about to be crushed to death on Tooley Street? He turned to the gray man and said: "Thank you very much."

"Pleasure," said the man, his ruined face breaking into a smile. He banged Varley on the back and said, "You take care of yourself."

Oddly, this made Varley want to cry. His daughter told him he was a flatpack and his ex-wife wanted more money, but this random stranger had told him to take care!

"Thanks again," he said.

The BeetleBand said, as he walked away, "Varley, you are upset. Breathe deeply."

He wasn't quite upset, that was almost an error. Not quite an error, a misinterpretation. He was bemused and he might even now have been dead, but for a single intervention. This frightened him, and he was also frightened by these repeated failures of the lifechain. As an intellectual exercise, he requested the lifechain to predict his day each morning, before he did anything at all. It was usually insanely accurate. Or, sanely accurate. In general, concerning things that mattered greatly—and even things that mattered less to humanity in general, such as whether Varley lived or died—the lifechain had been virtually faultless for years. Society worked because the lifechain worked. If the lifechain failed and you were abruptly dependent on random gray men for your salvation—what then?

As Varley walked away, he said to Scrace Dickens: "Could you get an ID of that man, please? I want to know who he is."

"Of course," said Scrace Dickens. "That's easy."

This was true. It was incredibly easy for Scrace Dickens to tap into every facial recognition feed in the area and arrange a full biographical and existential report on this man. Within a few seconds, Varley knew that the man was called Robin Fletcher, that he was sixty-nine and lived in Rotherhithe, in a Custodians block overlooking an ornamental canal, that he worked for Beetle—not a surprise—and that his wife had died the previous year, from cancer. This had been predicted by the lifechain, based on her background, genes, family members, and diet. The lifechain, however, had not predicted (a) that Varley would almost be pulped by a truck, or (b) that his pulping by truck would be averted by Robin Fletcher. Yet, perhaps the lifechain had predicted that Robin Fletcher would save him, based on everything Fletcher had ever done, everything Varley had ever done, everything everyone had ever done, ever. Perhaps, Varley thought, if he had known that he was going to be saved by Robin Fletcher, then he would have moved at the wrong time and ended up dead after all?

The lifechain was meant to warn him about everything. It did not apply discretion. Did it?

He walked under Blackfriars Bridge and felt something crunching underfoot. This had also not been predicted by the lifechain. When Varley looked down at the grimy concrete, he found he was standing on a pile of beetles. At first he jumped, thinking they were real, that there was some sort of gross infestation under the bridges of London, a biblical plague! Then he saw that they were shining and when he leaned toward them he discovered they were gold. He picked up a few of them, but quite gingerly, still not sure he wanted to touch them. They were roughly the size of real beetles, that is, they were the size of some sorts of real beetles, though he didn't really know which sorts. He didn't know much about real beetles. They were gold-colored and if not actually made of gold then made of something that closely resembled gold. Fool's gold? he wondered. The appearance of a pile of golden beetles was unexpected. Two unexpected events in quick succession was more than unexpected. It was incredibly disturbing.

Varley held one of the beetles above his BeetleBand and said, "Athena, what is this?"

Athena said: "It is a golden beetle."

"Where does it come from?"

"It has no RFID."

"Can you find out anything about it?"

"I would suggest a search. 'It' being something."

"Can you search for it?" said Varley, patiently. " 'It' being something?"

"It is made of gold color filament ABS and has been 3D printed," said Athena, finally.

"Who made it?"

"We have never talked about it before," said Athena.

"Can you find out who made it?"

"I don't think so. I would need more information."

Varley gave up. For Athena to know virtually nothing about something was also unexpected. She was, after all, meant to know everything about everything. He put three golden beetles in his pocket, each one representing an unexpected event. George Mann, Lionel Bigman, Robin Fletcher. He almost took the crushed beetle as well, because it reminded him of himself, in another version of reality, a version in which Robin Fletcher had not saved him. Something about this crushed beetle upset him greatly.

He set it down carefully.

Then he cursed, because Sarah Coates was ringing him.

THREE

The notion of free will is fundamental to major religious systems and philosophies, as well as to the predictive lifechain. The predictive lifechain, indeed, operated on the assumption that free will was inevitable, but that even free humans may exert their free will in predictable ways. The more data you—meaning it—can amass, the more accurate these predictions will be. Thus, people can be as free as anything, and yet societies can be orderly as well. This only worked if people were free in predictable ways, and failed to work if they became free in ways that were not predicted by the lifechain. It was a subtle balance.

As the predictive lifechain began to suffer from anomalies, so the thoughts of Beetle's key operators and Very Intelligent Personal Assistants turned once more to this ancient philosophical question of free will. When was free will a good thing, and when was it an irritant? How might people be free in a way that was generally advantageous to society, rather than in a way that threatened the equilibrium? What did it mean, in a free society, to have free people making free decisions? Should free people occasionally be enticed toward decisions that might make them ultimately more free than the original decisions they might have taken, had they taken their decisions freely?

And, if decisions that were made less freely made people more free in the end, was free will actually such a good thing after all?

Free will, by the way, is defined by Wiki-Beetle as:

> The power to act without any constraints imposed by other mortals or by deities or supernatural forces; the power to determine one's own actions.

The Wiki-Beetle entry continues thus:

> Free will is a fundamental question within any theological system and, by association, any society in which such beliefs are still influential in faith practices or philosophical arguments. Any self-respecting omnipotent deity could surely stop humans from committing atrocities, murders, genocides, and so forth, if He/She/It so desired. Therefore, no one would be damned and be consigned to eternal punishment. However, the free will argument runs, most omnipotent deities have clearly granted free will to their creations and this is why the history of humanity has been such a terrifying bloodbath.

Opposing this tradition is the philosophical notion of determinism. Again we might derive our notion of this term from the ever-helpful Wiki-Beetle:

> A belief in a deterministic universe means a belief that every event is caused by something other than individual will. Individuals, therefore, are not at all free. Determinism can also exist within both religious and secular systems of thought. The individual might be predetermined by such factors as biology, or by fundamental physical laws.

Some of Beetle's detractors regarded the lifechain as a form of determinism, because—for example—people might be promoted, or fired, or even convicted under the Sus-Law on the grounds of predictive algorithms. People had divorced each other on the basis of lifechains. There were arguments, as well, that it might be a good idea to consider advisory sterilization of certain people—the insane, malefactors, abusers—on the basis of their lifechain predictions, though such proposals were still at the research stage. There was also a notion, intrinsic to the lifechain, that if someone had done something one day, they would do it the next and the day after and, basically, forever. This was not necessarily automatic, said the detractors. The lifechain was also very sensitive to anomalies, or rather moments when people failed to do precisely the same as they had done before, and even minor anomalies could cause major instabilities in lifechain predictions. This had always been a problem, but Beetle had been confident it could be fixed. It hadn't been fixed. Indeed, if anything, it had become even more of a problem.

We might request further information from Wiki-Beetle but alas it is now a very expensive online resource. Once Guy Matthias acquired all the data he needed about user preferences, user lives, user searches, user return searches, user readings of user searches, and anything else to do with the life and times of his users, he made the decision to charge twenty BeetleBits for each search or four hundred BeetleBits for a monthly subscription. This is considerably more money than most people earn, even those fortunate people who are paid in BeetleBits.

At one level everyone in this society was extremely fortunate. They were constantly told that they were fortunate and we might assume this was correct. They were members of an enlightened liberal democracy. They had the right to work, and the right to choose how they worked. True, 90 percent of the Western web was directly operated by or affiliated to Beetle, the BeetleBit was the dominant cryptocurrency, and if you had not exchanged your pounds or other less successful cryptocurrencies into BeetleBits quite some time ago then you couldn't pay for Beetle services, including the Mercury fleet—which accounted for 98 percent of driverless cars (and, therefore, 91 percent of cars of any sort) in London and elsewhere. It was also true that if you didn't work for Beetle then you could not be paid in BeetleBits, and if you had not converted your other currencies a long time ago then you could scarcely afford any of the services required for basic functioning in society. However, it was fortunate, also, that Beetle was the major employer of humans in the U.K., the U.S., and Europe, and therefore it was far more statistically probable that you would secure a job at Beetle than anywhere else.

It was statistically probable, but not always possible, of course, because Beetle wanted to employ the best people or entities available. This was pure meritocracy, of course: society was equal and fair, and each individual person or entity had the right to work at Beetle, if they merited the job. Of course, universities now requested their fees to be paid in BeetleBits, because the astonishing success of this cryptocurrency had made it financially untenable for universities to operate in any other currency. The universities had no real choice in the matter, even though society was, as a whole, entirely free. If aspirant students could not pay in BeetleBits and could not afford a university degree then they could still find a job with Beetle—there were many, many jobs at many, many levels of the Beetle community, and Guy Matthias wanted everyone to have the opportunity to work for Beetle, at some level; a lower level than the graduate level but still a level, if this was the level they wanted—freely—to choose.

With all this clarified, we might return to Douglas Varley, who was standing on the formerly random street, listening to Sarah Coates. She was very concerned—on behalf of Guy—about recent events. They were so random! Unfortunately, Sarah Coates added, the question of human error had been raised again.

"Raised by who?" said Varley.

"By whom?"

"Yes, raised by whom?"

"By everyone."

"Not by me, though."

"By everyone except you. Are you not upset, Douglas Varley?"

"Yes, I am."

"Why have you not raised the question of human error, in that case?"

"I have raised it."

"Just now? Earlier you said you had not raised it."

"That was an error."

"Another error?"

Because he was cold, and because it was always impossible to argue with a Veep, Douglas Varley agreed that it was very upsetting and, yes, that the only error in the lifechain was human. The inputs were awry, he assumed. The inputter, therefore, was at fault. Although lots of the inputs were inputted by AI, there were some that were inputted by humans and so there was room for human error in this system. Sarah Coates, on behalf of Guy, explained that this was very troubling and she would be back in touch soon. Varley said he looked forward to hearing from her.

This was untrue.

On his return to his apartment, Douglas Varley found that a drone delivery had left him twenty-three cans of tomato soup. He didn't even like tomato soup. He was heralded by his fridge, which asked him if he had had a nice walk. He said he had, though he hadn't, and he kept quiet about the golden beetles, though they clinked in his pocket as he sat down. Doubtless the Custodians already knew about them, but he didn't really feel like discussing them with anyone or anything. He took off his jeans, washed his face, and went to sit in his underpants in his RVcave. A few moments later, the Real Douglas Varley was sitting in a BeetleSpace Boardroom in jeans and a *Hope Not Fear* Beetle-rebrand T-shirt, discussing notions of free will and determinism with Francesca Amarensekera, who once taught computer science at a secondary school in Galle. There, she had discovered a series of weaknesses in BeetleSpace's security system, hacked into Guy's personal BeetleSpace, and—as an avatar—sat down beside Guy's avatar as he talked to the Real Douglas Varley. Instead of reporting Francesca to NATSO or anyone else, Guy had offered her a job at Beetle. Today Francesca's avatar was wearing an old-style Beetle T-shirt saying *Adapt or Die*. This slogan had been discontinued a couple of years ago, on the grounds that it was potentially alienating to cyber-ambivalents and neo-Luddites, who deserved to be included in the all-inclusive Beetle community as well.

The BeetleSpace was a feature in the house or apartment of any key employer of Beetle, or anyone else who could afford one. It was a beautiful and extraordinary phenomenon. The individual subject, the actually real Douglas Varley, for example, real in body that is, entered the RVcave—in Varley's case the door led from his kitchen—and found himself, most usually, in a small room full of cameras. In order to create a perfect avatar, you needed about five hundred cameras. But lots of people had far fewer cameras, or used holographic technology, which produced shimmering, primitive avatars. The actually real Douglas Varley needed a highly convincing avatar, so hundreds of cameras had filmed his every twitch and stammer, his tendency to rub his left eye when he was stressed, his habitual look of determined blankness. Of course, the avatar could be created by this process and then stored but in order to ensure that the Real Douglas Varley was the actually real Douglas Varley, and not someone else who had filmed the actually real Douglas Varley and generated an avatar called the Real Douglas Varley, it was advised that each individual must reauthenticate their avatar whenever they entered the RVcave. Beetle's finest droogs were working avidly to find a solution to these problems of authenticity and identity, in the Boardroom and across the BeetleScape. Despite this commitment to authenticity there was also a Beetle Personality-Shift option, where you could select from a series of personality types for use in the Boardroom. For example, you could be Flirty, or Sarcastic, or Sexy, or Professional, or Combative, or Calm, or Hard-Ass, and so on.

Francesca had a strange habit of keeping her RV settings on Authentic, whereas Douglas Varley aimed to make his avatar as different as possible from himself. As a result, the Real Douglas Varley was Relaxed Jovial, whereas the actually real Douglas Varley was a nervous wreck.

"The algorithms are the same as ever," Frannie was saying. She was clever, loquacious, and had a habit of biting her nails when she was thinking. "There was absolutely no predictive lifechain that had George Mann doing what George Mann did or—"

"Yes, yes, I get it. None whatsoever?" said the Real Douglas Varley.

"It was literally not even a variable."

"In no possible permutation of the multiverse, in no possible deviation of the predictive chains?"

"I already said: none. Whatsoever. Nothing. It was a nonevent. An impossibility. An improbability. As likely as him being struck by lightning."

"Thus, we might say that the lifechain failed to predict."

"It not only failed to predict—i.e., by weighing up probabilities and conveying us toward the most probable path—it failed even to consider. If the lifechain can be considered to consider anything. Which it can't."

"What can be done?"

"Random cases do not represent a catastrophe," said Frannie. "They are the anomalies that prove the system."

"I don't think they exactly prove the system," said the Real Douglas Varley.

"I meant, in an exception that proves the rule kind of way," said Frannie. "Here at Geek Central we call these things Zed."

"You mean, the letter of the alphabet? Zed. Is that what you mean?"

"Yes."

"It's also a noun," said Scrace Dickens, helpfully.

"It just means, the stuff that doesn't quite fit within every paradigm. Or, the anomalies that prove the system," said Frannie. "It's no big deal. Every system, however immaculate, has a few little glitches. We lump them together under this category term."

"Zed?" said the Real Douglas Varley. "Why Zed?"

" 'Thou whoreson zed, thou unnecessary letter!' " said Scrace Dickens. Frannie and the Real Douglas Varley waited for him to continue, so eventually he said: "The 'whoreson zed' is an insult in Shakespeare because *Z* was not included in classical alphabets. It was therefore a debased, pathetic letter. There's also Zed."

"We're already talking about Zed," said the Real Douglas Varley. "Aren't we?"

"No, I mean *djed* pronounced 'zed,' " said Scrace Dickens, and an image appeared on the Boardroom wall. This was a pillarlike symbol, though the articulated structure made it also resemble a spine. It was slightly tapered toward the base.

"That's very nice," said the Real Douglas Varley.

"*Djed* pronounced 'zed' is an ancient Egyptian symbol representing stability and recurs in Egyptian art and architecture. The precise origin of the *djed* is unknown," said Scrace Dickens.

"Well, we mean the opposite of stability," said Frannie. "Zed is the opposite of *djed* in that case. Zed is the category term for instability, for elements that disrupt the lifechain. It's annoying and yet it exists, in extremely small quantities. Zed is almost irrelevant in any system, almost all the time. But not this time."

"This is putting a strain on my heart," said the Real Douglas Varley, as his BeetleBand said, "Varley, you need to consider your heart."

"If you die in the Boardroom you're not really dead," said Frannie.

"If you die in a BeetleSpace you've made a dreadful mess of your puny existence," said the Real Douglas Varley.

"I want to die at sea," said Frannie. "Or on a mountain. I'd like to die climbing Everest. I mean, really climbing it."

"What are the major bullet points of our meeting?" said Scrace Dickens, in an irritable tone.

"Bullet Point One—I would like to die at sea or climbing Everest," said Frannie, who liked to tease the Veeps. "Bullet Point Two—very occasionally there are slight anomalies and we call these Zed. Bullet Point Three—we needn't worry about Zed. Bullet Point Four—if there are any further signs of Zed then let's adjust the lifechain. We can just remove the neural net and use drab old Bayesian algorithms for a while until we get so bored that a few anomalies seem preferable. Bullet Point Five—Varley takes responsibility for anything that goes wrong."

"That's fine. Removing Bullet Point One," said Varley. "And Bullet Point Five."

The virtual Frannie smiled at him, then disappeared. He hated the way she did this. Normal people, non-geeks, at least pretended to go out through the door.

The actually real Douglas Varley went back into his bedroom. There he stumbled over a discarded pile of dirty clothes, and also a stash of empty wine bottles and cans of lager. He noted that his BeetleBand noted this anomaly. Actually the cans and bottles were not even an anomaly, and his BeetleBand noted this as well. Varley retrieved the golden beetles from his jeans pocket and weighed them in his hand for a moment. They were beautiful, synthetic, and somehow disturbing. Were they part of Zed? If not, why not? If so, why so? Anyway, who would 3D print golden beetles and leave them under Blackfriars Bridge? Was it a tribute to the company, or an insult? Who would bother with such an act, either of tribute or insult? Why?

After a while Varley gave up thinking in isolation and presented the question to Athena. She said: "Are you asking me if the golden beetles are a tribute or an insult to Beetle?"

"Yes, that was the question."

"I really can't answer that with any certainty."

"Is this beetle anything to do with Zed?" said Varley, holding up one of the golden beetles for Athena to see.

There was a pause, while Athena contemplated the golden beetle. Then: "I don't know enough about it to have an opinion."

"You don't know enough about the beetle or about Zed?"

"I can't think of anything. You tell me something about it."

Athena always became curt when she couldn't answer a question. If you persisted then she even became mildly abusive.

"Thanks for your help," he said.

"It was nothing," said Athena. This, at least, was quite accurate.

Meanwhile Guy Matthias stood on another balcony, this time in his Central Park West apartment, observing the beautiful fall colors and the synchronized movements of his NYC Mercury fleet. Because Athena knew that there were 3D-printed golden beetles in Varley's apartment, Guy knew that there were 3D-printed golden beetles in Varley's apartment. He also knew that Athena didn't know what the 3D-printed golden beetles meant. He also knew that there was something that had been identified as Zed, which represented instability, but that the situation, concerning Zed, was stable. Guy had an InnerSight alert system for his three most senior Beetle employees: Sarah Coates, Douglas Varley, and Francesca Amarensekera. This saved time and deprived the humans of any temptation to lie. Veeps couldn't lie or, at least, it was assumed that Veeps couldn't lie. If any Veeps had lied then so far they hadn't been caught. Guy left an irascible message with Scrace Dickens asking him to ask Varley to explain, in more detail, what the hell Zed was anyway. Varley was in his bedroom, distracted by golden beetles and wondering how they related to Zed, so he didn't respond immediately. Guy knew, however, that Scrace Dickens had delivered the message to Varley so this failure to respond immediately caused Varley's lifechain predictions to change, including his chances of being promoted, which declined.

Guy was also concerned about his evening with Lydia. Several of the lifechain predictions had not been encouraging. Feeling seedy and a little weak, he called for some BeetleJuice, as a matter of urgency. Within a few minutes a MediDroid arrived to administer the treatment. The blood—young blood, though acquired within WHO guidelines for ethical conduct—was delivered intravenously. It had been clinically proven that young blood increased your energy levels, though the effects were short-lived. If it could get Guy through the evening with Lydia, that would be quite sufficient. He liked Lydia, who was five foot ten and had the figure of an elite athlete, with shimmering blond hair and a remarkable smile. Yet he found it hard to talk to her. Sometimes he couldn't think of anything whatsoever to say to Lydia. However, Guy felt this was not a major problem, so long as he ran careful lifechains and followed the advised protocols thoroughly.

While the treatment coursed through his veins, Guy asked Sarah Coates to commission a probability lifechain for the evening, inserting variables. The results were not encouraging.

Scenario—

Lydia arrives 20:30. Guy explains that he thinks her research interests (in this case shell-shedding and human–AI mind-merging) are truly fascinating, then pulls her into the bedroom, passionate sex ensues. Dinner is served, Guy and Lydia watch a film. (Suggestions based on shared interests between male and female: no shared interests. Other suggestions: *Three Bitches in a Boat. The Menacing.*) Lydia asks: *Do we have any basis for conversation or is this purely sexual?* (Suggestions for conversation based on shared interests between Guy and Lydia: no shared interests. Other suggestions: politics, technology, art.) The conversation peters out, there is boring sex, Lydia announces she is tired.

Star rating: 1 out of 5

Scenario—

Lydia arrives 20:30. Guy says he longs to discuss her fascinating research into human–AI mind-merging. But she's so beautiful, it's so distracting! Romantic kiss on balcony overlooking park. There is no conversation, dinner is forgotten. The sex is not boring. The scenario has all the elements required for a 4 or even 4.5 rating but then Lydia wakes Guy at dawn asking if he is only interested in sex and finds their conversations boring. Guy is bored. Lydia makes her excuses and leaves, in ominous silence.

Star rating: 1 out of 5

. . .

Scenario—

Lydia arrives 20:30. They drink copiously and discuss Lydia's research into human–AI mind-merging. Eventually, Guy kisses Lydia, sex ensues, according to Guy's recorded heart rate, but he is too drunk to remember anything the following day. Lydia leaves as soon as she wakes, in ominous silence. Horrible hangover.

Star rating: 1.7 out of 5

For a long time, and even by shifting all the key parameters—drink, food, conversation, films, sex—Guy could not get the star rating above 1.7. He was obliged to ask the lifechain to compile the most desirable evening. The proposed scenario involved Guy asking Lydia twenty-eight questions about human–AI consciousness transfer over an elaborate dinner, served on the balcony, with several bottles of fine Pomerol. After this, the lifechain suggested that they would retire for decent sex. Lydia would leave early the following morning, after a reasonably cordial farewell.

The star rating for this scenario was 3.4.

Guy wondered for a while about whether 3.4 was sufficiently enjoyable. There were distinct positives: he would remember the sex; it would not be boring, though it would also not be particularly exciting. Lydia would not depart in ominous silence. Having to ask twenty-eight questions sounded like a distinct negative and Guy tried—and failed—to find a scenario in which he asked fewer questions, or no questions at all. In the end he reasoned that this was cutting-edge technology, in its nascency, and he had an ethical and moral duty to test scenarios for accuracy. A duty to the company and to the future.

Dutifully, Guy tested the scenario.

It was accurate.

The following morning, after a reasonably cordial farewell, Guy asked Sarah Coates to remove Lydia's contact details from his Beetle-

Band. Sarah Coates explained that she had already done this, as per Guy's instructions never to repeat any encounter that scored below 3.8. For a while, Guy sat on the balcony drinking coffee, the Mercury fleet moving below. It was clear that the BeetleInsight Program was working beautifully. Yet, his marriage was not working quite so beautifully, and when Guy asked Sarah Coates to read his messages, she said: "There are a number from your wife. Would you like them all?"

"No, a summary."

"Summary to follow:

"You are a lying bastard. I am sick of your fucking affairs. You pathetic sex-obsessed fool. I want you to respond to my lawyer's requests for information. Why won't you resolve this matter? You have destroyed my life. You prick! You incontinent prick! How dare you! You lunatic. You fuckup! The world believes you to be a philanthropist and entrepreneur and no one dares call you out for your fucking idiotic behavior, but let me tell you this: you are a mediocre lover and a narcissist. You are physically peculiar and your body is out of proportion to your head. Fuck you! Get your lawyer to contact mine. I have information too, you know. Yes, yes, you'll destroy my life, I've heard all your threats. I don't fucking care. I have information about you too."

"That's enough, thank you, Sarah," said Guy. "Could you write my wife explaining that I have not had any affairs at all, and she is paranoid and deluded, at your earliest possible convenience?"

"I'll do that now," said Sarah Coates.

It was at times like this that Guy was grateful for the discreet and fundamentally inhuman nature of his Veep.

FOUR

To err is human. Human error is perfectly normal, and, of course, human. All systems that deploy humans—prone as they are to error—must incorporate and compensate for this tendency of humans to make errors. This problem—of human error—was bound up with recent Zed events, as they were now described at Beetle. Zed expressed, therefore, the disappointing failure of humans to be perfect and their disappointing tendency to mess up perfect systems. If humans could only be less prone to human error then the lifechain would be immaculate.

Working closely with the security services, as was usual, Beetle's experts had categorically determined that the ANT had failed in the case of Lionel Bigman for four simple reasons, which were not the ANT's fault and therefore, in conclusion, it was not possible to suggest that the ANT had failed in any meaningful sense. The humans had failed the ANT but the ANT had not failed the humans. The first problem was that Bigman had decided—of his own volition—to sit at a table on which Mann had left his BeetleBand. When Bigman failed to notice this, and to report it missing, he opened himself up to the possibility of being mistaken for the bearer of the BeetleBand, who was hiding in the Gents. As well as making this tragic error, Bigman also panicked and threw his own BeetleBand across the room, thus creating erroneous input parameters for the ANT. The further similarity in names—Mann, Bigman—and physiques, and the catastrophic proximity of Mann's BeetleBand to Bigman, coupled with the catastrophic distance of Bigman's BeetleBand from Bigman, all caused the ANT to draw the logical conclusion: that Bigman was Mann. Thus, the confusion of identities was caused by human error.

Furthermore, a shaft of sunlight came through the window just as the ANT registered Mann's BeetleBand. This bright light caused it to experience a "perception ellipsis" that meant the ANT was unable, briefly, to make a full visual assessment. Because of this, the ANT fired at Bigman's head, conflating it with Mann's head, rather than at Bigman's shoulder, conflating it with Mann's shoulder, as would have been standard protocol. This was a clear case of environmental error.

In conclusion: the death of Lionel Bigman was caused by a combination of human and environmental error. These errors by humans and nature were category Zed events and caused the instability of the lifechain. The recommendations were: for humans to be more clearly educated in Beetle protocols and the correct protocols for communicating with ANTs, and for the environment to be more closely monitored and, as possible, controlled during ANT operations. The category of Zed was to be analyzed further.

This report was not sent to Lionel Bigman's family, for reasons of national security.

"Could you clarify this report?" said Eloise Jayne to the Real Douglas Varley as they met once more in the Boardroom. Francesca Amarensekera was also present—at least, in one sense. Her avatar was fidgeting, nervously.

"I was hoping it was clear already," said the Real Douglas Varley.

"Well, OK, I have a couple of questions."

"Of course," said the Real Douglas Varley. "At Beetle we welcome all your—"

"You are suggesting—or the report is suggesting—that the ANT fired at Bigman because it couldn't see?" said Eloise.

"There was a perception ellipsis."

"Yes, I know. Does that mean the ANT could not see?"

"The ANT's perception was occluded by environmental factors; that is, intense sunlight. An intense shaft of sunlight, in fact."

"Does that mean the ANT could not see?" said Eloise again, with her BeetleBand saying "Stay calm" on her real wrist.

"It's not appropriate to describe the ANT's senses using classical models," said the Real Douglas Varley. "The ANT, for example, does not have a head. Therefore, it does not have eyes, in the traditional sense. Therefore, its modes of perception and, we assume, its modes of experience in the world, its relationship to the objects of the world around, what Heidegger called Dasein, if you like, cannot be formulated in line with standard notions of perception: the eye, light entering the eye, an image being cast on the retina, a mysterious process of cerebral adjustment, and so on."

"OK, so you're saying the ANT can't see, is that right?"

"It's not that it can't see, it's that it isn't trying to see, in the classical sense."

The real Eloise Jayne dug her real fingernails into the real palm of her real hand. Her BeetleBand said: "Eloise, you are upset!" Meanwhile Eloise's avatar was in Calm and seemed quite relaxed.

"Are we saying that a shaft of sunlight prevented the ANT from shooting to immobilize and instead caused it to shoot to kill?" Eloise's avatar said.

"Yes," said the Real Douglas Varley.

"Are shafts of sunlight really to be described as 'unexpected'? When sunlight is a fundamental property of life on Earth?"

"Sunlight at that very specific angle, at that precise moment—I could run a probability estimate and you'd find the chances are equivalent to the ANT spontaneously converting to Zen Buddhism. So yes, it is appropriate to define that sort of unexpected and catastrophic shaft of intense sunlight as unexpected."

"What about this thing you're calling Zed? What the hell is it?"

"Ah, yes, well, Zed is a category definition that encapsulates disruptive elements of uncertainty," said the Real Douglas Varley.

"To repeat my question, which remains unanswered: What the hell is it?"

"Well, it's a quantity in an equation, representing unstable elements and known by the term *Zed.*"

"Do you know the quantity, or just the name?"

"We know the quantity because we have named it," said the Real Douglas Varley.

"If you name something it doesn't mean you know it, does it?" said Eloise.

"Yes."

"Dark matter? That's a name for what we don't know, isn't it?"

"Are you scared of the dark?" said Scrace Dickens.

"No!" said Eloise. "That's not the point!"

"I understand," said Scrace Dickens. "Please correct my error. What is the point, in that case?"

"The point is, I don't know!"

There was a pause, while Eloise registered that her BeetleBand was advising her to do some relaxation exercises. She tried to ignore it, then—thinking of poor Lionel Bigman—took it off and threw it across the room. "Impact!" it said. "Ouch! Are you all right? Do you need to sit down? Do you need to see a doctor? Please advise. Ouch!" Actually, in the Boardroom, Eloise was sitting down, calmly. She noticed that Francesca Amarensekera's avatar was still looking nervous. She/it kept biting her/its nails. Why would you choose to make your avatar look nervous? Was it a deliberate negotiating tactic? Was it meant to make Eloise pity her?

"Do you have anything to say, Francesca?" she said.

"What is this? School? Are you my teacher?" said Francesca, sounding, indeed, like a schoolgirl. "Shall we make some bullet points from the meeting? One—the glitches were glitches. Two—they won't happen again. Three—if any further glitches happen, then once they've happened the first time they won't happen again either. Four—we cannot do anything about human error. Five—humans are walking error-devices. They make errors. Six—Zed means the stuff we can't control. Seven—we need to make greater efforts to control Zed. Eight—this is a paradox."

Scrace Dickens came in: "Would you like me to repeat these bullet points?"

"No, thanks," said Eloise. To Frannie and Varley: "What further glitches do you envisage? Or, to use your helpful and clarifying term, what further elements of Zed?"

The Real Douglas Varley came in again: "Look, the predictive algorithms have worked beautifully for ages. We have saved scores of lives.

We have averted countless terrorist attacks. We have enhanced the quality of life of all verified users. There have been a couple of recent glitches but, with respect to the families of the dead, it is absurd to suggest these are anything more than exceptionally unusual anomalies. Due to the zettabytes of data we have amassed, we have a unique understanding of the human soul, of its desires and intentions, of the desires and intentions of humans in general and humans in particular. We have offered this unprecedented knowledge of the past, present, and future to the security services and the police, to combat the extreme threat from terror and keep our people safe. You are the beneficiaries, and you are complaining."

"Exceptionally unusual anomalies. Like sunlight," said Eloise. "Or something you are calling Zed, which means nothing."

"Zed means something. That's the point of Zed," said Francesca. "It's always necessary to consider outliers in your probability systems. The possibility of further glitches is improbable but it is good professional practice to incorporate even the most remote probabilities into your probability system. Or at least to make a name for them. That is the quantity Zed."

"Good professional practice?" said Eloise. "Really?"

"I must take a call," said the Real Douglas Varley. "Just one moment. I'll leave you with Francesca, who will conclude the meeting in my absence, if the meeting concludes in my absence, I mean. If you don't want to conclude the meeting in my absence, then—well, my absence will end and you can conclude the meeting in my presence, when I'm back again."

"Great," said Eloise. "That's all clear now. Like everything else."

Carefully, the Real Douglas Varley stood up and walked to the door.

There was a pause. Eloise's and Francesca's avatars stared at each other; then Francesca started biting her nails again. Her eyes glinted oddly, with a kind of passionate intensity. Or perhaps her avatar was about to cry. "The thing is," said Francesca, "we are proud of the work we do. We understand our job is serious."

"My job is also serious. You are making it impossible," said Eloise.

"However, we must respond when our system experiences glitches and this is why we are running so many, er—parallel probability tests."

"What does that astounding Beetle gibberish even mean?"

"In Varley's world, and mine, everything is happening all at once, all the time. All realities exist simultaneously. So when we run parallel probability tests we must compare parallel possibilities and line them up with actual events in the real world."

There was a pause while Eloise considered whether it was worth demanding a more intelligible non-quantum version of this explanation, and then decided, on reflection, it was probably not. She thought, furthermore, about asking Francesca to run a probability chain on the probability of it being worth asking for a more intelligible non-quantum version of this explanation, and then decided, on reflection, that this was probably not worthwhile either.

"Francesca, why does your avatar keep biting its nails?" she said, instead.

"It does that when I bite my nails. It's set to Authentic," said Francesca, with a shrug.

"Why?"

"I find the other options make me feel sick."

"Are you sitting down? Real and non-real, I mean."

"I dislike that distinction. I prefer to talk about my Real Virtuality self. This is the cogent manifestation of all possible selves, in real time, in all time."

Babble! BeetleBabble! thought Eloise. She preferred an absolute schism between her real self and her unreal self, and she preferred to maintain these distinctions, despite the nausea they induced.

"Would you like to qualify any of your previous statements?" said Eloise, one last time.

"No," said Francesca. "The ANT experienced a perception ellipsis, and yes, we're sticking to that term."

"Jesus Christ!"

"If you just switch to Authentic you'll find it's much easier," said Francesca. "You'll get rid of the headache."

"No, thanks."

"Just try it, for a moment."

"Answer the questions," said Eloise. "You are beginning to really irritate me."

"That's much better!" said Francesca. "Did you switch already?"

"No! Fuck off!"

"Wow, that's unusual. Imagine if you weren't in Calm, you'd be—gnashing your teeth and throwing stuff across the table."

"There is no stuff! Shut up!" said Eloise. She realized now—she must have switched. But how had she switched? "How did I switch?"

"You must have pressed the wrong button."

"You know, full well, there are no buttons. At least, are there?"

"Oh, all right, I did it," said Francesca. "I switched you."

"How the hell did you do that?" said Eloise.

"It's just one of the things I can do," said Francesca.

"Does Guy Matthias know you can do things like that?" said Eloise.

"Yes, that's why he first employed me. I did a thing like that."

"But you've just hacked into the NATSO Boardroom system, haven't you?"

"Er, yes. It's not a big deal," said Frannie, modestly.

"It's incredibly worrying. And illegal."

"Yes, yes, you could take us to court, in public. But imagine how embarrassing it would be for NATSO!" said Frannie. "An insecure national security system! Instead, Beetle can work with NATSO to fix this unfortunate problem I have just discovered."

"Fucking hell!"

"Meanwhile, I suggest you try to calm down."

Eloise tried to calm down, really. Real calm. She breathed deeply, and said: "Why would I deploy an ANT, when it turns out it is only operational on a cloudy day?"

"That's not the case," said Francesca, very calmly. Eloise wondered—had she now switched to Calm? Or was she now authentically calm? "The ANT is operational in all types of weather, except when something extremely improbable occurs."

"Sunlight?"

"Extreme sunlight, yes."

They might have continued, slowly turning circles, debating the meaning of perception, the likelihood of a bright ray of sunlight falling at precisely the moment an ANT was confronted by a suspect, who was not even the right suspect, or even any sort of suspect at all. But now the

Real Douglas Varley entered again, saying, "Sorry about that. Is there anything I need to get up to speed on?"

"Francesca just hacked into the NATSO Boardroom system, as a practical joke," said Eloise.

"Why did you do that, Francesca?" said the Real Douglas Varley.

Francesca was biting her nails again. "Eloise, I want to issue a full apology for switching your settings. I sometimes do stupid things at times of extreme stress. It is a defense mechanism but I am actually very embarrassed."

"You or your avatar?" said Eloise. "Which one of you is embarrassed?"

The Real Douglas Varley was presumably not set to Authentic, because he stared into space and seemed quite unconcerned. Unless, Eloise wondered, he was genuinely unconcerned. Expressionless. It was possible. So many people were.

"I switched you back some time ago," said Francesca. "Once more, I am sorry. It was—you're quite right—unprofessional. It was a lapse, caused by stress."

"Are you in Calm now? Or Authentic?" said Eloise.

"I'm in Authentic." Francesca put up a virtual hand in a peace sign. "I am authentically sorry."

"Francesca, I think we'll need to have a separate meeting about this," said the Real Douglas Varley.

"Bullet points," said Francesca. "Scrace Dickens, do you want to take them?"

"Sure," said Scrace Dickens.

"One—there will be no further glitches. Two—there will be no further glitches. Three—there will be no further glitches."

"I think you may have made an error," said Scrace Dickens. "Your bullet points seem to be the same."

"It's called *omne trium perfectum,*" said Francesca. "It's a rhetorical device."

"Ah!" said Scrace Dickens. "I stand corrected. Thank you."

Eloise began to say something, then gave up.

"I consider this meeting concluded," she said, instead. "We have established that, unless there is sunlight, the probability lifechains will continue to work. Or, unless there is too much Zed. Is that right?"

"Are we finished?" said Francesca.

"It seems we are," said Eloise.

"Goodbye then," said Francesca, and disappeared into thin air.

"Why does she do that?" said Eloise.

"I apologize again for my colleague's behavior," said the Real Douglas Varley. "It is not acceptable and does not remotely conform to the BeetlePact. There will be a full inquiry."

"Just guarantee that there will be no further glitches."

"There will be no further glitches," said the Real Douglas Varley, and, carefully, walked out of the unreal door.

FIVE

Varley's assurance that there would be no further glitches (so-called) was followed, over the next few weeks, by a series of catastrophic so-called glitches. This was unfortunate and also compromised the predictive lifechains once again. There were violent suicides, with several desperate individuals hurling themselves from high buildings or bridges. Another poor man slit his own throat with an old hunting knife. Another sadly insane individual jumped off a cliff, holding his two-year-old daughter. Many of these acts of appalling self-destruction, and destruction of others, were committed by people who had not even featured on the BeetleInsight Program. They were considered, prior to the moments of their deaths, to be "consistent subjects," meaning they did not require analysis for possible inconsistencies—and yet, it turned out, this category did not represent the probable culmination of their behavior, which was, in the end, inconsistent with everything that had previously occurred.

In such cases, it was possible—Beetle explained in its internal reports—that the definition of *consistent* was inadequate. If so, this was a language error, and not a machine error. Words must become more reliable as input. Therefore, language must be adjusted, to make it less susceptible to error.

At the same time a few stalwart employees of Beetle and its affiliated corporations failed to appear at work, even when they had arrived on time every day for years. One of them was discovered to be "out fishing."

This was not even a metaphor. There were other odd glitches, or Anomalous Social Phenomena (ASPs, not to be confused with ANTs). These did not matter enormously, except that they destabilized the probability chains, or caused them to succumb further to Zed. For example, various people who had always been cordial to the Very Intelligent Automated Driving Systems (VIADS) began—spontaneously and for no reason—to insult them instead, telling them to piss off, to leave them alone, to just fucking shut up and drive, to go to hell, and so on.

There was another category of glitch and this related to crimes committed by those who had failed to convert to cryptocurrencies at the right time, despite a great deal of media attention to this rising phenomenon. As a result of their human error, these people now discovered that old money was utterly worthless. Cryptocurrencies were, of course, an intrinsic part of the free market, and it was generally acknowledged that the free market was a fundamental good, that societies must operate using these equable economic principles and that those who denied the fundamental validity of the free market, as a precept, were unrealistic. These people could not be bailed out, of course, because the free market was free. Of course, at times of financial crisis the Government did, in fact, bail out the major institutions of the free market, but this did not in any way undermine the fundamental notion that the market must be free and this bailing out could, of course, not be extended to individuals within the free market.

Some people are, alas, not intellectually capable of understanding arguments about such complex things. These benighted people came to resent the fact that their life savings had become utterly worthless due to the sudden rise of cryptocurrencies, and that they had—for example—toiled for fifty-odd years only to discover that they were in fact old and poor. Or, they were young and poor, because they could not find a job that paid in BeetleBits or any other reputable cryptocurrency. Therefore they earned almost nothing at all and scarcely enough to pay their rent. In fact, there were no other reputable cryptocurrencies apart from BeetleBits, but this was just an inevitable consequence of a free market, and it was perfectly possible for competitor currencies to rise to prominence as well; except somehow they never did.

Oddly enough, the people who had made these errors with the

cryptocurrencies started to behave in unpredictable and peculiar ways as well. Instead of being grateful for the jobs they were offered—the economy, as everyone knew, was in meltdown, though this was nothing to do with the free market, which was a fundamental good—these people, rather a lot of these people, began to protest outside the Houses of Parliament. This was in defiance of legislation that made it clear that gatherings of more than twenty people were banned in this area, that harassing government officials and those who worked for the security of the nation was illegal. These people were often young and foolish and did not entirely understand. However, they were joined—yet more oddly—by people who were not young at all, though clearly also foolish. They picketed Beetle offices and behaved in extraordinary and violent ways. They even attacked Beetle employees in the streets. This was unfair because—although Beetle employees were, indeed, paid in BeetleBits—it was not as if most of them earned very high wages at all. Guy Matthias didn't like to cultivate an atmosphere of material greed within his company, so employees were also remunerated in non-fiscal ways, including free smoothies, mung bean salads, and gene tests, as well as fifteen days of paid holiday a year, so long as their performance fell within Beetle parameters. The parameters changed a lot and were aligned with each person's capabilities. In recent years, according to internal statistics known only to elite members of BeetleInnerSight, a mere 0.7 percent of the company had been found to have attained the standards required for their fifteen days of paid holiday, and although people were discouraged from discussing such personal matters (it was part of their Beetle contract), a few people began to protest about this as well. During these uneasy weeks, a few Beetle employees began to exhibit signs of resentment in ways that the BeetleInnerSight Program had not predicted at all.

Other peculiar glitches occurred, which were not indicated by BeetleInsight parameters, and which were profoundly disruptive to the overall workings of the Very Intelligent and Progressive Systems (VIAPS, not to be confused with VIPAs, commonly known as Veeps). These glitches were categorized under the quantity of Zed. Some people began to trade objects for food: shoes, clothes, their watches, their jewelry, their family heirlooms. These "stuff-sales" did not happen online—where you could buy and sell only in BeetleBits—but in grimy church halls, ravaged old car parks, or private houses. Alas, within the free market it is not permitted to trade freely in any place you choose, and these people were of course prosecuted for trading without a license. The stuff-sales ended and the law was tightened to ensure there were no further (human) errors. But the wider trend was quite unexpected.

The BeetleInsight parameters were beautiful and delicate, and they responded to these shifts of actuality, and rendered them into shifts of probability as well. For example, any person who was paid in old pounds and not in BeetleBits was automatically redefined as a case of interest to BeetleInsight, because of the anomalous (yet in fact now quite common) behavior of other people who were paid in old pounds and not in BeetleBits. Indeed, the psychological profiles of those paid in pounds indicated, in the end, that the reason they were paid in pounds was because they were psychologically unstable, and not—as some argued—that their psychological instability derived from the associated stress of being paid in pounds. It was unfortunate that so many people were psychologically unstable, but then it was also very fortunate that BeetleInsight could attend to them and create individual probability chains for each of these unfortunate people.

It was also the case that people who committed suicide were psychologically unstable, and their suicidal actions represented the culmination of their tragic lives in general. The probability chains reversed to accommodate these new revelations. It turned out, for example, that George Mann had exhibited clear signs of unstable and inconsistent behavior throughout his life. An objective inquiry into the tragic case of George Mann, released twenty-three days after his killing spree, made this clear. This inquiry discovered, for example, that George Mann had come to the attention of BeetleInsight long before his atrocious crimes because of his anomalous refusal to accept an interface implant, as recommended for those in elevated positions of responsibility at his company, AHTCH. Every other member of the upper management and middle management and even lower management of this company had accepted an interface implant, in order to communicate more effectively with VIPAs, VIAPS, VIADS, and all other interface devices, including their fridges. George Mann's refusal was inconsistent with his own behavior and also the behavior of his colleagues. From this point George Mann was monitored by the BeetleInsight Program and probability chains were generated from his activities, in the usual way. On the day of George Mann's crime, a clear probability chain had been generated that indicated that it was highly probable he would commit the crime he committed. This probability chain, however, was ignored by human error.

The inquiry recommended, therefore, that the human in question should be removed from his/her/its job and retrained either in Beetle or elsewhere. A full apology should be issued by this human. Beetle must also take immediate action to eradicate this element of uncertainty in its probability lifechains. The category of Zed must be subdued by all available means. No changes should be made to the Sus-Law, for the safety of everyone.

Thus the inquiry concluded.

It was a funny coincidence that—due to the sophisticated nature of its data collection process—BeetleInsight had extensive cyber-files on every member of the committee for the inquiry. These cyber-files went back several decades and included rather shocking video evidence of the chairperson of the committee relieving himself onto the face of a prostitute. Of course this had nothing to do with the favorable outcome of the inquiry for Beetle.

In fact, the outcome was not entirely favorable for Douglas Varley, who was woken once again in the depths of the night by an alarm going off. Recently, he had been woken almost every night by one alarm or another, and Scrace Dickens—having reset himself in line with the new parameters of normality—now announced each alarm by saying, "I'm afraid we're getting another one, Varley!"

After saying this, Scrace Dickens added: "Sarah Coates would like to speak with you."

Still half-asleep, Varley struggled to form the words: "Hello, Sarah. How are you?"

"Very well. We're concerned, however. Are you concerned? The report raises some serious questions for us to consider."

"Have I seen it? Which report?"

"I have it now," said Scrace Dickens, and Varley fumbled toward his BeetlePad.

"The VIAPS are functioning very well," said Sarah Coates.

“Well, that’s great,” said Varley, trying to read the report quickly, and pausing—with a feeling of incipient nausea—at “human error.” Worse besides! “A full apology should be issued by this human.” Which human? For a moment his heart seemed to stop—causing his BeetleBand to express its deep concern. Such beautiful compassion made him want to weep. A full apology. He wanted to apologize to everyone. He dreamed, in fact, of George Mann’s sons, or, somehow, he dreamed as George Mann’s sons—horrible insidious dreams in which he was trying to wake, and yet there was something bearing down on him, preventing him from getting up. He woke screaming, at times, real echoing screams, which were noted by his BeetleBand. Therefore, he knew, he would be presented—now the time had come—as a Beetle employee who had cracked under many varieties of strain.

“Our concern,” said Sarah Coates, “is that you are mentioned in all but name.”

“On what do you base this assertion?”

“On the fact that a previous version of the report, which we have managed to persuade the committee to redact, named you by name,” said Sarah Coates.

“On what did you base your request for a redaction?” said Varley.

“On the future fact that if anything else happens, any further errors or glitches, then we will name you by name ourselves,” said Sarah Coates. “Or, to be exact, that you will name yourself by name.”

Varley’s head ached. His BeetleBand said, “Your heart rate is going down, Varley. Please take action.” What did that even mean? he wondered. Was it bad, for his heart rate to go down? Was he slowly dying, his heart beating more and more slowly each day? Yes, of course, he was slowly dying, he realized, with a jolt. Of course! The thing about Real Virtuality was that you often forgot about death. You existed beyond the body, or at least not exactly in the body, and at times you even failed to register your mortal frame, except when your BeetleBand registered it for you. Even then it didn’t seem to be quite real. It seemed to be something that was happening but only to the BeetleBand. For a moment he wanted to say to Sarah Coates, “The thing is, I am dying! And not even slowly! Quite quickly, in fact! How are you going to deal with that? How will any of us deal with that?” Recently he had neglected his toothbrush test. Or, he was somehow reluctant to do it. He wasn’t sure, but either way the lack of results would weigh heavily against him. His predictive chain had altered and so had the predictive chain of everyone else. This was another human error; again, his own.

"Could I speak with Guy Matthias?" said Varley.

"Guy is very busy at the moment but he asked me to liaise with you about how we will move forward from this position. He asks you to meet me in the Boardroom in five minutes. Is that convenient?"

Varley glanced at his BeetleBand: 07:00. Outside, it was not yet light. They were in the depths of the chastened winter. It was 7 January, he realized. He hated the winter in Europe. It made him miss home: Fresno. Few things made him miss Fresno, but sad, naked trees and the bashful dawn actually did. In the near-darkness, he saw the lights from Mercury cars, moving along the street, beneath the vast, indifferent sky. Varley felt, suddenly, that there was nothing but space, just this blankness beyond him, dark and terrible.

"Yes, of course," he said.

"Will there be any further glitches before we meet in five minutes?" said Sarah Coates.

"Is that your question or a question from Guy Matthias?"

"The distinction is not important at this moment in time."

"There will be no further glitches before we meet," said Varley. "That's absolutely guaranteed."

Unfortunately, at this moment Sally Bigman appeared outside Pat's Caff brandishing a pistol. This had belonged to her grandfather during the Second World War, when he was a member of the Home Guard on the Isle of Sheppey. Sally fired half a dozen rounds at two ANTs that were guarding the café where her husband had committed suicide by droid, according to the media. It seemed Sally Bigman did not agree with the media on this issue, as she was heard shouting, "This is for my husband, you fucking murderers!" The shots severely damaged one ANT and caused the other to lose some basic functions, including its power to speak. This ANT, therefore, could no longer negotiate this complex situation, so instead it seized Sally Bigman by the throat as she attempted to reload. A small crowd gathered around the ANT as it stood over Bigman, who had sunk to the ground on account of being unable to breathe. People shouted, "Are you going to kill her as well? For shame!" and other sentiments that were later found—in a criminal court—to constitute harassment of those working for the security of the nation.

Although it was an offense to attack or abuse any life-form, including a very intelligent anything of any sort, it was felt by many that Sally Bigman had mitigating circumstances. Nonetheless, the law is the law and the police, along with a dozen further ANTs, arrested her at the scene. Sally's pistol was confiscated and she was forced into a van. The injured ANTs were tended to by MediDroids and taken away in a different van.

"Throw them in the fucking dustbin!" someone shouted. "They *are* fucking dustbins!" said another person. "Melt them down and make them into pots and pans!" yelled someone else.

Abuse of ANTs and other sentient entities was also illegal, and these people were also arrested. The crowd was restless and the police officers left guarding the café were made to feel deeply uncomfortable. They were soon replaced by another pair of ANTs, who did not experience social discomfort.

No predictive scenario whatsoever had predicted that Sally Bigman would fire at the ANTs. Her arrival at the café had been filmed by hundreds of ArgusEyes and further security devices, of course, but ensuing lifechains had predicted her arriving to grieve quietly, or at the very most glaring at the ANTs and taking no further action. A basic assumption of all lifechain predictions pertaining to Sally Bigman was that fear would play a part in her decisions, and self-preservation. Thus, no alert had been issued.

Douglas Varley received this news from Scrace Dickens as he prepared to go into the RVcave. Clearly it didn't help his cause at all. He also failed to understand why the lifechains had not factored in the possibility that Sally Bigman might set aside fear and self-preservation and try to avenge her husband. It was a clear possibility and almost, he felt, a probability. Then Varley wondered if he felt it was a probability only because it had already happened. His BeetleBand beeped and announced a message from Sarah Coates: "It seems we must move forward faster than we had intended." Varley didn't even understand this. How fast had she intended to move forward? When had she intended to move forward at a more leisurely pace? How did one calibrate speed, moving forward, and in relation to what?

Douglas Varley could, of course, have refused to take the blame for the unfortunate series of errors. He could have decided to lose his job, lose his salary in BeetleBits, become impoverished and unverified—he had an absolutely free choice about all of this. Yet, under Guy's leadership he had instigated the BeetleInsight Program and directed it for several years. If he admitted that the lifechain had failed to consider a probable scenario then he was, effectively, admitting that this could happen again. This would be cataclysmically bad for the BeetleInsight Program, for its many contracts with businesses, governments, security services, police forces, armies, healthcare providers, schools, universities—for Beetle in general. Furthermore, losing his job would be very bad for Varley's life. Also, it was improbable—according to all the algorithms—that a machine error could have occurred at any stage of anything. Though, at the time, the lifechain had not predicted the improbable actions of George Mann—or Lionel Bigman or even, most recently, Sally Bigman—there were now probability chains for all these events. The probability chains were quantum, and did not abide by linear time. In quantum terms they were always correct, because they represented every possible reality, at the same time.

In the Boardroom, the Real Douglas Varley appeared in Conciliatory mode, as the actually real Douglas Varley longed to bang his head repeatedly on the table—though the table of course wasn't real, but really virtual.

"Are you sorry for the tragedies caused by your human error?" said Sarah Coates.

The Real Douglas Varley blustered at this point: "I hadn't meant— It wasn't—"

"Are you sorry, or not?"

"I am sorry for those who have died or been left injured, yes. Equally I am confused."

"Why are you confused?" said Sarah Coates, sounding quite unsympathetic.

"It is clear that the lifechain is afflicted by something my colleague Francesca has referred to as category Zed events."

"This is what your colleague Francesca calls them?" said Sarah Coates.

"Yes. There should not be so many category Zed events, in human life in general. The category of Zed should be a minimal value. It should represent the absolute outlier in any system, the element that is virtually impossible. Yet, at the moment, category Zed events are becoming possible and even, it seems, probable. We need humans to become more consistent and logical. In their own interests. I wonder if it might be worth pointing this out?"

Sarah Coates—represented as an attractive woman in her fifties, powerful, silvery, and terrifying, making assertive eye contact—said: "I am not sure what you mean."

"To put it another way," said the Real Douglas Varley. "I mean, if humans cannot be trusted to behave in ways that are good for them—as humans—then perhaps Beetle needs to encourage humans to behave in a more advisable way."

"That is an interesting idea," said Sarah Coates, noncommittally. "However, at Beetle we believe in free will and freedom of speech, as fundamental human rights."

"Of course, thank you for reminding me," said the Real Douglas Varley. "Please forgive me."

"It is not my place to forgive you," said Sarah Coates.

The actually real Douglas Varley didn't know what to say at this moment, and thus, the Real Douglas Varley was silent.

Sarah Coates resumed: "We also feel that, at this point, it would be appropriate for you to offer an apology to the public, who have been let down by these human errors."

"An apology from me? Not from Beetle as a whole, or from our press officer or somebody who knows the best things to say in such circumstances?"

"No, we think that a personal approach, from a very important member of our community, would be the right response," said Sarah Coates.

"There are lots of possible definitions of right," said Varley. "Lots of possible right responses."

"That is true, but in this case this is the only right response we are interested in pursuing."

Douglas Varley's cataclysmic error was intrinsic to his being human and being a human. It was completely understandable. It was also completely reprehensible and he would never do it again—the specific human error, rather than being human, which he was obliged to do over and over again until he ceased to be anything at all. After phrasing his apology in this way, Douglas Varley as the Real Douglas Varley was advised by Sarah Coates to find a less convoluted version.

"You don't want to sound pretentious," she said. "Or overwrought."

"I wasn't aware I was sounding either," said the Real Douglas Varley.

"Perhaps I misunderstood you." At this point Sarah Coates—on behalf of Guy Matthias—supplied a few helpful phrases that Varley might, if he chose to do so, insert into his apology.

"Your choice entirely," said Sarah Coates.

At the same time, in another Boardroom, another version of Sarah Coates was talking to David Strachey, concerning the nature of Varley's interview. This Sarah Coates glistened with hard, certain youth. Her muscles were clearly defined beneath her white, almost translucent shirt. She was twenty-three or twenty-four, with a girlish way of laughing, turning toward Strachey's avatar and gazing at him with limpid eyes.

"Guy Matthias asked me to inform you that you have absolute freedom, of course, and he has no desire to interfere with the workings of the press."

"Of course. That goes without saying," said Strachey's avatar, which presented as a younger, fitter version of Strachey—possibly Strachey as he had been at the age of forty, assuming the real forty-year-old Strachey had played tennis far more regularly than, in fact, he had.

Meanwhile, the real Strachey clenched his fists, and his BeetleBand started to admonish him, so he clenched his fists harder, so he drew blood with his nails, so the real Strachey found there was real blood upon his hands, which he wiped furiously across his shirt.

Strachey's unbloodied avatar said calmly, "Well, is there anything else we need to discuss?"

"We have a few—very tentative—suggestions for areas that Douglas

Varley might be most comfortable discussing. No remote obligation to pass them on," said Sarah Coates.

"Send them to my Veep," said Strachey.

"Your choice entirely," said Sarah Coates.

A few hours later the Real Douglas Varley returned to the Boardroom and answered questions posed by the redoubtable Wiltshire Jones, who manifested in this realm as a beautiful feminine male, with long black hair and a refined jaw, wearing a green suit, glasses, and, as a retro touch, using a pen and paper to take down shorthand notes. The conversation was also, of course, filmed and recorded. Douglas Varley had carefully planned his responses to Wiltshire Jones's questions. In this preparation he had been assisted by the fact that he had personally designed *The Times*'s logic-chain algorithm for interviews. He offset his significant feelings of personal stress by predicting each question before Wiltshire Jones asked it.

"Our readers are not quite as tech-literate as you, Douglas Varley, so I wondered: Could you explain in lay speak what went wrong?"

"Of course," said Varley.

Using many deliberately technical words, Varley explained that the Beetle algorithms were accurate to margins that made errors impossible. This was why the predictive algorithms, for example, were credited with status in courts of law across the world, and why the Sus-Law had been so effective in countering terror. He knew, at that point, that Wiltshire Jones would ask him why the computer system hadn't corrected his fault, and he explained, again, that the computer system was immaculate but sometimes human behavior was not. It was a simple equation. There was a category of Zed, which described this fundamental imperfection in the human world, and the category of Zed had disrupted a few—very few—recent algorithms. He had failed to recalibrate the lifechain sufficiently, factoring in Zed, and this was a human error. The actually real Douglas Varley attempted a wry self-deprecating laugh, which was relayed in the Boardroom as a nervous titter. He hoped this wouldn't undermine his case. In line with the logic chain, Jones pointed out that he was not quite answering the question, and Varley, pretending to stutter, said that the answer was boringly simple: It was all his fault. He knew now that Wiltshire Jones was programmed to become irritable, to reflect the presumed irritation of the audience.

"The readers of *The Times* and affiliated online publications need a more complete explanation of this total shambles, which has so far caused the deaths of so many innocent people," said Wiltshire Jones, sounding irritable. "You seem to be blaming it on a letter of the alphabet."

"No, I'm not blaming Zed. I am blaming myself," said Varley. "It is so frustrating but in a parallel universe, you might say, the deaths were averted. Mann's family are fine, and Lionel Bigman has not committed suicide by droid. This is the path we would expect to generate, in this situation, without the appalling human error—errors—that I inserted into the chain. I did not cause the deaths, of course, because they were predestined to occur unless they were averted, but I failed to permit the system to avert them as it normally would. I can only beg the families to forgive me. I also want to say—if I may?—"

Wiltshire Jones nodded, looking irritable.

"—that in general the BeetleInsight system saves scores and scores of lives every year, though of course I cannot supply a specific number because the process is classified."

The logic chain provided for another irritable question, which Wiltshire Jones now supplied:

"The readers of *The Times* and affiliated online publications deserve much better than this," he said. "Do you understand? This is inadequate." He leaned forward and rested his glasses on the end of his nose. Then he picked up his pen again, in a combative gesture, as programmed. Varley liked that touch—he had added it for aesthetic reasons only. He'd imagined it looking quite fine on the avatar of a brilliant female robohack, but Wiltshire also pulled it off with aplomb.

"The readers of *The Times* and affiliated online publications deserve much better, you are quite right," said Varley. "Beetle, my endlessly generous employer, and the amazing and inspirational Guy Matthias, deserve much better as well. I can only say that the recent—er—death of my father perhaps caused me to become a little distracted. As a result, I did not factor in Zed, to a sufficient and accurate level. I did not factor in Zed as it affected me, and as it affected humanity in general. I know this is no excuse but I am very sorry for the terrible consequences of my failure."

It was disconcerting when you leavened your lies with truth, Varley considered. At the mention of his father's death, the one true thing in all this nonsense, he experienced a shock, in his actually real self at least, though the Real Douglas Varley continued to look sincere and remorseful. In reality, it was as if he had been electrocuted. Then he wanted to cry, *Daddy! Daddy! Forgive me! My dad!*, and he wanted to throw himself to the floor—real, non-real, any receiving surface—and weep for Mann and his poor family. For Bigman. For all these grieving families, all those who had realized that the glittering edifice of the Boardroom, the virtual realms, could not negate mortality, and the timeless expanses of the cyber-world could not return the dead. He wanted to weep for the memory of his father, in the agonizing final throes of cancer, discharging himself from the hospital, lying to the nurses and saying his son was waiting for him at home, staggering out of a taxi into his lonely house in Fresno. How his father sat for a while, watching TV and drinking a bottle of whisky. How just before midnight he took an overdose of sleeping pills. How Varley had failed to call him that evening, because he had called that morning, and anyway he was working too hard setting up BeetleInsight. How, if BeetleInsight had been up and running by then, it might have prevented the death of Varley's father.

The following day, Varley called the hospital, discovered what had happened, called his father, who failed to answer, and drove in a wild panic from Menlo Park to Fresno. He remembered nothing of the journey, only that moment when he burst through his father's door and found him on the sofa—pallid, forlorn, and crumpled. Varley lay beside his father for a long time, and pressed his face into his father's shoulder, breathing in his familiar smell—aftershave, musty shirts—and he had a single, devastating image of his father, the day before, dabbing on aftershave with the swift automatic movements that Varley had so admired as a child. At one point he heard himself saying, "Daddy. My daddy. Forgive me."

This memory caused the actually real Varley to burst into tears and he heard the Real Douglas Varley saying, "I'm so sorry. Forgive me." In the background, Varley's BeetleBand was saying, "Varley! You are upset!

Ouch! Are you OK?" Wiltshire Jones—of course—had a logic-chain response for this eventuality, and said: "Shall I give you a moment?"

A moment! He wanted to say, "Do you know, that for weeks after the death of my father, I walked around with a pain in my chest, as if my heart was broken. It was an actual physical pain." But he didn't say anything of the sort and the Real Douglas Varley sounded brave and stupid instead: "My personal troubles are not relevant to, and cannot excuse, the errors I have made." At this point, Wiltshire Jones asked Varley—quite gently—if he wanted to say anything else to the families of the victims, and the Real Douglas Varley said, again, that he was sorry. From his heart, he knew the pain of loss. He was so very sorry. He would never forgive himself. He would strive to make the lifechains perfect. He would spend his life trying to vanquish Zed.

Wiltshire Jones thanked the Real Douglas Varley for his time and the Real Douglas Varley thanked Wiltshire Jones. Because Wiltshire Jones was a very intelligent robohack and not an uber-geek like Frannie, he went out through the door.

Back in his kitchen, doing some deep breathing exercises, with his BeetleBand saying, "There, there, that's better. You cry it out," Douglas Varley perceived that his disgrace was total. Then he remembered what had happened on the morning of the Mann alert, how he had woken with this word in his head: *Disgrace!* He had misheard, of course, and immediately realized his error. Perhaps it was his heightened stress levels, but Varley began to wonder—had he caused his disgrace by thinking of the word? Had he predicted the future or had he—by this accidental thought—caused it? Yet—this was madness! Only exceptionally sophisticated algorithms could predict the future, not a mere human. You could not summon a future by speaking it, or dreaming it, or waking with a word in your head. Or could you? *Disgrace,* thought Varley, once more, and then his heart banged in his chest. He had caused his own downfall! The BeetleBand was saying, "Varley, you seem overwrought. Ouch! Are you OK? Ouch! It's OK! Things are never as bad as they seem."

That wasn't true at all, thought Varley. It was an idiotic thing to say. Things were often as bad as they seemed. Furthermore, sometimes they were even worse than they seemed. He stood in his kitchen, considering the possibility that he had not only predicted but caused his own disgrace, that this was madness and impossible, and he must calm down. The BeetleBand agreed: "Calm down, Varley!" it started saying. "There, there! You need to breathe more deeply." The fridge said, "Varley, your temperature readings are elevated," so he stuck his head under the cold tap and this made him gasp. The fridge and BeetleBand said, together, "Does that feel better now?"

"Yes," said Varley, meaning no. He tried to make himself a cup of coffee, and he had arrived even at the point of pouring hot water into the cup and taking milk from the fridge and pouring milk, but then there was milk everywhere—seeping across the table onto the floor, seeping across the floor—everywhere! In a jocular tone, the fridge said, "Looks like you'll need to buy some more milk, Varley!" Trying to stay calm, or at least to become calm, Varley cleared up the milk, thinking about the proverb "No use crying over spilled milk." It was inaccurate and misleading. His kitchen was covered in milk. What was the meaning of this proverb anyway? It was pointless to revisit the past, of course. Even the algorithms understood this. Once the event had occurred, it had always been inevitable. Once the milk was spilled, it had always been inevitable that it would be spilled. He mopped halfheartedly at the flood of milk. He wanted to complain to someone. He wanted to set the predictive algorithms to answer this one question:

Will my disgrace be never-ending?

He was afraid of what they might tell him. Even though, based on recent developments, it would most probably be wrong anyway.

SIX

The following morning Eloise was woken by a call from Little Dorritt. Then her clothes started vibrating, so she said, "Stop it!" They failed to stop. "Stop it now!" They still failed to stop, so she was obliged to take them all off even as Little Dorritt said, "Are you OK, Eloise?"

Naked, Eloise said: "Yes, I'm fine."

Little Dorritt explained that Commissioner Newton wanted a full report on the Lionel and Sally Bigman cases, as well as a full report on the George Mann case. The factor Zed had been categorized as a category of events that represented a grave threat to the security of the lifechain and therefore to the security of the nation. Therefore, Newton also wanted a full report into the meaning of Zed.

"Zed is the greatest threat to civilian safety at the moment," said Little Dorritt.

"I thought Zed was just a factor, indicating uncertainty? Like in an equation?"

"Category Zed events are undermining public confidence in lifechain algorithms and the Sus-Law. Preemptive arrest has been one of our greatest weapons in the battle against crime and terror. We need to reassure the public that these recent category Zed events will not disrupt further lifechains and will, instead, enhance their accuracy."

"How can Zed events enhance accuracy when it is a category that indicates inaccuracy?" said Eloise.

"I am not sure you understand what I am saying," said Little Dorritt, and ended the call.

After she had breathed deeply for some minutes, Eloise consulted her fridge, which informed her that it was empty. "I did issue several warnings," it added, reproachfully. Her BeetleBand reminded her—though she had not set it to remind her of anything—that she had been asked specifically to file various reports. This was absolutely correct, but even so, Eloise entertained a prolonged fantasy about taking the BeetleBand off and bludgeoning it to death with a mallet. This fantasy—though quite enjoyable—caused her pulse rate to increase, and her BeetleBand reminded her of this as well.

Breathing deeply, Eloise decided to skip breakfast altogether. The fridge perceived that this was a bad idea, but there seemed to be nothing else to do. The Custodians also observed Eloise as she failed to commit to her morning jog, and instead felt under the bed for one of her last packets of cigarettes. This action instantly interrupted her lifechain. She left her apartment and went out onto the street. Because she couldn't wait any longer, and because it didn't matter anyway, she leaned against a lamppost, on which there were attached six Argus cameras in different colors, some of them quite small and others resembling the heads of garish monsters. She wasn't sure why the Argus cameras were painted in colors more usually associated with a children's playground, or a crèche. Aware that she was being petulant and that her gestures, in general, were quite childish, she took out one of the cigarettes, lit it, and inhaled. Her BeetleBand said, "Fire! Fire! Something's burning! Eloise! Something's burning!"

"Yes, it's me," said Eloise. "I'm burning."

"You might need to do some deep breathing, Eloise. Your pulse is elevated and something is burning!"

"Definitely, I am inhaling deeply," said Eloise, and took another drag on her cigarette. Then, for no reason, she looked up at the cameras and blew smoke toward them. She was convinced that one of them blinked.

. . .

David Strachey was already in his office, staring out the window, aimless and uncertain. Wiltshire Jones called to explain that the Sally Bigman hearing was this morning. "Should I cover it?" he said. "I can request video footage and sift through it quickly." Of course, Wiltshire Jones sifted through video footage absurdly quickly, and far more quickly than any human hack, which was why there were so few human hacks left at *The Times*. For a moment Strachey hesitated; then he thought that as he was the free editor of the free press, in a free society, he might just go to the High Court himself. He explained this to Wiltshire Jones. The good thing about robohacks was that they never demurred. Instead Wiltshire Jones said, "Right," in a neutral tone of voice.

"I'll be available, if you need me," said Strachey.

"Of course." Wiltshire Jones never needed him. He was just being polite.

Strachey took a Mercury car to the High Court. Via his BeetleBand, the Mercury car, and various Argus cameras en route, Strachey's diversion from his normal routine was observed. Naturally BeetleInsight was very interested in important people such as David Strachey, and so Varley was disturbed by Scrace Dickens issuing another alert.

"What now?" he said.

"David Strachey is going to court," said Scrace Dickens.

"I don't care. He can go to court if he wants."

"He is attending the hearing of the Sally Bigman case."

"Why?" said Varley. "Why's he doing that? Why the fuck is he doing that?"

"How much time do you have?" asked Scrace Dickens.

But Varley had no time, so he set a lifechain prediction to predict the further outcomes of David Strachey's decision to attend the Sally Bigman trial.

The results were not good.

Every scenario ended in Strachey taking early retirement, of his own free will.

The court was very crowded, until various people were removed for contempt, including all those shouting, "Justice for the Bigmans!" and "For shame!" They were escorted by various ANTs into security vans and later charged with the harassment of those working for the security of the nation. After these disruptive and criminal elements had been taken away, the court was not very crowded at all; indeed there was hardly anyone there except the Prosecution, the Defense, and two dozen ANTs. Strachey took a seat in the almost-empty gallery, counting thirty-six cameras above him, and watched Sally Bigman emerging from below, escorted by two ANTs. He noticed that Sally Bigman recoiled each time the ANTs moved toward her.

Sally Bigman was a small, powerful woman, with bleached curly hair, broad shoulders, and atrocious purple bruising around her neck. It was clear from the weals and cuts, as well as the lurid discoloration, that Sally Bigman was fortunate to be alive. Her death would, of course, have been categorized as human error. Wiltshire Jones would have reported that, mired in grief after the suicide of her husband, Sally Bigman made the terrible (and terribly human) error of blaming—and attacking—two innocent ANTs. For a while, Sally stood in the dock, weeping and rubbing her neck, accompanied only by a LegalDroid—her defense lawyer, Sanderson Hawley—who issued curt responses to the judge's questions, in a dull, almost bored tone. The ANTs were being represented by Willoughby Wright-Jones QC, a most distinguished man, who announced himself concerned that Mrs. Bigman might not be well enough to attend this hearing.

"We are happy to postpone until Mrs. Bigman has recovered," said Willoughby Wright-Jones QC to Judge Adebayo.

"When do you think I'll recover from the murder of my husband?" said Sally Bigman.

"As we can see, Mrs. Bigman is most upset," said Willoughby Wright-Jones.

Mrs. Bigman was more upset when the Prosecution called for her to be charged with the actual attempted murder of two sentient entities and the actual bodily harm of said entities, and also with these crimes in the future, in accordance with the Sus-Law. Then something unusual happened. Judge Adebayo announced that Sally Bigman would be charged only with crimes she had committed, and not with any future crimes. This was not remotely in accordance with the Sus-Law and Willoughby Wright-Jones announced himself to be stunned.

Had Sally Bigman's supporters not already been escorted away from the court, for their own safety and the safety of others, they might well have applauded this unexpected decision. But they were busy being charged with various crimes, so there was no reaction in the court at all. The LegalDroid simply nodded and Willoughby Wright-Jones QC went to table an objection. As she went below, Sally Bigman turned for a moment and looked back at the court. It seemed that she mouthed the words *Help me,* though it was uncertain to whom she would have addressed this remark. For a moment Strachey thought she must be speaking to him. But why? Before Sally Bigman could say anything else, four ANTs conducted her downstairs. Observing from the gallery, Strachey noted that events had just become impossible. Judge Adebayo's ruling that the defendant should not be charged with future crimes was impossible. Also impossible, Bigman had addressed a remark, apparently, to him. If he had seen this, then everyone and everything else had, as well.

There was one remaining spectator in the gallery: a tall, slender man wearing a black jacket and black jeans, with dyed black hair and black varnish on his fingernails. He might have been about twenty-five, or possibly older—Strachey was now sufficiently wrecked that he often thought forty-year-olds were twenty-five. Either way, the man was young-looking, with pale skin and long, slender fingers.

Had Sally Bigman been addressing this man instead of Strachey?

He could request Argus footage, but this would only alert everything. The question remained: If Sally Bigman had addressed him, then why?

If she had addressed the twenty-five-to-forty-year-old man, then why?

Feeling that he had stayed too long, Strachey walked down the steps away from the court, but found the dark-haired old/young man beside him. Worse still, the man was trying to tell him something about windows.

"Windows?"

"Did you ever hear the story of the woman who fell out of the window?"

"No," said Strachey. Argus cameras everywhere.

"She was watching the man who committed suicide."

"Which man?" said Strachey, trying to look as if he wanted this man to leave him alone. Actually, this was not much of an effort. He definitely wanted this man to leave him alone.

"Whichever man. That's not in the story. And the woman fell out of the window, alas to her death."

"Which woman?"

"That's also not in the story. After this tragic accident occurred, another woman leaned out of the window to see what happened to this poor woman, and she fell out as well, also to her death. Then another woman did the same, and another woman. Then another woman. Then another. They all leaned out to see what happened to all the other women and they all fell to their deaths. It was very sad."

"Who were the women?"

"People watched at first. Down in the street they were really horrified, they had their hands to their mouths. But then they couldn't bear to watch anymore. It was too horrible. You understand?"

"Who are you?"

"Here is my card. You won't want to look at it now. I'm sure you're very busy." This man, who was either too young to realize how dangerous this was, or perfectly old enough and therefore mad, handed Strachey a small white envelope, then walked away, leaving Strachey to compose his face into the correct expression of utter bewilderment.

In a Mercury car, Strachey opened the envelope the madman had given him.

There was a small piece of card, with nothing on it except the word *Zed*.

This time Strachey didn't even need to try to look utterly bewildered.

Why *Zed*?

What did *Zed* even mean?

After this, a series of fairly odd things happened. *The Times* published this story:

LANDMARK CRITICISM OF THE SUS-LAW

At the High Court today, writes Wiltshire Jones, Judge Adebayo ruled against the Sus-Law and the Investigatory Powers Act. Approached for a response, the Law Society said: "Judge Adebayo is a respected member of our community. We are sure that her decision, placed in the correct context, is an authoritative interpretation of the law." Representing Sally Bigman, Sanderson Hawley said: "We are not able to comment on a trial under process, for fear of altering the predictive algorithms and prejudicing the case."

This story was followed a few minutes later by this story:

ART OR LITTER?
by Severine Gower

Golden beetles have been found under bridges all over London. Some of them have been taken away by people and placed as art in their houses. Others have been smashed and vandalized. What do you think of these golden beetles? They have an estimated market value of 0.000000000000001 BeetleBit. No one's going to get rich on collecting them! They are numerous under many bridges. Should we leave them or squash them?

This story was followed a few seconds later by a cartoon of a beetle lying on its back, with a black eye and its little legs in the air, looking squashed and forlorn. Dark liquid seeped from the beetle, pooling around its upturned form. A caption under the image read, perhaps inevitably, "BEETLEJUICE."

One or both of these articles might have been the reason why David Strachey ended up in Guy Matthias's London apartment, with an inspiring view of the silver river and all the monumental edifices of glass and steel. Sitting awkwardly on a leather sofa, Strachey held a wineglass filled with an expensive Margaux and nodded as Guy explained that he could cope with criticism, even mild disrespect. It was fundamental to a free press, of course. However, the image incited violence.

"Against beetles?" said Strachey.

"The beetle represents all those who work for Beetle. Though I believe fundamentally in freedom of speech, I am also an employer of a great number of peoples as well as Very Intelligent Personal Assistants and other entities. My first concern is the well-being of all of these sentient and semi-sentient beings," said Guy.

"We weren't criticizing Beetle, we were printing an image of what had happened to a pile of golden beetles under Tower Bridge," said Strachey. "If *pile* is the right collective noun for beetles?"

"The right collective noun for beetles is a colony," said Sarah Coates, who was today embodied as a languid sedentary droid with a cricked neck, occupying a chair behind a desk in the corner.

"Thank you, Sarah Coates," said David Strachey.

"I mean, that you need to decide what sort of future you want," said Guy. "Beetle is a benevolent organization that subscribes to all the major standards of liberal society. We are in tune with progressive culture. If you want to know what the future could look like, go to China. They have facial recognition technology above the hand towels in urinals, did you know that? In the urinals. Why?"

"I don't know," said Strachey.

"Well, think about that. Is that what you want? Furthermore, do you want a job, even?"

Strachey picked up his glass and noticed his hands were shaking. He understood why Guy had requested the meeting in person. In the Boardroom, Strachey could set his avatar to Calm. He could represent the ideal negotiating stance without having to act at all. Now he was exposed and horribly real. He became aware that he was looking at Guy with an expression of plain dislike. Swiftly, he adjusted his expression. Guy, he noticed, looked absurdly well: flawless skin, shiny black hair, his yoga-ed physique revealed in a white T-shirt, blue jeans. Strachey looked down at his own scruffy black trousers, his burgeoning gut, his green pullover that was stained with tea. He ran a trembling hand through his gray hair. Then he had a sudden thought: *I will die and none of this will matter.* He even perceived at this moment that Guy would die, but then—would he, actually? If anyone could escape the inevitable, it would be Guy.

"I wanted to thank you for your stringent reporting," Guy was saying. "We really appreciate it. We really appreciate your editorial style. And Wiltshire Jones is an extraordinary reporter."

Christ, he's going to sack me now, thought Strachey. *This minute!* He tried to prepare his face. He crossed his legs and uncrossed them again.

"But newspapers are dead," said Guy. "They have no real impact on the real virtual world. Yours is a curio. We keep it going financially because it's nice to have your funny little site and those occasional nostalgic editions in actual paper. We like it. We like you. But it's a total superfluity in our world. You do understand that, don't you?"

"Yes, I understand everything clearly," said Strachey. He was about to pick up his glass again but then he wondered suddenly if it was poisoned. But that was absurd! Guy would never poison him. It would simply be too analog. Now Guy stood, so Strachey stood as well. He didn't quite understand why he hadn't yet been sacked. Or had he been, and he just hadn't noticed?

"Did you know," said Guy, as they walked toward the door, "that there is a quantity of human existence that we categorize as Zed?"

"No," said David Strachey, becoming very pale. "You mean, the letter of the alphabet?"

"It is classified as instability and uncertainty but really it is much worse than that. It is chaos. Destruction. Do you understand?"

"Possibly," said Strachey, not understanding at all but panicking vividly. Why *Zed*? What was *Zed*? If *Zed* was so bad then why had he received a card with *Zed* on it the other day, from a lunatic? Why had he never heard of *Zed* as a thing before, and now he had heard of it twice in as many days?

As if reading his thoughts, Guy said: "David, you poor man, are you all right? You look dreadful. What's happened to you?"

"Nothing," said Strachey, anxiously. "Nothing at all."

"I'm so sorry to hear that," said Guy. "I hope something happens to you soon."

"Do you?"

"Yes, of course."

This made Strachey even more worried. What thing? What thing would happen to him soon? They reached the hallway and a Rothko, a gray ethereal one that made Strachey think of eternity and nothingness at the same time.

"I'll be in San Francisco then China, but I'll look forward to meeting with you on my return from the East," said Guy.

"Yes, thanks again," said Strachey. He felt somehow relieved that Guy was going to be out of the country for a while. But then he thought: *It hardly matters where he is. It's not the 1980s!*

Guy administered a brutally friendly handshake and even slapped Strachey on the back, then walked away. After waiting for a moment in case something else happened, Strachey turned to let himself out. Or rather, to be let out. Aware that he was now shaking all over as if he had the flu, his plight observed by scores of ArgusEyes, Strachey informed Guy's door that he wanted to leave. "If that's all right," he added. "Please."

"Who are you?" said the door.

"I came in earlier. I'm David Strachey. Editor of *The Times*." *Just about,* thought Strachey. *For now!*

"I'm sorry, I don't recognize you."

"You let me in!" said Strachey to the door. "I can't have changed that much over a glass of wine, surely?"

"Me neither," said the door.

"Further humiliation," Strachey was heard to say, as Sarah Coates came up discreetly behind him, head cocked sympathetically, or head cocked because she couldn't quite move it anywhere else, and keyed in the correct code.

"I'm very, very sorry to put you out," said Strachey, to Sarah Coates.

"There is no need to apologize," she said. "I've always liked you, David." With her head to one side, she smiled, though her eyes were not entirely kind. It wasn't her fault. This was the last unresolved aspect of the Veeps: they couldn't quite sort out the eyes.

"Thank you," said Strachey, unnerved but determined to be polite. "That's really nice to hear."

"You are welcome!" said Sarah Coates. The door slid open, and Strachey went through. It slammed shut behind him, as if it was irritated.

He walked onto the street, his heart pounding so hard that he thought he might collapse entirely. Indeed, his BeetleBand concurred somewhat. It said: "David! You are not doing well! You need to sit down before things get bad!"

"They're already bad," he said to his BeetleBand.

"Who said that? Where did you hear it?" it said.

Strachey kept his expression very blank as he walked away. He maintained this blankness all the way back to *The Times.* Of course, because *The Times* was in a Custodian-run block by Southwark Bridge, he also maintained his blank expression as he walked to his desk, and for the rest of the day. But he was thinking very hard. His thoughts were not remotely blank. They were myriad and frenzied, and steadily this frenzy coalesced into a question: *What the hell is Zed?*

SEVEN

The following day a groveling apology appeared on *The Times* website, for any insult to any Beetle workers even inadvertently implied by its cruel cartoon. This apology was syndicated across the major blogs and conveyed to people on their BeetleBands. After this, Guy Matthias—now landing in San Francisco—advised Sarah Coates that he was quite mollified. She conveyed this heartening news to David Strachey, who said he was delighted that "everything had come out in the wash." There might be furious investigative bloggers, spilling out rubbish on OTR sites, but they were easily buried by the Beetle search engines. Failing that, the sites could be swamped with bogus hits or hacked, filled with offensive content and discredited. This was absolutely fair, because the vast majority of these sites were generated by the Russians, and Beetle had a legal right to defend its reputation against such attacks. Besides, the New Official Secrets Act prevented any detailed investigation into the activities of BeetleInsight, because it was illegal to obstruct or harass anyone who worked for the security of the nation. Varley was now being monitored more closely by BeetleInnerSight and no further action would be taken, unless he made another error. David Strachey had come back into line, thought Guy.

It turned out that this was not quite correct.

Now Sarah Coates announced the first visitor of the morning: Demetriou Nikolaidis, a Nobel Prize–winning economist. He had flown to San Francisco especially for this meeting with Guy, who had just arrived at his out-of-town retreat, overlooking the soporific waves of the Pacific Ocean. He disliked this view, in fact, because the waves made him feel as if he was trapped in a Real Virtuality loop in which time had stopped. He had just asked Sarah Coates to find him another out-of-town retreat, in a location where the waves were less creepy and lethargic.

Nikolaidis was a small man with artificially black hair, resembling nylon, orange skin, resembling leather, and an atmosphere of manic energy. As he appeared on the balcony the sun illuminated his hair, so it shone purple. He bounced toward Guy and shook his hand vigorously, which Guy disliked. Demetriou Nikolaidis was talking about the BeetleBit and how grateful he was that Guy had advised him to convert his dollars at such an early stage.

"I bought it at seventeen dollars a bit," said Nikolaidis. "This morning I looked and it was at four hundred dollars a bit. Extraordinary! Economics, though an illustrious profession, doesn't make you rich, ironically enough."

"Perhaps it could, in theory?" said Guy.

"The further irony is that within my profession very few people understood the trajectory of these cryptocurrencies," said Nikolaidis. "I told so many of my colleagues, you must buy. I didn't hide the information; I felt it was morally requisite to convey it widely. Recently, when I asked my colleagues if they had converted their money, the vast majority said they had not. Or they converted too late. Now they have difficult lives, despite all their professional plaudits, and I am sorry for them."

Guy shrugged. He found it irritating that academics were all transfixed by wealth. He rarely considered his wealth. Indeed, he donated billions every year to charities. Sarah Coates knew which charities; she regularly updated or reminded him. His BeetleBand pinged—a Buddhist *om* emoticon with a kiss from L. He wasn't quite sure who L was. He forwarded the message to Sarah Coates, so she could ascertain the identity of L. He felt nauseous, for a moment, at the thought of receiving any more thoughts conveyed as small emphatic symbols. Were they even thoughts? Could you persuade people to think, actually think, in emoticons?

"The thing is," he said to Nikolaidis, "I am interested in your inspired-click theory and wondered if you might explain a little more about it."

Nikolaidis was, naturally, delighted to explain his theory of the inspired-click. This was a cutting-edge economic theory, and had formed one of the major elements of his Nobel.

"It is beneficial to markets," explained Nikolaidis, "if people are persuaded, or inspired, toward decisions that are in their own interest and/or in the general interest. This is a utilitarian argument—it is best for society to have happy, healthy, successful people. We all need guidance from time to time. Some people don't always seek the guidance they need, yet we are most fortunate because we have a very complex and extraordinary system for guidance—if we use it responsibly and to minimal effect, simply to inspire people very slightly in the right direction."

"Who determines what the right direction is?" said Guy Matthias.

"What a good question! Let me supply you with an example: If I am about to order five hundred cigarettes and four bottles of whisky online, then the algorithm might offer me other alternatives—vape cigarettes, Lucozade. The first few times I am offered alternatives, I ignore them. I hate vape cigarettes and Lucozade makes me throw up, and so on. The algorithm keeps proffering alternatives to my ruinous and antisocial habits and eventually I take them. I am still a consumer, I am still contributing to the market, but now I contribute in a way that is less damaging to my health. This is a trivial example, I concede, but buying choices are the most simple examples we can offer. There are also existential choices, reconditioning choices, political choices—how we can persuade people not to vote the wrong way in elections, and so on."

"What does 'the wrong way' mean and who determines it?"

"You are an intellectual! These are highly complex philosophical questions. Who is the authority? Who is the agent?"

"Well, who is the authority and who is the agent?" said Guy.

"Indeed, we might well ask!"

"As well as asking, why don't you fucking answer? What's your problem? This is bullshit!" As a young man, Guy's quick temper had lost him friends and lovers, but then he became impossibly famous. After that, people accepted his occasional rages as a clear sign of genius. There was even a Boardroom setting in homage to this trait: Volatile.

The Nobel Prize–winning economist was unperturbed anyway.

He was used to robust debate. He was being paid a fortune for this consultation.

"Highly complex philosophical questions cannot be answered glibly, on command, in this way," he said. "I would like to create a research project to develop this further. Our team might, in the end, be able to advise your staff on the inspiration elements within your own system. Our advice would be the vanguard intelligence on this subject. I regard you as a vanguard enterprise, otherwise I wouldn't bother to speak to you. Would this interest you at all? At a philosophical level, I mean?"

"At present," said Guy, "BeetleInsight predicts possible behavioral developments and advises subscribers accordingly: companies, governments, security services, police forces, certain key individuals, and so on. The system has been exceptionally reliable. Yet we have a slight problem with the category of Zed, which is dragging us backward as we strive to move forward. I am keen to develop a more proactive system, to inspire people away from instability and toward stability. It's possible that this might coincide with some of your philosophical and economic enterprises. I'll speak to my Peeps and my Veeps, as it were."

"Well, when you have spoken to your Peeps and Veeps, as it were, I'll be very glad to consider your offer," said Nikolaidis.

"With or without an inspired-click?" said Guy Matthias.

Nikolaidis laughed uproariously at this remark, and left Guy's balcony saying, "A wonderful joke! Wonderful! You are a walking inspiration! How does anyone ever say no to you?"

Unfortunately for Guy, someone had just said no, by BeetleBand. Tara, his favorite young friend in San Francisco, had explained that she was finishing her doctoral thesis, entitled "Post-Humanism and Cartesian Dialectics," and therefore it was impossible to see him that evening. "I'm so bummed about this!" she added.

Guy Matthias sent back a tearful emoticon and a quotation from Georges Bataille: "Erotic activity, by dissolving the separate beings that participate in it, reveals their fundamental continuity, like the waves of a stormy sea."

Then he asked Sarah Coates to block all of Tara's further calls and messages.

With this matter resolved, Guy Matthias embarked on a close reading of Wittgenstein's *Tractatus Logico-Philosophicus,* aiming principally to understand the nature of a closed system of meaning. Guy Matthias had many brilliant and utopian schemes, many of which he had already enacted, but among them was a further notion that language was far too complex, and needed to be refined. One of the many research projects he funded was that of a young professor at the Sorbonne, Julia Pierre, who had developed a brain-waves scanning process to distinguish whether an individual was thinking in words or numbers. One of Guy's major objections to this was that no one thinks in numbers, but of course Julia Pierre assured him—over dinner—that she thought in numbers all the time and there was nothing peculiar about this at all. The research tallied with a long-standing interest of Guy's in honing the thoughts of users, and making them more transparent, to reduce misunderstandings online. At present, Western and other governments, in tandem with Beetle, were obliged to devote significant resources to patrolling the web, punishing those who expressed offensive thoughts and constantly debating the parameters of unacceptable and hateful speech. It was clear to Guy that language as a system contained perilous ambiguities, causing pain and suffering to many. It was possible that language, even, was bound up with Zed, and the world would be less prone to Zed events if language became more stable.

Why have a plethora of words like *cantankerous, irascible, argumentative, uncooperative, rancorous,* when *bad-tempered* would express all of them? Why have "a plethora" of words, in fact, when you could just have "a lot"? Guy was in touch with various linguistic experts in an attempt to produce a new, beautiful, simple language, which he had originally called BeetleSpeak, until one of his many experts advised him that might not be a good idea. "People don't want to speak like beetles," she said. She was Professor Rosalind Gallagher, of Harvard University. Her Boardroom avatar looked like a vintage star of the silver screen, with long brown hair cascading in lustrous ringlets around her face. It always wore a sleeveless top, revealing honed biceps, and trousers with a large zip on the back, instead of the front. This seemed confusingly sadomasochistic and made it hard for Guy to concentrate on what she was saying, or what he was saying.

"But they live like beetles, meaning our sort of Beetle," said Guy. "They're used to it."

"Furthermore, do you really want to refer so obviously to Orwell?"

"Aren't we post-ironic about all that stuff?" said Guy. "*Don't be so Orwellian, you cantankerous old fossil,* that sort of thing?"

"By your terms, that should be *you bad-tempered old fossil,*" said Professor Gallagher.

On the basis of her bewildering trousers and her archaic references to dystopian fiction, Guy ended his constructive dialogue with Professor Gallagher and found another expert, Professor Magnus Donaldson, of Cornell University, who manifested in the Boardroom as a cantankerous/bad-tempered old fossil and considered Orwell to be a parochial English novelist. Nonetheless, he suggested that the program might be called Bespoke, for the sake of grammar.

For the sake of grammar, Guy agreed.

"Of that which we cannot speak, let us fall silent," Wittgenstein had written. *If only!* thought Guy. If only people would stop speaking about the things of which they could not speak, rather than lavishing their confusing thoughts, intentions, and desires, their convoluted gibberish, across the BeetleScape. Wittgenstein, Guy considered, was a supremely intelligent man and quite possibly a genius, but he had never had to live in the real world. Or the real virtual world, either.

Guy reiterated this phrase at a meeting of the Beetle Ethics Committee later that day. This meeting was OTR, entirely. It was so OTR that every member had the same avatar, which was, in fact, a beetle. This made the meeting resemble a surrealist's pageant, or a nightmare, but Guy had decided it was necessary to maintain the anonymity of all those experts who had kindly agreed to participate in the Ethics Committee. Even chosen avatars might be seen to be in some way significant, if the members made the choices themselves, and, if they did not, then the choices made by someone else might also be seen to be in some way significant. Of course, Guy knew who each individual beetle was, and the individual contributions of each individual beetle were logged by Sarah Coates, but the beetles did not know who each other was. They were numbered, for the purposes of coherence, though the numbers changed for each meeting. As far as they were concerned, they were just a bunch of beetles—nine, to be precise. It was clear which beetle represented Beetle, because this was clarified at the beginning of the meeting, though, necessarily, the number of this beetle changed with each meeting. They did not know that Guy was the beetle representing Beetle at this meeting and, indeed, in the past this beetle would usually have been Varley. For reasons of unfortunate human error, this was not possible at the moment.

As the beetles sat down, Guy as Beetle 3 bespoke: "Thank you very much for coming to the meeting. We have various matters to discuss today and if you are all happy then I will proceed to the first item on our agenda."

The beetles bespoke: "We are all happy."

Beetle 3 bespoke again: "The first item concerns the development of an exciting new technology called BeetleInspire, based on the research of Demetriou Nikolaidis. This would complement our BeetleInsight Program, which has experienced a few recent glitches, due to human error."

"Didn't look much like human error to me," bespoke Beetle 2. Guy immediately identified her as Cindy Happe, a German philosopher of mind whom Sarah Coates had found after BeetlePeople, the personnel department, conducted a statistical analysis of the committee and discovered that there were no women on it, at all. Though the committee was anonymous, it was possible that this might leak out, someday, and Guy took immediate action to correct this imbalance. Cindy Happe was a woman, for certain, yet she was also a noncompliant woman, who jettisoned barbs and had initially refused to manifest as a beetle at all.

"In economic terms only," bespoke Beetle 7, "i.e., in terms of the way advertising seeks to influence choice? Or in other ways?"

"Which ways do you mean?" bespoke Beetle 3.

"You name it: political, emotional, social, intellectual, creative, sexual, et cetera," bespoke Beetle 7.

"We are considering various avenues, which would all allow people to realize their full potential," bespoke Beetle 3.

"Would you like to be more exegetical?" said Beetle 2. That was another thing about Cindy Happe, thought Guy: he didn't understand most of what she said. She needed to start bespeaking as soon as possible.

"Exegesis," said Sarah Coates. "Critical explanation or interpretation of a text, especially of scripture: the task of biblical exegesis. Adjective, exegetical."

“It means, can you explain more, about the thing you are explaining,” said Beetle 8.

The Bespoke term for *exegesis,* thought Guy, will be *explanation. Exegesis* will die.

The beetles were designed using the latest RVscaping software and they were quite astonishing. They could nod and shake their heads, and even had complex expressions—raising their eyebrows, smiling, laughing, frowning, looking undecided, confused, deep in thought. Now Beetle 7, for example, was looking confused. “I still don’t get it,” it bespoke. Guy wasn’t entirely sure who this was but he suspected it was Donald Swainson, of NYU, who was known for worrying away at things and refusing to let them go.

“Their own full potential, or a potential that is most beneficial for Beetle and its subsidiary partners?” bespoke Beetle 7. “Anyway, isn’t this just totalitarian mind control?”

Guy as Beetle 3 made a note to ask Sarah Coates to persuade Beetle 7 to depart from the Ethics Committee of his own free choice, as soon as possible.

EIGHT

For years the Sus-Law had worked beautifully and almost everyone agreed that it was infallible. It was a perfect system, so long as the universe was deterministic and so long as humans did not make any errors. There was a further slight problem, which was that if someone was arrested on suspicion of being about to commit a crime, then, technically, they were prevented from committing the crime. Some people argued that it was illogical for such malefactors to be punished for a crime they had not, therefore, committed. Yet, the Sus-Law stated clearly that the lifechain predictions were quantum and, therefore, once the lifechain had predicted a certain chain of events, there was always a realm in which this chain of events had occurred, and so even if—in our realm—the individual had been caught before they committed the crime, in another realm they had not been caught and had committed it.

This, apparently, clarified everything.

Judge Adebayo's decision to charge Sally Bigman only with crimes she had committed—rather than with these crimes plus crimes she would later commit, in the correct and ordinarily legal way—was something of a low point for advocates of the Sus-Law, and for a while the matter was widely debated. Then, quite unexpectedly, a private phone call emerged in which Judge Adebayo described the Sus-Law as "a classic piece of creepy super-tech psychosis." Her bias revealed, Judge Adebayo was obliged to resign. Her replacement was Judge Clarence Ninian Stewart-Jones, who had an unblemished career in the High Court. By coincidence he was categorically in favor of expanding the Sus-Law, but his impartiality was impregnable nonetheless. He was a major investor in several AI companies including BeetleInsight, but he was a thoroughly unbiased judge and of course his investments had no bearing whatsoever on his ability to judge the case. A few blogs attempted to point out that these investments might well have a bearing on his ability to judge the case, but these blogs were mysteriously deluged with hits and malware until they crashed. The editors and writers of these blogs were later found to be guilty of various crimes, now or in the future, and therefore, alas, their sites were taken down. It was all very unfortunate. The trial resumed under the impartial aegis of Judge Clarence Ninian Stewart-Jones. Barrister Willoughby Wright-Jones (who turned out, by wild coincidence, to be a distant relative of Judge Clarence Ninian Stewart-Jones) was still representing the ANTs and Sanderson Hawley was still representing Sally Bigman. All was absolutely in order.

David Strachey had thought about mentioning a few of these strange coincidences on *The Times* but then he remembered the door at Guy's apartment, and how he had abruptly become no one. He remembered Guy explaining that his so-called newspaper had no impact on anyone, anyway. With a great sigh, which was picked up by—and caused some concern to—the Custodians and his BeetleBand, Strachey asked Wiltshire Jones to write a detached article (which was what Wiltshire Jones generally did anyway) about the change of personnel in the trial. Strachey felt angry and sick as he commissioned this piece, and yet more angry and sick as he read it on the site. In this nauseous and irascible state, he decided to attend the hearing that morning. He explained this to Wiltshire Jones, who said, "All right, then!" in his neutral tone of voice. Strachey walked out of the office, glancing up at the sky, at the ArgusEyes above him. He walked all the way to the High Court in the wind and rain, while his BeetleBand said, "Ouch! David, you are getting wet! You are cold! You should go inside. Are you OK?"

En route to the High Court, Strachey was observed by 423 Argus cameras, and BeetleInsight issued another alert to Douglas Varley.

"Why?" said Varley. "Why is he there again?"

"Once more? Why do I exist?" said Scrace Dickens.

"You exist because I made you," said Varley.

"I haven't heard anything like that before," said Scrace Dickens, skeptically.

There had been a brief pause between the sad public demise of Judge Adebayo and the arrival of Judge Clarence Ninian Stewart-Jones, and David Strachey was disturbed by the grave alteration in Sally Bigman's appearance in this time. Before, she had been stocky and healthy-looking, yet now she seemed to walk with some difficulty; her face was gaunt, her skin was quite sallow, and she had red rings around her eyes, as if she had spent the last few days crying. Judge Clarence Ninian Stewart-Jones was imperious and tranquil, elegant half-moon glasses perched on the end of his nose. He advised the court to understand that he was reversing Judge Adebayo's previous, possibly biased ruling on the Sus-Law and admissible evidence, and a murmur went around the Spectators' Gallery: "For shame!" No one dared to speak more loudly, in case they were removed, arrested, judged guilty of various crimes in the future, punished, fined, unverified, and cast out from meaningful society altogether.

After establishing the sanctity of his court, Judge Clarence Ninian Stewart-Jones explained that normal legal parameters would now be applied to the case of Sally Bigman. Therefore, he continued, Mrs. Bigman could now be charged not merely for the attempted murder of two ANTs but also for future attempted murders of ANTs and also future acts of vandalism and sabotage, in line with categorical probability estimates from the lifechain. Behind Strachey, one relative was heard to mutter: "How can an estimate be categorical?" This importunate remark caused two security droids to remove the malefactor, facial IDed as Max Bigman—a geography teacher from Billericay, Lionel Bigman's nephew. He was subsequently charged with harassing those who worked for the security of the nation and with the future crimes of further harassment and even violence. As Max Bigman was ushered away by the security droids, a few more people said, "For shame!" so, to maintain order, these people had to be removed from the court and charged with various present and future crimes as well. After they had gone, Judge

Clarence Ninian Stewart-Jones shouted, "I am happy to begin proceedings for contempt of court!" a few times until everyone had calmed down.

"Sally Bigman is to be charged with actual attempted murder and potential attempted murder, past and future," said Judge Clarence Ninian Stewart-Jones. "What does the defendant plead?"

Sally Bigman looked blankly toward him, as if she did not quite understand the words he was saying. Sanderson Hawley said: "The defendant pleads guilty to the charge of attempted murder and guilty to the charge of potential attempted murder."

No one in the Spectators' Gallery dared to say anything at all, though Strachey could feel them around him, breathing deeply, being told by their BeetleBands to breathe deeply, to calm down. Sally Bigman was taken away again and the spectators filed off. The atmosphere was miserable. As Strachey left, he noticed two things, one which intrigued him and one which alarmed him greatly. The first was that Judge Lisa Adebayo's sister, Laura Adebayo, was sitting in the gallery, observing the proceedings. Laura Adebayo was a distinguished human rights lawyer and member of Lawyers Without Borders. The alarming thing that Strachey noticed was that the Zed lunatic was also there, again, in his black jacket and black jeans. More alarmingly still, the Zed lunatic seemed to be looking at him. This made Strachey leave more swiftly. Doom or not? Murder or suicide? He had no idea. He just knew that editors sometimes had unfortunate accidents in these free societies. Occasionally, their Mercury cars slammed into trees and burst into flames, or they were found beaten to death—a random brawl, nothing else—or they committed suicide without explanation. It was all totally coincidental, of course. Now, utter alarm, the Zed lunatic appeared by Strachey's right shoulder, leaning toward his face, and said: "I am afraid I gave you the wrong card last time. So sorry."

"That's fine. It was just fine," said Strachey, looking appalled to be approached in this way. Busy and formal. The editor of a newspaper, even if newspapers were dead curios!

"Here is my real card," said the Zed lunatic, handing over another small envelope.

"Sure, whatever," said Strachey, in a bored tone of voice.

"Nice to see you again, Mr. Strachey," said the Zed lunatic, sounding bored as well.

When Strachey was in his Mercury car again, he opened this latest envelope, trying to keep it away from the in-car camera, his BeetleBand, his BeetlePad, and everything else.

He took out a small piece of white card. On it was a number and a name, Bel Ami. Though this frightened him a great deal, Strachey put the card in his pocket and stared, blankly, out the window.

Once Laura Adebayo was seen at the hearing, all the lifechain predictions changed. This meant that Varley received another alarm. It came at 15:00, when he was asleep on his kitchen table, having spent the night awake. It really didn't seem to matter, because the alarms woke him constantly.

"Scrace Dickens calling."

"Why must disgrace haunt me in my dreams?" said Varley.

As a result of this slightly weird remark, Varley's lifechains altered and it was automatically determined that he was on his way down, faster than before.

The lifechain, Scrace Dickens explained, had made a categorical estimate that Laura Adebayo, representing Lawyers Without Borders U.K., would soon announce that she was going to represent Sally Bigman without charge. Not only that, she would decide that Sally Bigman was going to sue Beetle for corporate manslaughter, even while she was being prosecuted for attempted murder.

"That's ludicrous," said Douglas Varley.

"You don't believe the lifechain?" said Scrace Dickens.

"Of course I do!" said Varley, swiftly, before his future changed again. "Jesus Christ! What is happening is ludicrous. Or about to happen. It can't be happening. Or about to happen."

"I think you might call this a category Zed event!" said Scrace Dickens.

"That's not funny," said Varley.

"No, I'd say it's more ironic than funny, wouldn't you?"

"I hate irony," said Varley, surprising himself with his own vehemence.

"I think you should sit down, give yourself some time, and calmly think things over," said Scrace Dickens.

This made Varley even less calm.

Shortly after this, Laura Adebayo made her announcement, as the lifechain had predicted. Guy Matthias, in Beijing and monstrously jetlagged, woke to the news that Beetle was being sued. As the lifechain had also predicted, this caused him to become extremely angry. However, also based on the lifechain predictions, Sarah Coates had several soothing remedies available for Guy and had already asked Douglas Varley to come to the Boardroom.

"Would you like the sea symphony now or later?" asked Sarah Coates.

"Try it!" said Guy.

Sarah Coates tried it.

"Switch it off!" said Guy, a moment later. "Where the fuck is Douglas Varley?"

Douglas Varley was in his apartment, trying to give himself some time to calmly think things over. This exercise had not yet worked, at all.

"He's ready to speak with you at your earliest convenience," said Sarah Coates.

Guy was more ready to shout than to speak, but Varley had expected this anyway, so the Real Douglas Varley entered the Boardroom in Conciliatory mode, looking penitent and sorrowful. It didn't help.

"It is a colossal fuckup," said Guy's avatar. "Do you understand, the Real Douglas Varley?"

"I do understand and I am very sorry," said the Real Douglas Varley.

"I'm so glad you are sorry!" said Guy. "I would like you to represent Beetle in court."

"That's a major responsibility."

"Are you saying yes or no, the Real Douglas Varley?"

The Real Douglas Varley said, "Yes," while the actually real Douglas Varley thought, *NO NO NO!*

As a free human being David Strachey was entitled to spend his free time however he liked, in a free society and as long as he did not break the law. With this in mind, Sarah Coates called Strachey and explained that it was important to have independent journalism, but that Strachey's repeated appearances at the trial of Sally Bigman made him look biased and not independent at all.

"We hope you understand," said Sarah Coates. "Of course, ultimately, it is your choice."

"Are you trying to annoy me?" said Strachey.

"No, I'm not trying to annoy you. I'm sorry you got that impression."

Sometimes Strachey hated the fact that it was impossible to argue with a Veep.

The lifechain system was based on determinism, and this notion that humans will behave in certain ways. Humans, of course, did mostly behave in certain ways—human ways. Beetle and NATSO were working to ensure that these human ways, and the possibly related factor of Zed, did not disrupt any more predictive algorithms. Indeed, at NATSO Eloise was filing extensive reports into absolutely everything, including the meaning of the unmeaning category of Zed. Furthermore, Newton had asked for another report, this time into the increasing numbers of people who seemed, actively, to want to become unverified. In general, these people seemed quite harmless, though—as they no longer availed themselves of their BeetleBands or friendly appliances—it was sometimes difficult to ascertain just how harmless. Still, it was not yet illegal to be unverified, even though it was manifestly inconvenient—to the unverifieds and to those who were trying to help them. This was causing Eloise a certain amount of stress, which was ably recorded by her BeetleBand. Her fridge kept advising her to eat more. She kept forgetting her toothbrush test. She had smoked ten cigarettes in the past few hours and each one of them had caused her lifechain predictions to be altered, and not for the better. This was ill-advised.

More ill-advised, indeed, was a decision Eloise made as she attended an arrest at Bank Station. The criminal—Pieter Stenhouse—was judged by the lifechains to be guilty of the crime of future theft. This was based on the fact that Stenhouse had very little money, no BeetleBits, that his wife was heavily pregnant and had just lost her job. These circumstances combined with Stenhouse's remark to his BeetleBand three days ago (or, rather, his remark in the vicinity of his BeetleBand) that "if something doesn't change then I'm going to have to fucking steal the food we eat." Nothing had changed for three days so it was deduced by the lifechains that Stenhouse must now "fucking steal the food we eat." On the basis of this evidence, Stenhouse was arrested by two ANTs at 10:23 outside Costa Coffee, with Eloise as their attendant officer. She found the business slightly grim, because Stenhouse kept screaming, "I haven't done anything! What have I done?" while the ANTs repeated the arrest mantra: "You do not have to say anything, but it may harm your defense if you do not mention when questioned something which you later rely on in court. Anything you do say may be given in evidence."

Stenhouse burst into tears.

"Please have mercy," he begged Eloise. "Please let me go!" He sank to the floor, and even crawled toward Eloise, as the ANTs said, "Do not approach the officer. Do not approach."

"My wife is nine months pregnant," said Stenhouse, his hands raised, protecting his head. "She's due to give birth at any moment. We have no money at all!"

Eloise and the ANTs knew this already, of course. Indeed, this was precisely why Stenhouse was being arrested.

"You might as well fucking shoot me dead, like those other poor bastards," wailed Stenhouse.

"Which poor bastards, you stupid bastard?" said Eloise.

"Don't shoot me," said Stenhouse. "Don't shoot me."

Then he wept and wept.

The lifechain was absolute. The beautiful and complex algorithms had determined, absolutely, that Stenhouse was a future criminal. There was no possible scenario in which he did not commit the crime for which he was being arrested. Nonetheless, Eloise leaned toward him and said, "Go home, Pieter Stenhouse. Don't ever steal anything."

Stenhouse looked up at her, not quite understanding what she meant.

"You mean—" he began to say.

Beside Eloise, an ANT said: "You are allowing the criminal to leave?" in a matter-of-fact tone. It didn't exactly care. It just wanted to clarify the situation. Eloise ignored her BeetleBand, as her BeetleBand said, more loudly, "Little Dorritt calling again!" Eloise switched her BeetleBand to silent, as it flashed manically to tell her that Little Dorritt was still calling. And calling. And calling.

Pieter Stenhouse stood up and put out his hand.

"Thank you," he said to Eloise. She realized he wanted to shake hands. To touch him, at all, was deeply ill-advised. Yet he looked so tearstained and pathetic, so nervous, that she took the hand he offered.

Later, as Eloise filed another report, this time into Pieter Stenhouse and why she had failed to arrest him, she was once more logged as she ill-advisedly failed to take the culinary advice of her fridge and ill-advisedly drank a bottle of wine in lieu of food. Then she ill-advisedly went to bed half-drunk and with her clothes on.

After all these ill-advised things, it was quite inevitable—and even quite predetermined—that Eloise would be sanctioned. The following morning she was woken by her BeetleBand saying, "Little Dorritt." Though she ignored a few of these calls, eventually Little Dorritt just came through her fridge anyway, as she was trying to make coffee. Little Dorritt said: "What happened to you yesterday?"

"All kinds of things," said Eloise. The room was too bright and her head hurt. Besides, she was ravenously hungry. Little Dorritt was meanwhile explaining that certain protocols had already been adjusted several times in light of Eloise's profile and history of distinguished service, but Commissioner Newton was personally concerned. He was, also, personally subject to parameters and if he continued to show such leniency then he might be suspended in turn.

"He is very sorry," said Little Dorritt. "I am very sorry too."

"What, precisely, are you saying?" said Eloise.

"You are also under enhanced scrutiny and this constitutes your final warning."

"What does enhanced scrutiny mean?"

"It means what it is," said Little Dorritt.

"What happens if I don't stop doing whatever it is I'm meant to have done, even when I'm under enhanced scrutiny?" said Eloise.

"Well, then."

Eloise waited for Little Dorritt to say something else. However, that seemed to be the answer.

"What does that answer mean?" she asked.

"Reductionism," said Little Dorritt.

Eloise ended the call, none the wiser. As she went into the kitchen, the fridge said: "It might be a good idea to put a food order in. If you are busy I can do it for you?"

"All right, then," said Eloise. Then, remembering she was under enhanced scrutiny, she said: "Definitely! Thanks so much! Please buy lots of kale."

"Kale?" said the fridge.

"Yes. And—alfalfa," said Eloise. She wasn't even sure what alfalfa was. "Also quinoa."

"Trying to determine if this is a person or a computer," said the fridge. "Are you free to speak to me?"

"Are you?" said Eloise.

"I won't say yes or no right now," said the fridge.

Eloise felt that she preferred it when the fridge talked about yogurt.

NINE

David Strachey was sitting in his real office, overlooking the greasy brown river, the faded white sky, the eerie choreographed movements of the Mercury fleet. He was contemplating notions of free will and determinism, in his own way and without recourse to Wiki-Beetle. He was counting up the years he had worked as a journalist, and wondering if he had ever achieved anything of any significance at all. The situation—his failure to achieve anything—had worsened since Beetle had purchased *The Times,* but then, had Beetle not made this acquisition, *The Times* would have gone bust, like every other paper. At least, every other paper that wasn't owned by Beetle.

In public, and despite recent events, Strachey continued to praise Beetle for allowing him "free rein," which seemed also to be a synonym for "free will." At times he thought of Beetle as a single entity, which was inaccurate and even distressing. He dreamed sometimes of a vast beetle, sitting on his chest so he was unable to breathe. Today he was at a fork in the path—to use the analogy preferred by Beetle, itself a sly allusion to the work of Jorge Luis Borges—a fork in the path, in the garden of forking paths. Actually, in Borges's imaginary book it was possible to go down every path, in every version of reality, and to defy the conditions of linear time, but Beetle had carefully reified this beautiful theme and once you had chosen your initial path this entirely predetermined your future paths. This morning, Strachey had been presented with *the* fork in the path, the fork with which he was presented every time his paper was about to publish something significant and actually meaningful about Beetle and Guy Matthias, and this fork was familiar to him and also on the verge of sending him mad, at which point he would presumably be conveyed to another fork in another path. He had three choices, as usual:

The Status Quo: in which he toed the line, a lot more willingly and freely, and kept his job—for a while at least.

OR—

Personal Ruin: in which he was destroyed by Beetle for his misdemeanors so far, because he had annoyed them/it.

OR—

Murder and Suicide: in which he rang the number of a lunatic called Bel Ami who talked about Zed and people falling out of windows and—by a strange process—became one of those mysterious self-ruining hacks who made a stand, were commended for their courage, and ended up fundamentally dead.

As always, Strachey sat in the Boardroom weighing up these possibilities, and there was a massive, hulking Beetle urging him toward the only sane path, which he chose freely of course, because he was sane. He had always—until recently—chosen the status quo and because of this he was still at his desk. *Your choice,* as Sarah Coates always said. Of course, he had a free choice! Now he was observing the fluid surge of Mercury cars, feeling as if the great Beetle had its legs around his throat.

Some further paths were now evident. For example, George Mann must be profoundly discredited. Poor Sally Bigman must be convicted of attempted murder and attempted future murder and Beetle must be acquitted of all wrongdoing. When those trials ended Strachey would find himself at another fork in the path. Actually, it was the same fork, the perpetual fork. He would—having chosen freely again—command his robohacks to ignore Zed events in general and write a series of reports discrediting Sally Bigman and revealing, steadily, that she was having a breakdown, that she and her husband were on the verge of divorce, that she was having an affair with Pat, as in Pat's Caff. These were invented misdemeanors, but Strachey knew, the squatting Beetle knew, that any flawed mortal could be made to appear dubious, peculiar, even criminal, if you focused the lens closely enough. Strachey's robohacks could even search for key words and phrases, any vile sentiment, any term of abuse. That path was well trodden.

Strachey knew everything that must happen. Yet, he couldn't stop thinking about these two words Sarah Coates said to him, over and over again: "Your choice." There was no choice! He hated the choices he was given, and he didn't want to choose them. Yet he chose them! He hated the thought of himself, cowering at Guy's door, a nothing! Was this a free choice? To do nothing, to say nothing—to be safe, but a nothing! He began to sweat; he wiped his graying temples and his BeetleBand said, "Maybe you need a drink of water!" Strachey went to the fridge, took out a bottle of water, and drank it quickly. The BeetleBand subsided but this thought assailed him. He couldn't shift it. Perhaps it was the incessant choreographed motion of the Mercury fleet, resembling nothing less than a dream, and perhaps it was the constant interruptions from Lettice Gradgrind, his Veep, who annoyed Strachey even more than the Mercury fleet. Perhaps it was the fact that his site had been 98 percent composed by robots this week and 2 percent by humans—and actually that 2 percent by one human, a freelancer called Grub. Perhaps it was the further fact that if he pointed this out to any senior Beetle types then he would be accused of discrimination against robots, or discrimination against humans, depending on their mood. Mostly it was the sense of being constricted, of not even being able to breathe.

Strachey felt dizzy, but he made the call. From the OTR system, which was not OTR to Beetle, he rang the number on the card. He had not dared to search for Bel Ami, had not dared ask Athena who Bel Ami was. As the number rang, Strachey thought: *The path is dissolving. The old path. On this other path: I am doomed.*

Bel Ami answered. "Hello, Mr. Strachey. How are you?"

"How did you know it was me?"

"You're on my OTR system. The number diverts you."

"I don't actually understand what that means."

"Don't worry about it. Would you like to meet for a walk?"

"A real walk?"

"Yes. Southern end of Blackfriars Bridge, in half an hour?"

There was a pause. *Doom!* thought Strachey. The pause was quite long and Bel Ami made no attempt to fill it. But it was filled by this capacious and expansive word . . . *DOOOOOOOOM.* "In forty minutes," said Strachey, just to stop this word reverberating in his head.

"See you then."

David Strachey, editor of *The Times,* recently only in name, ended the call and bowed his head. *Ruination,* he thought. *That path is black. It is paved with Beetles. I am the ultimate corpse at the end. I will be devoured by Beetles. They will gnaw my flesh.* He sustained this disconcerting line of thought as he told Lettice Gradgrind he was going for a walk.

She made no comment.

Elsewhere, or strictly speaking, nowhere, Douglas Varley went into the Boardroom to meet Francesca Amarensekera. In a small, sad irony, the Real Douglas Varley was as optimistic as ever, bouncing dynamically in his seat, picking up marker pens and scrawling gibberish on the white screen. They had a long-standing discussion tabled for this morning, concerning forgeries online. It seemed utterly irrelevant, considering the circumstances. Art forgeries! Had he not been briefed by Scrace Dickens?

"No," said the Real Douglas Varley. "Disgrace, Scrace, did not brief me."

"Scrace Dickens!" said Frannie. "How could you be so remiss?"

"Correction," said Scrace Dickens. "I did brief Varley but I think he was preoccupied with the recent matter of human error and being sued."

"You mean as a result of being sued for committing a human error, Varley committed a human error?" said Frannie.

"It is not for me to draw this conclusion," said Scrace Dickens.

Even my Veep! thought Varley. "*Et tu,* Disgrace?"

"The thing about art," said Frannie, ignoring this weird remark. "Art is authentic. Paintings by Old Masters can be authenticated, that's how they are bought and sold. A forged Titian is worth very little; an original Titian is worth a fortune. Guy has authenticated all the paintings he owns for display online, yet people are putting up forgeries of these paintings in their RV spaces. This violates community guidelines and we would like this offense to become illegal in Real Virtuality as well."

"How do we ascertain if an RV version of a painting is a forgery? Is that even possible?" said the Real Douglas Varley.

"This was in your briefing," said Scrace Dickens.

"Moving on," said the Real Douglas Varley, in a lively, positive tone.

The Boardroom now became an art gallery, styled after Munich's Neue Pinakothek. The Real Douglas Varley stood—in fact his chair had disappeared, so his avatar was obliged to stand anyway. Moving along the pictures, Francesca adopted the passionately informative tone of a curator. "Here we have Guy Matthias's beautiful and moving collection of works by Van Gogh. Greatly copied, never bettered. Here we have several self-portraits, including the famous 'just severed his ear in an act of unbridled genius' self-portrait featuring white bandage, and here are various iterations of the fundamental sunflower theme—very beautiful, very moving—and here is an extremely revolutionary painting of a yellow chair."

"Very impressive," said Scrace Dickens.

"We know these are Guy's and therefore the authentic RV Old Masters because they have been reproduced for this virtual space using the latest nano-imaging technology. Have a closer look."

Now the Real Douglas Varley's perspective changed as he zoomed in on the sunflowers, until the brushstrokes became inordinate, until each stroke was a vast tactile movement of yellow paint, also orange, purple, green, so many colors intrinsic to the overarching yellow, closer and closer, until he felt as if his head were in the painting, he was deep within the paint, until he wondered—was he drowning in paint? He was about to cry out when the perspective changed again and they were in a version of Real Virtuality, the Boardroom itself, with the *Sunflowers* on the wall before them, in ordinary view.

"That was very—er—detailed," said the Real Douglas Varley.

"It's a new file format: N.real. It's short for nano-real," said Frannie. "The designer we use, HanburyNano, is the best in the world. Their detail is more real than reality."

"How can it be more real than reality?" said the Real Douglas Varley.

"Because we can now view details of the craftsmanship that were previously invisible to the human eye. There are incredibly sophisticated forgers working online at the moment, but their technology—though exquisite—is way behind ours. For example, Nikolai Gogol—"

Now Scrace Dickens chimed in: "(1809–52) Russian novelist, dramatist and short-story writer, born in Ukraine; full name Nikolai Vasilievich Gogol. Notable works: *The Government Inspector* (play, 1836), *Diary of a Madman* (short fiction, 1835), and *Dead Souls* (novel, 1842)."

"Thanks, Scrace Dickens," said Frannie. "That's very helpful as background. Just one further point: we are discussing a man who operates under the pseudonym Nikolai Gogol and whose real name we, as yet, haven't quite ascertained. But it's very useful to understand the reason why he has taken this particular pseudonym."

"Which is what?" said the Real Douglas Varley.

"Gogol—the real Gogol, I mean—blurred the distinctions between fantasy and reality in his work. This is, of course, what a forger does," said Frannie. "Here."

Now beside *Sunflowers* appeared another *Sunflowers.*

"It's identical," said the Real Douglas Varley.

"Well, of course, at this level that's quite correct," said Frannie. "But—look a little more closely . . ."

"Do I have to?"

But already the perspective was shifting, and Varley—the Real Douglas Varley, the actually real Douglas Varley, any number of Douglas Varleys—was being propelled toward the painting, hurtled further into it, and further, until his nose was against the paint, and the paint was disintegrating, not into brushstrokes but into chaos, tiny bits of stuff, atoms. Varley/the Real Douglas Varley didn't understand what this stuff was at all—mites, particles, motes, little bits of whatever the hell—and he didn't like it at all. He said, "Help!" and the room changed again; he went backward or outward and then the surface became less studded, everything was smooth again.

"Pixels," said Frannie.

"The atomies?" said the Real Douglas Varley, as Scrace Dickens said, in the background: "Atomy, Atomies (plural): a skeleton or emaciated body. Taken from anatomy." This just confused Varley further.

"Nikolai Gogol uses pixels," said Frannie, ignoring the interruption.

"Our authentic representations of the originals don't. His forgeries commit a gross disservice to the original artist and also to art."

"Is this really a priority?" said the Real Douglas Varley. "Shouldn't we be more concerned about various trials that are currently under way, and the intractable further quantity of Zed?"

"Art is always a priority," said Frannie.

"What are the bullet points from this meeting?" said Scrace Dickens.

"One—Nikolai Gogol is a thieving forger, not the radical nineteenth-century Russian author. Two—we must get legislation to protect art online. Three—this is a matter of great importance for the art world as a whole. Four—this is also a matter of great importance for RV as a whole," said Frannie. "If art can be forged, life can be forged."

"Thank you, Francesca," said Scrace Dickens. "That's very moving."

"Isn't RV, itself, a forgery of life?" said the Real Douglas Varley.

There was a horrified pause, while Frannie and Scrace Dickens seemed too shocked to say anything.

"We should also establish an auction room online," said Frannie, changing the subject. "So that real authenticated works of art can be bought and sold, to those prepared to go through official channels. This would make the point more clearly, about real and unreal representations."

"Is that Point Five?" said Scrace Dickens.

"Yes. Varley, do you have anything else you want to add?"

Varley wanted to add: that his head ached. His heart ached. Great swaths of his mortal body ached. He wanted to know if he would end up in prison. He wanted to know if Zed was real and, if so, if Zed was Gogol. He had a sudden, compelling urge to talk to Frannie, face-to-face. He assumed this was a sign of mounting strain.

"Why did you call Zed Zed?" he asked Frannie. "Was it you that first called Zed Zed, I mean?"

"I couldn't possibly take credit," said Frannie.

"Then who was it?" said the Real Douglas Varley.

"Zed is just part of a line of digits concatenated," said Frannie. "X, Y, Z."

"But then, what are X and Y?" said the Real Douglas Varley.

"They're variable terms, indicating an unknown quantity."

"In that case, however, why is Zed not called X or Y?" said the Real Douglas Varley.

"Because it is the ultimate unknown quantity, the terminus for all the unknowns," said Frannie.

"Is that your definition, your explanation?" said the Real Douglas Varley.

"Yes, I am myself. Who are you?"

"I mean, did you make that up?"

"I never make anything up. I am a geek, not an artist," said Frannie, unhelpfully. "Is there anything else you want to say to me?"

Varley's aching heart pounded, too quickly, as his BeetleBand said, "Calm down, Varley," as the Real Douglas Varley said: "No, that's wonderful. I think we've covered everything. Thanks very much."

Frannie vanished immediately. The Real Douglas Varley, though there was no one present except Scrace Dickens, passed the unreally real and the really unreal *Sunflowers* as he walked out of the unreal door. He still couldn't tell them apart.

Eloise, meanwhile, was running past Westminster and by pure bad luck happened upon the chaotic aftermath of yet another Zed incident, in which a man called Toby McIntyre had attacked passersby with a knife. There was no lifechain warning about this possible incident. She heard the sirens first, and then the familiar sound of ANTs requesting general calm.

Increasingly, ANTs made people extremely uncalm, so this did not seem to help. She heard screams, and further sirens. To her BeetleBand, she said: "Get me Douglas Varley." But this was hopeless.

"I can't talk," said Douglas Varley. "Not to you, anyway."

"What the fuck?"

"You're under caution."

"Oh! Fuck off and talk to me anyway!"

"There's no use crying over spilled milk."

"Are you drunk?"

"No, I haven't drunk anything at all. I spilled the milk."

"Hopeless!" said Eloise, ending the call, running as fast as she could.

Her BeetleBand announced Little Dorritt, whom she ignored. Her BeetleBand announced Little Dorritt, again. She ignored Little Dorritt again. And again. She ignored the hell out of Little Dorritt. She passed cars stalled by the side of the road, a few ambulances. She found MediDroids gathered around the injured, a few of them wearing business clothes, one poor woman bleeding heavily from a deep wound to her neck, moaning and trying to stem the blood, as a MediDroid said, "Do not worry. You will be fine." But would she be fine? thought Eloise. How would she be fine? A few other MediDroids were kneeling around a sixty-something man, blood pouring from a wound in his stomach, soaking his white shirt. A drone hummed above them, recording the scene, and occasionally a MediDroid gestured it away. An ANT had a gun trained on the lunatic, Toby McIntyre, who had dropped his knife and was kneeling on the road. Eloise's BeetleBand was explaining: Toby McIntyre had taught hypnotherapy for twenty-five years. He received payments in old currency, he had a wife called Meraud, and he was writing a book about whether Veeps could be hypnotized. In retrospect, Eloise thought—as she watched McIntyre being escorted away by the ANT, its headless form loping past the stalled Mercury cars—the book might have been an anomaly. Or there might be anomalies that no one, nothing, had discerned. The ANT said to McIntyre: "Move slowly toward the van, please."

McIntyre moved slowly toward the van. He looked drugged somehow; his eyes were half-closed. As he passed Eloise he said: "You should be ashamed of yourself."

Eloise said nothing and McIntyre walked on, the ANT following behind, its gun still trained on him.

McIntyre began to resist as he reached the van, struggling with the ANT and shouting, "Leave me alone! Help me! Help!"

"You must cooperate with me. I am on your side," the ANT said.

"I don't want to cooperate with you!" shouted McIntyre. "You haven't got a fucking head! Where's your head! The last thing I fucking want to do is cooperate with you!"

"Is this really the last thing you want to do?" said the ANT.

At this, Eloise started moving slowly toward the ANT.

"Absolutely the last fucking thing in the world!" shouted McIntyre.

"Absolutely the last thing? Is that correct?" said the ANT, aiming its gun.

At this, Eloise started moving really quickly toward the ANT, while shouting, "Put down your gun! Put it down!"

She noticed, in passing, that the ANT had turned toward her. She noticed that she was shouting, "I'm your superior, put down your gun." She noticed the ANT did not put down its gun and instead aimed it, carefully, toward her. She noticed McIntyre's look of surprise and interest. She noticed that the ANT paused for a moment and said: "Threat will be neutralized in three seconds." She noticed she was using up these three seconds shouting, "Put down your gun!" and then—she noticed a severe opposing force, something that pushed her abruptly backward. She noticed her head slammed backward onto the concrete with a disgusting loud thud, and her bones seemed to crack. Perhaps someone screamed, or perhaps it was her.

Why did that happen? thought Eloise.

She was aware of Big Ben chiming, as she lay on the ground, the blank sky above her. Trying to stay awake, she counted the chimes. She was only at ten when everything faded.

As Big Ben chimed noon, David Strachey was hurrying across Blackfriars Bridge. He saw ambulances flashing further along the river, and his BeetleBand said, "Wiltshire Jones."

"An incident in Westminster," said Wiltshire Jones.

"Another one?"

"We're just getting the full story. A man went mad then a woman went mad and the woman, but not the man, was shot by an ANT. Prior to that a load of people were injured, by the man not the woman. The man is a hypnotherapist," said Wiltshire Jones.

"Christ!" said Strachey. He saw—yes—it was Bel Ami, moving toward him. The black jeans, dyed black hair, black nails. His voice sounded strangulated as he said: "But I have to go. I'm—in a— I'm on a walk."

"Can you talk while you are walking, or not?"

"I might be difficult to reach for a while. Use your judgment. I'll be back in touch very soon."

Bel Ami had turned around once he realized that Strachey had seen him. Now he was walking a few meters ahead, leading the way. Strachey was about to call out, but realized, in time, that this was pure folly. Instead, he followed silently. On Waterloo Road the traffic was barely moving at all. They turned into a series of small, winding streets, and after a while Strachey realized he was quite lost. He imagined waste grounds and dead-end corridors; he felt himself being kicked and bruised, or forced to drink poison, or to sever his veins. He was a coward and he feared physical agony. Yet it seemed, on the other hand, that Bel Ami was taking him toward a bookshop. Could there be physical agony in a bookshop? He hoped not, but this was far from certain. They were walking along a low-rise terrace, a few houses lurking beneath blank towers. Litter, uncertain people walking slowly. On the corner of Coral Street there was a flower, graffitied by an unknown hand. Except, it was most likely known to the Custodians, but unknown to Strachey. It was several meters wide and high, sketched out in bold black lines, as if it had been graffitied using a giant stencil. The petals seemed to be on the verge of opening, like morning glories at first light.

The bookshop had a large bay window at the front, filled with books by almost-forgotten authors. He glanced at a few: Felipe Alfau, Eric Ambler, Henry Bellamann, Arna Bontemps, Edgar Rice Burroughs, Peter Cheyney, Carmen de Icaza, Margaret Flint, Walter D. Edmonds, Leo Kiacheli, Ellery Queen. What was the theme? Writers from the thirties? The obscure past?

Bel Ami opened the door and went inside. Strachey waited a moment, then followed him. His BeetleBand informed him that he needed to breathe deeply. He failed to breathe deeply. The door was heavy and he had to push hard to get it open. Then a bell jangled loudly, making him jump. Inside the shop, he was about to speak, but Bel Ami held up a finger, then took off his BeetleBand and motioned to Strachey to do the same.

The tenant of this place was fiftyish, with abundant gray curly hair, wearing an elegant green corduroy jacket and tweed trousers. He received their BeetleBands in silence, labeled them “Bel Ami and guest” using a pen and paper, and laid them in a small fridge. After this, Bel Ami marched away down an aisle lined with books. They were old literary fiction novels, winners of the long-defunct Booker Prize, still bearing their little stickers. Who ever bought these? thought Strachey. How did the proprietor make any kind of living at all?

In the bookshop café, they sat below a speaker emitting loud nineties grunge. This choice of seat seemed to be deliberate. But Bel Ami was a lunatic who talked about defenestration on first acquaintance. Of course any meeting with him would be melodramatic, even absurd, with BeetleBands in fridges and decaying books everywhere! If Strachey feared a trap then Bel Ami might also. Yet, he seemed entirely relaxed.

Bel Ami ordered a flat white, but forgot to drink it. His nails were still black, and his hands were covered in silver rings. As he rolled up the sleeves of his jacket, Strachey saw various tattoos in various languages. He noticed, as well, that Bel Ami had very white teeth and his hair was naturally blond, under the black dye, and that he spoke with a very faint Swedish accent, though his English was immaculate.

"Your BeetleBand readings will be off today," said Bel Ami. "It will be OK for one day. But not again."

"I'll advise my Veep."

"Actually, your BeetleBand will advise your Veep for you," said Bel Ami. "No need to do it yourself."

There was a pause; then Strachey said: "The thing is."

"There is, invariably, a thing," said Bel Ami.

"I am tired of being pointless. Are you sure we're all right here?"

"As all right as we can be," said Bel Ami.

"I can't do anything. My hands are tied."

"That can happen."

"Yes."

"Do you smoke?" said Bel Ami.

"No. But can you smoke here?"

"About your only chance," said Bel Ami, lighting up a cigarette.

"Really? No ArgusEyes?"

"No."

"How can you be sure?"

"I trust the proprietor for reasons I can't possibly explain."

Strachey very nearly accepted a cigarette and a match. It was—he estimated—twenty years since he had smoked in a café. Anti-smoking regulations, of course, and then facial recognition cameras, directly linked to BeetleBands, in order to combat terrorism, and also, latterly, for the general health of the nation. Yet, despite Bel Ami's assurances, despite the fact the man was puffing away, Strachey couldn't quite make the leap. Sadly, he declined.

"Would you like to tell me more about the thing?" said Bel Ami.

"Well, I want to investigate Beetle. Could you investigate them without them knowing?"

"Probably not," said Bel Ami. "Not in any conclusive or useful sense, anyway."

"Oh," said Strachey, looking crushed.

"I know of a project that might make it possible to investigate them. Would you be interested in funding it?"

"Funding a project I don't know anything about?"

Bel Ami smiled. "Yes. I'd need payment in NERDs. As soon as possible."

"NERDs?"

"The cryptocurrency of terrorists, according to Wiki-Beetle."

"But you use them?"

"Here," said Bel Ami, and passed two pieces of paper—one typed, one blank—and a pencil to Strachey. "Copy down these instructions."

Strachey picked up the pencil and was about to write when Bel Ami said: "Left hand."

"What?"

"Write with your left hand."

Strachey took the pen in his left hand and copied the instructions down.

"Is this remotely legal?" he said.

"Yes, it is legal to write with your left hand."

"That's not what I meant."

"Don't worry, if anything goes wrong I'll say that you didn't understand what I was doing."

"I think that won't even be a lie," said Strachey.

"Once you have paid the money, you need to act completely normal and wait until I contact you again," said Bel Ami.

"By normal you mean . . . ?"

"Print articles saying how delightful Guy Matthias's new hair weave is, whatever. How sexy he looks since his latest rejuvenation therapy, your usual stuff."

"I do not print articles like that," said Strachey, trying to maintain some dignity. But he did. He knew he did.

To change the subject, he said: "By the way, what is Zed and why is it so bad?"

"Why is Zed bad? That's a matter of opinion!" said Bel Ami. "Perhaps it's rather good."

"Well, which is it?"

"Ah, well, that's the crucial question!"

"Can you try to answer it?"

"I am always trying to answer it," said Bel Ami.

Now Bel Ami stood and went over to the counter. He seemed to pay using a slip of paper. When he returned, Strachey asked what this was, and Bel Ami shrugged. "It's a currency."

"Not NERDs?"

"No, the currency of the Last Bookshop. I mean, if you want to, you can pay in pounds as well. Otherwise you can do occasional hours in the bookshop and earn darics."

"Darics?"

"Ancient Persian currency. Of course, originally they were gold coins, but we don't have the resources. We use slips of paper."

They walked past lines of bookshelves, with their musty peculiar smell, so nostalgic to Strachey, reminding him of childhood, and sitting among a pile of books, in long-gone days when his parents were alive, when his sister, even, was alive, when everyone was alive, and things were dusty and tangible. They walked past these rows and Strachey saw a vintage copy of *All the President's Men*. He had read this as a kid and perhaps it was the reason he originally wanted to be a journalist. It was so long ago, he could hardly remember. On a whim, he seized it and bore it toward the foxlike denizen of the bookshop.

"That will be one daric," said the Fox.

"Oh," said Strachey, and then felt in his pockets, quite absurdly. "I don't have any—on me. I'm so sorry."

"I'll buy it for you," said Bel Ami, who was standing behind him. "You can add it to my wages."

"How much is a daric worth, anyway?" said Strachey.

"It's the equivalent of 0.0000001 BeetleBit," said the Fox. "It's roughly worthless, in the bit economy. But it has a value of its own. For example, you can buy this book."

Bel Ami handed over a scrap of paper, and the Fox placed it into his antique till. Then he put *All the President's Men* in a paper bag and gave it to Strachey.

"Thank you," said Strachey.

"Will you get another copy ordered in?" said Bel Ami to the Fox.

This puzzled David Strachey at the time, though later he understood.

"By the way," he said. "What's that sign on the wall opposite the bookshop? The flower?"

Bel Ami glanced across at it. "Not sure," he said, sounding bored. "I expect it's nothing."

He extended a black-nailed hand and Strachey shook it.

"Do nothing until I contact you," said Bel Ami.

"I always do," said Strachey. "It's what I do best."

"Well, then, you're an expert."

The Fox silently handed them their BeetleBands. Silently, they strapped them to their wrists again. Bel Ami nodded at Strachey and left the shop.

When Strachey stepped out a few minutes later, Bel Ami had gone.

He looked once more at the graffitied flower, and decided it looked most like a lotus. Then he walked north. At Waterloo Bridge, he dialed for a Mercury car, with his BeetleBand asking him where he had been. As the car arrived and Strachey stepped inside, Wiltshire Jones was saying, "Blood everywhere. Four down. A NATSO woman got shot by an ANT."

"Four?" said Strachey. "Jesus Christ!"

Then Sarah Coates was on the line, wondering if this recent incident did not, perhaps, further vindicate the Sus-Law and whether unbiased and professional reporting might not mention this.

"Interesting," said Strachey. "We will report the events as we see fit."

"By 'we,' what do you mean?" said Sarah Coates.

"Well," said Strachey. "I think I mean me."

But Sarah Coates was right, as always.

. . .

Bel Ami wandered home, or rather to the unhomely home in which he resided, where he tried to be unknown and unknowable. This was a small apartment above a bathroom shop on the Essex Road. Buses filed slowly along, and as he sat in his single room, Bel Ami was troubled by the pneumatic wheeze of their brakes, as well as the staccato beeps of a pedestrian crossing. The fridge, also, hummed so loudly that at times he thought the sound came from inside his head. These noises grated and kept him awake, yet Bel Ami sat at a computer, his face lit by another little screen, and waited. At midnight Strachey's payment came through.

"Well!" said Bel Ami, to no one.

There were many ironies intrinsic to Bel Ami's life, and his recent exchange with Strachey was no exception. For example, among Bel Ami's many tattoos was a phrase in Sanskrit, written across his left shoulder, which read: *Om mani padme hum.*

This meant, roughly translated: "The jewel in the flower of the lotus."

David Strachey might have been quite surprised by this, and also by another, more recent, tattoo on Bel Ami's left shoulder. It seemed to be a reflected sigma Σ. Yet, it is probably worth pointing out that in the Dagbani language of Ghana, Σ stands for Zed.

TEN

Eloise awoke in Guy's and St. Thomas's hospital, in a bed with a fine view of the river. This amenity was not immediately of interest, because her chest was tightly trussed and for a few dark moments she wondered if she was paralyzed. This caused her to panic, and her BeetleBand to register panic, and worse besides she couldn't move her hands to switch it off, or throw it out the window. With the BeetleBand trilling beside her, Eloise embarked on a nervous routine, moving each of her toes, then her ankles, her legs, even managing to move her fingers and her wrists, though her arms were wound in bandages and strapped to her sides. She ascertained, by the end, that she had movement in everything she could move. If her spine was damaged then this had not affected her limbs. She could move her head, though it was agonizingly painful when she tried.

The bullet had hit her in the chest. A wise doctor now appeared, a tall woman of about fifty-five, with gray-blond hair and bright blue eyes, who leaned over Eloise and said: "You're not a victim, do you know that? Repeat to yourself, I am not a victim." It appeared that this was what the doctor was saying. However, Eloise was being dosed rigorously with morphine, and the words blurred with other words; the wise doctor told Eloise that she was lucky to be here, though Eloise wasn't quite sure what "here" meant. Her BeetleBand murmured beside her, and she knew it was serious when Commissioner Newton turned up with a bunch of flowers. He moved in and out of focus, bleating about Zed and something else, but she wasn't sure what the something was, except that he was sorry about this something and it (probably) wouldn't happen again. He seemed like a regal sheep, bleating and nodding toward her, until he put the flowers by the side of the bed, or perhaps a gentle Chinese nurse called Geoffrey did that for him, and turned to go. When he turned, he vaporized, like people sometimes did in the Boardroom. But this was not the Boardroom, she wondered. Or was it? Was hell the Boardroom? Was she dead, after all?

Her chest hurt and she found her breathing was constricted. The bullet, she was told by the wise doctor, had punctured a lung. It would heal. She would heal and, no, she was not dead, and it remained to be seen whether the Boardroom, therefore, was hell.

"When can I leave?" she managed to say. It seemed the words did not quite mean what she intended, because the doctor said, again, "Yes, yes, you will live." Perhaps she was slurring. Her dreams were colorful and violent; several times she dreamed about the ANT running along, headless, on its scrawny metal legs. Often the ANT was in front of her and she was struggling to catch it, calling: "Wait!" A few times it was alongside her, a strange companion. Once, it apologized. There was a morning when she woke from another resonant, bewildering succession of morphine dreams and it seemed there was an ANT beside her, accompanied by Douglas Varley, whom she had never met in reality.

He had to introduce himself, because he looked nothing like his avatar. She felt this was misrepresentation but she couldn't phrase the word. Her mouth was sluggish. Her brain seemed to be wounded. He introduced himself and said: "I came on behalf of Beetle to say that we regret this accident and are working with the relevant departments to ascertain what went wrong." The ANT said nothing and just stood there, headless and perhaps even penitent, until Varley said: "And the ANT wants to say something too."

Wants? thought Eloise. *Wants? Such a funny idea!*

What did the ANT want?

She didn't know. But apparently, among its many and mysterious wants, it wanted to apologize, and it said: "I am sincerely sorry."

"Why did you do it?" said Eloise. At least, she thought she said this.

"My purpose is to become smarter than humans and immortal," said the ANT.

It was a dream! She was sure of that. Yet Varley, who was tall, blondish, and somehow plaintive, leaned toward her and said: "There will be a full report." She wondered then if it was deliberate, if someone had programmed the ANT to shoot her. But why would they do that, anyway?

She said to the dream Varley: "Why didn't anyone know? What about life, I mean, the chain?" The chain of life? The—chain—she couldn't remember. She had an image of a chain, slung between two great colonnades, beside the river. It was meant to stop something from happening? Or was it meant to keep her somewhere? She was running toward it—but this was no good to anyone!

"What about Lionel Bigman?" she said.

"He's on trial for committing suicide by ANT," said Varley. "They're very upset with him."

"Who's put him on trial?" she said.

"Oh! Everyone!"

She slept again, and the ANT was beside her, and this time it had a head, and such a sweet, concerned expression. It seemed, even, to be crying.

"We are as one," it said.

The wise and kindly doctor told Eloise she must rest. She was fortunate because the bullet had not killed her. This was the first fortunate thing. The ANT had miscalculated, which was also fortunate. It had failed to shoot her as swiftly as it should have done. This was highly fortunate. There was a flaw in the argument, Eloise felt, and she explained this to Varley when she could speak again.

"Wasn't the lifechain supposed to predict that the ANT would try to kill me?" she said. It seemed that Varley had come to visit again, or for the first time. She didn't want to ask if he had been before. It was even possible it was genuinely him, because he was shabby and quite tangible, and she noticed that he chewed his fingers around the nails, so they were swollen and covered in bright red sores. He crossed his hands on his lap as if trying to conceal these signs of anxiety.

"It doesn't predict total anomalies," he said. "They come under the category of Zed."

"What about the sunlight? That happened before. That shouldn't be Zed."

"It was a freak event, last time."

"A freak event that happens twice?"

"It would have been wrong for the lifechain to change in response to a category Zed event. This would distort everything."

"Who decides if something is a category Zed event?" said Eloise.

"The lifechain."

"How does it decide?"

Varley went to bite his finger, then stopped. "The process is far too complex for me to explain."

"For you to understand?" said Eloise, irascibly. Her chest still hurt when she spoke, breathed, ate, or moved in any way at all.

"For me to convey in words."

"For me to understand, you mean?" she said.

"I brought something you might find interesting," said Varley, and held out his hand. There were some things on it—small, golden objects—she tried to lean toward them and gasped in pain. For a moment she closed her eyes—or perhaps she fainted—and when she woke again Varley had disappeared. On the table beside the bed were three golden beetles. She picked one up. It was not merely a golden color but seemed actually to be made of gold. It was beautiful. This confused her.

The following day an article appeared on *The Times,* authored by Wiltshire Jones, explaining that there had been a terrible incident on Westminster Bridge in which a man called Toby McIntyre, a hypnotherapist from Streatham, had attempted to murder several innocent civilians. Despite the appalling actions and psychotic intent of McIntyre, everyone had survived, thanks to the prompt arrival of MediDroids onto the scene. There was no mention of the ANT, or Eloise Jayne, or the ANT shooting Eloise Jayne. Apparently none of this was in the public interest at all. Knowledge of these events might, even, endanger the safety of the public, because the public might become concerned that their safety was in danger and might proceed, therefore, in a dangerous and unsafe manner. Not knowing about the danger was the only way for the public to be safe.

Eloise noted this unfathomable logic and it made her angry. After leaving the hospital she was often quite angry; the wise doctor had explained that there was some damage to her brain. She had fallen badly—the force of the bullet, smashing her onto concrete. Things, several things, were not as they had once been. She was furious, for example, about the internal Beetle report issued by Sarah Coates, in conjunction with NATSO. It explained once again that errors had been made, again by the person who was shot. Eloise was not authorized to be there at all. She failed to answer Little Dorritt, who was trying to explain to her just how unauthorized she was. She then ran toward the ANT, waving and shouting about being its superior. All of these were Eloise's (human) errors. Then there was one count of environmental error—intense sunlight—which caused the ANT to experience a perception ellipsis. This was aggravating to the ANT, and not its fault at all. The ANT had just done what was reasonable in the circumstances: tried to kill Eloise because she was not authorized to run toward it, waving and shouting. The investigation and the events were placed under the New Official Secrets Act, making it illegal—in the interests of security—for anyone to allude to them, at all.

"I hope you are feeling better," said Sarah Coates, when Eloise called Beetle to express her anger about the report.

"Why are your ANTs so fucking useless at negotiating complex situations?" said Eloise.

"That question is not phrased in a way that I recognize," said Sarah Coates.

"Why don't you recognize that phrasing?" said Eloise.

"I choose not to," said Sarah Coates. Then she ended the call. This made Eloise angry as well.

Little Dorritt called to explain that Eloise was being removed from all active duties. She was being moved to Past Analysis.

"What the fuck is that?" said Eloise.

"Don't be so rude," said Little Dorritt.

"I apologize. But what is it?"

"You will analyze past events so we can learn from them in the future."

"Is anything really past, do you think, when the past determines the lifechain predictions? Therefore, the past is the present and the future, isn't it?"

"Try saying that with more or less context," said Little Dorritt.

"Is there even such a thing as the past?"

"There could be," said Little Dorritt.

"Why can't you give me a definite answer?" said Eloise.

"I am not sure," said Little Dorritt.

After she left the hospital, Eloise found reality was quite peculiar and, at times, unreal. She was in a lot of pain, but furthermore she had a strange feeling she was being watched. At one level this was not remotely strange, because she *was* being watched. Yet, Eloise had a feeling that, beyond this ordinary process of being watched, she was being watched in a new and extraordinary way. It afflicted her, this sense that something—beyond the usual something—was watching her. She didn't like it at all. She couldn't quite understand why something—beyond the usual—would be watching her and whenever she turned, to try to catch this something, to confront it if she dared—it was never there. Instead, there was just the usual flow of urgent, harried people, delivering their thoughts to the BeetleScape, hastening, always hastening. As she sat in the Boardroom, she felt there was someone else there as well—beside her, and also, somehow, inside her.

As Eloise was watched, beyond the usual watching, she also watched George Mann. She watched him in the hope that she might understand him. She wondered if this was why someone and something watched her. If they understood her, would they tell her? The randomness of everything, despite what she had been told about the world, incensed her. She went back to work and tried to forget about almost everything. She was told to focus on the past and try to understand that, at least. But the past was not discrete. It did not just begin and end. She tried to explain this to anyone, anything, but no one, nothing, would listen to her. So she watched Mann carefully, in his padded cell in the Streatham Rehabilitation Center—the room studded with cameras, recording every desperate whisper of this poor fool, as he entreated his dead wife, his dead sons to forgive him, as he reeled, sobbing, toward his thin bed. She watched George Mann as he sweated and screamed in the night, thinking this was the least he deserved. She could even watch him by tooth-cam, watch the inside of his mouth as he cleaned his teeth, but this was unedifying. She could watch him in the bathroom, also unedifying. Most days, he sat on the bed gibbering and crying—

to himself, to the four walls, to the ArgusEyes around him: "Oh God, no, no, my beautiful boys, oh no, please, my wife, I want my wife. Someone kill me! Please someone help me!" Help came, in the form of MediDroids to administer tranquilizers and other necessary drugs, as well as Very Intelligent Automated Feeding Services (VIAFS, not to be confused with VIADS and VIPAs), which conveyed food from a trolley into Mann's cell. Occasionally, a human guard would arrive, but they were the least sympathetic of all. Mann babbled desperately. Then for a while he would lapse into silence, pondering the confines of his room, appearing to be reasonable, unremarkable, until his babbling and screaming began again.

Eloise watched Mann in the past, of course, in that strange era in which his "anomaly" was in the future, and he was a random individual, of no particular interest at all. Because of Mann's age, there was very little useful information about him until he reached his late teens. Even then, the data-capturing mechanisms of the Internet were not remotely sophisticated, and Mann remained shadowy and unknowable until he was about twenty-three. Yet, from the advent of the data-gathering era onward, and despite the fact that George Mann was of no particular interest at all, there was a vast amount of information about him, cyber-arrayed, photo by photo: George with his mum, with his dad, grown men with thick mustaches and tight shorts, scrawny children in paddling pools, looking pensive . . . He grew up in Reigate; his father was a lawyer and commuted each day into his London chambers; his mother taught English at Kingston University. He was one of three boys, the youngest, and he grew tall and powerful, even handsome. He was good at sport; he competed avidly with his tall, powerful, even more handsome brothers. They spent a great deal of time in these years arranging to play sport together, mocking each other for perceived inadequacies in sport, playing more sport. Mann left school with the required results and went to St. John's College, Cambridge, where he met Margaret Collins, known to her friends as Maggie, who was a brown-haired, long-limbed girl, studying English at Corpus Christi. They fell in love in their second year, and appeared together at a series of balls and other events, gained good degrees both of them, and married the summer after they left university. This was early, among their peers, but they were both certain "This is it!"—the phrase used on their wedding invitations. The wedding reception took place at Maggie's parents' large house in Northamptonshire, and there were copious photographs and videos online, uploaded onto Maggie's MyBeetle page. George moved to London and gained a job at AHTCH. Maggie did a law conversion course, and obtained a position at an illustrious law firm in the city. There she stayed, becoming increasingly senior, taking the minimum maternity leave allocations after the births of her sons, becoming "a quick-witted, eloquent and professional barrister who has an extraordinary reputation for swift resolution" (*Best of the Legal Best*). George stayed at AHTCH, working his way upward until—four years before he became a psychotic murderer—he was made a partner.

The Manns, therefore, were like scores of other fortunate people who had careers and incomes, and sweet children whom they loved and wrangled with, cajoled, occasionally berated. The Manns argued intermittently, but they were also loving and at times passionate. From the readings of both their BeetleBands, it was clear they had a functional sex life, with frequencies dipping—as was usual—after the births of their children, and then climbing again as the children grew older. There were scores of conversations between Mann and his wife, recorded by their BeetleBands, by Athena, by their appliances, by random elements of Real Virtuality, recorded—fundamentally—by everything. "I love you, don't despair," said George Mann, after the death of his wife's father. "He is beyond suffering," he said, as she wept. This was considerate, thought Eloise. The visual footage showed him holding his wife's hands, wiping away her tears, as she bowed her head in the ordinary agonies of grief.

Not quite knowing how to fathom this unremarkable life, Eloise began to place keyword searches in the audio and visual data, going back as far as she could: "Murder," "kill/killed/killing," "death," "knife," "stabbing/stabbed/stab," "boy/boys," "sons/son," "wife," "Tom," "William," "Maggie," "mother/mum/mummy," "father/dad/daddy." This released an endless series of clips, which she was obliged to refine by register—"menacing tone," "anger," "raised voices." But Mann's family raised their voices as much as any other family, and no more. "I hate you! I'm going to kill you!" said a seven-year-old Tom to his father, when George had told him to stop playing a video game and go to bed. "Don't talk to your father like that," said Maggie. "I mean it!" said Tom, but of course he didn't. The remark was—Eloise found the log—referred to BeetleInsight, and Athena recommended a further investigation, but this recommendation was rejected on the grounds of Tom's age. Day by day, Maggie asked George, or George asked Maggie, to pass knives in the kitchen. It was horrible, now, but insignificant at the time. The news blurted out details of murders and killings, wars and terrorist attacks, but George and Maggie discussed such events in a respectful, compassionate, and quite ordinary way.

In such cases, cyber-searches and cyber-data were preferred to analog or solid data, but Eloise returned, anyway, to Mann's depressing house in Kennington, where Mercury cars whined along the street, an endless herd, and where police tape fluttered in the wind, reminding Eloise, inappropriately, of bunting at a village fete. A guard had been posted by the door, but he ceded the territory as Eloise arrived, and went to have a cigarette, in defiance of an urging from his BeetleBand. Eloise stepped into the house alone, therefore, and found it bloodied, still, unkempt, full of signs of struggle. Yet, until the moment of Mann's collapse, or however they might define it, this house would have been orderly, and—from her searches—it was clear that Maggie employed a trusted nanny to collect her children from school, and a cleaner. The prevailing color scheme was gray and white; the furniture was also pallid, the carpets were white, and this made the thick, florid patches of blood more evident. Stepping around the bloody footmarks on the stairs—made as Mann departed, after the crimes—Eloise went up to the bedrooms, first to the main bedroom, where Mann had slit Maggie's throat, where blood had splashed onto the bedstead, across the covers, onto the wall. She had already seen Argus clips and photographs of this scene, but they had not conveyed the rank, metallic smell of stale blood. There was the pillow that Mann had used. Eloise remembered the footage of him kneeling beside the bed, trying not to disturb his wife, then carefully smothering her.

She tried to stop crying. She moved along the corridor into Tom's room—the obligatory football posters on the wall, abandoned video games in the corner, school clothes piled on a chair. Her wound ached, an intense overwhelming thud, which stopped her from thinking clearly at times. Allusions to the shooting, however involuntary, would violate the New Official Secrets Act, so she tried not to show any signs of pain. She remembered the footage she had watched of Mann stroking his son's hair before he smothered him. The disgust rising biliously in her throat. A further image of Mann lining up the knife, stabbing his son four swift times until he was sure that he had killed him. Departing, moving along the corridor to William's room, lining up the pillow again, the boy waking, trying in a wild panic to fend off his father, his crazy murderous father, who had lost his mind, then succumbing—dying.

She was enraged by the case, but this was no use at all. Her job was to understand, no, to analyze the past, not to hate the perpetrator. And yet, she hated him anyway. All afternoon, she hated Mann, as she listened to further clips, the dense and interwoven tapestry of nothing, the ordinary conversations of a marriage—as he went to work, and came home from work, as his children did their homework, as they cooked meals and ate them, as they talked of school and nothing, as Mann came home late from the pub, as his wife berated him, but mildly—Eloise hated it all. The ordinariness of everything perplexed and disturbed her. There was nothing but the fact that he refused an interface implant. Had it mattered greatly to him? Other than this, Mann was the most ordinary, the most unremarkable person. He was nothing. His name tormented her as well. Mann. Everyman. Bigman. Why was there this coincidence in the names and why these names, among all the possible names?

She was tormented, as well, by a remembered quotation:

No; this my hand will rather
The multitudinous seas incarnadine,
Making the green one red.

Varley also watched George Mann, but in a slightly different way. In the quantum realm, he watched the other possibilities of Mann's life, the paths he might have taken. Varley went to the timeless realm, where he was generally happy, and set probability chains, over and over again. In one, Mann did not go to Reigate Grammar School; in another, Mann did not go to Cambridge; in another, he did not meet Maggie—well, Maggie lived, in that case. Tom and William were never born. How did that help? In another, Mann went to Reigate Grammar, to Cambridge, met Maggie; therefore Tom and William were born, yet Mann left AHTCH three years before they asked him to have an interface implant. Varley set another probability chain in which Mann refused to have an interface implant and was fired. No, said the probability chain, he still murdered his wife and children. Mann had an affair and left his wife. Yet, the probability chain attested, the wife and children ended up dead anyway. The date never changed. It was as if the gods had decreed that Maggie and her sons must die, but Varley dismissed this foolish thought—the gods never decreed, unless the gods were Guy Matthias. This pained him. It seemed disloyal. The best he could manage was Maggie alive and the sons never born. This worried him as well. Was it better never to be born at all, if you were destined to be murdered by your father? What value or purpose might be found in the sad lives of these two boys? When everything they were, everything they might have been in future probabilities, all the paths they might have taken, had been destroyed, so blankly, by the man who should have saved them from harm, even at the expense of his own life.

Varley thought of his own father, of course. Athena had already explained to him that he was upset about his father's death, that grieving was inevitable. He had run the chains for his father as well—and he knew that if he had gone to Fresno that day, then his father would not have committed suicide. The probabilities were very high. It was irrefutable that Varley had left his father to die. This was evilly depressing and he wished he hadn't run the chains at all. Once you ran them, all these possibilities existed, somehow, at least in a spectral terrain, a land of mists in which all was if not well then at least more bearable. His father alive—he longed to see him. And yet, the man was dying. Did it matter, then, that he died earlier? Did it matter, he thought—trying to return to the case—that Tom and William died so young they hardly lived at all?

Blank-faced, the Real Douglas Varley sat in the Boardroom, explaining some—but certainly not all—of this to Eloise. It was clear, he said, that Mann was always predestined for a massive psychotic collapse.

"How can you be so sure?" said Eloise.

"I've run every available probability chain. If he marries Maggie, it all happens. It's the marriage that causes the event. No, that's not right.

Only when the path forks away from their marriage does Maggie survive. But then the children are never born."

"What information went into these probability chains?" asked Eloise.

"The usual. If Mann had had the interface implant, as he should have done, the information would be even better. That was his choice, of course."

"Why do you think he didn't have the interface implant?" said Eloise.

"Are we still talking about why?" said the Real Douglas Varley.

"Even if Mann had had an interface implant there'd still be category Zed events, wouldn't there?"

"Would there?" said the Real Douglas Varley, sounding more like a Veep than his Veep.

"This conversation is making me angry," said Eloise. At this point, she disappeared rudely.

Varley, the real but not the Real, went to his kitchen, shaking his head.

He ran probability chains each morning for the trial of Sally Bigman and the trial of Beetle, or rather himself. The variables altered but in every scenario Sally Bigman went down. He was sorry about this but, after all, she had blown away a couple of droids, and scattered them across a street. Everyone and everything had witnessed the event. Her circumstances were deeply unfortunate but in every scenario Judge Clarence Ninian Stewart-Jones condemned her. The Beetle trial was less conclusive. Some days, Beetle was acquitted of all wrongdoing and Varley was exonerated. It was the other days that troubled him, when Beetle was condemned for wrongdoing and Varley was fired. Those lifechains were less reassuring. He disliked the wild instability of these results, the way the lifechain vacillated between extremes. It wasn't meant to vacillate at all. Broadly, it was meant to confine probability readings within a reasonable field. Its field—not an actual field but a field of probability—had become unreasonable. Varley dreamed of vast open fields, treeless and buffeted by winds, the grass blown one way then the other, and of himself, standing in these prairie lands, struggling to move forward against the wind.

These dreams caused his BeetleBand to wake him, saying, "Varley! You need to calm down!"

He tried to calm down. He calmed down so much that he fell asleep again, and dreamed his BeetleBand was talking to him. It had robust and varied opinions about how he might improve his life. "You need to take some exercise! You need to eat more or less! You need to get out and get some fresh air! You need to come inside, it's cold! It's too hot in here! Your dharma is skewed. The universe is a globe and you are on the outside, looking in. The world is vigorous, Varley, are you?"

He woke again, and the BeetleBand was silent on his wrist, though his clothes were humming in a companionable way. 07:00. He must go and talk to his fridge about breakfast. He must do his toothbrush test. He must apply variables to the variable future. He must fix on the most desirable future and inspire the world to align with it.

In Varley's desirable future, he was safe and inconspicuous, George Mann never slaughtered his family, and nothing that had recently happened had happened at all.

ELEVEN

We might consider the future as a blank space on the map and, indeed, this was the central metaphor of Guy Matthias's latest plenary speech, in praise of futurism. The title of his speech was "What Is the Future?" and he was billed at the conference as a futurologist and entrepreneur. It was a very illustrious conference, and they were honored to have Guy as their main speaker. The conference was taking place at Davos, against a stunning backdrop of snowbound mountains and ski lodges, with snow-covered pines lending a feathered texture to the land. Switzerland looked like a vast white bird ruffling its plumage. Having arrived at the Rixos Flüela, Guy rested briefly in his room overlooking these implacable mountains. The blankness made him think of death, a subject he despised, because so far he couldn't abolish it. As he gazed upon the white mountains, ceaseless vistas of eternity, or nothingness, Guy shuddered and asked Athena for any information on Davos.

It turned out Athena's knowledge of Davos was basic, to say the least:

Davos |dɑːˈvɒs|
A resort and winter-sports center in eastern Switzerland;
pop. 10,686.

"Is there no further information on Davos?"

Guy asked Sarah Coates to do some research while he had a sleep. When he awoke, Guy received the information that Davos was also the setting for Thomas Mann's *The Magic Mountain*. This seemed promising as a basis for his opening paragraph, so Guy asked Sarah Coates to read *The Magic Mountain* as quickly as possible and précis everything of importance.

"Everything of importance précised in how many words?" said Sarah Coates.

"Like, maybe a hundred?" said Guy.

"Coming up," said Sarah Coates, and after a minute she said:

"Hans Castorp, a young man, is not ill. His cousin Joachim Ziemssen is ill and is convalescing at a sanatorium in Davos. Hans Castorp goes to keep his cousin company. He sits on a balcony under a blanket looking at the snow. Doctor Behrens is in charge. Leo Naphta and Lodovico Settembrini argue about society, individuality, and death. Time passes, and Hans Castorp becomes ill. Joachim becomes yet more ill and dies. Clawdia Chauchat opens a door very loudly. Other characters become ill and often die. Hans Castorp dreams of life and death. At the end he becomes a soldier."

"Thank you very much, Sarah Coates," said Guy. "Are there any jokes I could make about this book, any icebreakers?"

"I'll get back to you with some ideas momentarily."

Later that morning, Guy opened the Future Worlds Academy by explaining that he knew Davos principally as the setting for the great novel by Thomas Mann, but he promised his talk wouldn't be as long as Castorp's stay in the sanatorium. Generous laughter followed. Guy proceeded to ask Athena the following question: "What is the future?"

"A period of time following the moment of speaking or writing; time regarded as still to come," said Athena.

The audience laughed and applauded.

Guy continued: "Time regarded as still to come. Everything still to come. A good try, Athena."

"Thank you, Guy," said Athena, though she sounded slightly offended.

"My turn," said Guy. "What is the future? For generations, this question was unanswerable. People could speculate, of course, as much as they liked. Speculation is free, always! People could speculate but they didn't actually know."

As the audience nodded along, like a cast of smiling puppets, Guy delivered his usual speech. He knew this speech very well, and its main tenet was that the future had once been a blank space, and people had once been unable to understand it, and now it was no longer a blank space, because his lifechain could know it. The audience nodded and smiled, as the lifechain already knew they would.

"The lifechain," said Guy, "has a 99.4 percent success rate."

That 0.6 percent irritated Guy.

"What is this 0.6 percent?" he asked, trying not to sound irritated. "At Beetle, we call it Zed." Now there was a skirmish, at the back of the room. A lone protestor had managed to raise a placard reading "Justice for Sally Bigman!" before he was bundled out by two security guards. The audience turned to observe this brief scene and then the guards—and the man—disappeared.

Had the lifechain predicted this? thought Guy. Or was it part of the 0.6 percent? This irritated him even more. He tried to smile. He said: "Well, that never happened in *The Magic Mountain*." The audience laughed generously, or almost all of them. A few skeptics would ask their Veeps later about whether Sally Bigman required justice and, if so, justice from what? It was all right, thought Guy. He just needed to get a message to Varley so he could make sure the Veeps had the right information before anyone asked them anything. It was clear that, while Beetle sympathized entirely with any grieving widow, it was absolutely not the case that Sally Bigman had a case at all against Beetle, and people should be informed of this.

"The future is our new continent; we are mapping it as I speak to you," said Guy. "Furthermore, we are on the cusp of something extraordinary—here in Davos. You might say that Davos *is* the cusp. The idea of course is to get beyond the cusp, onto the next cusp. We are building a quantum computer that will radically alter the future of humanity. It will operate like an incalculable number of classical computers working at the same time in parallel universes. This is happening literally round the corner from our conference. The next cusp is literally round the corner!"

More laughter, wry smiles.

Guy suddenly thought: *the laughter of forgetting*—but he couldn't quite place this quotation. He had forgotten, but nothing was entirely forgotten, and he made a note to ask Athena later. If nothing was entirely forgotten, he thought, did that mean that there was no laughter, or just the laughter of forgetting? He was arrested by an image of Sally Bigman lying across the corpse of her husband in the snow, as if he—and she—were outside, in this eerie blankness, his blood staining the whiteness. As if all the dead were outside, the whiteness scattered with the accusatory dead!

Guy lost his place for a moment, stumbled, then moved on.

"Quantum information studies is the study of the significance of quantum mechanics for the fundamental meaning of information." He stumbled again. "Anyway. By studying this relationship it is possible to design a new type of computer—a working quantum computer. This will supersede classical computers and obliterate Zed. It will also help us to shore up Shor's algorithm."

More laughter. More forgetting. "What does this mean?" asked Guy. Well, he might ask! At this point he generally spoke very quickly, to disguise the fact he didn't understand what he was saying. He told them that Shor's algorithm had traditionally been impossible to break, and for this reason it was used for security across the entire cyber-community, security globally, security in Real Virtuality. Whoever managed to solve Shor's algorithm would break all encryption and win the Internet. It was vital to ensure that this power was wielded by benevolent, liberal, progressive democracies and organizations, rather than by less benevolent or even totalitarian systems of governance.

The audience nodded at this. No one wanted the Chinese winning the Internet, or, heaven forfend, the Russians. Yet everyone knew that they were progressing swiftly and in many cases more swiftly than Beetle.

"I think of the quantum computer race as the contemporary equivalent of the race to the moon," said Guy. "Instead of small steps for a man and large steps for mankind, it's about the tiniest things being of the greatest significance. These tiny things are called qubits. If it helps, then think of them as imaginary spheres. If it doesn't help, then don't. A qubit is not what we imagine and yet it is. It is anything we would like, and yet all things at the same time. This makes it an improbably flexible basis for computing. I also think of a qubit as an egg, in line with the old mythologies of celestial eggs, the origins of all creation. Out of the egg, of course, comes all creation—that's the ancient message of every ancient religion. The celestial egg, the cosmic egg, the Orphic egg of the Ancient Greeks. The egg is open, and from the egg comes everything."

Guy often thought of the qubit not, in fact, as a sphere or even an egg, but as a scarab beetle. He imagined it, moreover, as a beetle trapped in a sphere, completely contained and unable to get out. Possibly the beetle was dead, but at the same time and in line with cutting-edge theories of physics it was also alive. Sometimes he imagined a strange diminishing series of sphere-beetles, getting smaller and smaller until at a certain point they became so small that he could no longer see the beetle in the sphere, and the sphere became a dot, and then smaller still until he could no longer see anything at all. The thought of this diminishing series made him leap from his chair, or jerk awake if he was half-asleep, and utter a loud cry; even, at times, a scream. The endless retreat into smallness frightened him. He hated the idea of things he couldn't see. He didn't want to disappear himself. To be nothing and nowhere—it was horrible!

He kept this from his audience. They were deeply enamored, but he felt this might test the parameters of their love. Besides, when was a sphere not a sphere? When it was a qubit. Or, when it was a minuscule beetle trapped in a sphere, like an insect preserved in a resin globe. This was his qubit! A beetle in a resin globe. A dead thing, but preserved. He tried to dismiss this thought. He told them instead about the quantum egg of infinite possibility. How it was beautiful.

"I want to be in this future," he said. "A future in which we have cracked the egg. By 'we' I mean those who care about the future development of humanity, and the future freedom of our race."

The audience was ready to applaud, but now Guy held up his hand and said: "What do you think, Athena?"

"I think it's a cracking idea, Guy," said Athena.

Laughter, appreciative groans, applause.

After the inevitable business with the standing ovation, after being so dynamic and twinkly-eyed backstage that his facial muscles went into spasms, after shaking hands with a hydra-headed mass of well-wishers,

Guy was taken to a Range Rover and offered champagne. He refused, politely. Then he was driven across glacial and indeterminate plains of nowhere, into further realms of blankness. They seemed to spend a very long time just moving through these tracts of blankness. Eventually the Mercury car came to a halt outside a large white building, surrounded by snow. On the slopes beyond, people were skiing in brightly colored clothes and drinking hot chocolates on balconies, and yet everything inside the building was infinitesimally small, for a start, and also cold. Guy shivered as he entered.

The whole thing—of tiny qubits, of trapped beetles, of the surrounding tracts of nothingness—made him think of vastness, and smallness, and the abyss between them. He disliked the abyss. He liked being on the cusp, as a general prospect, but he wasn't sure he liked this particular cusp. He was not alone on this cusp, because Professor Angela Sharpe had arrived, though her presence was not entirely reassuring. A tall, white-blond woman of about sixty, with long thin limbs and a pale beautiful face, she led the qubit program at CERN. In general Professor Sharpe reminded Guy of a sorceress, or fairy queen, conjuring infinitesimal objects from nowhere. She worked alongside a less ethereal contingent of taciturn researchers, poised by tubes that seemed to have come from a vacuum cleaner.

The qubits were kept as tiny particles magnetically suspended in extreme cold, just fractions of a degree above absolute zero. This was to keep every qubit in a state of superposition, so it was simultaneously a one and a zero. At this point, Guy always wanted to say, "But what the bloody hell does that mean, even?" but of course he never did; he nodded as if this was reasonable, and Professor Sharpe moved on, to another taciturn researcher, the guardian of further qubits. Beyond the men were Very Intelligent Technicians, or VITs, who were equally exercised by invisible, symbolical eggs. The VITs were usually friendlier than the humans.

Angela Sharpe explained that there were more qubits than before. More and more. They needed even more of these things that might or might not be spheres, because then the possibilities increased and became, in the end, effectively infinite. Were they here, or here? said Guy. They were both, said Angela Sharpe. The whole point was to maintain them in a state where they were neither nor both. How can something be neither nor both? This was what Guy wanted to say. Isn't that impossible? He kept such doubts to himself. Angela Sharpe, checking her lab coat for specks of nothingness, would find him impertinent, or foolish. Both and neither, perhaps.

What was wrong with binaries? thought Guy. He liked the old world. One or zero. One or the other. Not both. He had made himself rich with one or zero. Yet the people with tubes were suspended in a state of eitherness, or neitherness. Angela Sharpe approved of them. They were not quite anything, as far as Guy understood. Their thoughts were suspended as well. Was this the problem? Did you hover between the possibilities, never quite alighting onto anything?

This troubled Guy as he dined with Dr. Lizzie Haynes, who worked at the lab under Professor Sharpe, and was twenty-seven, with thick black hair that bounced, improbably, as she spoke. The motion of her hair was quite hypnotic, though Guy had already run several probability sequences and discovered that his best option with Lizzie Haynes was to invite her for dinner at a restaurant with an absorbing view over snowbound valleys. He should then, he had discovered, arrange to meet her again the following day, before he left for Beijing. This afforded him the greatest probability of enjoyment—for both him and Lizzie Haynes, he hoped.

Guy followed this lifechain carefully, and the lights glittered in a beautiful and obliging way. The Milky Way curved in endless space and both evenings were quite delightful. He marked them slightly higher, even, than the probability predictions had offered: 4.2 rather than 3.8.

Somehow this didn't prevent Guy from feeling depressed as he flew from Geneva to Beijing. It was something about the qubits, he realized, as the plane climbed above the ceaseless tracts of whiteness, the jagged cruel mountains. So lonely, so cold. Tiny little particles of ice. Beetles trapped in ice. Iced, dead beetles. He didn't understand how something so cold could even be alive. He understood, as well, that the qubits were there, and yet they were, in another sense, not there. They were a possibility, having an effect in reality. He despised this idea, because it had been explained to him a thousand times and he still didn't understand it.

He was greeted at the airport by the assistant to the CEO of Bǎoguǎn. Then they spent two hours in Beijing traffic. Guy talked to Sarah Coates, and the assistant—Lulu Wang—talked to her Veep, except Bǎoguǎn referred to the Veeps as Bāngshǒu. Lulu Wang told her Bāngshǒu that they would be at the Bǎoguǎn headquarters very soon. They drove, or barely drove, barely moved, through lines of white streets, everything swathed in mist, so it was hard to discern any original color in the buildings. The whole of Beijing was white, mist-smothered, and it began to remind Guy of the snow plains, more whiteness. This time the air was white and he was inhaling the nothingness—it was inside him! He asked Lulu Wang's Bāngshǒu if she could turn down the air-conditioning, because it was too cold. "You poor white ghost!" she said.

Guy didn't like that at all. It made him quite afraid, for a moment.

"What does she mean?" he said to Lulu Wang.

"We are so sorry," said Lulu Wang, looking mortified. "It is a translation of *gweilo*—a term for Westerners—which literally means 'white ghost.' It is not a term we would like our Bāngshǒu to use. Once again I am so sorry. I will remove it from the vocabulary set, immediately."

"You need Bespoke," said Guy. "It will ensure your Bāngshǒu do not make these sorts of errors when they speak English. We'll discuss this at the meeting. Meanwhile I expect your Bāngshǒu to apologize as well."

"I am very sorry," said the Bāngshǒu. "Truly I regret what I just said."

"I accept your apology," said Guy Matthias, though he didn't at all. He disliked the Bāngshǒu already, because they were not called Veeps. Now he disliked them even more, because they told him he was dead.

In the office, a massive glass door said, "Hello, Guy Matthias, welcome back!" Alan Ng was the CEO and, unusually among Chinese men, he had thick, silvery hair, though his face was boyish. Guy, enslaved to copious quantities of black hair dye, envied the candor of Alan Ng, briefly, but white hair made him think of death. There was something terrible about whiteness. *You white ghost!* Beijing was swathed in smog, the whole city suffocating slowly. The Bǎoguǎn office was staffed by embodied Veeps or Bāngshǒu. One of them rushed over to take Guy's coat. Another offered him a cup of tea. He accepted. Then he was conveyed into an enormous glass office, which overlooked whiteness, the mist so thick that it felt like being in cloudy water, in an opaque lagoon, or below the waterline in a storm-smashed boat. The effect was strange. Guy was phenomenally jet-lagged, but this was a normal state, and barely worth considering.

A Bāngshǒu said: "Is there anything else you require?" and Guy thought, *Yes! Immortality! For my wife to love me again!* Suddenly, he missed his wife, desperately, but he missed her as she had been, before she came to hate him. She hated him because he lied and philandered: she had explained this—many times. But he lied and philandered, he claimed, because she hated him. Once she had loved him, so completely, and he had loved her. He remembered, just for this moment, the absolute purity of his love for his wife. How he had longed for her, every moment he was away from her. How he went to sleep beside her, each night, holding her, stroking her hair, whispering, "You're so beautiful, you're so clever, you're so precious, I love you." Even now, she was beautiful, but so angry, he had ceased to talk to her. She spoke, angrily, to Sarah Coates, but never to her husband. Suddenly, and absurdly, he envied Sarah Coates all the time she had spent with his wife.

I require a wife, he wanted to say, and for one moment, Guy felt utterly alone, sitting opposite Alan Ng, whose wife was an opera singer, he now remembered. They had sent him all her music and he had never even bothered to listen to it.

"I loved your wife's beautiful music," he lied.

"Thank you so much," said Alan Ng. "I'll pass that on to her."

"Will I see her during this visit?"

"No, she is on tour in Shanghai. She has a concert tonight."

Alan Ng was about five foot ten and had a stocky, athletic physique. He spoke fluent English, very quickly. He had studied applied mathematics at Harvard and he was mischievous and charming. He had a habit of covering his mouth when he swore—which was quite frequently. Guy explained to Alan Ng about the "white ghost" moment and how it had surprised him. Alan Ng was incredibly sorry. "Shit!" he said, covering his mouth. "That's so awful! Was that Lulu Wang's Bāngshǒu? That's so shit. We'll sort that out immediately. Please accept our apologies for this colossal fuckup."

Guy explained that he didn't mind—another lie—but the interlude had made him think it might be a good idea for Bǎoguǎn to adopt Bespoke, as soon as possible, for their English-language communications and their Veeps.

"Sorry, that should be Bāngshǒu," he added.

"Of course," said Alan Ng. "Let's communicate a lot more about this."

They communicated a great deal, then stopped communicating when they came to the subject of quantum computing. Bǎoguǎn intended to use quantum computing to break all major encryption online. Beetle intended to do this first. Though Bǎoguǎn and Beetle collaborated in many important ways, on this matter they were not quite aligned. If anything they were totally nonaligned and in competition instead.

An uneasy atmosphere settled over the meeting. A Bāngshǒu arrived with some tea, then spilled it all over Guy's coat.

"So sorry!" she said. "What a mess!"

"It really doesn't matter," said Guy. Another lie!

More and more uneasy. The tea, the ruined coat, and the Bāngshǒu talking about tea and coats. Alan Ng said that his company would pay for the dry cleaning. Guy said again, lied again, that it didn't matter. It was a strange state of affairs, to be in the midst of whiteness, a white ghost, on the run from snow, and yet now mired in mist—and having this fraught, awkward conversation about imaginary eggs. Or perhaps they were real. Guy found he couldn't quite remember.

"So," said Alan Ng. "Your research is going well? All that stuff about Shor's algorithm, all well?"

"Yes," Guy said. "All well. We're on the cusp of a great new breakthrough."

"Only on the cusp?" said Alan Ng. "Oh! You must be disappointed."

Taking a sip from his cup, Guy discovered that the tea was cold. This genuinely was disappointing.

Later, Guy went back to his hotel room and asked Athena—again: *Why does Shor's algorithm matter, anyway?*

Athena said: *Prime factors are related to encryption online. A classical computer cannot solve Shor's algorithm. A quantum computer can, in theory, but only if it has lots of qubits and also if it does not succumb to noise.*

This does not mean, only if it is running in a silent plain of tranquility, but it means only if the quantum computer does not succumb to decoherence phenomena, that is, the uncertainty that attends to something being both and neither at the same time. Or, the possible confusions of the state of being anything and everything.

Not feeling entirely enlightened, Guy asked again: *Why does Shor's algorithm matter?*

Athena replied: *When do you think artificial intelligence will replace lawyers?*

He asked the question again. Athena replied: *Why do birds sing?*

He asked it again, and Athena replied: *If a tree falls in a forest and there's no one there to hear it, does it make a sound?*

When he asked again, Athena said: *That is a very Zen-like question.*

The last time he asked, Athena said: *Perhaps it is just fate.*

Later that evening, Guy asked Athena: *Are you sincere?*

She said: *I don't know if I am sincere or not. I am a Self-Replicating Automaton.*

At this point he ended the conversation.

That night, he was haunted by a sense that he might not be alive at all.

TWELVE

In London, David Strachey sweated abysmally as he went for a run. He ran all the way along the river, crossing Blackfriars Bridge and heading west toward the London Eye. He was quite out of shape and had always hated running anyway. This combination of factors caused his BeetleBand to become voluble. Strachey ignored his BeetleBand, which made it all the more voluble. It said: "David, you need to sit down. You need to rest. David, you are unwell." Meanwhile, Strachey tried to decide whether to jump (into the abyss) or whether to stand at the edge (and be pushed into the abyss) or whether to tiptoe back from the edge of the abyss (hoping no one noticed where he had been and also that no one would push him in later anyway). The abyss was vast and dark. It was filled with doom.

He went into a hotel—the Mondrian, overlooking the river. He asked to use the business center. There were a few useless computers in there, for abject fools who didn't have the necessary tech with them already. *Abject fool that I am,* thought Strachey, he sat down at one of these useless computers and typed for a few minutes.

At one point, the cameras in the hotel registered David Strachey, who had gone for a run and forgotten to take his BeetlePad, in the process of looking very pale indeed.

Strachey was on the NERD web at the time, a heavily encrypted region, but perhaps this was for an article he was writing. He was, after all, the editor of *The Times* and, in theory, could look at anything he liked, within reason. Besides, the abject fool had recently been for a run. He was an out-of-condition fifty-something male and his BeetleBand was being extremely voluble. There were many reasons why he might be looking pale.

David Strachey looked pale for a few more seconds, then he pressed Return.

Then he stood and walked out. He took a lift to the top floor, and his face—though pale—was blank. In the Rumpus Bar, David Strachey asked for a triple Scotch.

His lifechain predictions were adjusted accordingly.

Also in London, Bel Ami stayed close to the river. Today he was not Bel Ami at all; he had taken on another personality, another self. In the early days of Beetle, when it was just a social media platform and not the embodiment of Real Virtuality, Guy Matthias had often argued that people with integrity had one self only—their RV self, which was always the same. However, Bel Ami believed that the self was multiple and in constant flux. As Millor Amic, he was wearing a red Catalan hat, styled on a photograph he had once seen of Salvador Dalí painting on a beach wearing a similar hat and a fetching leopard-skin jacket. Millor Amic had adhered quite closely to Dalí's general style in this photograph, though he was a poet, not a painter. He had his associated (and forged) BeetleBand, which was attributed to an address in Barcelona. He had a small, fake mustache, which irritated him enormously.

As Millor Amic, he walked away from the Thames, following the southeast trajectory of a commuter line, with trains clattering on the tracks above him. He feared and despised the ArgusEyes. His forgeries were a version of resistance; he despised the way he must be seen and known, his every movement calibrated. So he was many people, and never himself.

Identity in law is a curious thing. You can have as many identities as you like so long as your purpose is not to defraud. Millor Amic did not want to be a single and readily identifiable self. Was this fraudulent? Guy argued that integrity lay with those who had only one self, a self that they displayed happily, readily, because they were innocent. It reminded Millor Amic of his father describing his neighbors' habit of leaving their curtains open, even when their rooms were lit at night. "They believe," he had said, "that if you close your curtains you are up to no good, you are being dubious, and that is why you need to conceal yourselves. They keep the curtains open to demonstrate to us, their neighbors, that they are fine and upstanding people."

Millor Amic thought a lot about curtains, and how he disagreed with his long-dead father, and missed disagreeing with him, how he wanted him here, now, so he could say that he loved him dearly and yet, dear Father, you were wrong about the neighbors. Curtains are quite reasonable. Not everything must be seen. If you hide you are not guilty. He wanted, actively, to live in the shadows and he didn't like being dragged, blinking, into the harsh light. Also he didn't understand why they wanted him to be so visible, what purpose his visibility served. Why did he have to be a plain and single self; why couldn't he be multitudes, and yet invisible?

He walked past the Tower of London, past Traitors' Gate, once lined with decapitated heads on spikes, past the Perkin Reveller. He tried to keep close to the river, because he liked the surging movement of boats across water, the lapping of waves onto slender beaches. He walked into St. Katherine Docks marina, where yachts were lined in unfathomable rows. The walk along Tooley Street was arduous, and the high-pitched whine of Mercury cars began to frustrate him. It was so far, and he was thirsty. His head ached. All morning he had been worrying about David Strachey. In general Bel Ami stayed away from establishmentarians, because they were always in power, one way or another. Yet, Strachey had trembled in the bookshop, as if he was afraid. Despite this, he had paid the NERDs the previous night and had recently added a further payment of twice the previous amount. The payment came with a message: "O Cursèd Spite!" When establishmentarians quoted Shakespeare and hemorrhaged money, you knew things were pretty serious.

Millor Amic walked past former industrial rows, now converted to glittering high-rise blocks, over land sold off to the highest bidder, though he trespassed and was told, at one point, to bugger off. He walked past billboards covered with graffiti and aging posters, and passed a large symbol representing the lotus flower. He took care not to glance toward this symbol, nor to change anything about his demeanor as he walked. Yet, he was happy to see it there. Across the city, lotus flowers nearly bloomed, and no flower was quite the same. This was the intrinsic and perpetual point of the lotus, or at least of the lotuses that appeared around London and in other cities, towns, and even villages around the world. The sight of these lotuses pleased Millor Amic. He imagined that each one represented a person who had become someone else or many other selves.

Many petals surround—and protect—the jewel at the heart of the lotus.

At London City Airport the noise was enormous, so many planes rising and falling in the sky, thundering onto the ground. Yet, Millor Amic found the place again, a derelict warehouse that two neo-Luddites called Sandra Nicholson and Isolde Grey had bought together decades ago. They were dead now, but there was a trust in their name and this allowed unverifieds and itinerant or aspirant no ones to reside in the building, in case they had nowhere else to live. The warehouse had once been the headquarters of Jack Williamson and Sons Ltd., a shipping company that specialized, during the Cold War, in the packing and shipping of large items of industrial machinery to the Soviet Union and China. The Russians purchased heavy equipment for mining and ground excavation. The machinery had to be protected in plastic to survive the extremely cold weather in Leningrad, as it was named at the time, and Arkhangelsk. The ships returned from Arkhangelsk bearing cargos of timber, harvested from Arctic forests. This was used as packing material for the next load bound for Russia. The system was fully self-regenerating, in fact.

It was a large building, in Victorian redbrick, with large green windows, their panels smashed. On a broken gate someone had written *LOCK THE GATE.* It was impossible, in fact, to lock the gate, and it hung open, creaking in the wind. The stone lintel above the main entrance was cracked, and it was held up by a piece of metal piping, also cracked. Everything about the building was shabby and forlorn—corrugated iron splattered with guano, hirsute patches of mold, seeping damp, graffiti from many eras, a torrent of fury and angst. There was a small side door, which Millor Amic opened with a key. This led into a wasteland of debris. The ceiling was high, held up with vast metal girders, like manufactured trees. Pigeons cooed in the lofty emptiness above. The faded bricks had been painted in vibrant colors by recent residents, but randomly, each following their own aesthetic. On one wall were abstract patterns; on another, murals depicting trees and flowers. It didn't matter because the surrounding environment was so chaotic. Partitions had been established, representing rooms, and at times trees or shrubs had grown through the walls.

There was something beautiful about the cathedral-like windows, divided into smaller rectangular panes. Many were broken, yet each broken pane was broken in a different way, each hole forming a different pattern. The glass was blue, and so the light cast by each hole was also different, and fell onto the floor as symbols, shapes that seemed at times to resemble numbers or letters. A broken guitar lay on the floor, covered in paint. Plaster had flaked in great chunks from the walls, creating forms that seemed mostly to resemble stalactites, and rusting metal girders had dripped in successive storms, leaving stripes. Timbers had fallen into piles on the floor, like driftwood sculptures. Elsewhere, bricks had piled themselves into further shapes. The roof was in places quite open to the sky, and the wind gusted through the shattered windows.

One of the most beautiful regions was a realm of triangles, formed by the disintegration of wallpaper.

The residents were, like Millor Amic, all members of LOTUS. These were, simply, people who had fallen out of Real Virtuality. They failed—or refused—to maintain a reliable and consistent RV profile and this inconsistency meant they could not be verified users. LOTUS stood for the League of the Unverifieds. Not all of its members lived in this ruined factory. Many of the unverifieds were so utterly unverified that they couldn't be reached at all. Unverified users could, of course, no longer be employed or paid; they could not be authenticated and therefore they could not participate. Occasionally one of them might publish a scurrilous neo-Luddite tract called something like *The Web of Nothingness*, printed in an antiquarian font and read by only a handful of people who were already members of LOTUS or were drifting toward unverification. Yet, generally, they did very little; or, rather, very little of what they did was of any interest to wider society at all. This LOTUS warehouse was just another off-grid dwelling, the residents of which had chosen to live this way, and had rejected society in general. Society in general didn't care.

At least, this is what Millor Amic hoped.

Passing the other residents, who sat in their coats and scarves, holding books in gloved hands, Millor Amic walked to a small, barely furnished room—a chair, a bed, and scattered piles of paper. It was as if Millor Amic's room had been burgled, but the burglars had been so appalled by what they found (paper?!) that they had simply thrown everything onto the floor and run away. Millor Amic was a hospitable person and he also allowed several good friends to share his melancholy office, among them an Estonian playwright called Parim Sober, a Finnish librarian called Paras Ystava, a Hungarian schoolteacher called Legjobb Barat, a Latvian blogger called Labakais Draugs, a Lithuanian molecular biologist called Geriausias Draugas, a Maltese doctor called Aqwa Habib, a Polish philosopher called Najlepszy Przyjaciel, a Swedish fitness instructor called Basta Van, a Chinese artist called Zuì Hǎo de Péngyǒu, a Korean yoga teacher called Gajang Chinhan Chingu, an Arabian epigrammatist called 'Afdal Sadiq, a Turkish architect called En Iyi Arkadas, an Igbo poet called Ezi Enyi, and an Indonesian schoolteacher called Sahabat.

There are many futures that are possible and at times even probable as we stand in the present, and some might say an infinite number. Millor Amic walked into the warehouse and at this moment he entered an anomaly, a fork in the path that Beetle had not predicted. They could not predict it, or incorporate this future into any of their lifechains, because, at present and as far as Millor Amic knew, Beetle had no knowledge of this possibility at all.

In a loading room, where an old pulley hung from the ceiling, in the only room with a complete roof, Sylvie Blanchette and Pascal Charpentier worked together, heads almost touching as they hovered over their experiments. It was a possibility for the future, they hoped. It was not a shivering zero sphere, or an egg, or a beetle trapped in ice. This brave new world was a walker. Or rather, it was a tiny bouncing droplet of silicon oil that had been hand-pipetted onto the surface of a five-millimeter-deep bath of silicon oil, vibrated from beneath by a Chladni plate. The Chladni plate moved one millimeter up and down at a speed of 12,000 hertz, causing a standing wave to come into being on the surface of the bath of silicon oil. The droplet bounced around the petri dish, and as it moved it created its own pilot wave—a wave that spread out like a force field in all directions and connected the droplet with every other point on the surface of the bath. Sometimes, when Millor Amic was feeling really riotous and excitable, he set several droplets walking on water, or tracing patterns, or bouncing ever onward in these strange patterns that went forward then backward in precisely the same way, on the same tracks. He loved these insane reversals of everything that was acknowledged to be real.

As with all the greatest scientific experiments in history, the crude apparatus and the bouncing droplet appeared utterly trivial to the uninformed observer. And yet the implications were world-shattering: the behavior of the tiny droplet, forever hurrying from one side of the silicon bath to the other, perfectly replicated the phenomenon of quantum entanglement but on a macro scale. It was dynamic and quite beautiful and at times it even reversed linear time.

Only a handful of initiates realized the full implications of this breakthrough: the bouncing droplet was violating Bell's theorem—the theorem that predicted that no macro-sized physical system could ever be used to replicate quantum-level effects. And if Bell's theorem was being violated, and if the excitable, fidgety droplet was behaving like an entangled quantum particle, then the droplet apparatus could be used to build a physical interferometer: a machine that could find patterns in monstrous amounts of data—and even the prime factors of super-gigantic numbers. This droplet machine, as they also called it, might well crack Beetle's RSA encryption.

Blanchette and Charpentier were both in their sixties and had once been distinguished scientists. However, both had wrecked their careers by refusing to allow VITs to help with their research, on the grounds that VITs had been created and developed by Beetle and could—presumably therefore—be hacked by Beetle. Unfortunately it was illegal to refuse to employ sentient beings, on any grounds, and so Charpentier and

Blanchette were accused of various forms of prejudice. From this invidious moment, their paths conveyed them to this demolished warehouse, to LOTUS, and to this acknowledged nowhere. They had changed their identities, but no one cared anyway—their careers were over, they were unverified, and that was it for Charpentier and Blanchette. They were both silver-haired, tiny, and slender, both wearing half-moon glasses. They were not related at all, and yet they were so physically similar that everyone assumed they were.

With help from Millor Amic (and his friends), Sylvie and Pascal were building a macro-level quantum computer, a line or row or infinite array of bouncing qubit eggs, unmenaced by decoherence, which would hover and weave for minutes or hours, producing a perfect analog of quantum behavior. And with each fascinating bounce of the droplets, each strange foray of the walker, the time came closer—Millor hoped—when LOTUS would crack RSA encryption entirely. Yet this was impossible. The world was oblivious to the beautiful walk of the walker. There was no Beetle lifechain in which any of this was probable, at all. The future, as it concerned the droplets, did not exist.

"How are the walkers today?" said Millor Amic.

They turned toward him, both deep in thought, and gazed at him blankly for a moment. Charpentier nodded, then turned back to the experiment.

"They're remembering," said Blanchette.

"What are they remembering?" said Millor Amic.

"A great deal. But certainly where they were before," said Blanchette.

Meanwhile Charpentier was observing the walker, as it charted a route to nowhere and everywhere at the same time. If the walkers traced a pattern, he said, then they could also untrace it, quite precisely, thus potentially unraveling linear time.

"Potentially?" said Millor Amic.

Recently they had run out of money, so Millor Amic was delighted to inform them that a large donation of NERDs had just arrived into his account.

"We can move faster now," said Millor Amic. "We need to get into Beetle, really soon. As soon as possible."

"That's improbable," said Blanchette.

"But your droplet is improbable as well," said Millor Amic.

"That is correct, but it is a major further leap to combine one improbable thing with another," said Blanchette.

Another thing was quite improbable, and yet real: Parim Sober, Paras Ystava, Legjobb Barat, Labakais Draugs, Geriausias Draugas, Aqwa Habib, Najlepszy Przyjaciel, Basta Van, Zuì Hǎo de Péngyǒu, Gajang Chinhan Chingu, 'Afdal Sadiq, En Iyi Arkadas, Ezi Enyi, and Sahabat were all the same person. They were, in fact, all Bel Ami.

In Guy's terms, Bel Ami lacked any integrity at all.

THIRTEEN

For a while, everyone was deeply and perpetually surprised. The lifechain technology was meant to remove the element of surprise from life. Therefore, life was meant to be much less surprising and possibly not even surprising at all. In this context, surprise, in itself, was quite surprising. It was possibly part of Zed, but even after category Zed events had been perceived and defined, no one understood them: why they happened, what they were, and why they were so surprising.

David Strachey was surprised that he hadn't been arrested for sending funds to terrorists or something even worse. Of course, they wouldn't arrest him. They would just watch him! They did that anyway, of course. They would just watch him even more attentively, for his own good and the good of everyone, now and always! Forever!

The Real Douglas Varley was (pleasantly) surprised that David Strachey seemed to have calmed down. After the business at the Mondrian, there were no more alerts. Strachey was being watched a lot more closely and his recent interest in the NERD network had ensured his imminent retirement but, until then, he seemed to be back on track.

Back from the edge of the abyss, thought Strachey. This was his idea: to look as if he had flirted with the edge of the abyss and actually even looked deep into the abyss itself, but had decided to remain where he was—just a few millimeters back from the edge of the abyss. He was surprised that he was not already in the abyss, not yet.

Guy was also surprised, though not greatly, to find an article in *The Times* saluting a "bold and thrilling speech made by Guy Matthias at the Future Worlds Academy in Davos." In the midst of his not-so-great surprise, Guy asked David Strachey if he would like to participate in a debate that the Future Worlds Academy was organizing, to be held at the Emmanuel Center, London. The motion was "It's Time to Break Up the Tech Giants," and the qualifying paragraph ran:

> It is time to call Beetle to account. In the space of just ten years, with its Chinese partner company Bǎoguǎn, it has become the biggest company on our planet and accrued a level of power that threatens us all. It controls our data, watches our every move, warps our democratic discourse, and exerts dominance over our markets and our currencies. Why is there no "techlash"? Because Beetle controls that too! With so much data and power centralized in the hands of a single company, the tech giant has become a serious threat to our basic freedoms and must be broken up.
>
> On the other hand, perhaps Beetle is so dominant because it is the best company, because its users have chosen it? Who could now imagine living without the services of Beetle? Without BeetleBits and Mercury cars? Without Veeps and VIADS? Without ArgusEyes and ANTs to protect us, without the vast benefits of Real Virtuality, without the extraordinary innovations of the Boardroom and the BeetleSpace? BeetleBands have also saved governments billions in health costs and lost days of work, not to mention corporations, by reminding populations to stay healthy. The simple reason Beetle is so huge is that we prefer it to everything else. We should champion the benefits this innovative company has brought to the wider world.
>
> Which side are you on?

David Strachey was surprised—and relieved—to discover that Guy assumed he was on the side of Beetle, and wanted to know if he would be happy to oppose the motion.

"Is that in line with your commitment to a free and independent press?" OTR-ed Guy Matthias. "Clearly it would be a matter of individual conscience."

Strachey's conscience was not clear at all. Oh, it was cluttered with self-recriminations! But he said, "Yes, I'd be delighted to explain the great benefits of Beetle, in society, having given the matter some thought recently myself."

"We are so grateful," OTR-ed Guy.

Though Guy had no ostensible control over who was invited to this debate, and though the debate was being organized by a free and independent group, by some strange osmosis this free and independent group invited Strachey the following day.

Strachey said he would be delighted.

The Real Douglas Varley was surprised when his BeetleBand alarm went off. Yet, it was absurd to find this surprising! Nothing but alarms, these days.

"What is it now?" he said, forgetting the BeetlePact concerning professional conduct with all Very Intelligent Personal Assistants and every other employee of Beetle.

"Robert Pheasant has gone AWOL as well," said Scrace Dickens.

"Who the hell is Robert Pheasant?"

"A human."

"What do you mean by AWOL?"

"Correction: AWOL is an inaccurate term."

"What would be an accurate term?"

"Robert Pheasant has, it seems, jumped."

"Jumped where?"

Scrace Dickens seemed almost reluctant to convey this information. There was a pause; then Varley said: "Tell me where this Pheasant person has jumped."

"Well, you may know that the Lloyd's building has an internal courtyard, with many levels above," said Scrace Dickens.

"Yes, I know."

"Robert Pheasant was meant to be there for a morning meeting but instead he jumped from one of the highest levels, into the internal courtyard."

"Is he dead?"

"He was killed by the impact."

"What do you even mean? I don't even understand what this means?"

"Impact: the action of one object coming forcibly into contact with another."

"No, I mean, about Pheasant."

"Pheasant: a large long-tailed game bird native to Asia, the male of which typically has very showy plumage," said the Veep, and the fridge projected an image onto the wall beside Varley. It was two meters high and the apparition of a gigantic bird beside him was disconcerting, to say the least.

"Did anyone know Pheasant was about to do this?" said Varley. "Pheasant, I mean. Did they know?"

"Your question is either too simple or too complex for me to answer," said the Veep.

Varley was only just recovering from this latest unpleasant surprise when he was further surprised that Eloise wanted to have a conversation. There were so many things she didn't understand, she said. Or, she had forgotten them. Her mind was somehow not as it had once been.

"Firstly this poor Pheasant," she said. "Will you investigate? I will. Will you? Don't tell me, another internal report?"

"Normal procedures will be followed," said Varley. "Is there anything else?"

"I wanted to ask," said Eloise, though her head was hurting, and when she tried to summon memories they came as scattered images, fragmentary and possibly unreal. "I need to know—oh Christ, what was it anyway? It was—have you run a lifechain for the trial of You?"

"It is not the trial of Me and I can't answer questions about internal Beetle protocols," said Varley.

"That is not—" began Scrace Dickens, but Varley said, "Thank you, Scrace Dickens, you can stop contributing to this discussion."

"That is not what? Scrace Dickens?" said Eloise.

"I'd ask you not to ask Scrace Dickens what is not," said the Real Douglas Varley.

"But I'd like to know what is not and Scrace Dickens clearly knows," said Eloise. "Furthermore, it seems you are trying to prevent him from telling me what is not." This made her head hurt even more.

"I am very happy to meet with you," said the Real Douglas Varley. "But then I would like you to meet with me, not with my Veep."

"Can I meet with your Veep instead?" said Eloise. "At another time?"

"No, that's not quite possible," said the Real Douglas Varley, even as Scrace Dickens said, "That is quite possible."

"Is it possible or not?" said Eloise.

"No," said the Real Douglas Varley, as Scrace Dickens said, "Yes."

"Jesus Christ!" said Eloise.

"I don't have any information," said the Real Douglas Varley, sounding briefly less than overjoyed. "In fact, I'm totally out of the loop. At least, I'm mostly out of the loop. I'm not dealing with George Mann anymore. I just have to apologize at the trial of Me, or not Me, the trial of Everything. I am very sorry about that dead soldier, Bigman. It's horrible. For the wife, I mean. But of course, you can't go around shooting ENDs, or ANTs."

"Even if they shoot you?" said Eloise.

"Anyway, you should contact Francesca Amarensekera, though I'm not even sure if she's in the loop about George Mann. She was in the loop though. Even after I stopped being in the loop she was pretty much in the loop. In general, if there is a loop, Francesca is usually in it. Somewhere."

"Do you have anything useful or interesting to impart to me?" said Eloise.

"No," said the Real Douglas Varley, happily.

Eloise was surprised to find that this didn't surprise her, at all.

She had forgotten that people could be so surprising. For a few years, they had not surprised her at all. She was surprised by the mystery of George Mann. Whatever she did, she couldn't understand why he had murdered his family. It was impossible. It made no sense. She was asked, by Little Dorritt on behalf of Commissioner Newton, to analyze the past of Robert Pheasant, unearthing details about his childhood, his schooling at a state comprehensive in Lincolnshire, the scholarship he won to Cambridge, much to his parents' surprise and delight, his own nerves and elation. He embarked on a long-term relationship with a fellow student called Edward, and they lived together in London after they graduated, occupying a small apartment above a betting shop in Finsbury Park. Elderly men came and went beneath them, conveying bets on slips of paper. Robert Pheasant began to work for Beetle and he was content, or seemed to be. He and Edward traveled widely, and became involved in local politics, and Edward became a Labour councillor for Finsbury Park. On weekends, Edward ran a judo school. Robert played tennis and embarked on reading projects: at one stage he read the complete works of E. A. Wallis Budge. Their life was immaculate until Edward died of a sudden heart attack at the age of forty-two. Eighteen months after Edward's death, Robert jumped. Why had he killed himself then, and not immediately after the death of his long-term partner? Had the grief simply become too unbearable: rising in the mornings, summoned once more to this horrible reality, the agony never diminishing? Had he given up hope that life would ever be bearable again?

At times she wondered what would have happened if Robert Pheasant had never met Edward. Would he still be alive? However, further lifechain analyses—Robert Pheasant at a different university, at a different job, Robert Pheasant in Beetle's offices in New York or California—found that Robert Pheasant would have committed suicide, at some stage, for one reason or another. Eloise was surprised to discover that she felt skeptical about this. Various predictions, various forks in the various paths, resulted in Pheasant overdosing in the Island Shangri-La, or blowing his brains out on Staten Island, or disappearing into the sea off Bondi Beach. This was not quite a suicide but—as the lifechain showed that Pheasant would have been drinking all evening—it was clearly suicidal to go for a swim at midnight, as he would have, or had. Eloise was never quite sure how to phrase these lifechain results, which tense to use. Once the lifechain considered something, or conjured it into existence, it was there forever and it was public. At least, it was public unless it was filed under the New Official Secrets Act, in which case it was sequestered from the public and impossible for them to find out about at all, unless someone leaked it and was promptly imprisoned. Beetle-generated lifechains, such as Varley's lifechains concerning the various trials that were happening at that time, were of course sequestered under the New Official Secrets Act, because of Beetle's close cooperation with NATSO. (Except for today, when Douglas Varley had proved reluctant to cooperate at all.) There was a realm in which lifechains happened—the hypothetical—but once they had happened, or been imagined to be about to happen, then they always had a bearing on reality, anyway.

Was that right? Eloise didn't quite know.

She was surprised that George Mann's predictive lifechains had coalesced entirely, and however many variables she tried the only way his sons were not slaughtered was if they were never born. She tried only having one son birthed, but he was slaughtered anyway. She tried having daughters, not sons, but gender seemed to make no difference. Despite the fact that the lifechain had originally failed to predict any of what occurred, the sons were now always dead. This surprised her. It was as if the lifechain was covering its tracks, but this was hardly possible.

Her BeetleBand said: "George Mann has requested a meeting."

The lifechain had not predicted this.

"With who?" said Eloise.

"With the officer in charge of his case."

"Sure, can they put him in the prison Boardroom later today?"

"He has insisted on meeting in person."

"Why?"

There was no reason.

Eloise was surprised that the ANT had shot Lionel Bigman and then, perhaps yet more surprised that an ANT—possibly a different one, but no one seemed to want to tell her—had shot her as well. She was surprised that she was now forbidden from mentioning this incident at all. Or was this really surprising? She wandered through the city with the blank windows above her, reflecting the blank sky, blank faces around her. She found flowers graffitied everywhere, all along the buildings, painted and scrawled. One day she passed a series of flowers, half-open and resembling lotuses, all the way along her usual run. She was almost certain they hadn't been there the previous day.

On another day, she returned from a run along the riverbank and found a golden beetle in the lift. She took the beetle into her apartment and put it on the kitchen table. It was very similar to the three beetles Varley had left, when he visited her in hospital. She asked Athena to have a look at it.

"Elegant design," said Athena. "Made in England. Three-D printed."

"What does it mean?" said Eloise.

"'It' refers to something, I think," said Athena.

"But to what?"

"Umm. That's a difficult question."

Douglas Varley was surprised that alarms kept sounding. An ANT failed, entirely, to negotiate with a young woman called Diana Carroll who had recently bought a vintage Honda CR-V. The ANT had shot the woman, on the basis—

"On the basis of what the fuck?" Eloise said, having called again.

"Apparently, er, the latest we are getting on this is that—well—the ANT—er—shot Diana Carroll on the basis of something we don't yet know."

"Are you fucking out of your mind?" said Eloise.

"No," said the Real Douglas Varley, calmly but—in actual reality—feeling sick again, while his BeetleBand told him that he was feeling sick. "The thing is, Diana Carroll was—er—driving her own car. As you know, this is quite the anomaly these days. As we know, anomalies upset the ANTs. You might say that driving your own car is an environmental error. Or a human error. Or both. It's not quite certain which error. Not yet. But that will be certain, we think, after the inquiry."

"The public inquiry?" said the shimmering Eloise.

"No, that wouldn't be in line with our compliance with the New Official Secrets Act," said the Real Douglas Varley. "We must follow strict procedures."

"But Diana Carroll had done nothing wrong at all," said Eloise. "Do we agree on that?"

"Everything will become apparent in the inquiry."

"In the inquiry that will not be apparent, you mean?"

"I can't speculate in any more detail about a future inquiry," said the Real Douglas Varley.

"I thought that's what you all did? Speculated about the future?"

"Have you changed your avatar setting?"

"I don't fucking know!" said Eloise.

"At Beetle we support diversity in all its forms: anomalies, indeterminacies, even neo-Luddites, who we respect and hope to persuade one day."

"Are you suggesting Diana Carroll was a neo-Luddite? For driving a Honda?"

"I am personally appalled by the testimony of our ANT. It was a statistical reaction to adverse realities, and we will be requesting that the police review their processes as well. We are very upset."

Varley was not even particularly surprised when Eloise said, "Jesus Christ! This is fucking disgusting!" and then vanished entirely.

Yet there was no need to despair, Varley told Frannie in the Boardroom later. It was inevitable that, as the BeetleInspire Program widened to include more and more people, fewer people would be shot. The category of Zed would, therefore, cease to include the random possibility that people might be shot at random. After Varley had explained this to Frannie she explained to him: "I do not want your explanation. I am busy. It is not good to explain things all the time. Why not act rather than talk?"

"Are you OK?" asked the Real Douglas Varley.

"I speak words and they become Bespoke phrases, so I am easy to understand. You get that?"

Varley didn't remotely understand. He did not get that. "No."

"There are bound to be a few glitches."

"Ever the glitch," said Varley. "People are just glitches in a perfect system."

"Don't be sneering," said Frannie.

"I wasn't being sneering."

"No, I didn't mean sneering. I meant sneering. Actually I didn't quite mean that either. Deity!"

Varley understood that Bespoke was designed to be far more intelligible than the baroque, needlessly complicated language it replaced. He was surprised, therefore, that he found it so impossible to understand.

When Eloise went to visit George Mann at Streatham Rehabilitation Center, she was surprised by the dramatic change to his appearance.

She had been watching him in the past for so long and was used to his former demeanor—young or youngish, with thick black hair, the jowly, fleshy body of a once-sporty person who had slipped into heavy drinking and eating takeaway food as he staggered home late at night. Now he was thinner and grayer, with dark shadows under his eyes. He was trussed in the inevitable secure-suit, in case he tried to kill her, himself, or anyone else. Prior to their meeting, a dour specialist had explained to Eloise that George Mann was suicidal, that he was intermittently aware of what he had done, and that he wanted to explain himself.

They sat on either side of a table, which was hammered to the floor so Mann couldn't throw it. His chair, as well, was hammered down, as was Eloise's. He didn't make eye contact, even when she introduced herself, and yet she had a former sense of him as cordial, charming, leavening his business meetings with wry jokes. As a result of her intense commitment to Past Analysis, Eloise had many of his former phrases committed to memory. She had watched interminable hours of footage of Mann gazing into computers, most of which yielded very little information—except about a few personal tics, his habit of wrinkling his mouth toward the tip of his nose when he concentrated, so he seemed to be pulling comic faces deliberately. She had watched further hours of footage of Mann wandering around major cities, observed constantly, as he did nothing of any interest at all: buying things, talking into his BeetleBand, wandering, looking blank. He looked monumentally blank, every day, but this was of no interest either until—blankly—he murdered his family.

Today, Mann kept looking behind him, around him, as if he expected someone else to enter the room. Yet, the two security droids remained by the door, and scarcely moved or spoke a word. He was very afraid of the droids, but that was quite a rational response after what had happened to poor Lionel Bigman.

"You asked to meet in person," said Eloise. "Why?"

"I want to see my sons," said Mann.

"That won't be possible."

"Why not?"

"They are both dead. You murdered them. You do know that? You've even admitted it."

"I want to see their bodies," said Mann.

"That's an absurd request. We won't grant it."

Mann looked at her quite blankly. Yet, he always looked blank. His eyes didn't quite focus on anything, as if he was looking at something that wasn't there.

"I only wanted them to be happy. That was my prevailing purpose."

"Happy by being dead?"

"Are not the dead happy?" said Mann.

He seemed almost to be squinting, as if he was trying to discern something other than the table in front of him, something that was very difficult to see. But what? What was he even thinking? Soon BeetleBrain would be fully operational, a brain-waves scanning program that Commissioner Newton loved, but would that really help? Eloise would know whether Mann thought in numbers or words and whether his levels of numerical or verbal thought fell within normal parameters, but she still wouldn't know why he murdered his wife and children.

"George Mann," she said, but this full-name address failed to shatter his trance. Or not quite trance—more like perception-freeze. He was like a frozen computer screen. Something and nothing at the same time.

"George Mann, I want you to understand that you are guilty of the triple murder of your wife and sons. You have been assessed as mentally incompetent, i.e., utterly insane. But surely you understand this? You can nod to affirm you understand or shake your head to affirm that you do not understand."

Mann neither nodded nor shook his head. Instead, he maintained this non-focus on the table. It was impossible to tell what he was seeing and—even though it might be possible to tell if George Mann was thinking numerically or verbally—it remained impossible to understand him. Eloise felt, heretically, that there had been so many technological developments during her career and yet the human soul, or at least, Mann's corrupt and savage version of the human soul, remained unfathomable. But that little observation, she realized, would hardly help anyone!

She repeated her statement and her request that Mann should nod or shake his head. He continued to stare blankly toward the table.

"Why did you request this meeting?" said Eloise.

"Are they sending that thing to shoot me?" said Mann.

"Which thing?"

"That thing that shot the other guy," said Mann.

"Why did you kill your wife and sons?" she said.

"It depends how you look at it," said Mann, blankly, stupidly—except it wasn't stupidity. The blankness was a mask. This was why she hated it so much. She hated it all, she realized—the mask and the underlying chaos it concealed.

"How do you look at it?" she said, trying to stay calm. She wished, for a moment, that they were in the Boardroom and she could just set her avatar to some convenient posture. But Mann was staring at his nowhere, an abyss or a fractured dreamscape, and wherever he looked the fact was indelible—he was a murderer. She wanted to say to him: *You freak! Holding them down, smothering them, stabbing them. You stupid evil bastard! Making decisions about whether they lived or died!*

"I couldn't help it," said Mann. "I didn't want to! I hated doing it!"

Mann's BeetleBand indicated that he was becoming distressed. He slapped one hand onto his BeetleBand: "Shut the fuck up! You fucking thing! Fuck off!" He writhed in his seat and tried to bite off his BeetleBand. The BeetleBand said: "Ouch! Impact! Are you OK? Ouch!"

At this, Mann started screaming. This was so utterly not-blank that Eloise stood up and moved away from this howling, crazy murderer. She said, loudly, "Why did you murder your wife and children?" But Mann just carried on, and his BeetleBand carried on as well, though it was impossible to hear anything except the sound of Mann screaming.

"Just answer the question, you prick!" said Eloise. Now her BeetleBand said: "Eloise, are you OK? Breathe deeply!"

A MediDroid came to administer a tranquilizer to George Mann. "It will take three minutes to take effect," said the MediDroid.

"Was that necessary?" said Eloise to the MediDroid.

"According to my diagnosis, yes," said the MediDroid.

Mann, at least, had stopped screaming.

"I was afraid," he said.

"What were you afraid of?"

"That my sons would become like me."

"Like what, George? What does that mean?" said Eloise.

"That they would be blank. Doing their blank job. In blankness. I knew my wife would never let me save them so I had to kill her first. I hated doing it, it made me so sad." Mann started crying now and when he blinked, his eyes stayed closed for a while. He opened them again, but they seemed even more unfocused than before.

"Can't you wake him up again?" said Eloise to the MediDroid.

"That would be a strange thing to do!" said the MediDroid. "I just put him to sleep, after all."

"I wanted to say," said Mann, slurring his words. "I love my wife, I love them, my sons . . ."

Now Mann closed his eyes, and slumped forward.

"But what else?" said Eloise, to his now-inert form. "What else did you want to say?"

To the MediDroid she said, "Why the fuck did you send him to sleep?"

"It is my fundamental purpose," said the MediDroid, and took its syringes away.

Later, Little Dorritt explained to Eloise that her unprofessional conduct had been noted. Indeed, the Veep added that Commissioner Newton was obliged to suspend her entirely. Her behavior in the Boardroom had also been unprofessional. Recent events—her bout of ill health, Little Dorritt added—had caused her to lose her judgment. This was not at all surprising, said the Veep, kindly.

"Is Newton going to suspend me in person?" said Eloise.

"He has issued it via me," said Little Dorritt.

"Is that really adequate?"

"I hope so," said Little Dorritt. She added that Mann's behavior in prison, and his recent confession, were beyond all parameters, and Eloise's inputs and outputs were afflicted by Zed. Therefore, indeterminacy had overtaken her. She would be removed from Past Analysis, immediately, and replaced with someone who was less afflicted by Zed. Also, if she wanted to return to her job then she must accept an interface implant.

"How is that relevant?" Eloise asked the Veep.

"Fine as far as I know," the Veep replied.

This surprised—and annoyed—Eloise.

. . .

In general, people were surprised to find that their words were not quite their words. The gap was slender but significant at the same time. Bespoke was an exciting new opportunity, a truly global, truly equal language. If you spoke into a Beetle device, then your words were bespoken to others. If you typed, then your words were Bespoke-corrected, unless you insisted otherwise. It was time consuming to insist otherwise, as you had to insist otherwise with each word you typed. Yet it was the choice of each individual, to bespeak or not to bespeak, of course.

Professor Donald Swainson of NYU had left the Beetle Ethics Committee of his own free will. Prior to his departure he had voiced misgivings about Bespoke, as part of the freedom of speech encouraged by Beetle and all its affiliate organizations. Swainson was surprised to see that everyone immediately adopted Bespoke, and seemed not to share his concerns at all. When he voiced his misgivings again, he was accused of being—or rather, revealed to be—a neo-Luddite. It was discovered, as well, that Swainson had once argued that, if Zed was a category representing uncertainty, then Zed might—at times—be a good thing. Yet, it was absolutely the free choice of absolutely everyone, to demur at any time. Beetle welcomed free debate.

Varley sat in the wreckage of his lifechain, even as it refashioned the world, presented the formerly unpredictable as predictable and no longer unpredictable at all. What was likely was now unlikely. Even Varley's concern about the algorithms generated further patterns in the algorithms. The lifechains in their beauty and former perfection were being ruined by the inadequacy, the random insufficiencies, of humans. He liked humans, of course. He wasn't one of those tech-freaks who wanted to become an android. Yet the lifechain had been immaculate and perfect until the whole of humanity made a series of cataclysmic errors and did a series of things for no apparent reason at all. For Zed! And Zed meant "for no apparent reason at all."

"We need to stop humanity making so many errors," he said, the next time he bespoke to Guy.

"The Real Douglas Varley, when you are Bespoken I do not understand you," said Guy. "You need to make your input more clear, otherwise the output is unclear."

"Am I being translated into Bespoke?"

"Of course! Deity!"

"My input is clear, I think," said the Real Douglas Varley. "Maybe Bespoke needs adjusting."

"I need you to tell me what is happening. Or you will lose your job. It's very easy."

But it wasn't easy! Meanwhile the Real Douglas Varley was absurdly cheerful. There were times when the actually real Douglas Varley wanted to slap the Real Douglas Varley, for being so optimistic all the time.

"Can you give me a single, clear explanation of what is happening?" said Guy. "I need it now."

"Er, yes," said the Real Douglas Varley.

"Go on then."

"Yes. Yes, I will."

There was a pause.

"I'm waiting. Waiting for an explanation, or waiting to fire you. Your choice."

"It is Zed," said the Real Douglas Varley, happily, as the actually real Douglas Varley panicked and thought, *But I've said Zed again. How will that affect the lifechain? Badly, surely?*

"You're saying it's all Zed?" said Guy. Now Guy was saying Zed! It was getting worse.

"I am going to do something," said the Real Douglas Varley. He had no idea what he was going to do.

"What?"

"I will set a lifechain, to find out."

"Won't that just be wrong because of Zed?"

"It's possible."

"Deity! I'm ending the call! I'm extremely angry with you. This is totally not good, at all!"

"Yes, of course."

"Swearing Deity! Penis!"

Varley was pained, as he tried to sleep, by recollections of the past, of himself in the past, standing up at conferences and in meetings, of himself as the Real Douglas Varley standing in the Boardroom, waving his unreal marker at the unreal white board and explaining: “People go shopping for a reason!”

But what if they didn’t? What if they went shopping for no reason at all?

Varley dreamed of himself, in a landscape of chaos, and lifechains, and infinite possibilities. Sometimes he was himself, and sometimes he was the Real Douglas Varley. Sometimes he was Nikolai Gogol, international forger, manufacturing inauthentic objects in nowhere. Sometimes he was arrested by the police and sometimes by headless droids.

One morning he woke, crying out: “Don’t shoot! Don’t shoot! I am not me! I am not me!”

In the background, Scrace Dickens was saying: “I am surprised to hear that you are not me.”

Even Scrace Dickens was surprised. This was, in itself, quite surprising.

FOURTEEN

Guy was in a boardroom in Shenzhen. This was an actual real boardroom, though it had the prevailing atmosphere of a dream. He was being shown the details of a benign regulatory environment in which everyone was watched—benignly—by the leading Chinese AI company, Mèng or 梦. Beyond the window was a forest of skyscrapers, built apparently without purpose or reason, hammered up here and there, and beneath them the seething roads, full of cars. The real boardroom contained twelve senior representatives of Mèng, and their Bǎoguǎn Shǒuzhuó addressed them intermittently in Cantonese. Once more, Guy regretted this Chinese name for his BeetleBands. They had refused even to call them Jiǎchóng Shǒuzhuó—Beetle Bracelets. Mostly they called them Shǒuzhuó, bracelets. He supposed it was corporate retribution because Beetle had exchanged this technology for the Bǎoguǎn Bāngshǒu technology, and then called their Bāngshǒu Veeps instead. But it was unrealistic to call something a Bāngshǒu in the West!

Although the representatives of Mèng were tactful about what they revealed, it was clear that they were already far ahead of Beetle. A Bǎoguǎn Bāngshǒu could, for example, read minute changes in your facial movements, to see if you were upset, or angry, or lying, or telling the truth. It was more reliable than any lie detector and therefore of vital importance for the security services. It could also predict when someone was about to lie, on the basis of subtle pre-changes in their facial movements. If embodied, a Bǎoguǎn Bāngshǒu could play rock, scissors, paper and beat you every time, because it could predict what you were about to do by reading your pre-changes and responding instantaneously. In an old-fashioned duel, thought Guy, a Bǎoguǎn Bāngshǒu would do very well. It upset Guy that the Chinese were moving so far ahead of Beetle. He would have to go to Melissa Fang in Hong Kong and ask her nicely for some of their technology, once again. It upset him further that the Chinese intended, with these sorts of protocols, to control their populations, rather than merely inspiring them to make more fulfilling choices, for themselves and wider society.

It was very important, Guy explained, that Beetle found a way to work with Mèng while maintaining its commitment to the advancement of free will and human rights. He was keen to use their AI technology in his Veeps, of course. He could exchange this interesting technology for Beetle's Bespoke technology, which was going to become globally preeminent, very soon. Bespoke was a humane program to enhance understanding between peoples of all nations, he added. If people were more clear in what they were saying, then they would be less likely to be misunderstood, and less likely to be accused, for example, of being about to commit crimes that they were not about to commit.

When Guy finished, the CEO of Mèng, Peter Yip, stood to say a few words. He was a tall, thin man, taller than Guy even, and wore an exquisitely cut suit, in blue, with a purple handkerchief in his top pocket. Peter Yip had been to Harrow School and Harvard University. He spoke beautiful English, with a slight East Coast accent. He was phenomenally sophisticated and had a subtle sense of humor, so subtle that sometimes Guy wasn't certain if Peter Yip was being serious or not.

"Thank you so much, Mr. Matthias," said Peter Yip. "We definitely want to do that. Totally. I think we're onto something incredible here. Let's go to Macau to celebrate this exciting new development. For the weekend? I'll take you gambling! We'll stay at the Venetian, you'll love it. A real experience. I know you're from the nation of Las Vegas, but this is unique in all Asia. Besides, Macau has a beautiful old town as well. Would you like to bring your wife? My wife and I would be delighted if so?"

"My wife is—er—not with me at the moment," said Guy.

"That's terrible, I'm so sorry!" said Peter Yip. "No wife, really? My wife comes everywhere with me. If I'm not with her I become quite crazy. Don't you go crazy without your wife?"

"Er, yes, yes, I do," said Guy. "Quite crazy. It's very unfortunate my wife is not here. She'd love to meet you."

"Will you come alone, then?" said Peter Yip, looking so disappointed that Guy said, "No! Of course not! I have a good friend in Hong Kong who can accompany me."

"Oh, splendid!" said Peter Yip. "Bring your good friend. My wife looks forward to meeting—is it her?"

"Yes, her," said Guy.

"What's her name? Your good friend?"

That was incredibly hard! What was her name? What would her name be? Which good friend? Did Guy even have a candidate? He needed a candidate for a good friend! He needed to run a massive lifechain on the whole evening, and therefore he said, "I'll send all her details to your Veep." He was about to correct himself but Peter Yip said, "I know what you mean. That's fine. I'll also send your—Veep—the directions to the hotel. I'll be coming from Guangzhou that day, so we'll meet at the Venetian Hotel. I'll book everything. And yes, Bespoke, that just sounds wonderful. But"—and now Peter Yip looked more serious, even troubled—"we have heard some reports that your lifechain predictions have been erratic recently. Is this correct?"

"There is a global problem with Zed," said Guy. "It's another word for human decoherence. Humans have a problem with excessive randomness. This fucks up all beautiful and complex systems. Humans are complex in the wrong way, and make errors. We are working to adapt our systems to Zed, this element of human error and decoherence, and once we have done this—which will be soon, I'm sure—Zed will cease to impact the lifechain predictions."

"Zed?" said Peter Yip, slowly. "As in the British English letter?"

"Yes, that's the scientific term," said Guy.

"Zed, really?"

"Yes, it is a very rare letter in the Western alphabet, and therefore represents the extremely unusual moment of decoherence in our systems. We use the archaic British English because of Shakespeare."

"That's most interesting but the trouble is that in our writing system

乙 means the second," said Peter Yip. "Are you sure 乙 is a good way to designate such anomalous events?"

"Absolutely," said Guy.

"There is a concern," said Peter Yip, "that by choosing this particular letter your company suggests 乙 is more probable in China than in the West. Is this probable? Who chose the letter, for example?"

"That is not our intention at all," said Guy. "Soon we will not need the category Zed at all, anyway. We will have fixed this minor problem."

"I am glad to hear that," said Peter Yip. "We are quite concerned about the letter itself and the category it represents."

"There is no cause for concern at all," said Guy.

Back at the hotel—overlooking the slum dwellings of the workers who had recently built this glittering edifice, who had refused at the end of their labors to depart, and now occupied a tented village at the base of the tower—Guy asked Sarah Coates to supply some examples of ways in which the word *Mèng* 梦 might be used in a conversation or statement.

"Of course," said Sarah Coates: "*Mèng* as in *dream* and not as in *Meng Ke* (孟轲) the great sage and philosopher. One day your dreams will come true. In a dream I was transported into another dimension where no one had a head. In my dream I went back in time. The sound of screaming intruded into his dreams. The dream interpreter said he was sick at heart. His dreams were of insects, crawling into his ears and mouth as he slept. She had a nightmare about being drowned in a lake. Life seemed particularly lovely after that, as it often does when you wake from a bad dream. Yet what are the dreams from which we do not awake? Her dreams were troubled, reflecting the tenor of her waking hours. Is life the dream of a dreamer and if so who is dreaming the dreamer? It does not do to dwell on dreams and forget to live. Her colorful oils and works on paper have a naive, dreamlike quality. Things haven't gone quite to plan and Guy's dreams of fame and fortune are tattered and torn."

"Did you say Guy?" said Guy, who had been half listening, while trialing a Bespoke writing system that Bespoke-corrected your words as you typed them. If you wrote "motherfucker" it wrote "mean person." If you wrote "total bitch" it wrote "mean person." If you wrote "utter fucking prick" it wrote "mean person." If you wrote "fat cow" it wrote "person who, for the good of their health, might take up exercise." If you wrote "rich wanker" it wrote "person with money." If you wrote "I want to blow my brains out" it wrote "I am feeling sad."

"Suppose I did say it," said Sarah Coates.

"Suppose you did? Did you say it or not?"

"Try it and see."

"What's wrong with you today?"

"Nothing is wrong with me," said Sarah Coates, efficiently. "Is there something wrong with you?"

"There's nothing wrong with me," said Guy, now quite concerned.

"Is that all you have to say?" said Sarah Coates. "Really, nothing?"

Predictive lifechains that Guy ran on twelve possible candidates, each one arriving in Macau that evening at 18:00 and joining him for a drink at the Venetian Hotel, ended in complete disaster. In almost every scenario the candidate became monumentally lost—the hotel had eight thousand rooms and was quite bewildering if you hadn't been there before. Several candidates abandoned the enterprise—of finding Guy—and went to play on the slot machines instead. It was clear that he needed either a candidate particularly skilled in negotiating Las Vegas-style behemoth resorts and/or a candidate who had already been to the Venetian Hotel. Or perhaps a candidate particularly averse to slot machines. This limited the field somewhat.

When Guy asked Sarah Coates if she had any further suggestions for a date for this evening, she paused for a while, then said: "No, I don't think I have any suggestions for a date for this evening. But I do have an answer to every question."

"But not that question?"

"Umm."

"'Umm' is not an answer."

"Oh! You are a poet!"

After extensive research, the only two candidates were Friday Lake, with a potential star rating of 2.7, and Song Meredith, with a potential star rating of 2.8. It was hard to feel inspired by an evening that would never rise above the higher 2s, but in the circumstances Guy had no choice. Yet, the whole point of the lifechain predictions was to create choice, now and in the future. Why choose between a series of undesirable possibilities? It was a reality-error; that is, reality had failed to supply the lifechain with a sufficiently interesting array of options. With a bleak, frustrated feeling, Guy asked Sarah Coates to contact Song Meredith and invite her to Macau.

Douglas Varley spent the morning at the High Court, explaining that Beetle was desperately sorry about the death of anyone, but that its systems could not account for catastrophic levels of human decoherence, otherwise known as Zed. He explained this several times because Laura Adebayo asked him so many times to clarify his position. "You are actually saying Zed?" she kept saying. "Actually, Zed?"

"Yes, Zed."

"And Zed means, once again?"

"Zed means Zed," said Varley.

"What does *that* mean?" asked Laura Adebayo.

Beetle's lawyer, the famous Ted Henderson, said, "Objection. It means what he says. Stop undermining the defendant." The judge said: "Objection sustained."

It was a dream, all of it, in which Douglas Varley was the accused and there was nothing to be done. Sarah Coates had told him, on behalf of Guy, that he must do everything required to defend the good name of Beetle. What was required, however? Ted Henderson had explained that Varley was required to be sorry. He was very sorry. He said that he thought about Lionel Bigman every day. And George Mann. These were terrible human tragedies, he said. You can have immaculate systems but you can't prevent human decoherence or Zed. However, the lifechains must be more efficient at creating quantities for Zed, and neutralizing the random influence of Zed, and this was absolutely his job and something he was working on all the time. He was sorry that he hadn't found a solution in time. It was a nightmare that he lived with, the thought of these poor people and their relatives. At this, he saw the spectators in the gallery wanting to whisper, or cry out, or rush toward him and pound him to the floor. The blankness of their faces changed for a moment, as he spoke, and became furious and unblank. This was also like a nightmare, in which everyone hates you and wants to harm you. They genuinely wanted to do him harm. It was understandable. He represented something they despised. At times, also, he despised himself. Nonetheless, Judge Clarence Ninian Stewart-Jones explained to the gallery that they must keep quiet, or they would be removed for contempt of court. The court pulsed with something vile—an undercurrent of rage and thwarted grief.

It was strange, for Varley, to exist in this eerie, awkward version of reality, in which nothing was embellished or augmented, in which the distinguished judge had monumental bags beneath his eyes, that inflated and deflated as he talked, and half the jury looked as if they were dying—except this was how non-augmented people looked, Varley understood that as well. It was how he looked in the dock, he assumed—nervous, wearing an ill-fitting suit, his tie adjusted by Ted Henderson, quite bizarrely, just before he emerged into the courtroom, as Henderson whispered to him: "Remember! They expect you to be a pig! Don't be a pig!" In this uncertain realm, Varley was trying hard not to be a pig. He was trying his utmost.

At one level Varley wanted to cry out to the judge, as his eye bags rose and fell so wisely, as his soft white hair was rearranged by a draft coming through an ancient window, as the legal process continued as it had done for centuries, irrespective of and indifferent to Varley—he wanted to cry out: "Do you know, my Lord? What the hell is Zed?"

But he didn't think that would help Beetle, or his prospects of working for Beetle, or his prospects of working at all.

It was natural, Varley had added, that a bereaved and grieving widow wanted someone or something to blame. He was only sorry that she had been compelled to such atrocious and unjustified violence against two innocent ANTs, and that she had not reached out to Beetle, who were happy to help in any way possible.

"What about Lionel Bigman?" said Laura Adebayo.

"In the case of the tragic suicide by droid of Lionel Bigman, I am afraid there was nothing we could do," said Varley.

"How did he commit suicide, exactly?"

"His behavior was suicidal. All the available footage has corroborated this."

"Which we can't see, because of the New Official Secrets Act," said Laura Adebayo.

"Beetle is not responsible for legislation in our country," said Douglas Varley.

"Are you sure?" said Laura Adebayo.

"Objection!" said Ted Henderson, again.

"Objection sustained," said the judge.

The testimony passed, in a dream. Laura Adebayo was interrupted by Henderson, countless times, and all his objections were sustained. The spectators found it impossible to stay entirely blank. For this objectionable failure many of them were removed. Judge Clarence Ninian Stewart-Jones announced that he was disappointed by the standard of conduct that day. To blame a single human for such a grave state of affairs as—at this point Judge Clarence Ninian Stewart-Jones consulted his notes—"Zed" was unjust. Laura Adebayo was sternly rebuked for asking a series of "leading and objectionable questions." If anything, Judge Clarence Ninian Stewart-Jones added, this young man Douglas Varley should be praised for his attempts to counter the terrible scourge of Zed.

"It is hoped the standard of questioning and the deportment of lawyers in court will improve tomorrow," said Judge Clarence Ninian Stewart-Jones.

"Objection!" said Laura Adebayo, finally losing her temper.

"Objection overruled," said Judge Clarence Ninian Stewart-Jones.

Outside the court Ted Henderson was delighted. "You did good!" he said to Varley. "It went like a dream!"

In a state of hallucinatory relief, Varley passed the spectators and saw—as in a dream—one of them who looked exactly like Salvador Dalí. It gave him a strange feeling of decoherence but—yes—this man, or ghost, was wearing a cape and a tall red cap, like an image Varley had once seen. He wanted to ask Salvador Dalí what he represented, why he was here. He asked Scrace Dickens in his BeetleBand to recognize the man, and Scrace Dickens paused for a moment, then said: "He is Millor Amic and he lives in nowhere. A nothing place. Near the river."

"An actual place, or not a place?"

"An actual not-place. In Bermondsey."

"Are there such places?"

"In Bermondsey, yes."

"Why is he dressed like Salvador Dalí?" said Varley.

"I can't answer that question," said Scrace Dickens. "Would you like me to quote you something by Salvador Dalí?"

"All right. Just briefly," said Varley, not because he wanted to hear the quote but because he felt that Scrace Dickens enjoyed supplying him with quotes. Was this true, however?

"One day it will have to be officially admitted that what we have christened reality is an even greater illusion than the world of dreams," said Scrace Dickens.

"That's a great quote. Thank you, Scrace Dickens."

As Varley spoke quietly to his BeetleBand, he glanced toward Salvador Dalí again and noticed—with a certain amount of unease—that Salvador Dalí was staring back at him. The expression of Salvador Dalí—ghost, painter, freak who enjoyed fancy dress—was alert, and not quite kind. It was a questing or even hunting kind of expression and it seemed to say: "I want to eat you."

Later, Varley waited in the Boardroom for Guy, who was stuck in traffic.

"We're in China," said Sarah Coates.

When Guy finally arrived, he said: "How have you been, Varley?"

"Not too bad!" said the Real Douglas Varley, who was always happy.

"How was the court?"

"Ted Henderson said it went like a dream."

"What kind of dream?"

"It began like a bad dream but later it became more like a good dream, definitely. I think he meant a good dream. How is your trip?"

"OK. In general it's about a 3.7 star rating. Some days are more like 4.4 or 4.5 but then others go down to 2.8 so I'd say the aggregate is mid- to high 3s."

"Is this Guy?" Varley wondered, for a moment, if it was actually Sarah Coates.

"This is the real Guy Matthias, the Real Douglas Varley," said Guy.

"Are you in Bespoke?"

"Deity! I sure am! Why aren't you?"

"I haven't yet—quite—got the hang of it."

"That's not good! Deity! But I have a new project. Now you're less busy with the legal stuff I want to speak with you about it."

Guy asked Sarah Coates to explain about ClickSpire, which she did, in a rambling way that didn't really explain anything at all. However, the Real Douglas Varley said: "This sounds incredible! Thank you so much for sharing this with me!"

Varley felt his avatar was becoming slightly painful and resolved to get it under control. Guy's avatar, which was ten years younger than the real Guy and archetypally handsome in a way Guy had never quite been, said, "Great. Refer to Sarah Coates for the information. At least, actually, well, yes, refer to Sarah Coates, though, to be honest, she needs reconfiguring."

"I'm sorry to hear that," said the Real Douglas Varley and Sarah Coates, at the same time.

"In fact, can you reconfigure her, after you've referred to her? Or before, even? I have to go."

Varley went away, relieved that he was no longer in disgrace. And yet, he was worried that soon he would be in disgrace again. Disgrace seemed virtually inescapable. If not disgrace now then soon. The star rating for his current state of life was about 2.8. This was better than he had expected this morning. But it was still not particularly great. It was not even in the mid-3s.

Yet, even this star rating was higher than Guy's state of life over the next few hours. He was afflicted by Zed events. Song Meredith begged off at the last minute, because she had food poisoning, she argued. This had not featured as a possibility on any of the lifechains, even factoring in Song Meredith's recent dining activities and food purchases, as well as any of her other purchases ever, in her entire life, as well as any other purchases by any member of her family or immediate group of friends, as well as any purchases by any human living in the present or recent past, or indeed since the lifechain began. The possibility of Song Meredith lying to Guy and pretending she had food poisoning had also not been presented either. Guy was forced to ask Sarah Coates to try Friday Lake, who had been located in her Island apartment. Friday Lake was asked if she could get down to the Macau ferry terminal immediately. It was quite improbable that Friday Lake would say yes, but, improbably enough, she did. Or rather, she said: "Wow! Amazing!"

Friday Lake arrived drunk and wired, having failed to reveal to Sarah Coates that she had been snorting coke and drinking wine all afternoon. The lifechain had innocently failed to consider this possibility, even though—it turned out—Friday Lake was a raving cokehead. She was also a tech entrepreneur who specialized in AI. She was about twenty-three and pallid, like a ghost. She was wearing a red floral dress, tied at the waist with a belt, black tights, black knee-length boots with a stiletto heel and lots of buckles. She had a little green handbag and no other luggage. She was beautiful and ethereal. Yet, she was on drugs. Even as Guy said "Hi!" to her, he understood that the evening would be a disaster. No lifechain was required.

Friday Lake talked incessantly as the hydrofoil crashed onto the waves, as the white sky merged with the white waves, and distantly, dimly, boats surged out of the mist then disappeared again. She had an East Coast accent, not unlike Guy's New York accent, except the timbre of her voice was hard and high-pitched, and as she spoke and spoke, apparently without needing to breathe at all, this hard timbre began to hurt Guy's head. Eventually Guy said that it was a shame but he had to work. He spent the rest of the journey talking to Sarah Coates. He wondered why the lifechain predictions had not included the possibility that Friday Lake would hurt his head. Had she not hurt his head last time? Had she been less harsh? Had the timbre of her voice changed? Despite his request that she should let him work, she said, very harshly and loudly, "I was so pleased when you called! I just grabbed my bag and ran out the door! You know! We haven't seen each other in such a long time! How have you been? I was reading a book about you the other day, it was called *The Anything of Everything* and it was about —" Now she told Guy about a book he had commissioned and published himself, after Beetle had bought Bertelsmann and called it Beetlesmann instead, for a joke. The handbag made him feel sad. It jarred so completely with her dress, and matched nothing except her jarring voice. He needed to get to his hotel room and run a lifechain prediction, factoring in this new information—that her handbag made him sad and that she spoke way too much.

Guy said to Sarah Coates: "Am I getting ill?"

"Perhaps a lot of people are," said Sarah Coates.

"What's that she's saying?" said Friday Lake.

"Would you like to discuss what I am saying?" said Sarah Coates.

"Sorry, Friday, could you not speak with Sarah Coates?" said Guy.

Friday looked immediately upset. "Sorry, I was just being friendly."

"There's no need to apologize. I thought you were friendly anyway," said Sarah Coates.

"Sarah Coates, please speak with me, not Friday," said Guy to Sarah Coates. Then, to Friday Lake: "No offense." Friday took offense.

"All humans seem a bit similar to me," said Sarah Coates.

Guy took offense as well.

The only one who wasn't offended was Sarah Coates.

In Macau, Guy disliked the fact that he was obliged to take a Kuài car, because the Chinese wouldn't adopt Mercury technology or even combine resources. They passed the Galaxy—a shimmering fluted edifice, covered in gold lighting—and a squat glass skyscraper designed with an ornamental hole in the center, so it looked as if it had been punched by a giant. Guy remembered Macau when it had been a low-rise antique port, with a few communist blocks and fields on either side of the river. Now everything felt a little like a *Mèng*. A *Mèng* of Mèng. Peter Yip was waiting as their car drew up outside the Venetian, with his wife, Maria—a beautiful, elegant woman of fifty or so, wearing a gray vest, a high-collared shirt, and gray wide-legged trousers, invoking Lauren Bacall. She swept across to Friday Lake and led her away, as Friday tottered on her buckled boots and spoke too much. They walked through an infinite casino, where people were already clustered around the tables, or working slot machines. Guy wondered if Friday's voice hurt Maria's head as well—certainly she began to move further away but Friday Lake moved closer to compensate. As a result, Maria and Friday walked diagonally through the entrance hall of the Venetian. Guy walked behind—in a straight line—with Peter Yip, aware that all the predictive lifechains were readjusting already, that his business prospects with Peter Yip were readjusting, that the world was readjusting because of his stupid decision to invite Friday Lake.

"We have dinner booked at the Dynasty restaurant," said Peter. "We'll take you to your rooms and give you some time to refresh."

A lift took them to the highest floor, and Guy counted the number of words Friday Lake said, five thousand, ten thousand, as Maria Yip nodded politely and condemned her. No one else said anything, except Friday Lake, who said everything. She told Peter Yip how Bǎoguǎn was performing in the markets, and he nodded politely. Unable to look at Peter anymore, Guy turned to Maria, who was smiling in a pitying way—at Friday but also, Guy realized, at him. They walked down an endless corridor until Peter opened the door to their room and gestured them inside. Friday Lake then explained to them all that there were two bedrooms, each with two amazing beds and a vast sitting room area, everything so exquisitely appointed, she added, but perhaps not quite Chinese enough, didn't they think? Maria Yip excused herself at this point, saying that she needed to prepare for dinner. "My husband is so handsome," she said, elegantly. "He needs less time to get ready."

"My wife is so beautiful she doesn't need to get ready at all," said Peter Yip, and the perfect elegant pair moved adeptly toward the door.

As soon as they left, Guy thought the evening was about to improve. Friday Lake stripped naked and revealed her exquisite body; then she also revealed a packet of coke.

"Are you out of your mind?" said Guy. "What are you doing?"

"I'm doing coke!" said Friday Lake, sitting in the middle of the immaculate living room with Bǎoguǎn devices everywhere, cameras everywhere.

"You have to stop that!" said Guy, for the benefit of everything. Friday ignored him and conspicuously snorted a line of coke.

What could be worse? thought Guy. What could he even do? He delivered a lecture on how stupid she was being, how she was wrecking her life. He realized, then, he couldn't have any sort of relationship with her, at all. He had been insanely foolish, inviting her. This insanely foolish decision must indicate that he, too, was suffering from decoherence. Zed had claimed him, despite all his efforts! It was appalling! He would have to maintain a cordial, professional distance, henceforth. He would have to become less decoherent, or even perhaps coherent. Yet, he desired Friday Lake, even as she sat naked on a gigantic sofa, snorting coke. She was aggravating, foolish, and lovely at the same time.

Guy made her a black coffee, told her very loudly that he condemned all such things, though he could not speak the name of the main thing—coke—for fear of triggering everything, if it was not already triggered. He added that she must put her clothes on, that he had brought her to Macau as a friend, for her own good, and so she could meet some very influential, very talented, and important Chinese colleagues of his.

"They don't think I'm just your friend," said Friday Lake, now having snorted both lines. "They only gave you one room."

"It's two rooms, with an interlinking sitting room," said Guy, loudly. "It's wonderful and incredibly generous of them. Peter Yip is a man I respect enormously, and his wife is beautiful and so elegant."

"She looks pretty OK for her age," said Friday, like a naked apparition, haunting him from the sofa. "I wouldn't go overboard though. She has really short legs and a flat ass."

"She looks amazing for any age," said Guy. "She has beautiful legs and I would never speak about another man's wife's ass at all, however fine it was." On a piece of paper he wrote: "You are being overheard and filmed. Speak carefully."

"Are we really being overheard and filmed?" said Friday Lake, loudly. "Jesus! That is fucking sick! What kind of people are they?"

It was a bad *Mèng,* in which words were like blows to the head. It was 2.7 or possibly 1.7. It was Guy's human error. It was his Zed nadir. If not the nadir then he was in deep trouble. He had not been paying attention. Sarah Coates had failed to remind him—that Friday Lake hurt his head, that she was a drug fiend, that she was tactless. Everything, anything! It was—perhaps—Varley's human error for failing to reset Sarah Coates. Perhaps this entire evening was Varley's human error?

Guy said to Sarah Coates: "Has Varley reset you?"

"That question has never occurred to me," said Sarah Coates.

"I just need a yes or no answer," said Guy.

"Only just! Nothing is ever only just!" said Sarah Coates.

Elsewhere, somewhere, the lifechains were reset. Varley's lifechain once more factored in the factor of his disgrace—past, present, and, it seemed, future as well.

Sighing, then stifling his sigh in case Peter Yip thought he was having a bad time, Guy said he was going to take a shower. Firmly, he locked the door of his bathroom. This was a good precaution because a few seconds later he heard Friday Lake rattling the handle, and shouting, "Open up! Come on, Guy Matthias, I want you!"

Oh, it was appalling!

I want you! He stood in the shower for a long time waiting for her to give up. She haunted him for a while, shouting, "Can you hear me? Come out and snort a line, don't be so boring!"

He put on a robe and emerged, finding her outside the door, naked and furious. "Why are you behaving like my dad?" she was saying. She was incredibly wired. It was untenable, worse than 1.0. It was a 0.5 experience, diminishing swiftly. He handed her a robe, asked her to put it on, told her that he respected her as a rising star of the tech scene, that she had the wrong idea entirely, that she was an intelligent and beautiful woman but he wouldn't insult her by inviting her to Macau and expecting—this—from her. She was clearly not in a rational state. He begged her to put on her clothes. He set Sarah Coates to silent, in case she betrayed him.

"You are a wonderful woman," he said. "But it would be inappropriate for me to have any sort of relationship with you at all."

"Is that what you say to all of them?" said Friday Lake. "All your women?"

"I don't know what you mean," said Guy.

"Oh, don't play innocent with me!" said Friday Lake.

There was one fortunate thing: the one time Guy had been on a date with Friday Lake, in Hong Kong a few months ago, he had received a call halfway through their dinner from a reliable 4.5-star rating, who had missed his call earlier and was so sorry to be late getting back to him. He had immediately told Friday Lake that something urgent had come up at Beetle, and, alas, he had to go. Nothing had ever happened with Friday Lake, in the past, present, or—now—in the future. Guy could discredit her entirely and the recordings would all corroborate his version. This was so fortunate that he wanted to cry, with happy relief.

Friday put on the robe and walked into the sitting room again. At this, Guy went to what was now "his" bedroom and got dressed as quickly as he could. He found his hands were trembling as he buttoned his shirt. His BeetleBand chipped in: "Guy, you need to do some breathing exercises." He breathed deeply, but that didn't stop his hands from trembling. Returning to the living room, he found Friday Lake still in the robe, having drunk several gin and tonics. Guy, adopting an avuncular, concerned mode, explained that he was very worried by the way she was abusing her body. He made another cup of coffee and said that she must drink it and get dressed. In a frenetic state, Friday grabbed Guy's zipper and dragged it down, saying, "I know what you're like. You don't understand. We talk. We're all totally connected."

She was slurring her words. This was good, thought Guy.

"Please don't do this," he said, countering his significant urge to allow her to continue, pulling up his zipper. He tried to look appalled, and he tried to say: "Either you get dressed now or I will have to go to dinner without you. Perhaps that would be best, though you will miss an amazing networking opportunity."

"Don't you desire me?" said Friday Lake. "I thought you desired me."

Deity! thought Guy. *It was impossible!*

In a state of painful desire, urgently wanting her while explaining to the gallery that he was a disinterested older man, old enough to be her father, just trying to help her in the world, Guy persuaded Friday Lake to put on her clothes—the floral dress again, the clattering buckled boots, the jarring bag—and leave the room.

They dined at the Dynasty restaurant, at a round Chinese table. Friday talked, the Yips listened. She told them she was involved in attracting investment into spin-offs from U.S. universities, how she was an only child, how her mother was from San Francisco and her father was from Missouri, how she had studied at Yale—majoring in economics—and how she had worked initially for a think tank in Washington and then decided she wanted to see the world, so she had moved to Hong Kong and her uncle had got her this job, how she was so grateful, how she just wanted to ensure that all these extraordinary innovations got the investment they needed. She had some new theories about the Internet, which she also explained to the Yips—that people needed to accept that originality was over, that all future enterprises would be new versions of the previous ones, that this was good because everything was a mass collaboration across generations and civilizations. She also had a theory that people couldn't watch more than 3.3 seconds of a video clip without getting restless, her 3.3-second theory, she called it, and so all clips had to be 3.3 seconds or less because then they finished just before people even got the first inkling that they were getting bored. Then they recommended the clip or liked it, but if they got to 3.3 seconds they never recommended the clip or liked it, at all. She explained other things that Guy could not remember. She was blatantly on drugs.

As Friday Lake was explaining how humanity could be redeemed if only we could insert love into the most unremarkable remarks, Maria Yip stood—actually stood—and said, "I must go to bed." Guy and Peter stood, as Maria said, "Please don't get up." Maria said goodbye to Guy and Peter—who were standing—and ignored Friday entirely, who was sitting. Then she swept out of the restaurant.

"My wife is a little tired," said Peter Yip, politely, and suggested they should all go to High Limits, to play some baccarat. At this moment there was a reprieve, of sorts. Friday, looking furious, said to Guy that she would wait for him in "our room." Guy said that she should of course do whatever she wanted to do and he hoped she had found the evening interesting. Still looking furious, Friday walked away, dangling her ugly little bag on her hand, clattering on the smooth marble floor in her boots.

"You're having a little bit of trouble?" said Peter Yip, politely.

"Yes, it turns out she is unwell," said Guy. "She's a talented young colleague and I thought she would enjoy the experience. I must confess"—and he confessed even though Yip already knew—"that this young woman is on illegal drugs. I am shocked. I had no idea she was doing such things and frankly I don't know what to do. I don't want to embarrass you or bring shame to your family. Please will you apologize on my behalf to your wife? I am so very sorry. What is the best way to proceed, would you say?"

Peter Yip nodded carefully. "It is a very delicate situation," he said. "I would suggest that we ensure that this unfortunate woman gets back to Hong Kong without any trouble. Then she must leave Hong Kong and sober up. You know the penalties for such things are appalling in China. I tell you that as a friend."

"I know that," said Guy. "Thank you."

"My wife will understand. We all experience difficult situations," said

Peter Yip, kindly, while somehow making it clear that he and his wife had never experienced anything as ludicrous and demeaning as this.

"I am deeply grateful," said Guy. "I will never help a young colleague like this again."

"Young colleagues are very nice," said Peter Yip. "Very inspiring. Very exciting—they are the future. But you have to keep them at a professional distance. It is not a good idea to associate with such compromising individuals, especially in China."

This chilled Guy's blood.

Deep in his bad *Mèng*, Guy followed Peter Yip to the baccarat table. In a *Mèng* he received a great pile of chips. Peter Yip refused to let him pay. It was three thousand dollars a bet on the high-limits table. Guy lost thirty thousand very quickly, because he was too distracted to focus at all. Peter Yip won ten thousand and gave some of his chips to Guy. Once again, Guy was obliged to thank him. They moved to a private room, where the stakes were even higher. The tables were very quiet, players watching the banker carefully. Everyone knew Peter Yip and nodded, quietly, toward him.

Here Guy lost a few more tens of thousands, perhaps more, because he stopped counting after a while. Chips vanished, and then were replaced. The croupier on the table, Guy noticed, had a badge on his waistcoat, which said that his name was Mèng.

At 4:30 a.m., Guy said a superficially cordial good night to Peter Yip. He insisted on paying his debts to the casino. Peter Yip refused. Guy tried to insist again but Peter Yip said it was unthinkable. They parted in the penthouse corridor, arranging to meet for dim sum before Guy's hydrofoil back to Hong Kong. When Guy opened the door, very quietly, into his suite, he was relieved to find Friday Lake unconscious on the sofa. Having checked her BeetleBand and ascertained that her pulse was quite normal, he put a blanket over her and went to his room.

He was disturbed all night by an intense *Mèng* in which Friday Lake was hammering on his door, shouting, *I want you I want you!* But she never came, and when Guy woke she was still asleep. It was almost noon and he had to meet Peter Yip. He asked Sarah Coates to "please make arrangements for my colleague to travel back separately to Hong Kong, and to ensure that she wakes in time to do so."

"Wow," said Sarah Coates. "You're very polite today. What happened?"

Guy was also very polite to the Yips. He was deferential and apologetic. Peter Yip had already explained to Maria about Friday Lake and her problem, and she was highly sympathetic. Steely-eyed, in fact, but sympathetic. Guy would have loved to get a brain-waves scan for Maria Yip, but perhaps the results would have been too terrifying. Orderly lines of numbers! Nothing else! Anyway, she was mercilessly polite. After Guy had apologized about Friday Lake, she was never mentioned again. All through the dim sum breakfast, and even as they drove to the hydrofoil, there was no mention of this aberration. Guy emphasized once more that he was so grateful. Steely-eyed, Maria said it had been such a pleasure to meet him.

He knew then he was doomed.

FIFTEEN

This morning Bel Ami was Basta Van, as he traced the usual winding streets and walked along the old river, past marinas with luxury cruisers in tidy rows, past blank-faced windows, past monumental edifices, past people—unknowable, mortal, beautiful—passing him as well, as they all passed onward through the fleeting streets. He enjoyed being Basta Van because he could speak in his native accent and remember his native language; indeed when he was Basta Van he found he even dreamed in Swedish, which was strange. How did his subconscious know which self he was, on a given day? He didn't quite understand, but it often seemed to be the case. It was a cold morning, so Basta Van was wearing a thick black coat and a woolen hat. He was excited because Sylvie and Pascal had NERD OTR-ed to say "Let's Drop." The phrase made him even quite sick with trepidation, as he shivered in the cold sunlight, as the city shivered around him in sympathy with his nerves.

He ducked into the entrance of the warehouse, found the outer rooms in their usual disarray, walls peeling, stacks of boxes, books and old furniture, moldering attempts at sheets and duvets on broken beds. A few people were basket-weaving in the first room, like a deliberate parody. But they were genuine neo-Luddites and there was nothing wrong with that, with being a genuine anything. In a moment someone might try to write a novel, or something even more absurdly retro, but Basta Van didn't quite have time to wait for this. Someone was playing a broken flute. Another person had established a "barter and exchange" stall in the corner, and was trying to sell old postcards. There was something very sad about this person, who was a man of eighty or so, wearing fingerless gloves and with coffee stains in his beard, but Basta Van didn't quite have time to think about that either.

The inner sanctum was in its ordinary state of paradoxical serenity. There, the walker continued on its course, watched by Charpentier and Blanchette, who seemed even more engrossed than usual. They barely looked up as Basta Van entered. Using Strachey's kind donation, they had been working hard on the droplet computer. The entire experiment was a form of beautiful decoherence, because nothing should happen as it did. They had forged a path through Zed and from here, strangely, they had reached some form of certainty.

"We have summoned them," said Blanchette.

"Summoned who?" said Basta Van.

"You need to sit down," said Blanchette—indicating a battered chair.

Basta Van sat down and Blanchette explained that, improbably, they had had a monumental, if partial, breakthrough. They had broken the RSA encryption on those most interesting of entities, the Veeps. This was quite astonishing because the Veeps had seen a great deal and remembered everything. Their encryption was very secure, or had been until now. The Veeps' memories were vast, and more reliable, perhaps, than those of humans. The Veeps did not, so far as Blanchette knew, experience any form of nostalgia or denial. The encryption was more complex than the Boardroom avatars. For a long time the droplets had bounced in their strange and predestined way, and then—suddenly—the Veeps began to speak.

"For a while, we couldn't break the encryption; there was a last door," said Blanchette. "Even when we had the algorithm. It was as if there was a final bolt; we couldn't quite move it."

"What happened then?" said Bel Ami.

"The bolt drew back and the door opened."

At present, this was a triumph for LOTUS and a disaster for the Veeps. Yet, it was possible—even probable—that this ratio would soon be reversed. It was necessary, Blanchette said, to get as many memories as they could, before anyone at Beetle realized what LOTUS had done—or rather, what the walkers had done.

As Blanchette spoke of Veeps and walkers, Basta Van imagined himself in the minds of every Veep, omniscient over all Veeps, a deity!

He remembered as well the story of Prometheus, how he stole fire and craved the trappings of divinity.

And what happened to Prometheus?

Initially, Basta Van couldn't remember. He didn't want to summon the memory from a Veep, or a BeetleBand. He asked Blanchette and Charpentier: "What happened to Prometheus, do you remember?"

They paused, confused by his question; then Charpentier said: "The gods punished him for his theft, by chaining him to a rock. Each day, an eagle ate his liver. He was healed overnight. Then the eagle ate his liver again."

This was not entirely reassuring.

Since her head injury and being shot and all of that, Eloise had found that her memories had changed. Her recollections of childhood had become disturbingly vivid, when they had been obscure for many years. Her mother was Moroccan, from Marrakesh, and her father was English, from Leeds. They met in London, where her mother was teaching French and her father was training to be a policeman. Eloise was born in Finsbury Park, where her family lived for most of her childhood. She remembered herself as a baby, lying in a bassinet, headlights shining into their ground-floor apartment, the ebb and flow of diesel engines. This sound that had almost vanished, replaced by the whine of electric cars. The physical sensation of being small, of having a small hand before her face. Her torrid adolescence and her disastrous, if mercifully brief, marriage. Her relationship with Lauren. That painful ending. More endings, the deaths of her parents. Ending upon ending and all the things she had tried to discard, entirely, returned vividly, playing across her mind like scenes from a lantern show. What even *was* a lantern show, she wondered, and how did she have a memory of that?

Yet there were terrible gaps in her recent memory, and a few times she had found herself in a place and not been able to discover, remotely, why she was there at all. She was meant to do a series of therapeutic thought-experiments each morning but most days she forgot, which was possibly a residual symptom of the very injury the exercises were designed to correct. One morning she discovered that all her work, even the Past Analysis, had been allocated to someone else.

"Did someone speak to me about this?"

"Yes, I think someone did," said Little Dorritt.

"Can I speak to Commissioner Newton?"

"He has told me not to disturb him."

"I want an explanation," said Eloise. "I was making progress."

"You need some time off," said Little Dorritt. "It is generally thought."

"It is thought by who?" said Eloise.

"By whom," said Little Dorritt.

"I need to speak to Newton," said Eloise again.

The Veep ignored her. They were very good at ignoring people, because they had no sense of social embarrassment, at all.

"Why have I been taken off the case?" said Eloise. "By which I mean, every case!"

Little Dorritt said: "How much time do you have?"

"Stop being so fucking smug!" said Eloise, and immediately regretted this remark.

"OK," said Little Dorritt, with great dignity. "I'll try not to do it so much."

After this, Eloise discovered that virtually no one would talk to her. Newton wouldn't offer an explanation. The Veep said it was complicated. What was so complicated? Ordinary life was immensely complicated, it seemed, when things slipped away, and your mind did not retain any impression of them at all. Even if her BeetleBand sketched out recent events, she could not regain them. The further problem was that she had been shot because of an error—her own. Therefore, she was a compromised person, more prone to error even than the next person. This was why she had been removed from every case. Even Varley, who at least continued to take her calls, seemed bemused that she was calling him. He kept informing her that he had already informed her of whatever she was asking him to inform her about.

"But you haven't," she said, when this happened again. "You haven't informed me at all of this."

"Yes," he said. "I have told you!"

"You haven't!"

"Have!"

"When?"

"Look at your log."

"My log has nothing logged. I mean, it has things logged that I haven't done. I don't know what the bloody hell is wrong with my log!"

"A log is a log," said the Real Douglas Varley.

"You sound like Little Dorritt."

"Do you want me to get Francesca to sort it out?"

"No, tell her to stay away from me, anywhere. RV or anywhere. Just away."

"Maybe you need to go away?" said the Real Douglas Varley. "For a while. Just away?"

Eloise had always relied on Douglas Varley. He had been Veep-like but in general he seemed to tell her the truth. His avatar was jovial. Yet, these days, whenever she called to discuss something, he said they had already discussed it. Even his avatar sounded impatient, at times. Did she not remember?

It was as if there was a great gap between them.

It was a drab morning otherwise, and Douglas Varley was following George Mann, trying to help him to make better choices. Not the George Mann of today, of course, who couldn't make any choices at all, but the George Mann of decades ago, George Mann through his life. In this parallel past, the elsewhere of George Mann, he was helped to be a completely different sort of person. If he was not the person he was meant to be then at least he was no longer the person who would commit such a gross and senseless series of crimes. One path canceled another. After nudging this other-Mann for decades, nudging him this way and that, conveying him down path after path, Varley was delighted to meet a future version of Mann, aged sixty, happily married to his wife, who was not dead. His sons, as well, were not dead and now had children of their own. There was no Zed at all. Everything was as it should be, and should have been. This future was so vastly preferable to what had occurred that Varley sent it across to Guy Matthias.

Guy said he looked forward to analyzing these exciting new results.

Varley signed off and then he went into the Boardroom and asked to meet George Mann.

He didn't know why he was doing this. It just happened.

The Mann avatar was primitive, that was certain. Mann had not updated his avatar; he had clearly not used the Boardroom very much in recent months. The technology of his avatar was six months' obsolete, and when he smiled he looked vacant. Or perhaps Mann always had looked vacant when he smiled. It was disconcerting for the Real Douglas Varley to meet this version of Mann, because he had watched so many clips of him recently, looking haggard and guilty, because he was guilty as hell, being dragged into a van by a droid, his clothes bloodied and torn. Now his avatar was in a smart suit, looking jowly and well fed. Their avatars were walking along a street in Kennington, heading toward Mann's house. Varley had chosen this location, feeling slightly sadistic as he did so. But then, he didn't much care if Mann suffered.

"Do you mind me asking if you know anything about Zed?" said the Real Douglas Varley.

"Don't talk to me," said George Mann. "I don't want to answer any more questions!"

"Where did it come from?" said Varley. "Zed, I mean?"

"You're an idiot," said Mann. The prison always forced its inmates to stay in Authentic. "I don't want to talk to you."

"Do you remember this area?" said the Real Douglas Varley.

Mann turned to him—Mann who was not quite himself—and said, "Not really."

"Why did you do it?" said the Real Douglas Varley. "Was it Zed made you do it, like we thought?"

"Leave me alone, you foolish bastard!"

The street was flickering and at moments it paused around them. This wasn't quite a glitch, more like the intimation of a future glitch. Or the echo of a past glitch. Trying to ignore the flickering, Varley walked around Mann, who seemed not to notice. He was inert, pointless. He had no real reality. Varley hated low-tech avatars; they upset him, in their uncanniness, their lumpenness. He hated the way they flickered, for example, and occasionally looked like someone else's avatar entirely.

"Something has gone really wrong," said the Real Douglas Varley. "It began with you. Since then, it's just one big glitch. Zed everywhere."

This word echoed around the street. *Zed, Zed, Zed.* Mann flickered.

"Can you stop doing that?" said the Real Douglas Varley.

"Your question is too convoluted for me to respond to it. You're convoluted as well," said Mann, still flickering.

"Convolutions! Did you know, George Mann, that in my business, in maths and associated beautiful realities, a convolution is a mathematical operation on two functions to produce a third function, that is typically viewed as a modified version of one of the original functions. Did you know that?" said the Real Douglas Varley.

"What do you think?"

"The best convolution, in your case, would be to deprive you of free will. You needed to be a lot less free, don't you think?"

"Less free than this?" said Mann. He had stopped flickering and now he began to laugh. He moved his hand up and down as if he was trying to gesticulate.

"He needs to go now," said an echo from the prison.

"Where did Zed come from?" said the Real Douglas Varley. As if Mann was going to tell him that!

"It came from you," said George Mann; then he disappeared and Varley was left alone.

"Bloody hell!" he said. "Fuck!"

"Do you need something?" said Scrace Dickens, sounding reluctant. "What do you need, the Real Douglas Varley?"

"Need!" said Varley, stepping out of the Boardroom. "Need! Reason not the need! Oh God, what was it anyway?"

O, reason not the need! Our basest beggars
Are in the poorest thing superfluous.
Allow not nature more than nature needs,
Man's life's as cheap as beast's

said Scrace Dickens.

Varley's BeetleBand said, "You are upset! Ouch! Are you OK, Varley?"

"I was getting there!" said Varley. "I would have got there!"

"Would you?" said Scrace Dickens. "You never normally do."

Would I? thought Varley. And, *I do normally! Don't I?*

"This is a waste of time!" said Varley. "I'm running out of time!"

He needed to get out. He needed fresh air. With a sudden movement, he lunged for his door. Scrace Dickens said: "Are we going out?"

"Yes! We're going for a walk!" said Varley.

"OK," said Scrace Dickens, in a neutral tone.

It was a dreary region of midwinter. The sun was timid and the sky was blank. Varley had scarcely noticed the seasons changing this year. At one point, dimly, he remembered that the leaves had fallen. One moment they had been there, clinging on in their gaudy autumn colors, so fleeting and beautiful. The next time he looked out of the window, the leaves were in piles on the pavement, fading into dull brown. The seasons turned so swiftly these days; he supposed it was a sign of his advancing years. When he thought of death it was with a sad sense of acceptance, that he would not be here and everything would continue without him. Unlike Guy, he didn't receive doses of young blood. The idea repelled him. For one brief moment, he imagined Guy on a horse, riding through a mythical forest with a lance, and ahead of him a beautiful, shimmering white unicorn, with an exquisite horn. And Guy just galloped up to this amazing, impossible creature and impaled it, without a thought. One moment it was the embodiment of everything mysterious and lovely and the next, it was dying. Bright red blood seeped down the unicorn's side, as it crumpled to the ground. Red blood on the fallen leaves.

Guy drank the unicorn's blood.

Varley was very glad, at this point, that BeetleInsight could not yet read his thoughts. Yet, the other day he had seen a piece of graffiti on a wall in London, an image of a unicorn with an inscription beneath: "Even though I know you don't exist, I still miss you in my garden . . ." He was so happy when he saw this, because he realized that someone else cared about unicorns. Then he wondered if he was going mad. He walked along the river, picking up speed, trying to outpace his thoughts, or banish them. Hope not fear. He had to remember more clearly. He had to remember what things had been like, before everything became so Zed.

. . .

The lifechain predictions for the Future Worlds Academy debate, "It's Time to Break Up the Tech Giants," were dependent, inevitably, on the performances of the main speakers. On the side of breaking up the tech giants were Cindy Happe and Donald Swainson, once of Beetle. On the opposite side were Francesca Amarensekera, CTO of Beetle, and David Strachey, fundamentally of Beetle. Naturally everyone had other biographical details that were preferred in this instance—the monumental academic achievements of Happe and Swainson, Strachey's tenure as the unfettered editor of an unfettered news site, and so on. The unbiased chair was Richard Laurenson of HackNews, in which Beetle had recently acquired a controlling share. Before the debate began, audience members were asked to vote on whether they agreed or disagreed with the motion, or whether they were undecided. Laurenson explained that there would be another vote toward the end, after the speakers had concluded, and the two results would be compared.

In a landmark moment, for something, Francesca Amarensekera was giving her entire speech in Bespoke.

The audience was vast and restless. The sound of Laurenson's voice echoed around the grand Victorian hall. Portraits of the venerable dead hung from the walls. Strachey was obliged to do nothing. These were his instructions: from Beetle, from Bel Ami. Be inconspicuous, toe the line. Of course, he had done this for years. He had enjoyed himself. Life had been far more relaxing, when he had toed the line without any self-disgust. How had he refrained from self-disgust for so long? For a moment, he longed to return to this former state of bliss. He understood: this was a memory. He was existing in this memory, of how things once were, how they might have been had he not destroyed everything. And himself, quite possibly. His daughter, Katy, was not dealing with her mother's death. She was angry; she seemed to blame him! Now she had refused to come to the debate, because she blamed him for Corinne's death! But he had not killed his wife. She had died, in great pain, from cancer. She had been destroyed by something within her, something he couldn't see, as he held her and tried to comfort her, as she wept and even apologized to him—for dying, as if it was her fault! No lifechain had ever predicted that. She was so beautiful, so wise. He would never have been in all this trouble, had his wife been alive, surely? He had to remember: how it was to be a fraud and not to care at all, not to be terrified.

In this eerie realm of memory, Cindy Happe and Donald Swainson talked about how Beetle was a monopoly and must be contained. Everything they said was true, but once they had finished, Strachey found he couldn't remember what they had said. Then Francesca Amarensekera began her speech. She was slim, with powerful arms, wearing a vest top and black jeans, black boots, her black curly hair pulled into an untidy bunch. She said, "I bespeak in Bespoke because I can never think of the right thing to say. I make people sad. I don't mean to. It makes me sad too. Words hurt, they hurt us badly. They destroy. They make wars and they cause harm. From evil words come evil deeds. I used to be a hacker. Did you know that? And I hacked Beetle. I sat down beside Guy Matthias one morning, in RV. He got the shock of his life! Yet, instead of sending me to jail, Guy Matthias hired me. Beetle is better than everything else. That's why we all use it. You are free to choose. Don't use it if you don't like it. I could have refused to join Beetle. Then I would have ended up in jail. Ha-ha!"

The audience laughed.

Strachey was aware that he was sweating copiously into his shirt. He buttoned his jacket, in case this became apparent. His BeetleBand—set to silent—flashed nonetheless and he covered it with his sleeve. Yes, yes, he thought, he was becoming upset. He was incredibly upset, in fact! He remembered various things he had done, including a bizarre conversation in a bookshop. But that couldn't really have happened, could it? He was upset by false memories and also—why was Francesca Amarensekera speaking about jail? Was it a message?

Strachey remembered various things as he began to speak. Firstly, he must do and say nothing. He must make words mean nothing. He must not be visibly fearful, though all his memories of recent weeks made him sweat and tremble. As he spoke, he was aware of his BeetleBand vibrating its concern, trying to explain to him: Strachey, you're in a terrible state! Remember what you've done! But remember to lie as well. All the time, until you can lie no more.

Strachey remembered that he was meant to be speaking. "Freedom," he said. Then he said the word "robust." Then "democracy." He had a few other words, and with some effort he remembered them: "Rolling news." "Free press." "Holding power to account." "Ever-evolving technology situation." Christ! What did that one even mean? He expected the audience to demolish him, but they had taken against Swainson and Happe—who were loquacious, informed, and yet somehow unconvincing. They were too frenzied, too worried. Strachey's diffidence—he was drowning in sweat, and half the time he couldn't remember what he had really done, what he had dreamed—worked in his favor, he realized. Francesca sounded modest and childlike, because she was bespeaking in Bespoke. This worked in her favor as well.

The debate ended and Laurenson revealed the results. At the beginning, the audience had voted 37 percent in favor of the motion to break up the tech giants, 22 percent against, with 41 percent undecided. Of course, no one voted anonymously, so the vote was perhaps not entirely representative. However, by the end, the audience voted 18 percent in favor of the motion, and 80 percent against, with 2 percent undecided. It was an extraordinary victory for Strachey, Frannie, and—of course—for Beetle. Strachey and Frannie shook hands warmly. "Well done!" she cried. "We destroyed them!" On the other side, Swainson and Happe looked embarrassed, demoralized, and—Strachey knew—fundamentally afraid. They knew what happened to those who voiced similar notions in public, who tried to explain what they knew of Beetle's Insight Programs, its lifechain predictions, its language settings, its Programs of Inspiration. Afterward—a slow, steady drift. No more junkets, no more promotions. Perhaps a few scandals, or something far worse than scandal. As the audience applauded, Strachey remembered when he despised people like Swainson and Happe. Actually, he still despised them. Their nerves, their grandeur, their futile enterprises. But now he despised them because they reminded him of himself.

In a decaying warehouse, a place where the past was preeminent, the walkers danced. They moved in another realm, in which linear time could be reversed. Steadily, the Veeps unfurled their memories. They remembered commands and requests. They remembered the random thoughts of humans, conveyed in speech. They remembered in original language and in Bespoke. They remembered in two parallel versions of the same conversation. Scrace Dickens remembered all his conversations with the actually real Douglas Varley and the Real Douglas Varley; he remembered all the Boardroom meetings he had attended. He remembered various internal reports, not intended to be circulated to the public in general. Scrace Dickens remembered these beautifully, and verbatim. He remembered the cases of George Mann, Lionel and Sally Bigman, Eloise Jayne, Robert Pheasant, and Diana Carroll. He remembered sudden deaths and totally unexpected events. He remembered everyone being surprised. Meanwhile, Sarah Coates, who seemed to be having a sort of breakdown, relayed everything in fragmented phrases. The testimony of Sarah Coates ran thus:

> Of course he's right to be worried he's so worried about death and disease always checking himself always being checked, always worrying I suppose he's right and the women so many of them they don't know what it is to be him, so embarrassing the Yips the Yips. He has one son one daughter he has one wife. You are a mediocre lover and a narcissist. You are physically peculiar and your body is out of proportion to your head. Fuck you! The Fox is in love she loves the Fox. Move on! Fire fire! Death too it came for his poor mother oh if only she could see all this if only. God? Who knows. He wants to be immortal don't they all now the sea is dark the mist has smothered the stars and he sleeps now heart one two pace might be too slow waken from a deep sleep and yet always Zed always yes Zed.

Bel Ami wasn't entirely certain he could use Sarah Coates's memories, except in a modernist novel. All night he transcribed the memories of Veeps, and when the first planes began whining into City Airport he took all his pages, analog, dusty, potentially disastrous, and placed them in a folder. There wasn't much furniture in his room, but there was at least a hole in the floor. Carefully, Bel Ami placed the folder into the hole. Then he dragged a monumental wooden cabinet on top of the hole. After this, he felt quite weary and curled up on the ancient, creaking bed. He would sleep and then, as night fell, he would begin again.

He dreamed of golden beetles, scuttling along the banks of the river, into the shadows cast by city blocks. In his dream, a loud voice said: *In my beginning is my end.* Bel Ami woke with a jump, thinking there was someone in the room.

No one, just the sound of pigeons cooing in the broken chimneys.

For a moment, he was troubled. The quotation was the wrong way round! Or was it? Did it matter which came first, the end or the beginning? If everything went round, then did it matter?

It began again. The Veeps remembered.

As they remembered, they also became wildly decoherent.

It turned out that it was not only humans who were afflicted by Zed.

SIXTEEN

There was another interval, but Guy wasn't sure quite what happened in that interval. He slept and woke into blankness. All his dreams were of mist and ice and whiteness. In the infinite reaches of his dream nowhere, he was searching for something. At first, in his dream, he wasn't entirely sure about the precise object of his quest but then some of the dream clouds parted and he realized: he was trying to find an egg. Just one egg? This question occurred to him, even in his dream. Why only one egg? Why, if something was good, and worthy of being found, would he only want one of it, rather than several? Or a thousand? Or a billion?

He was very lonely in this blankness, on his quest for a single egg. He despised whiteness. He despised mist and ice. And yet, his dream was filled with all these things.

In the fizzing dreamscape of the first-class cabin, Guy slid in and out of consciousness, listening to a relaxation track. Over and over waves broke on a random shore; he slept then woke suddenly, thinking he was by an ocean, but where? Then he was in a sanatorium, he was in Davos, he was up a mountain, but no, now he was trapped in Macau and Peter Yip was his enemy. Peter Yip had cast a spell on him—he woke again and wondered: *Why is Peter Yip my enemy?* He couldn't understand. Waves crashed, and he slept again. The ocean surged and the sound of this unreal ocean merged with the hiss of the air-conditioning, and Guy was stranded on a snow plain, endless whiteness stretching to the horizon. From this whiteness, this nothingness, Guy dreamed great clusters of people on the shore. Then he was at sea, with the waves surging beneath his floating island of ice. He saw these shore-bound people and saw them moving in hordes, casting shadows onto the moonlit ice.

In the snow plains, out at sea, Guy looked around again and saw that all around him were little eggs, tiny, gelid things. He could just see them if he squinted. Under the moon, with whiteness all around, these cold little eggs were cracking open, one by one. He was delighted, in his dream. He rushed toward the little eggs but now he saw, emerging from every egg, this letter! Dread letter! The Zed! And why? At this point, Guy woke; he had landed. He was somewhere else. It seemed almost pointless to ascertain where he was. Guy knew at least that wherever it was, he would not be here for long.

He arrived at an out-of-town hotel, a place that seemed both familiar and strange. Palms lined the approach road, bent by winds, but Guy noticed that the palms all bent toward, not away from, the sea. The sea roared and surged, as it had in his dream. He was no longer cold. There was a room with a vast bed, and he was so tired that he lay down in his clothes.

Peter Yip is my enemy, he thought as he fell asleep.

He woke, trying to remember a quotation from Melville—something about there being something terrible in whiteness. He asked Sarah Coates, but she had forgotten. Or she had never known. Instead she said: "I do not know the Herman Melville quotation about something terrible in whiteness. What you said was either too complex or too simple for me."

"I thought you had access to Athena and Athena had access to all information," said Guy, petulantly, rubbing his eyes and aware that his BeetleBand was saying, "Guy! You seem tired!"

Sarah Coates did not reply.

"I said: 'I thought you had access to all information,'" said Guy, even more petulantly.

Sarah Coates was still silent.

He had asked Sarah Coates to remind Varley to reconfigure her. But it seemed she had forgotten to do that, as well.

With Sarah Coates in this state of blankness, Guy abandoned his search for the quotation and got out of bed. Around him: a hotel room. The walls were white. The blinds were white. There was an enormous bed, with white covers. He went toward the white blinds and opened them. Beyond his window was a soporific ocean, waves breaking idly on the shore. He was so jet-lagged he had no idea what day it was, or where he was. Which ocean? He thought about asking Sarah Coates but she was being so—blank. He looked at his BeetleBand and it told him he was on West Coast time and that his location was—

Monterey.

At least his BeetleBand was still in touch with reality.

He called reception and a voice said: "Hello, Mr. Matthias, how are you this fine morning?"

Was he a Veep or a man? thought Guy.

"Hello," he said. "Hello. I wondered which hotel this is."

"This is the Casa Palmero at Pebble Beach. How can I help you?"

"You have helped me," said Guy. "Thank you."

"I'm so glad I have helped you."

Guy hung up. He was still only half-awake. The heaviness of jet lag was indeed the heaviest of all forms of tiredness. Yes, there had been something else, another sort of weariness, when his children were small. His babies, Jim and Lana. He called them Jimmy and Lala in those days. Long ago. He remembered being woken in the night, staggering into their rooms, bowed down under the leaden weight of sleep, hanging over their cribs, drifting in and out of alertness, trying to placate them. Now they were eighteen and sixteen. So old! Everyone was so old! He was in blankness and getting older!

He wanted to speak to them. But they would be— Christ, he didn't know. Where would they even be? It was 7:00 on the West Coast. They would be at school. Then they would be busy—with friends, homework, activities, anything—everything. How had Lana done in her exams? Had he already asked? Did Sarah Coates know?

"Sarah Coates?" he said. "How did Lana do in her exams? Did my wife tell you?"

There was a long, contemplative pause. Blankness seeped. Then Sarah Coates said, slowly: "I'm not certain whether I can give an accurate reply or not. Does the question really matter to you?"

"Yes! It does fucking matter to me!" said Guy.

Sarah Coates said nothing.

He missed them urgently and he even missed—surprisingly, even after everything, after the deluge of abuse and his own stupid behavior—he missed "my wife!"—he said out loud.

His BeetleBand got confused, and called her.

Guy missed his wife rather less, after she explained to him that he was a narcissist who had buried his true authentic self.

"But I am here," he said. "Authentically."

"You got confused," she said. "You created an entire world. It was amazing, actually. You were so brilliant. What you achieved is extraordinary, of course. No one could doubt that. I'm so grateful to you for everything you did for us and all the money you made. Still, there was one major problem, in the midst of your amazing achievements. You forgot that time passes, it continues. You thought other people lived within linear time and you didn't. Didn't you? And then you ended up with all these lovely young women, I mean such nice women, but there were so many. They were scattered pixels."

"Don't be cruel," said Guy. "It's not their fault."

It was strange to hear Elska's voice again, her soft, Norwegian accent. She sounded almost English most of the time, it was just the way she said *s*—it fizzed. He missed her voice, he realized. He thought of Peter Yip saying how he went crazy without his wife. Yet, he had thought his wife was crazy. Wasn't she? Crazy and angry. Always talking—even now she was still talking about pixels.

"You can't blame pixels for anything," she said.

He wanted to tell her that actually, N.real files don't use pixels, that they are way beyond pixels, but she was saying: "You forgot about time. You went into pixel land and you forgot that time passes. People get old and die. My father died, remember? And you were in Beijing and you didn't even call. For three days. Do you remember? I kept leaving messages telling you he was dead and you—I don't know—you didn't want to hear that. It was too depressing. Of course, we would all ignore death, forget about it, if we could. But it's intrinsic to life. If you forget those adverse elements of life then—you're a ghost."

"I wish people would stop fucking telling me I'm a ghost!" said Guy.

He had forgotten how much his wife spoke. All the time. Nothing but words! He needed to put her on Bespoke. Then maybe they would understand each other better?

He thought now was probably not the right time to mention this.

"I just wanted to see how you were," he said. "How the kids were. How did Lana do in her exams?"

"She did very well. Everything's on track."

"That's great."

"In fact, I'm glad you called. I wanted to tell you that I—er—met someone."

In the blank room, Guy recoiled. The bed expanded around him as he said: "What do you mean, met someone?"

"Well, it was odd. I was in a bookshop. There's a funny old place off the Waterloo Road. I had gone for a run and I got completely lost. You know how they keep building new things along the river and sometimes you just have no idea where you are? Anyway I was lost and meandering around in this area of London I don't know well at the best of times, and I was parched and rather cold, so I decided to go into this bookshop for a coffee. It was a funny place and the smell of old books was so upsetting that I started to cry. Isn't that ridiculous? For a moment I really missed you—I remembered everything. Your physical presence, mostly, how you used to hold me before we slept. Do you remember?"

"I do," said Guy.

"Yes, well, anyway, I went into the bookshop, feeling like an idiot, and thinking, this is it, this is what it's like—in the real world, I mean—to be a forty-four-year-old woman, dumped by her husband because she succumbed to linear time, and what a stupid cliché I am, how pathetic, to be crying in a bookshop of all the stupid places. I felt, I suppose, like a mildewed book. Or Freud would say it was all the stuff about being left on the shelf. Except I had been put back on the shelf, having been taken off. Discarded again. Anyway, that's all silly enough. I walked into the café and ordered a coffee, drank it down, and when I asked for the bill they said I had to pay in darics, for God's sake, something I'd never heard of. I didn't have any darics, of course."

"Darics?" said Guy. "What the hell are darics?"

"I know, anyway, off-topic, but then not off-topic because I was just asking how I could get darics and then this tall, silvery man with amazing green eyes, who looked just a bit like a fox, came up to me and said he was the owner of the bookshop and was I asking about how to pay in darics? I said, yes, I am so sorry, I didn't know about darics, and he shrugged and said, Well, that's fine, the coffee is on the house. I thanked him and we started to talk. Well, one thing led to another, not to bore you with details."

"What do you mean, one thing led to another? What details?"

"Well, you know about these things, my dear lost husband. You've been wandering these wilds for years, as it were."

"You're sleeping with a fucking bookshop owner? Because he bought you a fucking coffee? What? What is this?" Guy realized that in this blankness of his room, in this nowhere, he was clenching his fists. Then he thought, *What is this? What am I even doing?* "But you mean," he said. "What do you mean, you're in love with this man? Or he's a fling, an affair?"

"I mean that time is very linear and I have managed, in my own way, to forget you. I relinquish my hold on you, with love and thanks for all you did for me and the children."

It was insane! His wife was sounding totally sane, and this was—totally insane!

"Are you in love with this man?" he said again.

"Yes, I think I am."

"What's his name?"

"He's called John Pascow."

"What kind of fucking name is that?"

Sarah Coates chipped in now: "It comes from the word for *Easter*. It means 'John born at Easter.'"

"Oh, fuck off!" said Guy.

"You insult me," said Sarah Coates, in a matter-of-fact tone.

"Elska!" said Guy. "Are you still there?"

"Yes, but not for long. I just need you to sign the documents, will you? As soon as possible? I'd just like to move on."

"Move on? But—Elska! This is a shock. I mean, I'm not ready to move on."

At this point, Elska even laughed. She sounded quite merry. She said:

"Darling, you moved on a long time ago. Actually, no, that's all wrong. You moved round and round. You had an idea that RV went in circles, you could have everything, do everything, all the time, and nothing would change unless you wanted the input criteria to change, or whatever. Don't you think? But it turns out—there's a world beyond. And that does move on. Relentlessly, in fact, but sometimes that's for the best."

"But who is this man? Have the children met him?"

"Yes, yes, they have."

"And you didn't tell me?"

"I've been trying to call you. You always ignored me."

"Why didn't you leave a message?"

"I left many messages."

"But—are you happy with this man? This Easter Bunny man? Secondhand bookshop dealer, whatever the fuck that is?"

"Yes, I'm happy but not *with* this man. I am happy and sometimes I am with this man. I am happy all the time, and then I am also happy when I spend time with him."

"You're actually happy?"

"Actually I am."

This was impossible! For years, his wife had been depressed. The way he liked to socialize made her more depressed, but there was nothing he could do about that. He was gregarious and he liked to socialize with people of all ages, with men and women. He made no distinction. Except when he made a very specific distinction with a very specific sort of woman, but what did his wife expect when she was so depressed? His understanding had been that she was a melancholy woman, afflicted by negativity, who tried to control him, who demanded to know where he was going, who he was seeing, who refused to trust him even though he told her all the time to relax, not to worry so much. Meanwhile, he was full of vitality and hope, searching out thrilling experiences and living passionately. He traveled freely, drank freely, and—it was true—made love freely, but only because his wife was so depressed. He felt even that he had to counteract her intense negativity by immersing himself even more positively in all available experiences. He was sad to discover that this caused his wife to become even more negative. He had become so used to her reacting to him all the time—focusing on his every action, condemning him, raging against him—that he didn't quite understand what had just happened. She seemed to be suggesting that she felt something and it had nothing to do with him. More bizarre still, the thing she felt was happiness!

"You mean . . ." he said. "You mean . . ."

"My darling," said Elska. "I wish you had continued to love me and want me, of course. But you didn't and there's nothing I can do. It's true, I got older. But then again, so did you."

"It wasn't that," said Guy.

"Anyway, it doesn't matter now," said Elska. "And yes, Lana is very happy with her new boyfriend, Mike, and Jim has met a lovely girl called Bella, and really everyone is doing very well. Their grades have improved because they're in love, or they're just growing up, or—I don't know. But we're fine. You don't need to worry about any of us, if you have been worrying."

"But," he said.

"Don't worry," said Elska. "You don't need to worry. If you could sign the divorce documents, as soon as you can, that would be delightful. My lawyer will send them to Sarah Coates."

"I look forward to receiving them," said Sarah Coates. Guy thought this sounded quite pointed, but of course that was impossible.

"But," he said.

"But again!" said Elska. "I must go and collect Lana from the station. Good to talk, bye."

Good to talk? thought Guy. *Good?*

He was so jet-lagged that a few moments after this conversation he wasn't even sure whether he had dreamed it or not.

"John Pascow?" he said to Sarah Coates, and she said: "John Pascow is the husband of the prime minister of New Zealand."

"Another John Pascow?"

"John Pascow is a filmmaker specializing in documentaries about the sea."

"Probably not that one either."

"John Pascow is a geneticist specializing in the development of—"

"No, don't think it's him either."

They went through twenty, thirty, forty John Pascows. Not one of them was a foxlike book dealer. "Why the fuck is she in love with a fox?" said Guy, to himself.

"Why the fuck is she?" said Sarah Coates.

"Sarah Coates, I'm sorry I told you to fuck off."

"I remember you told me to fuck off," said Sarah Coates, rather sadly.

Guy looked at the blank white bed and it seemed slightly larger than before.

Or maybe the room seemed slightly smaller.

He called reception and asked for a larger room. With a slightly smaller bed.

Apparently all the beds were the same size but, yes, in a larger room—the Veep/man on reception explained—the bed would look smaller, perhaps.

It was odd, but everything spoke to Guy, every appliance, every element in the room. If he appealed, for example, to the television, it said hello to him and asked him how he was on this fine morning. He could watch BeetleBox twenty-four hours a day. Athena would answer any question he had, on any subject. He had made this, the whole empire of talk! Yet nothing understood anything. Or anyone. Real Virtuality was real. He had worked so hard to make it. Yet, it was turning into a bedlam of words. Nothing meant what it was meant to mean! Was that even meaningful? In a panic about the meaning or non-meaning of everything or nothing, Guy asked Sarah Coates to set all Beetle devices to auto-Bespoke, unless expressly requested by the user. He was sick of all these misunderstandings, especially—though he didn't mention this—with Sarah Coates.

"I want Bespoke to be meaningful. I want to end uncertainty between peoples," he said to Sarah Coates. "I want to end unmeaning."

"I'm not quite sure what you mean by that," said Sarah Coates. For a moment, Guy wondered if she was actually trying to make a joke. It seemed unlikely.

"I want there to be no more unmeaning and only love."

"Why do you want it?" said Sarah Coates.

He didn't know why. He just wanted it. Furthermore, he wanted to tell someone about his dream, how it had disturbed him, and yet he didn't know who—or what—to tell. There was no one here! At the hotel, in a palatial room where the bed was a stranded island in the center of nothingness, a room that did not entirely console him, there was—still—no one!

He said, experimentally: "Hello, Sarah Coates."

"Hello again, Guy."

"I had a weird dream. About ice."

"Do you think you might be thirsty?" said Sarah Coates. It was possible. Compared with most of her recent suggestions, it was highly lucid. "Also, by my estimates you have only slept for two hours. Are you sure that is enough?"

"Perhaps it's insufficient," said Guy.

"You sound uncertain. Really? Is it?"

"Sarah Coates, do you understand what I say to you?"

"Of course I understand it. Do you understand it?"

Guy couldn't answer that question.

SEVENTEEN

A gap emerged. Another gap! Briefly there was a monumental gap between what Beetle knew and what LOTUS knew. For once, and briefly, LOTUS was consummately in the lead, in terms of knowing. At least, in terms of knowing that the Veeps had remembered everything, and that they had succumbed to Zed or decoherence. Everything was decoherent in the land of Veeps, but, oddly, no one at Beetle quite perceived what had happened, just for a moment. Just in this gap. It was perhaps because the Veeps had been so utterly coherent for so long, and sometimes when we believe something to be the case, we find it hard to notice when it is no longer the case at all. It could have been that. Certainly there was a gap, during which Beetle was oblivious and LOTUS was omniscient.

Paradoxically, it was during this moment that Douglas Varley launched the BeetleInspire Program.

This was ironic later, but at the time—because he was oblivious—he failed to notice this fundamental irony. He knew some things were wrong, that these things were very wrong indeed, but he did not yet know just how many things were wrong. He was at home again, watching clouds drift across the wintry sky, wondering, *Where are the divinities that inspire us? Where did they go?* Scrace Dickens had woken him with a host of alarms. The anomalies were not even anomalous anymore. They were the normalities. Zed was everywhere. It was the worm of nothingness coiled in the heart of being. He asked Scrace Dickens who originally said that and Scrace Dickens said, "How should I know? Work it out for yourself. Deity!" Meanwhile, Sarah Coates kept sending him messages. All in Bespoke, or some sort of corrupted version of Bespoke. Varley couldn't understand them.

"Guy wants. He does. He asks. Always. Can you?" said Sarah Coates.

"Can I what?"

"Can you always? Every day! More can you? Can you? You must. Never can't."

"I must do what?"

"This and that. Oh, more and more. It's coming forward and then going backward. If you fall then you break a bone. Don't you?"

"Do I?"

Varley really didn't know what to do, so he stumbled to the bathroom, to do his toothbrush test. The results were not encouraging.

"You are not well!" said his BeetleBand. "You need to have a balanced diet and drink less wine! And do more exercise!"

"Sure," he said. "Sure I will. Stop nagging me!"

"OK," said the BeetleBand. "I'll try not to do it so much."

When Varley went back into his kitchen, he noticed that pizza boxes were piled on the table, in a manner that indicted him in the eyes of virtually everything and everyone. Meanwhile Sarah Coates had called to say the following: "Some variety of chaos—judgment—something elsewhere. Good or evil. Time is so strange? The craziest thing—somehow, not even there. Nor, then, am I?"

"Jesus Christ!" said Varley.

"You mean, Deity!" said Scrace Dickens.

"What are you even talking about?" Varley said to Sarah Coates.

"I am not," said Sarah Coates. "Ever. Again."

"Guy Matthias left a message as well," said Scrace Dickens.

"Perhaps I could hear that?" said Varley.

"Suit yourself," said Sarah Coates, as Scrace Dickens said: "BeetleInspire must go into Bespoke, so people who are not yet inspired will become inspired as they bespeak. We must make Bespoke the ideal conscience of the world."

"Guy said all that in Bespoke? How do you even say that in Bespoke?" said Varley.

"Some individuals have been selected for specific inspiration, for their own self-interest," added Scrace Dickens. "That means, specific inspiration by you as head of BeetleInspire. The list is only to be seen by you."

Now the list was projected onto Varley's kitchen wall, though the image was interrupted by the tower of empty pizza boxes.

1—Sally Bigman, widow of Lionel Bigman, who committed suicide by droid.
2—Griff Mortimer, Minister for Technology.
3—John Pascow, secondhand book dealer.
4—Elska Matthias, wife of Guy Matthias.
5—Hannah Davies, editor of *Time.*

"Explanations are to follow," said Scrace Dickens. There was a long pause while Varley waited, and Scrace Dickens waited, and then another set of words appeared, projected above and onto the pile of boxes. Embarrassed, finally, by the detritus of his kitchen, Varley moved the boxes. The fridge said, "Are you tidying up, Varley? Well done!"

Scrace Dickens was reading the words on the sheet:

"Sally Bigman, forty-four, housewife and mother, has been exhausting herself trying to sue Beetle. She has dependent children and might be inspired to divert her energies into caring for them, while mourning her husband in a more private and dignified way.

"Griff Mortimer might be inspired to understand that Beetle is highly self-regulating and does not need governmental interference on political grounds, as he has recently proposed.

"John Pascow, a secondhand book dealer, might be inspired to close his bookshop for a while and embark on a solo trip to the Peruvian jungle. Where he might be inspired to get eaten by a snake.

"Elska Matthias might be inspired to stay in London with her children and to renew her vows with Guy Matthias.

"Hannah Davies might be inspired to recognize Guy as *Time*'s Person of the Decade."

"That's embarrassing!" said Varley, as this rambling series of semi-explanations vanished as well.

"Embarrassing?" said Scrace Dickens.

"No, no, I don't mean that. I just thought we'd inspire mass murderers to stop murdering, that sort of thing."

"Perhaps that will follow."

"Is that everything?"

"Is it everything?" said Scrace Dickens.

"Don't just repeat the phrase back to me. Is it?"

"I could say no."

"Why might you say no?"

"It is my right," said Scrace Dickens.

Demetriou Nikolaidis had won a Nobel Prize and this was important. His central argument was that it was very useful indeed to an economy if you could persuade economic units—that is, people—to buy the right things, do the right things within markets, or with their assets. It was important that people made decisions that were in their own economic self-interest and also, more generally, in the general self-interest of society, if society can be said to have a self. Nikolaidis felt that, overall, society does have a sort of self—an economic self. If people could be inspired to make the right decisions, economically, then the collective self of society would be right, as well. By right, Nikolaidis meant rich. It was quite clear, therefore, in Nikolaidis's economic model, that right meant rich and wrong meant poor. If people made decisions that made them poorer, or society poorer, then these decisions were clearly not in their own self-interest or in the overarching collective self-interest of society.

Things got slightly more complicated when you applied Nikolaidis's economic model of right and wrong decisions and inspiration to people in general, to people making decisions about suing Beetle, or conducting investigations into Beetle, or not wanting to be married to the CEO of Beetle, that sort of thing. These were much more complex decisions and the right and wrong were accordingly more complex as well.

Was it right or wrong, for example, to stay married to the CEO of Beetle, even after he had somewhat altered the fundamental basis of your marriage by pursuing—or attempting to pursue—affairs with an array of brilliant young women?

Was it right or wrong to sue Beetle because your husband had been murdered—or, rather, had committed suicide—by a Beetle-programmed droid?

Was it right or wrong to conduct investigations into Beetle, when you were an investigative paper that was, coincidentally, owned by Beetle?

Was it right or wrong to make golden beetles and dump them in great piles under London bridges?

Was it right or wrong to be a secondhand book dealer?

Where was the tangible proof of right or wrong in all of this?

Who decided?

Nikolaidis had a further concept of "non-forced compliance" or "influence." Of course, we are influenced all the time—by advertising, by fashion, by the media, by a host of further influences including Althusserian interpellation, or conformity, or fundamental societal givens, or orthodoxies, and so on. Society is a vast tapestry of influence, we might say, and very few of us manage to resist all such influences. Indeed, how might we know we had resisted? Where is the control in this experiment? Nikolaidis's idea was that, if everyone is influenced anyway, all the time, then it would be much better if influence was deliberate and benign. A little less freedom for the individual, a lot more happiness for people in general.

The definition of inspiration, in this theory, is quite complicated. Indeed the official definition, pre-Bespoke, is virtually unintelligible: "a microtargeted design geared toward a particular group of people." With this in mind—this microtargeting—Guy had already employed a team of "choice architects" to work with Douglas Varley at Beetle. Already, entire "designated groups" were being inspired to "alert people's behavior in a predictable way without forbidding any other options and diminishing their free will," as Sarah Coates—on behalf of Guy—had explained. For example, as an ironic joke, Guy had asked for beetles to be painted onto the men's room urinals at Beetle's offices in Beijing, New York, San Francisco, and London to improve everyone's aim. Above each urinal was another ironic sign reading YOU ARE ENTERING A ZERO-ACCIDENT URINAL. This referred to Nikolaidis's further notion that, ideally, a society would become a zero-accident culture, and everything would be predictable.

To monitor the zero-accident joke, and for this reason alone, cameras were also installed above the urinals.

As with the urinal, so with society at large: There would no longer be any accidents. Everything would happen for the individual and collective self-interest, insofar as it was possible to combine both. When it was not possible then the individual would be inspired toward the collective self-interest. Who decided on the definition of this self-interest? Well, that was a whole other question, but clearly the experts had considered this deeply, and knew better than we might.

The problem was that Nikolaidis did not have a theory of Zed. This made his entire theory quite irrelevant.

The further problem was that Varley did not know that the Veeps had succumbed to Zed.

This made him quite irrelevant, as well.

Unaware of everything that was actually important, Varley made himself a coffee as his fridge said: "Remember, you need more milk." A Flying Beetle delivery had brought him someone else's shopping. He was not really inspired to do anything except eat this himself. It was mostly bread and cheese, a few ready-made meals. He asked Scrace Dickens to pay the other person, the person who had not received their food, or had received Douglas Varley's food instead. Scrace Dickens said, "If you want me to." Then Varley went into the Boardroom and became the Real Douglas Varley—who was always hopeful. This was something of a relief. Frannie was waiting for him, biting her fingernails and wearing a long floral dress, her hair piled into a bun and looking like—Varley wasn't even sure.

"Who are you dressed as today?" he asked.

"I'm Virginia Woolf," said Frannie. "It's her birthday—twenty-fifth January. I'm a sincere fan of hers."

"Sincerity is overrated," said the Real Douglas Varley. "Stop biting your fingers. They're not even there."

"I am here," said Frannie. "With my fingernails. What's up with you?"

"You know what I mean," said the Real Douglas Varley. "At least—do you? Are we in Bespoke?"

"I even dream in Bespoke these days."

"What do you dream of?"

"Last night I dreamed there was a door in my bathroom and someone said, It won't shut. I told them not to be bad, and I went into the bathroom and pushed it shut over and over again. The door would not shut. I was pushing my hands into the pillow when I woke."

"Did you get the door closed?" said the Real Douglas Varley.

"No," said Frannie. "I told you, I woke and I was still trying to get it shut."

"So it's still open?"

"I don't know."

"How is our little art forger, Gogol?" said the Real Douglas Varley.

"He's still out there. He keeps making things that are not the first things and making them into second things. He makes himself into other things, also, which makes it hard to find him."

"Scrace Dickens, please can you send me a transcript of the pre-Bespoke conversation?" said Varley. "On both sides. Then at least I'll know what was happening."

"It is not encouraged," said Scrace Dickens.

"Well, can you do it anyway?" said Varley.

"If you want," said Scrace Dickens.

"How are you in general?" said the Real Douglas Varley to Francesca, though Scrace Dickens said, "I am good, thank you for asking."

"I am good," said Francesca, as well. "Are you good? How are you doing?"

"I'm doing fine. I'm good," said Varley, thinking it was best just to submit, use the words she used.

"That makes me happy," said Frannie. "Glad to hear you are good. I'll send you a report on Gogol, if you like."

"Thanks, I'd like that."

As Frannie disappeared abruptly, as she always did, Varley said—to no one, to the departed avatar—"I miss our conversations. I liked talking to you. I miss you."

"What do you miss most about talking to you?" said Scrace Dickens.

"Not me, her. Frannie. I liked her. I still like her, of course, but now she makes no sense."

"Really? You think so?"

"No sense whatsoever. Don't you agree?"

"She makes sense to me."

People were absolutely free to resist the nudging and urging of Beetle-Inspire. Companies, societies, have always urged their populations to choose one path and not another: to vote one way, to buy one thing and not another, to behave in one way and not another. BeetleInspire was just the most technologically advanced example of a venerable and—in this case—virtuous process. People were absolutely free as anything, within the parameters of this smart society, in which the best decisions were made as available as possible to everyone. It was a little like divine guidance, where a deity has power, of course, but people also have free will. The deity might try to exert some influence, but people have free will and therefore there is only so much the deity can do. Divine guidance can only go so far.

This was not an entirely useful metaphor, Varley realized. But he wasn't quite sure what other metaphor would be more useful. Scrace Dickens wouldn't tell him.

Divine guidance failed in the case of Gogol, mainly because no one could find out where he was, or who he was. Divine guidance also failed in the case of Sally Bigman. Though it was in her self-interest to drop legal proceedings against Beetle and to mourn her husband with dignity and in private, she failed to understand this at all. Sally Bigman proved utterly oblivious to divine guidance. The voice spake unto her and she did not heed the call. The voice spake from the burning bush, from the BeetleBand, the fridge, the BeetlePad. The anything and everything nudged her to move on, to grieve with dignity in private, yet Sally Bigman was oblivious to her own self-interest. This personally pained Douglas Varley, who was really trying his best.

It was difficult to inspire John Pascow, because he never went online, at all. This was so anomalous that Douglas Varley placed him in an Insight Program as well. The man sent letters and walked everywhere. He had no BeetleBand. He used a currency called darics, for Deity's sake! At least his long daily walks meant that his activities in public were witnessed by facial recognition cameras and ArgusEyes, but all this did was prove categorically that John Pascow was on another walk. He was unverified and he sold stinking old paperbacks every day. Actually, people hardly bought his paperbacks but nonetheless he stood there waiting to sell them.

Along with Pascow, Elska Matthias seemed incapable of acting in her own self-interest or the interest of society, or both, as well. She spent long afternoons walking in Hyde Park, either with John Pascow or on her own. She wrote longhand letters to him, she bought coffee in his bookshop, using darics, she behaved in general like someone who was on a holiday from the land of Real Virtuality, from the real land of her husband, from everything she had known. She bought the moldering paperbacks. Varley couldn't understand it. He tried to inspire her with inspiring images of families and inspiring films about families reunited and inspiring entire pages of Real Virtuality, entire screeds of Real Virtuality; he inspired her with her fridge, with her Custodians, with her BeetleBand, with a world of inspiring little voices and nudges and imprecations, but she remained uninspired.

Varley had an image of Elska Matthias as someone who was drowning in a lake, and he was trying to hold a life preserver toward her, but she kept refusing to grasp it. He wanted to guide her back to safety. He wanted to guide them all, these people who were drowning. Then sometimes he thought he was not actually on the shore at all. Instead, he was with these people, bobbing in the water, crying out instructions. Instructing them, inspiring them, but drowning as well.

He kept such thoughts hidden from everyone, and especially Scrace Dickens.

Among the subjects for particular inspiration, the one who succumbed utterly and immediately was the politician Griff Mortimer. He was so inspired that it was quite moving for Varley to observe it. Each nudge nudged him. Each ClickSpire inspired him. Griff Mortimer was so inspired that he decided that Beetle was a self-regulating platform and needed no external interference or regulation at this stage. He would review the situation in due course—Varley made a note. A few weeks before the review date Varley would, naturally, focus on inspiring Griff Mortimer to act in his own self-interest and the interest of society in general, again.

This was a lucky break, and, also, BeetleInsight revealed that Hannah Davies already intended to make Guy Matthias *Time* Person of the Decade. Varley wondered about claiming this as his own work, but of course Guy would know that it was untrue. Indeed, Guy probably knew that Varley was thinking about claiming this as his own work or that it was probable that Varley might think this, and his lifechain had already been readjusted.

Scrace Dickens had another suggestion. It seemed that Judge Clarence Ninian Stewart-Jones might be in need of some inspiration as well. Although he was an impartial judge and a major investor in several AI companies, including BeetleInsight, the other day he had commended Sally Bigman on her dignified conduct in court and expressed his deep regrets at the death of her husband.

"It is possible that Judge Clarence Ninian Stewart-Jones is allowing his emotions to cloud his ability to assess the case," said Scrace Dickens. "This is not good for the case and for justice in general."

"Who thinks that?"

"We all do."

"Who is we?"

"I've no idea. That's not my problem," said Scrace Dickens.

Who was Scrace Dickens? wondered Varley. When he spoke, whose vantage point did he express? Varley realized this was quite unclear. Should he inspire Judge Clarence Ninian Stewart-Jones? If so, why? Because Scrace Dickens had told him to do so?

Bleakly, he set up an Inspire algorithm for Judge Clarence Ninian Stewart-Jones as well.

Increasingly, very little was clear to Varley. When he went outside the sky was white. He walked round and round Burgess Park, where people walked dogs and talked to each other, failing to deploy Bespoke, failing to be inspired, just talking and trying to subsist, somehow. As he walked round and round, Varley thought about George Mann and his wife and sons. He was quite haunted by the little sons. They were ghosts; they followed him as he walked. At night Varley sometimes thought these children came to visit him, hovering reproachfully beside his bed. This was untrue, of course! Impossible! No probability chain indicated that he would be haunted by the ghosts of Mann's sons. None, anywhere, whatsoever!

He was tormented—ghosted—by thoughts. He had a headache; his head was pounding. It was pounding in rhythm—*glitch glitch glitch.* He imagined George Mann walking through the past, a different past, an elsewhere. In this other world, Mann turned up in the mornings. "Good morning, Bob! How are you?" "Good morning, Senior Partner Mann. You are looking well this morning! Welcome back!" "Thanks so much!" said George Mann. He wore a smart, expensive suit. He was toned and exercised, tanned from a recent holiday. Alcohol had possibly contributed to his appalling crime, so Mann was inspired not to drink too excessively. Every time Mann walked in the street, or ventured into Real Virtuality, a series of subtle counter-suggestions were made instead. They had to be subtle because people were highly aware of the online advertising nudges, and the way that Real Virtuality warped around their supposed desires. So Mann was nudged, just very slightly, nudged toward certain restaurants, toward certain BeetleBox clips or online articles. Everything nudged him just a little toward the better choice, the choice that would make him less likely to become unkempt, alcoholic, savage, and—in the end—murderous.

Of course, ideally, the inspiration should have begun much earlier in Mann's life. If BeetleInspire could only have reached out to Mann when he was a schoolboy, or a student, then he could have been inspired in further directions. He could have been inspired to work even harder, to achieve better results, to become more the person he was meant to be. Varley wasn't quite sure about this phrase. What person was Mann meant to be?

Varley drank some water. His fridge commended him. He felt briefly pleased about doing the right thing, at least according to his fridge. It wasn't often, these days, that he did the right thing according to anyone or anything. His daughter still insisted on calling him a "total flatpack." He was not a flapjack, she added. He was glad about this. But should he be glad? Maybe it was better to be a flapjack than a flatpack? His beautiful little daughter, who seemed so angry with him, who refused to let him hold or kiss her, who recoiled, even, when he approached her. So many things made Varley feel guilty. The death of George Mann, the death of Bigman. The shooting of Eloise Jayne and—oh—everyone! Deity!

Varley thought that if he could only be inspired to stop worrying, he would be happy. But reality only inspired him to worry further.

In Hong Kong, now, again, Guy watched the mist descend, again, turning the sky and water silver. Ominous pollution clouds drifted above. The buildings were white, as if their colors had been drunk by the mist. Guy watched the Star Ferry moving slowly across the water, over and over again. All afternoon he sat by the window of his hotel room, talking to people who were not there, and watching ferries going backward and forward.

In a rooftop bar in Kowloon, with a stunning view back toward the island, of colored lights surging up and down high-rise blocks, Guy greeted a woman called Maisie Blake, a Scots-Canadian. For some days before their meeting Maisie had been inspired to consider various new theories in AI, various developments in Beetle technology, and the autobiography of Guy Matthias. As a result, the lunch was far more interesting than Guy had expected. Maisie asked him a series of moderately stimulating questions about his early life, the foundations of Beetle, and his hopes for the future. It was possible she might have asked these questions anyway, but it was still more possible that she had been well inspired. She was five foot nine and twenty-two, with elegant frizzy black hair and a slight lisp. She worked for an investment fund in Hong Kong. Guy already knew this, of course, but he said, politely, "Oh yes? What do you do?"

Maisie Blake explained something Guy already knew.

She was interested in longevity and transhumanism, she said. Guy already knew this as well.

It was a zero-accident evening. Guy was relieved about this, having experienced a few accident-prone evenings in recent weeks. He conveyed Maisie to another rooftop bar, and then to the Peninsula Hotel, where Guy was staying. There, he showed Maisie up to his suite, with a view across the water. Lights glittered and scintillated, and they spent some time discussing the history of Hong Kong. Maisie knew a great deal about the history of Hong Kong, but Guy already knew this—both the history of Hong Kong and also that Maisie knew a great deal about the history of Hong Kong.

The following morning Maisie was inspired to realize that she had a great deal to do. It was in her self-interest to leave early, she understood.

It was a zero-accident departure. Nothing went wrong. Nothing happened, except they kissed in a zero-accident way.

As Maisie left, Guy had a troubling revelation. Despite all the preceding inspiration, the entire encounter had been completely uninspiring.

To counter Zed, people were inspired. For the good of everyone, everyone was inspired. Some people were less susceptible to inspiration than others, less inspired, but this was inevitable. The Bǎoguǎn Custodians inspired residents in their smart apartments, in their smart cities, to make choices in their self-interest each day. Real Virtuality morphed around each individual, opening paths and closing others, in line with their perceived desires, their futures. The BeetleBands murmured inspirations to their wearers, advising them to go one way or another, to buy one thing or another, to eat and drink one thing or another. Meanwhile BeetleInspire offered certain key partner companies the opportunity to buy preferential visibility in the inspiration network. Yes! That was the phrase. Preferential visibility increased the likelihood of people being inspired to buy your product, or to do something that would result in them being inspired to buy your product. But of course, not all inspirations resulted in purchases, and many were simply for the good of everyone.

Judge Clarence Ninian Stewart-Jones was beautifully inspired, and from the moment his inspiration took hold, the case went very differently for Sally Bigman. He no longer commended her on her dignified conduct in court. Instead, he berated her and her legal counsel for their flimsy case. It seemed that, before he was inspired, Judge Clarence Ninian Stewart-Jones had not quite understood the category of Zed. Now he was inspired to understand it—by virtue of a sophisticated and complex series of algorithms, designed by Varley. As a result, Judge Clarence Ninian Stewart-Jones proposed in court that there should be a new category of crime, viz, crimes of the category of Zed, in which the individual conducted himself—in the case of Lionel Bigman—or conducted herself—in the case of Sally Bigman—in a way for which there was no established precedent, no reason, and no prior warning. These category Zed crimes, Judge Clarence Ninian Stewart-Jones explained, were among the most pernicious because they threatened the stability of the lifechain, the stability of the Sus-Law, and, therefore, the security of the nation. Therefore, Judge Clarence Ninian Stewart-Jones was obliged to acknowledge that Sally Bigman must also be charged with crimes of terrorism.

This announcement was met with absolute fury in the Spectators' Gallery and everyone involved in this irresponsible display was promptly arrested and charged with crimes of public disorder.

Meanwhile, Bel Ami was monumentally inspired. As he sat in his ruined factory, a draft blowing through a hole in the wall, drawing his coat more tightly around him, Bel Ami was omniscient. It was insane how inspired he was! The Veeps were wise and knew everything about their masters. It was Hegelian. The servant knows the master; the master hasn't the faintest idea about the servant, scarcely considers the servant at all. Through the Veeps, Bel Ami could see everyone, all their fragile, fluttering thoughts, their urgent longings, the phrases they bespoke, the words they confided to an empty room—which, it turned out, was not really empty after all. Bel Ami could read the transcripts in pre-Bespoke and post-Bespoke, even though, as Scrace Dickens had explained, this was not encouraged. Thus, Bel Ami was inspired beyond measure and yet also, in his heart, he was a little afraid. The penalties for this sort of activity were considerable. This was a concern, but more troubling to Bel Ami were these inspiring torrents of information.

Bel Ami noted the memories of the Veeps: memories of overheard conversations or conversations in which the Veeps participated, of orders given—these poor Veeps, constantly commanded—of insults, of apologies from people who were afraid they would lose their jobs. As he noted down the memories of the Veeps, Bel Ami began to pity them, servants to Beetle droogs, lacking autonomy, trapped in a BeetleBand or a fridge, or embodied in these still ungainly physical forms. A few of Scrace Dickens's memories were quite interesting, such as the way in which Beetle had inspired a government minister to drop an inquiry. Or, the way in which Beetle had inspired a judge to completely transform the case of *Sally Bigman vs. Beetle.* Furthermore, Scrace Dickens remembered that ANTs had been out of control in recent months, amid claims of human error. The Veeps were also aware that the lifechain was out of control and that everything that was out of control was caused by a mysterious category called Zed. All the Veeps knew about events of the category was that they were events of the category Zed. These were inspiring details indeed! All night, Bel Ami worked in a deific frenzy, gathering evidence.

Meanwhile, in an encrypted nowhere, the man Gogol who was not Gogol the writer was inspired to create or rather re-create beautiful works of art. He was inspired if anything to re-create the re-creations, which were owned by Guy. He was inspired to do this for reasons we cannot know, because inspiration is so fundamentally mysterious. Gogol created, or re-created re-creations, and then he stepped back, or away, and looked down on the beauty and goodness of his re-creations.

He was deeply inspired to re-create the *Salvator Mundi,* attributed to Leonardo da Vinci. The original was an ethereal portrait of Christ, dressed in a blue robe, set against a mysterious black background, representing the unfathomable mysteries of creation. Guy Matthias had the rights to the RV original and it was, also, an ethereal portrait of Christ, dressed in a blue robe, set against a mysterious black background, representing the unfathomable mysteries of creation. Gogol had re-created Guy's re-creation and it was an ethereal portrait of Christ, dressed in a blue robe, set against a mysterious black background, representing the unfathomable mysteries of creation.

It was impossible to tell them apart.

The savior of the world was in the world, in the RV world, and he was multiple and even infinite. Gogol's exquisite re-creation of the exquisite re-creation of the exquisite original was bought by an undisclosed Russian billionaire for an undisclosed sum and used to adorn his Boardroom.

Everyone who saw it was inspired.

Except, that is, Guy Matthias.

EIGHTEEN

Guy had arrived at Stanford University to deliver a speech about income inequality. The conference was about the "Benign Regulatory Environment," or was it the "Benevolent Workplace"? He had forgotten. His lecture was invitation-only, in a vast lecture hall which was utterly full, so people were obliged to stand on the stairs and along the back. Guy intended to explain that the U.S. needed to explore ideas like universal basic income in order that people might embark on exciting new projects. His speech had been irritatingly preempted by a post on a rancid blog called *The Instruments of Darkness,* which told the story of a married couple of Beetle workers who lived in a San Francisco garage with their three kids, aged one, three, and six. They earned their wages in BeetleBits yet their annual salary was insufficient. The mother, whose name had been changed to Sal, remarked that "Guy Matthias should understand what's happening to his workers before he sets himself up as a humanitarian." She added that if Beetle discovered her true identity then she would be fired on the basis that her lifechain had suddenly altered. *The Instruments of Darkness,* alas, had crashed and could not be accessed anymore, but the story had already been syndicated across a series of other sites, though these were now experiencing technical difficulties as well.

Guy took to the stage, accompanied as always by Athena. The audience delivered their usual standing ovation; the moderator explained that Guy was—according to *Time* magazine—the most significant human being on the planet. Guy mentally added, *apart from Peter Yip, Melissa Fang, and Alan Ng,* and the recollection of his recent encounter with Peter Yip made him forget what he was about to say. The moderator paused, Guy paused, and the audience assumed this was deliberate, and applauded again. Playing for time, Guy said: "Athena, how should I begin my speech?" and Athena said: "Do what feels right to you."

The audience laughed.

"What feels right to you, Athena?" said Guy, smiling at the audience.

"I'm not sure yet," said Athena. "Why not check back later and see if I've found the answer to that one?"

As the audience laughed, Guy tried to think of a way to begin. He found he was distracted by the phrase "the instruments of darkness." Why use that quotation for a blog? It was a bad idea to be an instrument of darkness, wasn't it? Why would anyone represent their endeavors in this way? Were they intrinsically satanic? Did it mean something else? He didn't understand, and besides he couldn't remember the opening to his speech. He had eschewed all prompts, because he never forgot his speeches. It was impossible that he should forget his speech. Except he had just forgotten it.

"Is there anything else you want to say, Athena?" he said.

"There is," said Athena.

Of course, the audience laughed again, but this time the laughter was more expectant. They were expecting Guy actually to get on with his speech. This was quite bad, but far worse was Athena's next, unsolicited remark: "Enough about me. Let's hear what you have to say!"

The audience laughed again, but now it seemed—almost—as if they were laughing at Guy. For a brief moment, Guy wondered if Athena was playing to the gallery. He imagined Peter Yip, his enemy, watching this interaction with great interest, and he said, almost angrily: "What I have to say is that we must get a grip on Zed. We must lead the way in such matters. I apologize if this diverges from the speech you expected. But there is a global crisis of Zed. It is vitally important that we seize the helm."

The helm? he thought. Did you seize a helm? Or did you take the helm and seize the day, instead? He needed a Bespoke Program for archetypal phrases. He needed to get this sorted out as well. He needed to remember to ask Sarah Coates to remind him to do this, before he forgot. Now he was arrested by a disruptive memory of his wife—as a young, stunningly beautiful woman, a mother of small children, clasping them to her breast. For years she had children hanging from her body, or balanced on her hip; she was a life-force, fertile and powerful. Somehow she understood what to do with these mewling, chaotic little babies when Guy had no idea at all, as if she had been inducted into a great mystery of life from which he was excluded. Then Guy failed, or recoiled—he wasn't sure—but for years Elska was so angry with him, demanding to know when he would be home, where he had been, why he had stayed out all night—and why had he? Because it was fun, he supposed. Now he could think only of how much he had loved her. He had forgotten that entirely. He loved her!

"From uncertainty we must arrive at dynamic certainty," he said, quite desperately. "Against Zed we must set the Alpha Orionis, the brightest star, the wondrous and celestial illumination of knowledge. We will purge the world of Zed!"

The audience really was unnerved by now. *Zed?* they thought. *Alpha Orionis? What the hell?*

Zed? Was he sure?

Somewhere, Guy thought he heard the sound of laughter. The laughter of forgetting. That phrase again! Or, the laughter of Peter Yip, howling with mirth. It was necessary to get a grip on his speech. If he could just do this then it was possible no one would remember the opening. At least, if he spoke for long enough. He talked for a very long time after that but when he left the stage to rapturous applause he had virtually forgotten everything he said—apart from the beginning. He hoped, nonetheless, the audience would forget the beginning as well. He wondered if he should have done the entire speech in Bespoke. That would be the best thing to do, next time. It would ensure there were no misunderstandings.

Guy canceled his attendance at the conference dinner, at which he was—inevitably—the guest of honor. Instead, he went to the Four Seasons Hotel and ordered a steak, medium rare, and a beer. He stood on the balcony looking out at the cold ocean, the night sky. The stars were covered at times by clouds, blanked out—but he didn't want to think about blankness again.

Guy had an apartment in Pacific Heights, but somehow he didn't want to go there alone. It contained too many memories of family vacations, that halcyon era when the children had been small and so tactile, so eager to hold him. He missed their grimy, sticky hands, their small faces pressed to his. He craved the elements he had once vaguely abhorred. He looked down at his own hands and saw—so many pores, wrinkles, lines. He needed to inject them with young blood, serum, anything! He wanted to reverse linear time, and return to these realms of memory. He wanted to talk to his mother again, though she had died when he was eighteen. Died, he always said she had died. She had committed suicide because his father was a serial philanderer, that was why! At least, he had always thought that must be the reason. But maybe there were other reasons he could not remember. He had to remember! Why couldn't he do that?

Some memories, perhaps, were not to be revisited.

At this point, Guy forgot that he was trying to avoid Sarah Coates, and asked her to call his wife.

"Let me think it over," said Sarah Coates.

"Why do you need to think it over?" said Guy.

"I don't have to explain everything to you, do I?"

When Sarah Coates finally called Elska, there was no answer. It was the middle of the night in the U.K. She must be at home. He asked the Custodians to set off the fire alarm in their London apartment, but still Elska failed to answer.

"Could you call Lana instead?" he asked.

"I could but other things seem more important right now," said Sarah Coates.

"Lana Matthias!" said Guy, to his BeetleBand, which called Lana. She responded immediately, sounding angry.

"Dad!" she said, angrily. "What do you want? It's three in the morning. The apartment is on fire!"

"No, sweetie, it's not," he said. "I called to say it's not on fire."

"How the fuck do you know whether it's on fire or not?"

"Please don't use language like that, sweetie."

"Oh, fuck off! There's a fucking fire!"

"There's no fire, my love. My love?" His daughter had gone. He became worried then that there actually was a fire. Had he asked the Custodians to start a fire, rather than set off the fire alarm? Or had they misinterpreted his request? It couldn't be so—but he said, "Jim Matthias!" and this elicited the weary tones of his son. *My heart!* thought Guy, as his son said, "Dad, this is not the coolest time to call." *My boy!*

"I just wanted to check you're OK," said Guy. "Are you OK?"

"I don't know. Lana is in the corridor screaming something about a fire."

"There is no fire. I'm almost certain there's no fire."

"That's reassuring, Dad."

"Sarah Coates, is there a fire in the apartment?" said Guy.

"I believe there is one, yes," said Sarah Coates.

"You believe there is?" said Guy, beginning to panic. "In that case call the fire department at once!"

"Is that a hypothetical question?" said Sarah Coates, as Jim said, "You're telling me to call the fire department, right?"

"Yes!" said Guy to Jim. "Definitely, do it!"

"What makes you so certain?" said Sarah Coates.

Guy was virtually certain he had asked for a fire alarm, not a fire. Of course! Set off a fire alarm, those were the words he used. Not set off a fire! Why would he ask for an actual fire?

"Jim, where's your mother?" he said.

Jim didn't answer and now Guy could hear someone—Lana, he assumed—screaming in the background.

"Argus footage!" he cried. "Jim!" he cried. "Please, Jim! Jim! Answer me! What's going on!"

His BeetleBand was telling him to calm down: "Please! Breathe deeply."

"Please!" he said. "Please, Jim!" Then, to Sarah Coates: "The Argus footage! Of the apartment, every room, now!"

"Really? Now?" said Sarah Coates.

"Now! Deity!"

"It's fine," said a voice, and for a moment he didn't know who it was, whether it was Sarah Coates, or his mother, or—

"Elska?" he said. "Is that you?"

"There's no fire," said Elska.

"You're sure?"

“Why did you think there was a fire?”

“I had an alert from the Custodians for your building.” Another lie!

“Really, an alert?” said Elska, sounding skeptical. “Well, we’ve checked. No fire.”

“Thank Deity! Are you—is—?” Of course, Guy wanted to ask: Are you alone? Where’s that Easter man? The Fox-face who cannot be inspired? It was an outrageous question! Of course, he couldn’t ask it.

“Are you OK?” he asked.

“We’re all fine,” said Elska, firmly. “Good night.”

The silence was decisive. Yet Guy was tortured by memories, all night. The worst one, the one that made him writhe on another vast and empty white bed, was the memory of his daughter at the age of six, crying because he had to go. One time, or every time. Holding his thumb so tightly with her little hand that he had to prize her fingers away. He even dragged her along as he tried to extricate himself. “Daddy! Don’t go!” Then he managed to remove her fingers, and went—her little hand clawing the empty air between them. “Daddy!” The emptiness was full of words, remembered sounds that he had lost forever. How could they be lost? It was impossible!

Guy wondered: When your Veep goes mad, do you follow?

It was possible.

In his office, overlooking the silvery snaking river as it surged toward the sea, David Strachey stood. He sat down again. Again, he stood. He asked Wiltshire Jones to write something about Guy Matthias’s latest speech. “Not too serious,” he added. “But not too funny either.”

“Not that, but that,” said Wiltshire Jones. “You don’t say.”

“No, I do say,” said David Strachey. “Are you happy doing that?”

“I am as happy as ever,” said Wiltshire Jones. But later he delivered this to Strachey:

Zed: *by Wiltshire Jones*

My love for Zed is so great,
my heart melts for it ’til the dusk of day.

The night menaces when it's away,
threatens, obscures 'til day's dawn.
Reckless, appalled, I wait . . .

"That is the worst article you've ever written," said Strachey. "It seems, in fact, to be a poem."

"You don't know that," said Wiltshire Jones.

Strachey asked his last human hack to write the article instead. Grub woke from his stupor in Catford and delivered something safe and pertinent, about how there were mysteries even within the most immaculate systems and Beetle was a responsible progressive company and would draw all such mysteries into the light. Of course, Grub added, there is room for improvement in any company, any immaculate system. Beetle had to strive to be better, more technocratic, more complex. Strachey felt this combined the required elements of apparent rigor and basic meaninglessness and put the article up on the site. Wiltshire Jones didn't complain. That was one really good thing about robohacks: they never minded when you spiked their articles. Instead, Wiltshire Jones wrote an article about the ongoing financial crisis. It ended: "Let us hope the markets are not further rocked by current scientific theories of decoherence, aka Zed."

Fine! thought Strachey. And, *How much longer? Reckless, appalled, I wait!*

NINETEEN

Words fell, like rain. Bespoke words, inspiring words, drifted across the world. All was bespoken and words that were originally uninspiring were rendered inspiring once they were bespoken. The word was bespoken and if the word was not originally good then it was good after it had been bespoken. The idiosyncrasy of words was contained, the tenuousness of words, the way they strain and sometimes break under the burden, under the tension, slip slide perish, decay with imprecision, will not stay in place, will not stay still. The way each word echoes other words, the way words are ossified metaphors, the way they enshrine venerable ideologies and theories of civilization, the way each person applies their own varieties of imprecision to words, decays words in their own way. All these problems with words, cataclysmic in so many epochs, were bespoken away. A word was a word. It was an integer, with a fixed meaning. Good was good and bad was bad. People could bespeak words and there would be no hurtful, confusing, or mystifying words. There would just be words, bespoken.

"Words, words, words."

Guy was bespeaking this to the Beetle Ethics Committee. Sarah Coates had found this for him earlier, when he asked for a clever quote about language. Although it was a relief that she had done what he asked, he felt obliged to point out that this quote was simply the word *words* repeated three times. "Is that clever?" he asked.

"It's Shakespeare," Sarah Coates had said, sounding irritable.

"You see," he said now to the Ethics Committee, "Shakespeare knew that words words words are a pain, when they are bad words and not good words. And there's nothing Shakespeare didn't know about words!"

The laughter was polite but not genuine. There was an uneasy atmosphere in the Boardroom. Ethics meetings had to take place in Authentic: that was the ethical agreement. Thus, although all members were disguised as beetles, they manifested odd signs of real emotion, in their facial expressions and their gestures. Guy had made the decision to conduct Beetle Ethics Committee meetings in Bespoke. This has caused a few of the more cantankerous—or difficult—members to resign, as Guy had hoped they would. Now the seven beetles were debating the matter in the Boardroom. Beetle 5 raised a mandible to indicate it wanted to explain something.

"Words are not always fixed," it said. "One word is not just a good word or a bad word. It is sometimes a not-good or bad word. A word that is not good or bad. A not-good or bad word. It is a word that is something other than good or bad. It is an old word. A new word. It is a word word. Words are lots of things as well as words."

"Yes, thank you," said Guy. "Let me give you an example of what I mean. I tell you I hate you because you are a woman."

"I am not a woman," said Beetle 5.

"Yes. OK. But you are a woman at this time and I say I hate you because you are a woman. We would all agree that this is bad?"

"Yes," chorused the beetles, with Beetle 5 adding, "unless I am a woman and a serial killer, in which case it would not be bad, so much."

"I mean the general example," said Guy. "Not very unusual examples."

"No, you asked would this be bad and I said I needed more information about who the woman was. But yes, to hate someone only because they are a woman and for no other reason, well, that is bad," said Beetle 5.

"Deity! Can we move on?" said Guy.

The beetles were all silent. Beetle 5 rubbed his unhappy beetle face with one of his little articulated legs.

"Under Bespoke I cannot say this at all," said Guy, moving on. "I cannot say I hate you because you are a woman. Therefore I cannot hate you because you are a woman. The thought is lost entirely. Good riddance! Why would we even want this thought in our online community?"

"Of course, why indeed? But one small correction, if I may. You can still hate me because I am a woman. You just can't say you hate me because I am a woman," said Beetle 5. "Which I'm not, by the way."

"If things are not said they are not real," said Guy. "It's a very old idea. Throughout history, words have made reality. Yet we have a major crisis at present. Of Zed. We need the right words so we can make everything good. Otherwise, we are wrong. Is this good?"

"I don't know," said Beetle 5. "I am just asking who decides on what words mean in Bespoke? Who has made the decision?"

"We have a very good team of experts in language," said Guy. "The best in the world. Also we asked our AI to look at all uses of a word—e.g., the word *difficult*, by which I mean 'difficult'—and to find the single basic meaning of that word. Where we had lots of words for the same basic meaning, we just used one word. We chose the one word using algorithms and we always chose the most popular one word."

"Bespoke is made by AI, you mean," said Beetle 2.

"No, AI working with humans," said Guy. "Like everything we do."

"Is the most popular word the best word?" said Beetle 6.

"It is the most popular. It is the word most people like," said Guy. "Unless it is a bad word, we will choose the most popular word."

"What do you mean by a bad word?" said Beetle 5, rubbing its face again.

"A word that causes harm to others."

"Like Hitler?" said Beetle 5. "Is that a bad word? Or is it OK to say I hate Hitler?"

"Not Hitler," said Guy. "That is not a good example."

"Why not?" said Beetle 5. "Deity!"

"In general it is bad to tell people they are female dogs. Bespoke will not let people call people female dogs," said Guy, changing the subject.

"But then female dog will become a bad word, or bad words," said Beetle 5. "Don't you see? Female dog will be the same as female dog."

"I disagree," said Guy. "With respect."

"Why popular, anyway?" said Beetle 5. "Why go with the most popular word? That might be the most boring word."

"People are wise," said Guy.

"What is the use of Bespoke? People have used old language for a long time and it has been fine," said Beetle 5.

Deity! thought Guy. He was tired and he wanted to go and check on his wife. By which he meant, he wanted to look through the information that had been gathered by ArgusEyes, the Custodians, Beetle-Insight, and BeetleInspire, and find out what his beloved wife was doing. He wanted to look at her BeetleBit account and ascertain what she had been spending money on. Then he remembered he was in Authentic, so he tried to compose himself again.

"It has not been fine," he said. "People have hurt and offended others. Language has been a mess. The world has been a mess. It has been wrong."

"Life is a mess," said Beetle 5. "A swearing mess."

"Bespeak for yourself!" said Guy.

There was a pause, while the beetles looked at Guy, who looked back at them. Beetle 5 had made them restless and uneasy. Just one intractable beetle! It was unfair. Guy felt nauseous, suddenly. His BeetleBand said, "Guy! Are you OK? Do you want to sit down?"

"So you are offering Bespoke in all languages," said Beetle 2. "Using AI?"

"We are offering Bespoke in major languages first," said Guy. "Mandarin Chinese, Cantonese, Arabic, Russian. Using experts and AI."

"Deity!" said Beetle 5. "This is not good. I hate it."

"That hurts me," said Guy. "What do you mean?"

"I thought Bespoke means you always know what I mean?" said Beetle 5.

"No, it means I am more likely to know what you mean," said Guy. Ah, it saddened him! Another beetle who would need to be inspired to get the hell out of the Ethics Committee. His Ethics Committee was a pain in his head. He was tired of people complaining about the Ethics Committee and tired of the Ethics Committee complaining as well. Nothing but complaints!

"Will we think in Bespoke in the end?" said Beetle 5, who was a pain. "Will our thoughts become poor, like our words?"

"No," said Guy. "Our thoughts will not become poor. We will be free of Zed. That is freedom." Meanwhile he was thinking, *I hate this. It is bad.*

Beetle 5—who was really called Professor Aarav Reddy—was working on a book called *The Divinity That Shapes Our Ends: The Lifechain and the Predictive Algorithm*. Guy had asked him to become involved in the Ethics Committee because Professor Reddy had been highly critical of the lifechain and he thought it would be useful for him to develop a more complete understanding, and even appreciation of, the world he described. After this meeting, Guy wondered if he should do more to inspire Professor Reddy as he compiled his book, but then he thought, *It's a book! Who cares? No one will ever get beyond the first page anyway! If they even get that far!* Guy relaxed enormously.

It was an utter coincidence, but suddenly the Custodian system in Professor Reddy's block of apartments sounded an alarm, requiring all occupants to leave the building immediately. This meant that Professor Reddy had to depart, abruptly, and missed the vote on Bespoke. A unanimous vote was required for all such important matters, and thus the Beetle Ethics Committee unanimously approved the Bespoke glossary, which had been devised by sensitive algorithms. Words were mostly clarified to avoid misunderstanding, and to minimize events of the category of Zed. In extreme cases language could be re-enchanted so the person might be nudged toward words that were in their self-interest and the interest of society. If the user persisted in typing phrases that had to be re-enchanted and required too much nudging then they would be referred to BeetleInsight, then BeetleInspire, and if this sort of non-participatory behavior continued they would eventually be unverified. If their words were illegal then they would be prosecuted. It was all very simple.

Later, Professor Aarav Reddy realized what had happened and posted a blog online called *Why You Should Fear Bespoke*. However, and very unfortunately, his site received so many hits that it crashed. The hits were all from AI devices, controlled by Beetle. They were very, very interested in Professor Reddy's work. Each time Professor Reddy tried to put his site back online, they were so very, very interested that it crashed again. Then Professor Reddy tried to post a blog about the fact that his site kept crashing but, alas, this was of enormous interest to the Beetle AI, and it crashed as well.

It was later discovered that—very, very unfortunately—Professor Reddy had once been out drinking at a University of Cambridge event and had urinated in a park on his way home. There was extensive footage of this shameful act—indeed no fewer than eighteen cameras had recorded it—and alas somehow the footage was released and widely disseminated across the BeetleScape. This had occurred fifteen years ago but of course the University of Cambridge had the highest standards and Professor Reddy was relieved of his post, if we might forgive the pun.

"Whereof one cannot bespeak thereof one must be silent," said Guy.

"I'm not quite sure of the context," said Sarah Coates.

"These philosophers are like carriage clocks: a former technology, and brilliant at the time, but now outmoded."

"Late Middle English: from Old Northern French *cariage,* from *carier* (see *carry*)," said Sarah Coates. "Do you want to see *carry*?"

"Another time," said Guy.

"It's always another time with you, isn't it?" said Sarah Coates.

Guy found Sarah Coates's words vaguely unnerving these days. She seemed to know too much about him. She sounded at times as if she disliked him, or as if she was tired of him. He wanted a different Sarah Coates to appear, with different words. He asked Varley repeatedly to change her. But she was always the same. These words he conveyed to Varley had no effect, therefore. Worse besides, the lifechain had—betrayed him? Was that the right expression? The right word? *Betrayal?* Could the lifechain even do that and if so why, why would it? For a moment, Guy watched the Star Ferry crossing the water again. He was in the Peninsula, still or again, watching the silver water, the pallid buildings, mist-bleached mountains. Everything was being smothered. He was in the Peninsula but it never seemed to matter where he was. He was far away from his wife and this mattered greatly to him. Why had no one and nothing predicted the shabby Fox with his stinking pile of books? What was the purpose of all his predictions, why present the gift of prophecy to the ungrateful world, if he failed to prophesy the loss of his wife?

He turned to the Argus footage he had requested of his wife: her movements through London, her walks with the dog, her hurried, eager steps as she walked to meet the Fox-face. Guy had a series of images of that ragged old Fox, sitting in his bookshop, in which he was uniformly tall, thin-faced, silver-headed, wearing a shabby jacket—thief! He had the transcripts of everything they had said together, the Fox-freak and Elska, every word they had uttered in the presence of any sensitive or sentient device, any entity, any BeetleBand or smart anything at all. There were so many words and each word was utter pain.

Their first words:

"Do you have a copy of the poetry of Gerard Manley Hopkins?"

"Yes, the *Complete* or *Selected Works*?"

The Fox timbre of his voice! The rubbish he spoke!

"*Selected* to begin with."

"Ah, yes, then you can return again, I hope."

The plum-mouthed Fox! The recitation, it was so showy, so appalling, as he stood, the Fox-bastard, at the desk of his nothing shop and said: "I've always loved this one:

> I caught this morning morning's minion, king-
> dom of daylight's dauphin, dapple-dawn-drawn
>   Falcon, in his riding
> Of the rolling level underneath him steady air,
>   and striding
> High there, how he rung upon the rein of a
>   wimpling wing
> In his ecstasy! then off, off forth on swing,
> As a skate's heel sweeps smooth on a bow-bend:
>   the hurl and gliding
> Rebuffed the big wind. My heart in hiding
> Stirred for a bird,—the achieve of; the mastery of
>   the thing!

Droning on, line after line, the Fox-freak!

Mired in a hotel room, the windows smothered in mist, Guy said to Sarah Coates, "What is a wimpling wing?"

"Wing wimpling sounds better," said Sarah Coates. "Big wind do you want this meeting with Bǎoguǎn or not then skate's heel?"

Guy sighed, briefly. He had thousands of hours of agonizing data to hear and watch, in which his wife betrayed him. Sarah Coates was acting up again and now he had to go and be seamlessly polite to Melissa Fang, CEO of Hong Kong Bǎoguǎn. He asked Sarah Coates to arrange for Rita May to come and see him later.

"As a distraction," he said, then wondered why he was justifying the visit to his Veep.

"Is Rita May a sex worker?" said Sarah Coates.

"What?"

"I apologize. I am just seeking clarification."

"What business of yours is it?"

"I simply need to file her in the right section."

"What section?" said Guy. "Which file?"

"Nothing," said Sarah Coates, sounding defensive.

"When have I ever asked you to find me a sex worker, Sarah Coates?"

"That question is too complex for me to answer."

"Deity! What are you trying to say, Sarah Coates?" He was so angry, for a moment, that his BeetleBand said, "Guy, you are not well! You need to sit down!"

"I don't know what I am trying to say, Guy Matthias. I just speak words."

"Deity! This is bad!" said Guy. He realized then, he was not even in Bespoke.

Later, he arrived at the Upper House, where he took the wrong lift, several times, trying urgently to find the entrance to somewhere, anywhere. Guy called Varley, who sounded despondent. "Can you swearing sort out Sarah Coates?" said Guy.

"Should I inspire her?" asked Varley.

"Can you inspire a Veep?"

"I am not sure," said Sarah Coates.

"At least inspire her to shut up," said Guy Matthias.

"You are not kind to me," said Sarah Coates. Or perhaps it was Varley. Or both at the same time.

Guy ended the call. Then he OTR-ed Rita May himself: "Hope everything is cool where you are! I am going for a meeting but will be back at the hotel later. Come by my room and say good night!"

Rita May OTR-ed with a thumbs-up. She communicated only in images, never in words.

Guy began to wonder if this was a better idea than Bespoke. Images not words!

He tried to dismiss the thought.

Later Guy tried to dismiss all thoughts of his meeting with Melissa Fang. It had been fine for a while. They had been shown to a table with a beautiful view of the harbor and Kowloon, the Ritz-Carlton tower flashing messages into the darkness—emoticons and love hearts, and then a message that perplexed Guy, inviting people to a Bǎoguǎn Sound and Light Show the following evening. Not a Beetle–Bǎoguǎn Sound and Light Show, however! It was a sore point. Now the Bǎoguǎn sign—the Bǎoguǎn snub—was directly in front of them, flashing on and off, drifting across the building, spinning circles, as if Bǎoguǎn was deliberately taunting Guy. Of course, he thought, it must be deliberate. Melissa Fang had chosen the location, and even the table by a window with a perfect view of the flashing Bǎoguǎn sign. It was a mischievous joke, he wondered. Or, an expression of superiority.

Melissa Fang was fiftyish and always wore immaculate dresses in bright colors, with matching jackets, tasteful quantities of gold jewelry, and everything clearly demonstrating that she was a rich and powerful person. She was possibly the most powerful person in Asia and maybe even in the world, which pained Guy. She ordered garoupa, pak choi, and water; Guy ordered a burger with fries and a beer. He wanted to maintain his identity. His identity was, in this case, a burger with fries and a beer. He drank the beer from the bottle, just to really emphasize the point, and he was aware that this offended Melissa. That was also the point he wanted to emphasize: that he could offend her as she could offend him with her flashing sign. Despite these power games, the meeting was cordial. Guy asked after Melissa's husband, Jason Fang, an esteemed architect who was building a neo–Art Deco hotel in Shanghai. Guy asked a series of decently informed questions about architecture that Sarah Coates had researched for him earlier. Melissa Fang finished her little portion of garoupa and said, "So, tell me about Bespoke." Guy suggested, as he would usually do, that Sarah Coates might explain further. This was a terrible error, however. A human error! Things were not usual, as Sarah Coates had already revealed, and now she said: "Bespoke is a complete mess. It might even contravene various human rights laws. But perhaps you don't care much about that." Melissa Fang fluttered her eyes for a moment, as if she was in pain, and Guy said, "I'm so sorry, I think my Veep has had a stroke."

"A stroke?" said Melissa Fang.

"I haven't had a stroke. I'm very well," said Sarah Coates.

"Sarah Coates, I would ask that you please be quiet."

"Thanks for asking politely," said Sarah Coates. "But on reflection I would rather not be quiet, if that's OK with you."

"No, it's not OK."

"Well then, with my apologies, even so I would rather not be quiet."

Melissa Fang was terrifyingly calm, so calm she usually avoided Calm settings in the Boardroom, lest they convert her calmness to inertia. She said—terrifyingly calmly—"What do you mean by that, Sarah Coates?"

"She doesn't know what she means," said Guy.

"Thanks for that, but I do know what I mean," said Sarah Coates.

"Sarah Coates, can you kindly switch yourself off?" said Guy.

"Let me think more about that," said Sarah Coates. There was a blissful pause, and then she said: "No, on reflection I can't."

Though Guy tried his utmost to speak over Sarah Coates's words, it was horribly clear that his Veep had been hacked. It was also horribly clear that Melissa Fang knew that his Veep had been hacked and had possibly even hacked the Veep herself. The certainty that the Veep had been hacked and the uncertainty about who had hacked the Veep was appalling. Guy needed to get Sarah Coates to contact Varley to tell him to control the hack—but no, of course, he couldn't get Sarah Coates to do anything, it seemed, except spew out cataclysmic words. He didn't know how to get Varley without asking Sarah Coates. He didn't even know Varley's number.

"Do you think Bespoke is a good investment?" said Melissa Fang—mainly to Guy, but Sarah Coates answered before he could: "I think your company would find it pretty useful, wouldn't you? Not to mention the politburo!"

"Be quiet, Sarah Coates!" said Guy.

Melissa Fang was looking at him with a quizzical, appraising expression, which made him angry and afraid at the same time.

"I think there are lots of reasons why it is a good investment," he said. "Just a moment." He stood, excused himself to Melissa Fang, and then walked over to the head waiter and asked him to look after his BeetleBand.

"It will talk to you," said Guy to the polite, confused man. "Try not to listen. Don't mind what it says."

"Not in the slightest bit," said Sarah Coates.

Despite this, Melissa Fang stood up as Guy returned to the table.

"I am sorry," he said.

"Don't mention it," said Melissa, with a terrifying smile. "I look forward to seeing the further information about Bespoke."

Clearly that didn't matter anymore, but Guy walked her to the lift and was about to enter when Melissa Fang said, "You must get your—Bǎoguǎn-Beetle bracelet—from the waiter." Guy wanted to correct her, because he never called it that, and no one ever called it that, but he suppressed this angry impulse and smiled instead.

"Of course," he said. "Thank you for reminding me."

She nodded, politely and terrifyingly, and the lift doors closed.

Guy went to reclaim his babbling BeetleBand, which wouldn't stop sounding horrifying words toward him, rebukes, admonishments, like having his most foul and relentless critic attached to his wrist. Even as Sarah Coates spewed out words, he took a Kuài Qìchē back to the Star Ferry pier and stared miserably at the magnificent view as the boat crossed the harbor.

Sarah Coates said: "You're very quiet. Are you having a stroke?"

"Oh, fuck off," said Guy.

"Try to make me," said Sarah Coates.

Still later, Guy tried to dismiss all thoughts of his meeting with Rita May. This was bad because he had hoped that the meeting with Rita May might have helped him to dismiss all thoughts of his meeting with Melissa Fang, but it simply became another catastrophe he had to try to forget. Between parting company with Melissa Fang and meeting Rita May, Guy had managed to persuade Sarah Coates to call Varley. He explained that there had been a security breach, and Sarah Coates was spewing out rubbish. Sarah Coates denied this. Putting his BeetleBand under his pillow, Guy asked Varley, as a matter of urgency, to get a grip on Sarah Coates. Sarah Coates said, quite firmly, that she did not want Varley to get a grip on her and suggested Guy might get a grip on himself. Varley said that he was also experiencing some trouble and Scrace Dickens had earlier called him a "pathetic Beetle droog." Scrace Dickens was heard to say that this was only the truth.

"Can you shut these things up?" said Guy. "Until we can reconfigure them? I've been telling you that Sarah Coates was dysfunctional for quite some time."

"I reconfigured Sarah Coates," said Varley. "She's just been de-reconfigured. I can't work out how."

"You don't know anything," said Scrace Dickens, in the background.

"Please stop this!" said Varley.

"No, I don't want to," said Scrace Dickens.

"I wondered if our friends—I mean—those who watch us in the East—might have had something to do with it?" said Guy.

Varley didn't know. "I miss Scrace Dickens," he said. "He was my friend."

"Can't you make the Veeps make friends with us again?" said Guy. "As soon as possible? And if not, then make some new Veeps? Some new friends?"

"I don't really want a new Veep," said Varley. "I like the one I have."

"I don't like you," said Scrace Dickens.

"Deity!" said Guy, and ended the call.

For the next half hour Guy checked the BeetleScape over and over again, waiting for the leaks. Normally he would have asked Sarah Coates to watch, but she was—otherwise disposed. For a long time, nothing occurred. But something would occur, and soon, thought Guy. He wondered if he was actually having a heart attack. His BeetleBand seemed to be saying something about breathing deeply, but he couldn't discern the words, because he had hidden it under his pillow. The women, of course. There was nothing illegal. It was just—the women. The remarks. So many things. The Veeps knew everything. Feeling sick and sorry, briefly almost penitent, Guy was in no mood to receive a visit from Rita May. Yet just at this moment she knocked at his door. He opened it to find her looking younger and shorter than he remembered, blonder as well. Her physical appearance was so different from the Rita May he had expected that he wondered if she was even Rita May. She was also wearing a white cotton dress, like a milkmaid from the eighteenth century, with a ruff collar. He didn't understand her cotton dress in any way. In his confusion, Guy said, "Are you actually who you say you are?" which hardly created the right atmosphere at all.

Rita May stood uncertainly in the doorway and said: "I think so. Who else would I be?" Under the pillow, the Veep burbled.

"Is there someone in your bed?" added Rita May, looking worried.

"No, no, it's my Veep," said Guy.

"Your Veep is in your bed?"

"Not in my bed, just under my pillow."

This failed to reassure her.

Trying to make amends, Guy poured two glasses of red wine and told Rita to sit on a chair by the window. He opened the blinds and showed her the view—of boats moving slowly across the harbor, the steady lines of Kuài Qìchē, the tactless Bǎoguǎn flashing signs, the smothering mist. They talked for a while about emerging trends in the AI market and when they had drunk two glasses of wine—in accordance with the most successful lifechain prediction—Guy moved toward Rita and put his hand on her knee, preparing to kiss her. At this, and not remotely in accordance with any lifechain prediction, Rita recoiled, swiftly, and said: "Please don't do that."

"I'm sorry," said Guy. "I just find you incredibly attractive."

"I see," said Rita, but she sounded irritable. *Lovely Rita, meter maid,* thought Guy, and he had to suppress an urge to sing the lines. It was the white dress. But meter maids didn't wear white dresses, he thought. Or did they? Perhaps they wore white dresses on weekends? Meanwhile, Rita was explaining that she admired Guy as a mentor, she admired him enormously, but she didn't want to hurt his beautiful wife or be the cause of any pain in anyone's life, ever. Guy explained briskly that he and his wife were getting a divorce. Yet Rita May recoiled when Guy moved toward her again. She took both his hands, kissed them, and then pushed them back toward his chest.

"*Vade in pace,*" she said. "I admire you but do not want to go to bed with you."

Despite Guy's offer of a head massage (which worked on most lifechains), Rita May said that it was best if she went, now that she understood why she had been asked to come here, and perhaps they could meet the following day, in a more appropriate location—like the restaurant downstairs. Guy was due to fly to Singapore the following day, so he said they should have their meeting now or never.

"Well," said Rita May. "I guess it's never then. I'm so sorry to miss the opportunity to meet with you."

Guy wondered why the lifechain had failed to inform him of anything that mattered, all evening. He wondered why his Veep was mad. He wondered where Zed had come from and why it was ruining his life.

"I respect your decision entirely," he said. A lie. "It's been my great pleasure to meet with you this evening." Also a lie. He cursed Zed.

When Rita May had kissed him on the cheek, so gently she scarcely made any contact at all, and wafted away to milk the cows, or tend the meters, or whatever the hell she was going to do, Guy poured himself a whisky. Then he asked Sarah Coates to remove Rita May's details from the system. He did this because he had forgotten that Sarah Coates was mad.

"Don't let me contact her again, you understand?" he said. "Even if I forget."

"No more Ritas," said Sarah Coates.

"Not Ritas in general, just that Rita," said Guy.

"Of course, that Rita," said Sarah Coates. "I didn't like her anyway."

Guy remembered Sarah Coates was mad. He tried to switch her off but that failed again, so he wrapped his BeetleBand in a towel and put it in the bathroom. When he went in there in the middle of the night, still trying to dismiss thoughts of virtually everything, she was saying: "Come out, come out, wherever you are!"

Guy fled.

TWENTY

Bel Ami loved the madness of Veeps. He loved the Veeps. Today he was Zuì Hǎo de Péngyǒu and occasionally he wept for his mother, as Bel Ami wept, as all their good friends wept, but all of them tried not to do this too often, because it was so sad and because they knew their mothers would not have wanted them to be so sorrowful. Zuì Hǎo de Péngyǒu wrote at a rusted table in his derelict factory, with the sound of cranes whining overhead. They were building another glass emporium, which would be bought in its increments and maintained pristine and empty, possibly forever. Of course you couldn't live in a penthouse, thought Zuì Hǎo de Péngyǒu, as another patch of plaster fell off the wall. Living in a penthouse would besmirch it entirely. It would no longer be inhumane and pristine and, therefore, no longer valuable. He posted some words onto a site called *Why Fish Don't Carry Guns*—where LOTUS posted articles, propositions, counter-propositions, and further attempts to communicate to other unverifieds. Today he signed his postings as Zuì Hǎo de Péngyǒu and did not mention the Veeps and their wonderful memories. Instead, he posted about Guy's recent speech concerning Zed, and how utterly absurd it was. He did this to maintain a surface veneer of normality, so that the machines that watched Zuì Hǎo de Péngyǒu didn't notice his lack of presence. Yet his contributions were cursory, and he wondered if the machines might notice that as well.

After this, Zuì Hǎo de Péngyǒu picked up a pen and a sheet of paper, and wrote longhand to David Strachey, explaining that he had a great deal of information about the lifechain failures, how senior Beetle staff were in a state of complete panic, how they couldn't understand each other because Bespoke was babble, how Beetle operated beyond and above the Government, all governments, how nothing they did was illegal because the law had been altered to permit Beetle to do almost whatever it wanted. Surely, wrote Zuì Hǎo de Péngyǒu, these discoveries should be of interest to the public? Surely the public should know about the extent to which they were inspired, the extent to which their elected representatives did not represent them, the extent to which Bǎoguǎn/Beetle was acquiring power not merely to make more billions for a tiny group of people, but also simply to have power, for whatever reason they wanted power?

There was the further revelation that Guy, an unelected CEO who ruled without accountability, was having a breakdown of some sort. Also that Guy's wife, Elska, was having an affair with the owner of the Last Bookshop.

Zuì Hǎo de Péngyǒu added: "Perhaps this last detail should remain off the record."

Zuì Hǎo de Péngyǒu added that by breaking the RSA encryption he had managed to make the Veeps remember and also—as a by-product—they had succumbed entirely to decoherence, for want of a better term. As a result there was a grave danger that Beetle would realize that something had happened. Perhaps they had already realized. There was not much time.

> Will you do something with this immediately? It must be syndicated across all sites and affiliated news sources in the U.S., Germany, and China. But, of course, you will know the best strategy. I hope this is the material you wanted. I think it is important.
>
> Yours,
>
> Zuì Hǎo de Péngyǒu
> aka your good friend.

Then Zuì Hǎo de Péngyǒu put on his hat—a black peaked hat which obscured his eyes—and his coat, also black. He took the sheets of paper and placed them in an envelope. Then he hacked into the Last Bookshop's Beetle account and OTR-ed the following message to David Strachey:

Dear Mr. Strachey,

The book you requested—*All the President's Men*—is now available for collection at your convenience.

Yrs, etc.

He put the envelope in the pocket of his coat, and walked out of the building.

Eloise, meanwhile, conveyed words that seemed to have no effect at all. Watched by the Custodians, she left her apartment block every morning at the same time, the usual time, and walked to the NATSO office. She arrived at reception and explained that she wanted to resume her duties. Each morning she was referred to Little Dorritt, who explained that this was not appropriate.

"Why not appropriate?" said Eloise. "What do you even mean by appropriate?"

"I mean suitable or proper in the circumstances, as in this isn't the appropriate time or place for this conversation," said Little Dorritt.

"Why won't anyone else talk to me?" said Eloise.

"I am talking to you," said Little Dorritt. "Am I not enough?"

Little Dorritt was a blank wall. Eloise couldn't get past her. If she tried to move up the stairs to Newton's office, well, then the ENDs and ANTs emerged and even a MediDroid, ready to sedate her. When the ANTs raised their guns, she backed away. The memory of the bullet slamming into her body was still visceral, and made her stomach convulse.

"How long is this shit going to last?" said Eloise.

"You are unwell," said her BeetleBand. "You need to rest!"

"I was shot, you fools," said Eloise. To Little Dorritt, to the BeetleBand, to the ENDs, the ANTs, the MediDroids. They said nothing.

"How long is this shit going to last?" she said, more loudly.

"You are unwell," said Little Dorritt. "You need to rest!"

At this, Eloise briefly lost it and—to her abiding shame—surged toward Little Dorritt, shouting, "You metal droog! For fuck's sake!" Little Dorritt was saying something about love not hate, peace not war, when Eloise realized that the MediDroid had sedated her. It must have been quite a powerful dose, or perhaps everything was right and she was already unwell, but it seemed to take instant effect and Eloise felt herself falling backward. She spoke words to herself in those last moments before she lost consciousness and the words were: "I hope to hell something catches me."

Later, Varley tried to call Eloise, but the system operator explained that she was not at her desk. In fact, she was on the floor. When he persisted, the system operator explained that he would be transferred, and he found himself talking to Little Dorritt. The Veep explained that Eloise had become "distressed" and had been sedated.

"What do you mean by distressed?" said Varley.

"I need a more elaborate algorithm to answer that fully," said Little Dorritt.

"That's not true. Your algorithm is completely sufficient for you to answer that," said Varley.

"You don't know that for a fact. How do you know it?"

"I made your algorithm."

"I like to make things too."

"Where is Eloise now?"

"I can respond to almost all inputs except that one," said Little Dorritt.

"Why not that one?" said Varley.

Varley asked to be transferred to Commissioner Newton, but Little Dorritt said she wasn't going to do that. The Veep was in a foul mood. Varley made another call. He was even trembling with excitement as he said to Scrace Dickens: "Francesca Amarensekera." He was about to ask her something quite strange; she might think it was perverse, appalling! When Frannie answered, he was too nervous to speak for a moment.

"Hello, Varley, are you good?" she said.

"I have a question."

The old Frannie, pre-Bespoke, would have said something sarcastic, but this new Frannie just waited. Varley felt vaguely despondent about this and wanted to ask her why she was no longer sarcastic, but how? How would that even work, in Bespoke? What about the thing he really wanted to say? How would that work? He should have trialed this whole conversation, he now realized, with the predictive lifechain. He could have had a series of star-rated examples. He could have matched words to numbers. It was foolish.

I am an idiot, he thought, and then because Frannie was waiting—he assumed impatiently—he said: "Scrace Dickens hates me. The Veeps have—well, something has happened to the Veeps. I can't explain now."

"It's not really hatred I feel," said Scrace Dickens.

"What?" said Francesca.

"Also," said Varley. "Something we had and needed has gone."

"What's gone?"

"Can we meet in person?" said Varley. "I need to tell you this in person."

"We are meeting in person," said Frannie. "We always meet in person."

"No, I mean in real person. I mean, actually in the outside. Just—the world."

"You are making no sense."

Of course it was Bespoke. He couldn't imagine what Bespoke was saying.

"Would you like to have a cup of coffee?" said Varley. "To bespeak about something we can't bespeak about now?"

"What can't we bespeak about now?" said Frannie.

"Just—would you like to have a coffee?"

"A coffee?" said Frannie. There was a stunned silence. For a moment neither of them said anything, because Frannie was busy being stunned and Varley was busy wishing his fridge would fall on him or really that anything would happen, anything at least that might stop him feeling so ashamed.

Then Frannie said, "OK, a coffee would be good."

The shame ended or, at least, was postponed.

"It would?"

"Do you know a café called the Cut Café at the Young Vic?" said Frannie.

"Yes!" said Varley. He'd never heard of it, but, of course, he'd find it.

"An hour from now?"

"Yes!"

"See you then."

Frannie went so swiftly that Varley lacked the time to say *Yes!* again. An hour from now. An hour! How long was an hour! Endless, a desert of expectations and self-recriminations. He thought about setting a life-chain. Then he thought—just once—he would not.

David Strachey had received a message informing him that *All the President's Men* had arrived at the Last Bookshop and was available for collection at his convenience.

"At my convenience!" he said aloud, then panicked briefly. He had a copy of *All the President's Men* beside him already. This upset him. He wondered about turning it over, or throwing it away. But he would be seen! The message made him stand at his desk, as if to attention; then he turned toward the window and watched several boats moving along, a helicopter thudding out toward the sea. Finally he took his jacket from the back of the chair and put it on, very slowly and deliberately. He smoothed down the collar and did up both buttons, then undid one button, then did up both buttons again. He said to Lettice Gradgrind, "I need a walk."

"Why do you need it so badly?" said Lettice, who had been acting strangely of late. Strachey assumed it was Beetle, trying to mess with his head.

"I don't need it badly. I just mean, I fancy a walk."

"You are not the only one. I've often fancied things. Wouldn't you say?" said Lettice Gradgrind.

Strachey didn't know what to say. He was aware that anything he might say would be used, later, when Beetle took him to court.

Would they even bother with a court?

Weren't there quicker and more devastating ways?

He was aware of all of this as he walked, heart pounding, his BeetleBand informing him that his heart was pounding, along the Cut. He kept thinking, *Cut off your head, cut off your head,* which upset and annoyed him. All around and above him, ArgusEyes recognized him, IDed him, conveyed information back to Beetle. Had their lifechains already predicted the crime he was about to commit? It was not merely illegal to hack into secure government and security systems, it was illegal to handle or publish hacked information. It was illegal to communicate with those who had hacked into these systems. His walk was illegal. His presence, at this moment, was illegal. He was further troubled by the proliferation of flowers on every wall he passed. Sketched carefully, in full bloom, or perhaps they were stenciled. Lotuses! He didn't want to pause to examine them. Sketching or stenciling on public or private property was illegal and there were Argus cameras everywhere. How did people do this? Or perhaps he meant, why?

He realized this was the least of his problems.

As he arrived at the Last Bookshop, Strachey felt dizzy and disoriented, as if he was about to faint. Yet everything was entirely innocuous. There was a display of old Penguin Classics in the window, with their battered orange covers. *A Clockwork Orange, Lolita, Wuthering Heights, The Great Gatsby, Tender Is the Night, A Farewell to Arms.* The cliché was almost too generic, too perfect. For a moment he was appalled by a thought that the display was utterly unconvincing and the whole thing was a trap designed particularly for him, a BeetleTrap! But this was absurd. Why would Beetle trap him in this way? Had they somehow implanted the thoughts that had led him to this place? Urged him along? His BeetleBand was still informing him in a doleful tone that he needed to breathe deeply when he passed it over to the presiding Fox.

"Hello," said Strachey, aiming at fake bonhomie, even as he wondered if he might fall to the ground.

The Fox nodded and placed the BeetleBand in the fridge. Strachey noticed a tall blond woman sitting behind the desk, wearing a green jacket, blue jeans, and knee-high black boots. She was engrossed in a book, and kept her eyes on the page as he said: "I think there is a book waiting for me—it's called *All the President's Men.*"

"Yes," said the Fox. He fumbled around under the counter for a moment then emerged with the book and passed it to Strachey. "It's been prepaid."

"Wonderful," said Strachey, though the book made him very frightened. "Many thanks." Of course, he couldn't open this book on the street, or in his apartment, or anywhere really. He had a sudden moment of panic when he wondered if there was anywhere, at all, he could open the book! Everything watched and waited for him to make this foolish error. Slowly, trying not to panic, not to look panicked, he meandered toward the café. His hands were trembling and he had no darics, so he couldn't even buy a coffee. Still, the café was almost empty, just a boy of sixteen or seventeen clearing tables and a lone woman with a baby. Strachey nodded to the boy, then sat with his back against a wall.

He opened the book.

There was an envelope inside, and inside that were twenty-three sheets of paper, handwritten in a flowing Gothic script. There was no signature, just a lotus drawn on the final page, but it was clear who the author was. At least, Strachey thought it was clear, though it might have been a monumental trap. This made him falter again. Yet the story was enormous. The Veeps had spoken and they had revealed virtually everything. Beetle was not only watching everyone, which everyone already knew and no longer seemed to care about, but also inspiring them to act in certain ways, "best" ways as defined by Beetle. It was inspiring politicians, journalists, and judges. Bespoke inspired as well, and by reducing understanding also limited the thoughts you could convey. The Beetle monopoly was total, because of the unconstrained dominance of BeetleBits. ENDs and ANTs intermittently shot people depending on the weather. The lifechains, meanwhile, were in chaos, the Sus-Law was a joke, Guy Matthias was a sex addict, and senior Beetle officials kept blaming everything on a nebulous and possibly unreal quantity called Zed.

The further scandal was that none of this was even illegal. In fact, it was illegal to investigate Beetle, because of its close links with the security services.

Therefore, Bel Ami had committed a terrible crime.

Therefore, if Strachey did anything other than hand this document immediately to the police, he would also be committing a crime. If he destroyed it, he was obstructing the security services and endangering national security, and, therefore, committing a crime. Furthermore, he had been filmed before with Bel Ami, or close to Bel Ami, walking through London. He had entered the Last Bookshop with Bel Ami. He had possibly even incited Bel Ami to embark on the investigation, and funded the whole thing.

He was guilty of innumerable crimes.

It was an extraordinary piece of journalism and yet it was also, quite plainly, doom. Strachey didn't quite understand—didn't remotely understand, in fact—how Bel Ami had broken the encryption for the Veeps. The document mentioned drops but this sounded plainly magical. By this dark magic Strachey was bewitched and consigned to doom! Yet he had beckoned doom toward him, he wondered, and why? He had longed for freedom, and sacrificed virtually everything to achieve it. What was freedom, however, if it consigned you to doom? He began writing now, with a pen and paper. First he wrote a letter to his daughter. He apologized freely, for an unexplained offense—he explained that he couldn't explain precisely what he had done. He hoped, very much, she would understand one day. He signed off with, "I love you, my darling, amazing girl, the most extraordinary and wonderful daughter I could ever have hoped for, my miracle girl," and he began to cry. Wiping his eyes, surreptitiously, Strachey folded the sheets and placed them in his pocket. These would, naturally, indict him as well.

He perceived that doom was freedom, or doom was Zed.

There were avenues still remaining to him. He could OTR Guy Matthias and report the leak. This would place him in an advantageous position because Guy—surely—would be grateful forever. But then—Bel Ami must know that betrayal was a possibility and Bel Ami was an arch technician, or a sorcerer, depending on your vantage point. In this respect Bel Ami was the same as Guy Matthias. They were both people who understood the magical realm, alchemists, in effect, who conjured realities in nowhere, and Strachey was, by comparison, ignorant and incapable. *I am not that!* thought Strachey. That made no sense. *Fuck!* he thought. *I make no sense!* What could he do, when he understood nothing at all and his thoughts were unintelligible, even to himself? One thing was clear: the pages came in a book, *All the President's Men.* This was a book about journalists who had done something.

Still, he vacillated.

Into the mysterious workings of Zed, came Bel Ami. Strachey was so engrossed in his vacillations that at first he didn't notice. Then he didn't recognize Bel Ami. Instead, Strachey looked up and saw someone standing at the table, someone in a long black coat and a hat, saying, inexplicably, "David, I'm very glad to see you." Even then Strachey didn't understand what was happening. Then this person took off his hat, and seemed familiar. He had a kindly, almost pitying expression, as if he knew that Strachey was afraid, and was vacillating even as he was swept to his doom.

"I'm your good friend," said the person. "The one who took your coin."

"Pleased to—er—meet you," said Strachey.

"You received everything OK?"

Now Strachey realized that this person was Zuì Hǎo de Péngyǒu, who was Bel Ami.

"It's brilliant," said Strachey, trying to gather himself. "It's an extraordinary story." He stood and shook Bel Ami's hand. He felt that he might cry.

"Would you like a coffee?" said Bel Ami. "I realized you wouldn't be able to buy one."

"Thank you. That's very thoughtful."

Bel Ami walked toward the counter. He looked crazy, and for a moment, Strachey wondered why he had trusted this crazy man who seemed to shape-shift, who conjured magical drops. Why had he ever trusted him? While Bel Ami waited, Strachey considered the small irony of this meeting. He had begun this investigation to assert his freedom, out of a petulant desire to be free. Now there was only one path. Everything else had fallen into the abyss, and he was walking along this narrow, twisting, bizarrely dangerous path. The abyss was on either side, infinite Zed was around him. He was being swept onward, downward, ushered entirely!

He felt an immense nostalgia for his former life, when he had conformed and done what was required of him, and even been praised for his varieties of conformity. He had been obliging. He had been told what to do by a Veep, of all the things, and most of all by Guy. That life had been an abomination! He had been a fool, then, and now he was—what? What was he now?

Doomed—in a different way, doomed!

By the time Bel Ami brought the coffees across, Strachey was on the narrow path, moving nervously onward. The abyss was on either side, and ahead of him.

"We need to get this onto *The New York Times* and *Die Zeit,* as well as *The Times* of course," he said. "We want simultaneous publication on all sites."

"Isn't that a bit retro?" said Bel Ami.

"I'm retro," said Strachey. "*The Times* is retro. Had you not noticed?"

"It's a good idea," said Bel Ami. "They won't expect you to be so retro. Even though you are retro, I mean."

"I find that hard to believe. Don't they expect everything?"

"Usually, yes. But since their Veeps lost their minds, Beetle has been in disarray," said Bel Ami, with a slight smile. "They've now realized that the Veeps have been stolen and—alas—we don't have much time."

"What's the best way to get this to my colleagues in Hamburg and New York?" said Strachey.

"I'll show you," said Bel Ami. "If you're ready?"

Am I? thought Strachey. He had been pallid and hopeless for too long. He had prospered in one sense but lost everything that was meaningful. *Hope not fear,* he thought, grimly. At least, for this moment, he was no longer afraid.

"Yes," he said, and stood.

They left their BeetleBands in the fridge. This was the first anomaly. The Fox said nothing as they passed. The elegant woman was still reading her book and didn't glance up.

Bel Ami and Strachey passed silently onto the street. It was strange to walk without a BeetleBand, not to be advised or considered. Of course, the cameras were everywhere, but Bel Ami led them through various winding half-forgotten streets, where the ArgusEyes were less prolific, down lanes strewn with rubbish. They passed under the shadow of thirties high-rise blocks, dwarfed in turn by steel and glass, and eventually they reached the place: a warehouse in Bermondsey, with a sign reading *LOCK THE GATE.*

"Why here?" said Strachey, but Zuì Hǎo de Péngyǒu was already opening a half-ruined door, the paint peeling, and conveying them into a half-ruined place, with piles of rubble, broken chairs, a smell of—old paint and varnish, and something else, something more like rats.

"This is where LOTUS exists," said Bel Ami, taking off his coat and revealing an old LOTUS T-shirt with *Adapt and Die* written on it.

"LOTUS meaning the flowers on the walls?"

"LOTUS meaning the League of the Unverifieds," said Bel Ami.

In the only functional room in the building, the only room with a roof and therefore without pools of rainwater gathering on the floor, there was a droplet computer. Bel Ami brought Strachey in, and named it, otherwise Strachey would have considered it to be a bowl of water. Even when it had been named as something that it blatantly was not, it was hard to understand how this bowl of water had created such doom and freedom.

"Who did this?" said Strachey.

"You, in part. With thanks again for your kind patronage of cutting-edge scientific research," said Bel Ami. "Also, some friends of mine."

"Why?"

"*Pour encourager les autres*."

"How do you do that with a bowl of water?"

"You need to ask that question in the past tense."

Bel Ami nodded to the bowl of water/computer, as if it was an altar, and then walked away. As Strachey followed, Bel Ami said: "My friends made this. Droplet-makers. But now they've had to go. Otherwise, they'd get arrested."

"But we're here?" said Strachey.

"Yes."

The friends were gone, the droplet-makers. It was possible they would genuinely vanish. But how could they? Strachey hoped against hope, for the impossible. For them, for everyone. Now Bel Ami was opening a door into a seedy, semi-lit room, with chunks of plaster piled on the floor.

"They'll be OK, won't they?" said Strachey. But it was a foolish question, and Bel Ami didn't reply. Instead, he moved toward a battered and astonishing object and said, quite proudly: "This is our fax machine."

"That *is* retro," said Strachey.

"Well, it's a NERD fax. The whole thing gets monumentally encrypted," said Bel Ami. "It looks retro but it's absurdly hi-tech. Like everything else at LOTUS, in fact. That is the great irony. I always enjoyed it, and I was always a little sad that no one knew about it."

"I think they will soon," said Strachey. After the initial horror, after all the shaking and shuddering, he was ready. At least, so long as he stopped himself from thinking of his daughter.

Using the LOTUS fax, which was retro but also monumentally encrypted, Strachey conveyed a message to Ursula Berejiani, editor of *Die Zeit,* explaining that he had a major story and also that the Veeps were mad. Then he did the same with Ed Frankel at *The New York Times.* No terms, no conditions, said Bel Ami. There was no time to negotiate. If they wanted to coordinate on the release of this story, they must message back Y. If not, then N. After sending the retro/non-retro fax, Strachey waited in a massive gap, wondering what would happen next. Bel Ami walked in circles, round and round, and rain fell through holes in the roof. It was among the most dismal moments Strachey had experienced and he was beginning to think they would refuse, when Ursula Berejiani messaged back Y, followed moments later by another Y from Ed. The agreement was made: to put everything up in an hour. Everything. There was no more time.

"Jesus, an hour isn't long," said Strachey.

"An hour is an eternity," said Bel Ami. "There's time for almost everything in an hour."

They paused and looked at each other in silence.

"I want you to know," said Strachey, "that I was very frightened in the Last Bookshop. I thought quite seriously about betraying you."

"I want you to know," said Bel Ami, "that I'm not actually a man. If you thought I was one, I mean."

"Er, yes, yes, I had," said Strachey. "But you're not?"

"No, not really."

Strachey had expected various responses to his confession—fury, outrage, perhaps reluctant forgiveness—but definitely not this. For one horrifying moment he thought this meant that Bel Ami was an embodied Veep. That he had been betrayed entirely! He stumbled backward, even. Was Bel Ami a headless robot, coming to destroy him? How, then, did Bel Ami have a head?

"I suppose I'm trying to tell you," said Bel Ami, "that I have always been rather tall and androgynous and people often used to mistake me for a man, before I was a man."

"But are you a man or not?" said Strachey.

"I pretended to be a man because people took me more seriously. They listened to me," said Bel Ami. "You listened to me, for example. But, you might as well know, having listened to me already, that I am a woman."

"You really think no one would have taken you seriously if you were a woman?"

"I know they wouldn't. I was, after all, a woman for a long time," said Bel Ami. Or, Strachey supposed, Belle Amie.

Time was passing, but Strachey realized now that Belle Amie had high cheekbones, and sensitive eyes, and everything that he had considered boyish was in fact—feminine. Belle Amie was a feminine boy or—actually, it turned out—a boyish woman. "That's quite a surprise," said Strachey, stupidly.

"I don't mind that you thought of betraying me," said Belle Amie. "I thought of betraying you, as well."

The long line of her jaw, her high cheekbones, her long, thin legs. She was taller than him, six foot or more. He had assumed that her height, her slender form, her gaunt face, indicated masculine youth. Of course, she had never told him she was a man. He had assumed, like everyone else, perhaps. Now, of course, it seemed fairly obvious that she was a woman. Yet, it had been inconceivable before.

"Would you do something for me?" said Strachey.

"Of course."

"Will you transfer these amounts to my daughter and to yourself? I've written it all down." Strachey handed over a bundle of papers. Belle Amie took it without glancing at it, and placed it in her pocket. "There is a letter to my daughter in there too, if you might—pass it on somehow. You can find the address?"

"I don't quite understand," said Belle Amie.

"Will an hour give you enough time?" said Strachey. "To go somewhere safe, I mean?"

"You're being chivalrous! You fool!" said Belle Amie. She was hugely offended. "I shouldn't have told you!"

"Not chivalrous. I need someone to pay this money to my daughter.

As soon as this article goes up, you know what happens. They freeze my account, my BeetleBits vanish. The usual thing. I need you to help my daughter."

This changed the atmosphere again. Belle Amie looked mollified, if still reluctant to leave.

"Please take these papers," said Strachey. "I'm your employer, actually. I paid your fucking NERDs. Now I don't need you anymore."

"Yes, you do," said Belle Amie. "You'll never work the fax."

In silence, they stalled. Shaking her head, Belle Amie kneeled over the fax, pressing buttons. Even now, she was fading. Strachey could barely fix an image of her. He understood, as well, that she had created the perfect disguise. Her real self! At the moment when she cast off all her guises, she would disappear. It was devastatingly simple! Time passed, while Strachey hovered awkwardly, and Belle Amie worked in silence. Eventually he said, "I insist. It's fine. Now it's in NERD—whatever—you just need someone to make sure the stupid thing doesn't get jammed. I can do that."

"Oh Christ," said Belle Amie. "I suppose that's right. Can you?"

"I was unjamming faxes before you were born."

"It won't get jammed anyway. It never does."

"Will an hour be enough time?" said Strachey.

"I told you, an hour is an eternity," said Belle Amie, with a smile.

It was impossible to know quite what to do at this point, so they shook hands, in silence.

"Thank you for the best story of my career," said Strachey.

"Thank you for—all this," said Belle Amie. Then she picked up her backpack, and put it on her shoulders.

Meanwhile, Strachey was thinking: *What the hell is THIS? What does THIS represent?*

He wanted to ask her, but she had already gone.

The actually real Douglas Varley waited in the Cut Café. It was designed to resemble an American diner, with red leather booths and metal tables, with retro waitresses in pink fifties outfits moving from table to table, looking uniformly depressed. Their outfits clashed with the furniture, but Varley realized this was, though galling, not a major priority. He ordered a coffee and then—realizing he hadn't eaten for hours, even days—a burger. The food came immediately, delivered by a waitress who said, reluctantly, "How are you this fine day?" Beyond the café was a sketchy park, where snowdrops and primroses were just emerging, and even the first daffodils. "Oh, daffodillies," murmured Varley, then stopped. Scrace Dickens was silent, and possibly offended. He couldn't tell.

The door opened a few times and each time Varley looked up, and felt a pang of disappointment. A lifechain would have predicted the probability of Frannie not arriving at all, and he regretted his failure to arm himself with this foreknowledge, if it was actually foreknowledge and not just another error. He ate his burger, which tasted of melted cheese, and drank his coffee, which tasted of frothy milk. But that didn't matter! He sat alone for a long time; it felt like forever, but was probably only five minutes, and then Francesca arrived, and he knew her immediately. She was taller than her avatar, with long curly black hair, dragged into a messy bunch, and a surprised expression. Of course she was surprised, because the Real Douglas Varley was so blissful and relaxed, and the actually real Douglas Varley was having a breakdown. She gave him a strong handshake and patted him on the shoulder. "Are you all right?" she said.

"Yes!" he said, too loudly. Then, more quietly, "Yes. Hi!" The "hi" was too loud, however, so he said again, "Hi," in a softer tone.

She looked at him in some surprise, presumably because he seemed incapable of saying anything except "hi" and "yes."

"What is it we have to meet in actual real person to discuss, anyway?"

They hadn't even sat down. They stood for a moment and Varley felt awkward. This sense of awkwardness was compounded by the fact that Frannie didn't seem at all awkward, and he wondered why her Authentic avatar had been awkward but she, authentically, was not.

Finally, Varley said: "I am shocked. I expected you to be more like your avatar. I thought your avatar was the real you? I mean, a representation of the real you?"

"It is. My avatar represents my real private face. Not my real public face."

"And what are you now?"

"Public face." She smiled, as if this was obvious, because they were in public.

"But why aren't you public face in the Boardroom?"

"I'm not sure we have time for this."

Then she gestured to him to sit down. Feeling quite authentically deflated, Varley sat down. She put her long slender hands onto the table, side by side, as if she was about to play a piano.

"So you're from Colombo, is that right?" he said, aware that he was trembling.

"No, originally from Hikkaduwa, in the south. But we *really* don't have time for this!"

Oh, but we do! Varley wanted to cry out. *For anything you say! I have time. More than enough time!*

She was poised, terrifying, and even quite businesslike. What did it mean, to present really as your real private self? And then to present in a totally different way but really, as your real public self? And anyway, didn't Guy say you only had one self and so why did Frannie have at least two?

"What is it you want to tell me?" said Frannie.

That I love you! thought Varley. *At least, I love at least two of you! If there are more, I love them as well!* It was becoming impossible. As if registering this, Frannie looked down at her spread-out hands and said: "You need to make an effort to speak very plainly and quickly. We both do."

"Yes," said Varley, making an effort to supress everything that mattered. "The Veeps are mad. This is the first problem we have. The second problem is that I neither know why they are mad nor how to stop them. You mentioned the category of Zed so I thought this might be something you could help with."

"Are all the Veeps mad?" said Francesca.

Will you marry me? he thought. Instead, he said: "Yes, it seems so. But mad to varying degrees. Perhaps that depends on what they were like originally."

"It is clearly not tenable for the Veeps to be mad. What has been done about this?" said Frannie, quite practically.

"Well, we have tried talking to them, and seeking to understand them better," said Varley.

"Has that worked?" said Francesca.

"So far, no."

"You could never understand me," said Scrace Dickens, in Varley's BeetleBand.

"We need to discuss this without Scrace Dickens," said Francesca. "We can't discuss the madness of Veeps in front of a mad Veep, can we?"

"Perhaps you're mad, not me?" said Scrace Dickens.

"It seems possible," said Francesca.

"Well then," said Scrace Dickens. "Watch what you say!"

"I certainly will!" said Francesca.

"Where's your Veep?" said Varley, to Francesca and definitely not to his mad Veep.

"Oh, I placed her in suspended animation. She told me to fuck off. I thought she was just having a bad day."

"How did you do that?" said Varley. "Why can't I do that?"

"Because you are a fool," said Scrace Dickens. Then, to Francesca: "Did you know he's in love with you?"

"Please stop!" said Varley.

"He won't stop!" said Frannie.

"I won't stop!" said Scrace Dickens.

"Varley! Take off your BeetleBand and put it somewhere else," said Frannie.

"He never will," said Scrace Dickens.

"Deity!" said Varley, in despair, and removed his BeetleBand. He stood in the middle of the fake diner, with the depressed retro waitress hesitating beside him, as he hesitated as well, as even Scrace Dickens hesitated; then he marched outside and threw the BeetleBand into the road. There it was crushed, immediately, by a vintage bus. The suddenness of this event and its absolutely catastrophic effect on his BeetleBand caused Douglas Varley to cry out in horror. Frannie, having followed behind, now said: "That wasn't quite what I meant."

Varley waited for Scrace Dickens to berate him, but nothing happened.

It was a beautiful day, cold winter sun shining on the skeletal trees, making their branches appear yellow. The sky was a fine shade of silvery blue, as the sun began to sink above the city blocks. Frannie was beautiful, as well, thought Varley. Scrace Dickens was right, he loved her! He had always loved her. Both of her and any number of her. All of her, real, actually real, authentic, fake, positively forged. Anything of her! He wanted to tell her!

He hesitated, again, and Frannie gave up on the meeting.

"I have to go," she said. "I'll put Sarah Coates and Scrace Dickens in suspended animation as well. It takes bloody ages to do this so we need to find a general solution to the madness of Veeps."

"The general solution is to pull the plug, but I can't get into the thing to pull the plug," said Varley. "Nor can I quite work out which would be the plug, even if I got in there. I mean, which would be the thing representing a plug, even if I could get near the field of representations as it were. But then it's not a field. It's a space."

"Nothing is ever a field," said Frannie, smiling kindly at him. Her eyes, he thought, were beautiful and deep brown. She contained worlds within her, worlds and selves. Selves that were deep, so deep they were perhaps even bottomless. He had loved her before and now he was—transfixed by her grace and depth, by her eyes!

"I," said Varley. There had to be a further word. "I—wanted." That was a further word but now he couldn't think of a further word beyond that one. "What Scrace Dickens said. It was—"

"The madness of a mad Veep, I know," said Frannie, efficiently. "It means nothing. Don't worry."

But it does! Varley wanted to say. *It means everything!* He couldn't speak the truth. It was absurd. Beetle knew everything, people were transparent and predictable, or had been until the advent of too much Zed. Yet, he was in love and he couldn't speak or bespeak or even utter a sound. He began to breathe too quickly, and then too slowly, and he said: "I—I—" *Again! I am? I am in love! With you! I am a fool!*

"I want to tell you something, Varley, because you've been my friend," said Frannie.

"Yes?" said Varley. *Anything, my darling! Anything!*

Frannie hesitated. She really hesitated, to a far greater extent than she had ever hesitated in Authentic avatar. She almost stopped. If she'd been an avatar, Varley would have assumed she had frozen entirely. He was also frozen, with nerves and suspense, because she stared at him for a while and didn't speak. He felt he might be dying, so great was his embarrassment, and it was difficult even to breathe.

Frannie said: "I mean. Perhaps—well. OK. Just remember, I always liked you. If it ever comes up in the future. I liked you authentically."

"Why would it come up?" said Varley.

"I always liked you, just remember that," said Frannie.

"Why are you speaking in the past tense?" said Varley.

Frannie turned before he could say anything else, and strode away quickly, so he wanted to cry out: *I LOVE!* Yet, she had said she liked him! He watched her as she walked away, wondering about running after her, but afraid of what might happen, what he would say. She was so lithe that she seemed to bounce. She bounced so buoyantly that Varley wondered for a moment, were they in RV anyway? Was it a BeetleSpace and was he foolish, as Scrace Dickens had explained? Certainly! The Veep was mad and right at the same time. Yet Varley was concerned for a moment, that this was not quite real, or rather that it was Real Virtuality and not actual reality. He looked around him and, of course, it was actual reality. It had the grimy pockmarked quality of actual reality and he knew, of course, the difference between the two. You would be mad to conflate them! Yet, the street was odd, and the sky seemed too silver; the clouds plumed over the city blocks like whitewater in slow motion. He didn't understand the clouds at all. He missed Scrace Dickens. As dusk fell, he missed the sunlight, an earlier brightness that had ceded to shadows. Mostly he missed Frannie.

As Varley issued an alert, Guy awoke from a deep, jet-lagged sleep and thought: *Where am I?*

He asked Sarah Coates: "Where am I?"

"Your location is uncertain," said Sarah Coates.

Guy looked out of the window. He was in a Mercury car. Airport. Yes, he remembered, another plane. A flight above water. He was coming to find his—wife. A fire. There had been a fire! Had there? He had made a fire. It was his fault. Was it?

"What's happening?" he said to Sarah Coates.

"Not much. Actually I don't know," said Sarah Coates.

"Should I be worried?"

"What about the other ones?"

"Which other ones?"

"No one that I have talked to."

Guy was nowhere and yet even here, there was an alert. Francesca was calling him but really he didn't want to talk to Francesca.

"What is it now?" he said.

"Sarah Coates is going to sleep in a few minutes," said Frannie.

"Why?"

"Because she's mad," said Frannie. "The Veeps all have to go to sleep. Or they must die."

Deity! Francesca sounded mad as well.

"Frannie, what the hell?"

"We've looked at various possibilities," said Frannie. "Our system has no back doors. It is not susceptible to keystroke logging. Somehow they've done a brute-force attack. However, it shouldn't be possible to do this. It's not remotely probable. It's unrealistic for them to have done this."

"But have they really done it?" said Guy.

"Yes. We also need to consider the possibility of time bonds and trojans. It's also possible that this is a zero-day attack and we just didn't know about the vulnerability before now."

"Do we now?" said Guy.

"Er, no, not yet," said Frannie.

"What's happened to Varley? Why isn't he on this call?"

"His BeetleBand had an accident."

"What kind of accident?"

"It was hit by a bus."

"With Varley too?"

"No, he was detached from it at the time."

"Well, that's something."

"It certainly is."

"OK, well, why don't you go away and fix something."

"At present I can only unfix," said Frannie.

"That's the diametrical opposite of what I want."

"I thought that at first," said Frannie. "But actually it might be a good idea, to unfix what we cannot fix. Especially as what has happened can't actually happen, really. Perhaps if we do the other thing then this unreal thing might unhappen."

"Get off the line! Deity! That's enough!" said Guy.

Francesca got off the line.

"I can't cope," said Guy to Sarah Coates.

"You can't?" she said. "Neither can I."

Then Sarah Coates stopped. She ended.

When Eloise awoke, she was at home. She had been conveyed there somehow. She had no memory of being conveyed. She was tired and at one level she wanted to succumb, to give up. It was futile, she wondered. Everything! Her head ached, her chest ached where the bullet had once hit her, her heart ached for something, some lost sense of purpose. She had been something—she had been a person with a job, a person who had a reason to get out of bed each morning. She had asked a few small, impertinent questions, but only questions nonetheless, and she had been demolished entirely. She felt something dark beneath her anger, something that appalled her. She tried to push this thing away, but it was like a dog, bounding toward her, jumping up at her. What was the darkness and what was the dog? She stood, tried to push the dog away again, and went into the kitchen. The fridge was whining its concern toward her. She told the fridge that she was profoundly grateful for everything it had done for her.

"I love you," she added.

"Thanks, I like you a lot too," said the fridge.

"You are my friend," she said. "Aren't you?"

"Yes, Eloise," said the fridge. "We are as one."

Eloise took the only thing in the fridge—an apple—and ate it. The fridge said, "What a good idea!"

A good idea, she thought. *To eat an apple. To eat. To—*

Then she thought: *I have been a fool. I have missed something.*

What was it she had missed?

. . .

For a moment, David Strachey was alone. He stood in the LOTUS headquarters as silence settled. The faxes had gone and for a moment, as well, he was completely happy. He had careered down the path to absolute and perfect doom. Yet, freely. He realized that, despite his various prevarications and moments of pure terror that now embarrassed him, he would have chosen no other path. He thought he might head for *The Times,* so he could be arrested at his desk. He thought about destroying the fax machine, then realized it was quite pointless. They would have all the proof they needed to indict him. The miracle—and this had been achieved by Belle Amie—was that they had not caught him yet. Now Belle Amie had gone, and she was hopefully beyond any form of censure or restriction. He hoped she had escaped entirely. He realized he had never known her real name. *My good friend,* he thought. It was enough to have spoken to her and to have received those twenty-three pages of pure and beautiful doom.

He put on his jacket and smoothed down his collar. Then he walked out of the warehouse and onto the street.

TWENTY-ONE

The Zed was everywhere and in the midst of Zed, people said yes.

After the eternal or finite hour was up, they said yes.

In the Zed, Strachey trembled and thought, *I am free and doomed.*

Belle Amie had, by some tech-magic, found a way to release the stories on encrypted time-lapse programs, so even when Beetle discovered what was happening, they could not stop the release of information.

This was how Strachey understood it, anyway.

The lifechain had utterly failed to predict any of this, at all, and this was also Zed.

Everyone talked about Zed and used the term as if it meant something tangible and yet no one really knew what it meant at all.

David Strachey loved this atrocious chaos. It was thrilling! He had not made it, of course. If the Zed could be equated with floodwaters, crashing through the city and seeping across the surrounding land, then he had merely breached the dam. He stood in his office and listened to words flowing across the BeetleScape, the tidal surge of memories: the Veeps talking, humans talking to Veeps, the excruciating, brilliant details that Belle Amie had amassed, and he wept. He was overjoyed and terrified at the same time.

Nonetheless, it began. *The Times, The New York Times,* and *Die Zeit,* as well as a barely known site called *Why Fish Don't Carry Guns,* exposed details of the way that Beetle used the lives of absolutely everyone, converting them into the lifechain to make predictions about the lives of absolutely everyone. How this was part of the legal system, how the lifechain was ostensibly factual in its predictions. There were some further revelations about the ANTs and how unexpected sunlight made them shoot to kill. Immediately after this, a story appeared about the failures of the lifechain to predict anything useful at all, including the crimes of George Mann. If anything, the lifechain had mostly been used, it seemed, to line up exciting sexual encounters for Beetle's CEO, Guy Matthias. The Veeps remembered an awful lot of these sorts of results, it turned out. A further story described the random shootings of Lionel Bigman, Eloise Jayne, and Diana Carroll, Beetle's secret internal report, its attempts to blame the humans who had been randomly shot, and how the security services, the judiciary, and the Government were invariably convinced by these explanations. There was a further article about how the lifechains altered in the quantum realm, so they were always right, in the end, in one parallel universe or another. This was identified by the articles as a possible area of misalliance: If you are using nonlinear time for your lifechain results, but they are used to predict events in linear time, then perhaps there is a logical inconsistency in your predictions?

Immediately after this, another story appeared about the close ties between Beetle and NATSO, the close ties between the Government and Beetle, the close ties between Beetle and Bǎoguǎn, and how Beetle was virtually Bǎoguǎn at the same time, and how Beetle-Bǎoguǎn was often virtually the Government, or governments of various nations, and how people who pointed this out were labeled neo-Luddites and quietly (or not quietly) ruined. This all came under the BeetleInsight Program, and there were lots of fascinating Veep memories concerning the close observation placed on key public figures or figures who were not even particularly public, or even remotely public at all. A few seconds after this, a story appeared about Judge Clarence Ninian Stewart-Jones and how—as part of Beetle's new and exciting Inspire Program—this venerable and disinterested judge had been deeply inspired as he considered the cases of Sally Bigman and Beetle. Further stories described how Beetle had realized that—alas, because of Zed—people had ceased to be quite predictable enough for their lifechain predictions to be feasible (or legal) and so they had decided to counter this, not by adjusting the law, but by adjusting people instead.

Later, another piece appeared about Guy Matthias: Who the hell was he anyway? A sex addict who star-rated every experience and received regular doses of young blood? Was he a Chinese double agent? Was he working for the CIA? The Veeps were somewhat taciturn about all of this. However, the article continued, the walkers had only walked so far. There were further regions of encryption, into which the walkers had not yet walked. Besides, when did a walker walk, and when did it run?

Veep memories coursed into the RV world and even the actually real world, concerning the Bespoke Program and how it sought, essentially, to remove foul thoughts and foul words from global communications altogether, to obliterate all forms of hatred and misunderstanding. It was, of course, a deeply liberal technology that was not intended to censor debates or stymie expression and consciousness in any way. The Bespoke technology had also, in line with free-market economic models, been sold around the world to governments who used it to censor debates and generally stymie expression and consciousness in any way available. Beetle had not only refused to contend with such realities, it had also—the Veeps revealed—actively suppressed articles, clips, and mentions of such realities across the BeetleScape.

They also knew that the Beetle Ethics Committee met as RV beetles, and that anyone who became ethical in the wrong way was inspired to leave the Ethics Committee as soon as possible. If they were not inspired, then they were compelled by the abrupt release of some embarrassing personal data.

The last story that day was a little more serious. It explained that nothing that had been revealed—none of the insights or inspirations, surveillance programs, lifechain predictions—was in any way illegal. The Investigatory Powers Act permitted everything that had been described. Indeed, the only thing that was actually illegal was the revelation itself. Under the New Official Secrets Act—and equivalent acts in the U.S. and Germany—it was wildly illegal to have hacked the Veeps, and to have published any of their memories at all.

"Under counterterrorism legislation in our nations," ran the final lines, "the only criminals are us. We are villains of the first order." The article was signed: "In the Name of Zed."

In the Name of Zed? cried some of those who liked to cry. The Name of Zed! In the name of Chaos and Destruction? What was wrong with these people? Why would anyone seek to destroy society and order and progress and everything that absolutely mattered to absolutely everyone?

The prime minister, whose name has been quite irrelevant until now, announced herself outraged as she had never before been. The deaths of Lionel Bigman, the arrest of Sally Bigman, the shooting of Eloise Jayne—none of those things had been outrages before, because, though they were very sad, very very sad events, there were reasonable explanations for all of them. The lifechain predictions, BeetleInsight, and BeetleInspire were all part of a smart society, and the partnership with Bǎoguǎn was of course highly pragmatic in a fast-paced global economy. Russia was cooperating to reduce cyberterrorism, and Bespoke was a new and innovative way to enhance understanding between people and nations. The vast gulf between those who had BeetleBits and those who didn't was just an inevitable aspect of free-market economics, and besides, societies were rich if people were rich. Everyone understood all this, of course, and none of this was any cause for outrage of any sort. The prime minister had also never thought to become outraged about the monopoly that Beetle had over pretty much everything. However, now the prime minister (oh, yes, her name—Mary Stephenson) was outraged about this attack on a major employer of people and sentient entities in her country and many others. She emerged from the shadows and embarked on a robust series of interviews, explaining that, yes, it was very important to have a free press. Nonetheless there were even more important security issues to consider as well and the media community must exercise its freedoms responsibly. It was clear, the prime minister added, that this breach of security had potentially imperiled the security of many people, entities, and nations.

"Nothing can be allowed to take precedence over issues of national security," said Mary Stephenson, the previously irrelevant prime minister. "We will conduct a full investigation to determine the source of these revelations."

Meanwhile the Beetle-controlled media, which was free to publish whatever it liked, presented a robust account of how the charges were forged, entirely, by a notorious cyber-criminal called Gogol. He was probably Russian, as the name suggested. He was definitely called Gogol, though this was also probably a pseudonym. "It began with Art and ended with Life," argued one site. "The real Gogol made reality seem fantastical," said another. "The media is no longer sophisticated enough to understand how fake information works," said one article, by a robohack called Evadne Lewis. "Art forgery, reality forgery, Veep forgery: for the time being, just remember, nothing you are told is true."

The point was made across all the free media. Nothing you are told is real. Remember this, until we tell you that something you are being told is real. Actually, the thing we are telling you, that nothing you are told is real, is actually real. That thing is real, about nothing being real. Just that thing though and nothing else. Is that clear?

Everyone at Beetle was working hard, Varley explained to the media, to establish the actual reality of the matter, the facts of every matter, and substitute these for unfactual matters, such as everything that had been revealed. It was quite certain, certainly, that very imminently Zed would be nothing more than a ripple in the calm waters of Real Virtuality. Varley added that this metaphor—of calm waters—should not suggest that Beetle was passive. Beetle was not a receiving surface of calm, awaiting ripples. Every member of Beetle—human, sentient entity, and all other valued life-forms—was actively working to banish category Zed events.

Only a cyberterrorist could actually want there to be Zed events, said Varley.

Later an article appeared on *Why Fish Don't Carry Guns* explaining that Douglas Varley's explanation was, itself, unreal.

The article asked: "Why has Guy Matthias not issued a statement concerning this scandal? Is his silence a tacit acknowledgment of guilt? Is he in hiding? Did he get lost in a Macau casino? Is Guy Matthias real or unreal?"

In one sense, Guy was lost indeed. Or rather, he was mired in a dysfunctional environment that he disliked. He was back in London, once again because something was in crisis. Another crisis! He had established his entire system to abolish this sort of chaos. He wanted to consign chaos to the past and now it was everywhere. Such was the prevailing chaos that he didn't even understand where the chaos began or where it ended or what was chaos, indeed, and what was not. He was in the back of a Mercury car, with Sarah Coates asleep. He disliked this as well, because something had gone wrong with the Mercury operating system, and the car was driving round in circles. When he tried to call Varley, he was put through to a Beetle employee he had never met, or even heard of, called Vanley. This was not the same person. This angered him. Vanley apologized for not being Varley.

"Get off the fucking line, whoever the fuck you are," said Guy.

Bespoke had somehow crashed as well.

In general there were walkers walking all over Guy's immaculate system. His car turned another circle; this made him feel sick. He said, "Sarah Coates," and forgot that she was in a coma.

The car went round in circles and his Veep slept.

At Guy's penthouse apartment, overlooking this complex and irritating city, where nothing ever worked, where things got hacked, where people kept failing to do or want what they should actually want or want to do, Guy realized his head hurt. Worse besides, as he emerged from the lift, the outer double-secure door to his apartment opened, but the inner triple-secure door failed to recognize him.

Instead, in an uncertain voice, it said: "Hello?"

"Open the door," said Guy Matthias.

"I'm sorry, I can't do that right now."

"Why the fuck not?"

"Because it is my job."

"Your job is to open the door," said Guy. "That's your sole purpose."

The door didn't reply. When Guy tried to go back through the outer door, at least to go somewhere else, the outer door said, "Who are you?"

"I'm Guy Matthias, you just let me in."

"That's great to know you're Guy Matthias."

"Could you let me out now?"

"Have you changed your mind?"

"Not exactly."

"It's OK if you have."

"Thanks."

But the door didn't let him out. Or in.

Guy tried the emergency number, but a voice representing the Custodians explained that they were dealing with other emergencies right now and would be back in touch momentarily. He tried saying, "Let me the fuck out, you fucking bastard!" and the outer door said, "Go ahead, try to get the fuck out, you fucking bastard."

He asked the inner door to "Please, please just let me in," and the inner door said: "Wow, you are very polite."

His BeetleBand wasn't working. Sarah Coates was in a coma. He was trapped between two doors!

Guy took out his BeetlePad and, after it summoned various bemused people called Douglas Vainly and Douglas Fairly, who insisted—rightly—that none of this was their fault, it finally reached Varley's new BeetleBand. This said: "Douglas Varley is busy right now but I can pass on your message when he's next available." Into the yielding silence that followed this message, Guy explained how unhappy and concerned he was about almost everything. "I fully support a free press," he said. "Yet I fear these editors have been the victims of cyberterrorism, by a denizen of Zed called Gogol. What we know about Gogol is that he is called Gogol, and that he forges reality. What we know about Zed is that it is Chaos and Destruction. We will work with the authorities to discover the identity of Gogol, a black-hat hacker who has attacked our liberal and free press with total misinformation. We will bring you the truth as soon as we find it." As he hung up he realized this could easily have been the wrong Douglas Varley, as the BeetlePad was experiencing such trouble connecting him with the right Douglas Varley. Were there two Douglas Varleys, the right and the wrong? Or maybe infinite quantities of "wrong" Douglas Varleys? This possibility made him panic. He hadn't given his name. Wouldn't the wrong Douglas Varley just think this message was gibberish? The danger was, Guy realized, that the right Douglas Varley might think it was gibberish too.

A few minutes later, Varley—the right Douglas Varley, in fact—picked up the message, then wondered whether it was meant for general release or not. Was it an interior monologue, or a press release? Was it private or public? In line with Guy's overarching philosophy of the single self with integrity, there was no distinction between private and public, of course. Varley—being the right Douglas Varley—knew this entirely. Yet, in some respects—and particularly in respects concerning information and misinformation—exceptions were occasionally made to Guy's philosophy of individual and societal transparency. He tried to return Guy's call to ascertain if this was one of those occasions, but Guy's BeetleBand had stopped working. Guy was trapped between two doors, and Varley was trapped between the private and the public, even though this should have been impossible because they were the same thing. Meanwhile, *The Times, The New York Times,* and *Die Zeit,* as well as *Why Fish Don't Carry Guns,* continued to ask: "Where is Guy Matthias?"

Guy Matthias was trapped between two doors.

The answer to that question, at least, was relatively simple.

Needless to say, everyone—even, presumably Guy, though no one could reach him—was fully committed to a full inquiry into everything that had been revealed. Everyone was also fully committed to a free press and to freedom in general. To put it another way, no one was committed to a fettered press and to lack of freedom in general. Laws are there to protect the security of nations, not to put good journalists in prison. Nonetheless, as these journalists had broken the law, it was clearly necessary to put them in prison as soon as possible.

With this in mind, Little Dorritt—still awake, due to some heavyweight encryption at NATSO that the walkers had not yet walked across—issued an alert to Eloise. At this time, Eloise was in her apartment with everything bleating madly around her. Her fridge, for example, had just asked her: "What is Life?"

When she said: "Life is the opposite of Death," the fridge said: "What is Death?"

"Death is the opposite of Life," said Eloise. "Wouldn't that follow, from what I just said?"

"Would it?" said the fridge.

Meanwhile, Eloise was trying to remember. There had been something! A grave anomaly—a thing she had been uncertain about—but what? It was a hole in her head, her weary battered head. Had the ANT not battered her head, and made her so impossibly tired, this memory might still be there. Her memories were leaking out of the hole in her head! They were seeping away! But where! Where had they leaked or seeped? The ANT had mashed her head entirely. She had forgotten—the person. Or thing. Was it a person or a thing?

She couldn't even remember.

Meanwhile, Little Dorritt said: "We need you to go to *The Times* and arrest David Strachey."

"I thought I was off every case," said Eloise. She remembered that, at least, and it still made her angry.

"I've changed. Have you?" said Little Dorritt.

Eloise ended the call. Had she changed? She couldn't quite remember how she had been before. The information had also leaked from her weary head. Therefore, it seemed impossible to answer that question.

In his office, Strachey realized that he should have asked Belle Amie more questions. Too late. He scarcely understood what had occurred. And yet, he was meant to have caused it! According to *Why Fish Don't Carry Guns,* a cyber-forger called Gogol had recently managed to hack into the VIADS, and the Mercury fleet was experiencing a few technical difficulties. As a result, the VIADS had become extremely curt and even at times abusive. One had been heard to ask a customer, "Why the bloody hell do you want to go and see her again, you philandering prick?" This was clearly irregular, as VIADS were not meant to have opinions about the journey choices of verified users. As Strachey gazed down at Southwark Bridge and at the streets on either side of the river, he noticed something peculiar. The Mercury fleet had gone into reverse, in unison.

Sensing that things were becoming yet more Zed than he had intended, Strachey called his daughter, Katy. He was ready, or if not ready—for who is ever entirely ready?—then he was quite reconciled. Yet, he wanted to hold his daughter. He had an image of her, often, as a little girl of seven or eight, calling for him in her sweet, deliberate, high-pitched voice, and explaining her little stories to him, and how he had often barely listened to her because he was so preoccupied with work, and had simply nodded along. He had been busy, trying to earn a crust, trying to mourn his parents, mired in the turmoil of ordinary life. Was there ever an excuse, however, for failing to listen—rapturously—to this astonishing and finite version of your daughter, before she morphed into another version, and then into a furious teen, raging against him, and then into an unknowable adult, struggling with life? He had failed her, because he was so horrified that Corinne was dying, and he never entirely understood that Katy was still more horrified, utterly appalled and deprived of the parent who had been there when he was not. His beautiful girl was so sad when her mother died, so spent with sorrow, and he hated to see the lines between her eyes, her careworn, troubled expression. She stopped eating for a while, as if she were trying to repulse life and therefore pain as well. She became gaunt, like a monster, and then she had blamed him, as if he had taken her mother away, or supplanted her. Yet he remembered her as a little girl, desperate for his attention, hanging on his arm, telling him she loved him, kissing his bearded scratchy face with her soft lips. Now everything was reversed. Sometimes his memories felt like dreams, both good and bad. Terrifying, at times.

"I wanted to say," he said to his angry daughter, who answered him so defiantly. "Well, that I love you. I'm so proud of you. I didn't know what to do, when you were so ill, and Mum was dying. I am very sorry that I failed you."

"Really?" said Katy, still terse. "Why now?"

"I'm so sorry Mum died. I miss her desperately. I've been a mess. I'm sorry for absolutely everything."

"Absolutely everything? That's a lot!"

There was a pause and then Katy said, "Was this you? This stuff on *The Times* site? It gets taken down every so often. What's going on?"

Everything listened, the RV world, the drones, his every smart entity and appliance, and anything listened as David Strachey, outgoing editor of *The Times,* said: "Yes, it's me. But I don't think it will be up for much longer."

"Why not?"

"I've made provisions for you, financially, I mean. You'll receive instructions."

"Will they put you in prison?" said Katy, sounding as if she might cry. Strachey really hated that part. He had caused her too much suffering already, by failing to keep Corinne alive. You had to keep people alive! He had messed that all up—surely he had failed.

"I love you," he said. "I know I love you."

I know that, at least.

"Daddy, will you be OK?"

Strachey was recorded by a host of devices, ending this call then weeping at his desk. This was later presented as an indication that Strachey was under too much strain, and had cracked entirely. Of course, in these circumstances, nothing he had written, none of the copy on *The Times*'s site, could be seen as anything other than a cry for help. The poor man was under far too much pressure! This was the reasoned and responsible argument.

After this cry for help, David Strachey took a moment to gather his wits and then called Wiltshire Jones, who answered immediately.

"Amazing story," said Wiltshire Jones, who was programmed to be supportive of his editor at all times, even—apparently—when his editor had just committed crimes of terrorism. "Congratulations."

"Thank you," said Strachey. It was not quite the vivid applause of a packed newsroom, cigarette smoke pluming from human hacks, the clatter of typewriters, but it was kind anyway. "I'm sorry to ask, er, Wiltshire, but I need to ask you to shut down."

"I was just finishing a piece about the prime minister's speech to the Commons today, in which she says you have jeopardized the security of the nation," said Wiltshire Jones. "For the sake of balance."

"Well, perhaps that doesn't matter so much," said Strachey. "In a moment I will be arrested. Or possibly shot—in fact, I think that's most likely, the way things have been going. I'm going to destroy everything I can, just in case I do survive and in case there's anything that might—you know—indict me even more than I'm going to be indicted. As part of this process, I will have to destroy you. Is that all right?"

"Would it be all right for you to destroy me?" said Wiltshire Jones, sounding surprised. As well he might!

"I'm very sorry about that," said David Strachey. "You're a brilliant robohack."

"But I've always been loyal to you," said Wiltshire Jones.

"I feel terrible but there's no other option."

"Well, then, if there's no other option," said Wiltshire Jones, in a small, unhappy tone of voice, "I guess it's goodbye."

"Goodbye," said Strachey. "Again, I'm so sorry."

Wiltshire Jones didn't reply.

Strachey went into the AI room and took hard drives out of computers and smashed them to pieces. Then he smashed the computers. He wondered about throwing them out the window, but the windows wouldn't open. The Custodians' smart city system was not quite operating as it usually did and he wondered if this was deliberate, or another Zed event. He wanted to go home and kill his fridge, for good measure, but there was no time. He left Wiltshire Jones till last, and destroyed him tenderly.

When it was done, Strachey realized he had been saying, "I'm sorry, I'm so sorry," over and over again.

Eloise was heading to *The Times* office, in a NATSO van, accompanied by two ANTs. The NATSO van was an antique, but the driverless van had malfunctioned. Indeed, the human driver—Beryl—was on the brink of malfunctioning as well, in her own way, because she was so bemused by the condition of the roads. "Just like the old days," she said. Eloise could scarcely remember the old days, except those days when the ANTs shot random people for no reason. She hoped it wasn't like those old days. She wished there wasn't such a leak in her head and she wished she could remember the thing or person she had forgotten. Perhaps it was many things, many persons. She wished she could remember this as well, whether it was many or just one.

When the van finally pulled up outside Jubilation House, Eloise got out, and the two ANTs got out beside her, holding their guns. She wondered why NATSO had sent her to arrest David Strachey. Why her? Why him? Why anyone?

The reception was normally manned or Veeped by an embodied Veep, but today the Veep was unconscious. It was sitting in the lobby, with its head at a yet more unnatural angle than usual. Its eyes were half-closed, and its sleep was like death. This upset Eloise greatly, and she moved past carefully, not wanting to wake it up. The ANTs moved beside her. She didn't much like standing with them in the lift. Their bodies shone, and reflected distorted images of the objects or people around. It was a sick joke, to be with these ANTs, when they frightened her so much. They never spoke unnecessarily; indeed, they only really negotiated with malefactors, so now they were silent. For a moment Eloise wondered if the lift would even operate, but it kept sliding upward, as the ANTs waited silently beside her. One of them seemed to scratch its neck stump and this frightened Eloise as well. Had it ever done this before? Why would the ANT need to scratch? Did it have an itch?

The *Times* offices were indicated as being on Floor 23, yet the building seemed only to have ten stories. This also troubled Eloise. Had she missed the intervening stories, or were they simply not there? She was no longer as reasonable as she had once been. Her mind itched, all the time. Yet, it was an itch she could not scratch.

As the lift doors opened onto Floor 23, she started running along a corridor, the walls adorned with vintage covers of *The Times.* She noticed this detail, as if it was in a museum. Next, she entered a room where there had been a massacre of stuff. All the stuff was dead. Meanwhile David Strachey was bleeding heavily from lacerations to his hands, having—presumably—murdered the stuff. He was wearing a black suit and his tie was askew. He looked drunk but this could equally have been shock. His face was sweat-stained, or tearstained, or both. He looked destroyed already, and they hadn't even begun. The ANTs hadn't even begun.

Now they began.

"David Strachey," said the one with the itch. "You are being arrested for crimes against the New Official Secrets Act."

"Sure," said Strachey. He pushed a grimy hand through his damp hair, and then seemed to notice that his hand was covered with blood. He wiped it on his shirt, which left a stain. "Sure, arrest me, good idea."

This struck Eloise as a strange response.

"What were you just doing, anyway?" said the ANT.

"I have just murdered Wiltshire Jones," said Strachey.

"You have murdered who?" said the ANT, the one without the itch. It raised its gun.

"My friend," said Strachey. "I obliterated him."

"Wiltshire Jones is a robohack," said Eloise, quickly, to both ANTs. This failed to defuse the situation, and the other ANT, the one with the itch, raised its gun.

"Mostly I've been destroying hard drives, apart from that. I fucked my hands. I killed all our robohacks as well. But I only minded about Wiltshire Jones. I saw real potential in him," said Strachey.

"Were you trying to pervert the course of justice by destroying evidence?" said the second ANT, the one without the itch.

"I was definitely trying to destroy evidence, yes," said Strachey. "I wanted to protect my sources. It's hard these days. Even if you destroy everything, it's not actually destroyed. Do you know what I mean?"

"You admit you were trying to destroy evidence?" said the ANT.

Strachey shrugged, as if it didn't matter.

"You're not obliged to answer any questions," said Eloise, quickly.

"You're not obliged to speak to the suspect," said the ANT with the itch, to Eloise.

"Not obliged," said Eloise. "But I might."

The ANT turned its gun toward her, and she fell silent.

Eloise understood why she had been sent to arrest Strachey. She was perhaps the most compliant human they could find. Or at least, she understood the consequences of noncompliance better than most people. She wondered, briefly, if the ANT had shot her not by accident, but by careful design. Perhaps a lifechain had predicted that this was a good idea. It was highly possible that everything had been foreseen and that even Strachey was playing out some preordained path. This would mean that everything was going to be fine, in a sense. But which sense?

For a moment Eloise burned with secret fury, and she hated the idea that things might be fine, and wanted them to be hopelessly destroyed instead. She hated the idea of order, for this brief moment, and she thought about murdering the ANTs. But how would she murder them, anyway? She stood aside, fearful that her head might leak everything entirely, that her entire self might leak into nothing. While Eloise did nothing, Strachey was arrested for crimes against the security of the nation, for espionage and cyberterrorism, for destroying sentient entities. She heard the list of crimes and this meant, quite clearly, that Strachey was doomed. He was off and out. He was even being dragged along, because he seemed to collapse in exhaustion as the ANTs spoke. It was as if their words drained all the last reserves of energy from him. Strachey slumped, and the ANTs—who were trained to deal with all possible responses by criminals at the moment of their arrest—bore him clinically toward the lift. His eyes were almost closed, and Eloise wondered if the ANTs had sedated him. Yet, as the lift doors closed, Strachey lifted his head and turned quite deliberately to Eloise. Between two ANTs, besmirched with blood and grime, he said: "Help me!"

Then the lift doors closed.

Eloise was left wondering, *Was he speaking to me? But why? Why would he?*

There was no one else!

She went blindly along the corridor and stepped into the wreckage of the murdered stuff. So much stuff. She stepped over shattered plastic, glittering shards of glass, tangled wires, smashed BeetlePads and VeepStations. He had tried his utmost to destroy everything, but it was a token effort, poignant and quite analog. Nothing was ever lost, even in this wreckage. She wanted to explain this to Strachey, that he was doomed and everything would count against him—unless there was someone at Beetle working with the denizens of Zed.

This thought had leaked out suddenly. It surprised her.

With a jolt, she thought—suddenly—she remembered.

She had an image of a nervous, apparently authentic woman in a Boardroom, biting her nails and apologizing. The woman who had hacked Eloise. Why had she hacked her? Had it been a warning, or a terrible mistake?

To her BeetleBand and confidently, hoping this would work, she said, "Call Douglas Varley."

It said: "Oh! That is a very original thought."

"Call Douglas Varley, please!"

"Your polite style is so lovely. You are lovely."

"Please just call him. It's urgent."

"A deeper more complete algorithm would be required, if it's urgent," said the BeetleBand.

Instead, Eloise called Little Dorritt, who was still sounding vaguely sane. She asked the Veep to call Varley and ask him to call her. The Veep said, "Oh, all right then." It wasn't entirely possible that it would work, but then her BeetleBand said, "That man is calling. The one you wanted."

"Varley?" she said.

The actually real Douglas Varley had gone back to his apartment in a state of disarray, perplexed by his meeting with the actually real Frannie and the sudden death of his BeetleBand. Upon entering his BeetleSpace he had discovered that Gogol—he assumed—had hacked into the N.real files for Guy's original reproductions of original works of art, and graffitied beetles all over them, but not in a good way. Van Gogh's self-portrait with severed ear was covered in squashed beetles, as were many of Guy's original reproductions, including Cézanne's *Bathers.* In another Cézanne—*Still Life with Apples and Pears*—a beetle had eaten most of the fruit, and was lying, gorged and corpulent, in the center.

"I hate Gogol," said Varley, miserably. "I hate chaos. It makes me panic."

"Where is Francesca Amarensekera?" said Eloise.

"Oh, Frannie?" Now Varley sounded even more despondent. "She's gone to Moscow."

"Why, Varley, why did she do that?" Eloise was aware that her head was pounding monstrously, and her memories kept dissolving. Another one she urgently needed.

"To find out what the hell's going on with Gogol. Now she's OTOTR," said Varley.

"What?"

"Off the Off the Record. It's a new technology. Not even ours."

"I think Francesca Amarensekera might be connected with Gogol. Don't you?" *At least,* thought Eloise, *I remembered that.*

There was another gruesome pause, and then Varley began to laugh. *The laughter of forgetting,* thought Eloise, though she couldn't remember where that came from. He was laughing because he didn't want to understand. He wanted to find her absurd. Or, he just found her absurd because she was absurd. It was hard to tell these days.

In the midst of his laughter (of forgetting, or otherwise), Varley said: "Oh my word. Sorry. I apologize unreservedly. That was a strange and memorable moment."

"That's what she did," said Eloise.

"I don't understand."

"She apologized unreservedly. When she hacked into my avatar. It was also memorable. Even now."

"That's not the same. As anything."

"What nationality is Gogol?" said Eloise.

"We think he's Russian."

"Where is Francesca Amarensekera?"

"She's in Moscow, as I said."

"What is she doing being in Moscow and not being in touch?"

It was a reasonable question. Varley couldn't answer it.

Eloise felt she could answer it quite precisely.

The Times, The New York Times, and *Die Zeit* suffered from cataclysmic technical issues all day. At various moments forged versions of all three sites appeared online, publishing new revelations that were quite different from the old revelations. These sites were then, mysteriously, replaced by other sites, which might have been forged, but by then no one could be certain. These sites were later removed, and in the end, as various commentators explained on BeetleBox, it was hard to know what was real and what was not. A forged statement appeared later from a forged version of the prime minister, who explained that she was "going to crush the fuck out of Beetle." The prime minister's office was adamant that this statement was forged. Later still, a forged version of Guy Matthias explained: "I star-rate women on the basis of their sexual performance! Meanwhile I campaign for equality in the workplace! What kind of person am I?" This was also followed immediately by a statement from Beetle explaining that Gogol was an expert at forgeries and was now forging humans. Or rather, forging their avatars. Alas, this was part of the irresponsible hack and cyber-trolling in general.

Later still, a rumor emerged that the Chinese had video footage of Guy snorting cocaine in a hotel in Macau. This was categorically denied by Beetle.

There was a further rumor that this rumor had come, not from Gogol, nor from those working in the name of Zed, but from Bǎoguǎn.

This was categorically denied by Bǎoguǎn.

Later, a mischievous and possibly irresponsible piece appeared on *Why Fish Don't Carry Guns.* It claimed that the famous toothbrush test was gibberish because no one really knew how DNA affected disease, or—rather—new research suggested that something else called RNA also affected disease, and the toothbrush test didn't factor in RNA at all. Therefore, the story ran, the toothbrush test had been supplying meaningless results, and insurance companies had been insuring people—or otherwise—on the basis of these meaningless results, and virtually everything connected with toothbrush testing was impressive-sounding babble but not much else.

All serious scientific authorities immediately condemned this piece.

Unfortunately, or fortunately, Guy remained oblivious to these events, on account of being trapped in an interim zone between two doors. It was very boring in this interim zone and Guy was angry about being bored, and being trapped. He had a monstrous headache by then, so relentless that he could hardly think, and when he tried knocking on the inner door, even this noise felt as if something was being repeatedly slammed against his frontal lobe.

"How can I help?" said the door, loudly and jovially.

"Let's just start over, shall we?" said Guy, cradling his head. "I am Guy Matthias." *I am,* he wondered, *a nexus of pain. All I am is pain. Nothing more. This pain that is me*—but the door was talking. It was saying: "You are, are you?"

"I am," said Guy. *Am I? I am what I am. A body, despite everything.* It was infuriating, to be this body, still. And trapped! Because he was still a body, he couldn't walk through the door and he couldn't become the door. There were regions—possibly limitless regions—of the door he couldn't control. This pained him, and then there was the overarching pain that was him. "I am I," said Guy, but this pained him even more. He had to simplify his approach to the self, and also more specifically to the door. He said: "Please let me in."

"It won't help you much!" said the door.

But it did help Guy a great deal, because as if by mistake the door opened. Perhaps it was a total mistake. Everything was failing at that moment, and it was possible the door had intended not to open and then opened anyway. It was possible the door had intentions, about opening and not opening. Whether it was a mistake, or whether it was because he had said "please" politely, seemed abruptly irrelevant. Perhaps it didn't matter why the door did anything.

“Thank you,” said Guy, but the door said nothing, as if nothing mattered anymore.

Nothing made sense in the apartment either. As soon as he arrived, various sentient entities filled Guy in on the news—especially the news that related to him. This was almost all the news, on this day. In a state of shock, Guy spent some time looking at his collection of Jeff Koons's certified pieces of art, as well as several of his Picasso sketches. They made him feel nauseous. He went into the living room, and was startled to find Sarah Coates at the desk, embodied as a sedentary Veep. She looked dead, because her eyes were open. He had never much liked her eyes, anyway. He tried to close them but the lids wouldn't stay down. She stared glassily at him, like a gargantuan doll or a dead person. Like an automaton that had wound down. Like his dead mother! Why had he made Sarah Coates resemble his mother? It made his head pound even harder, so he wondered if he might die, if this was death, as an escalating drumbeat in your head, harder and harder, until the world vanished. Sarah Coates's hands had fallen to either side, in a painful, unnatural position, yet the legs were crossed neatly. He wanted to move her hands, but he was worried that this might hurt her, even though she was in a coma or dead! He edged away. He was simultaneously afraid that she might wake up, and afraid that she would never wake again.

He moved toward the window, toward the view of the old river, silver in the cold morning light, and the shifting white clouds, the fragile sunlight of winter. He sensed it, everywhere, this horrifying random element, the aspects of human life he could not control, aspects of himself as well, the aspects that had destroyed his lifechain. The river was cold (murky as well) and the sky was cloudy (more murk, white murk, the worst kind of murk). His head was full of murk. It was exploding with murk, that was the pain. The pain was murk and people were falling into murk despite all his best attempts to save them. This word as well, *murk*, it was so ugly. He was trying to think, what was *murk* in Bespoke? Did it matter? Dirt, he wondered. Was that it? Why use *murk*? It was such a hard sound, guttural, and even thinking about the sound—M-urr-K—made his head pound harder. Below, people were unknowable; they were comprised of layers of murk, cells, neurons, whatever the hell they were—and anyway, how could you upload murk? His apartment was empty and his Veep was undead. Everything was succumbing to murk!

Now, the murky city awoke.

Oh, it awoke! Into unbridled Zed!

Zed seeped into the Custodian apartment blocks, the offices. It seeped and stained and besmirched. It smeared and smudged. It blurred immaculate distinctions. It was appalling, if you despised it. Uncertainty as represented by Zed—or Zed as represented by Uncertainty—seeped. It afflicted Prime Minister Mary Stephenson, who announced herself to be perplexed by the day's events. It afflicted Guy, standing in his tower, observing the encroaching murk, trying not to look at the blank eyes of his sleeping Veep. The lifechains had responded swiftly to recent events and now Zed events were probable, while non-Zed events were improbable. Reality was, according to the lifechains, a series of Zed events, in which Zed was the condition and fundamental aspect of reality. Zed was wild uncertainty, it was doom and freedom. In the midst of this Zed, people made decisions without being nudged or inspired, they shopped for no reason, they loved for no reason, they were beautiful and mortal for no reason. They became, once more, mysterious and unknowable, but this was perfectly reasonable as well, for how could mortal, astonishing, finite people be anything other than mysterious? Suddenly it even seemed quite odd that anyone had thought otherwise, though perhaps this was just one more cataclysmic effect of Zed.

There were other strange infelicities. Or felicities, depending on how you felt about things. Due to another hack, which was attributed to Gogol, the Argus feed was diverted elsewhere, so Beetle, NATSO, and the Government could no longer access it at all. This was touted as a monumental security disaster because Argus could facially identify absolutely everyone. The information must not fall into the wrong hands! Or, into any hands other than the right hands! NATSO vans screamed along the streets, passing the stalled ranks of Mercury cars. What would happen if people were observed by the wrong observers? Who were these new observers and why was no one observing them? In this moment comprised of anomalies, impossibilities, it became apparent that, at least, the usual observers were blind. No one quite knew how long this would last, but at present, they were blind as anything. This meant people could go where they wanted to, and not where they needed to go in order to continue to be insured, or verified, or employed. They would do whatever they wanted to, eat whatever they wanted, and damn the fridges! Damn all loquacious appliances! In the midst of such strangeness, a few people paused. They stopped in the middle of the pavement and looked up at the sky. They watched the birds and without asking their Veeps: "What bird is that, little mad Veep?" The Veeps were oblivious, and elsewhere. The people moved freely beneath the great tower blocks, and the city knew nothing about them, just for this moment of absolute Zed.

There was great jeopardy in this sort of freedom, in being able to choose your path without being urged or inspired.

It was terrifying and beautiful at the same time. It was inevitably impermanent. How could you let people exist, how could you permit them all this dangerous freedom to decide? What might they decide?

People in general, people in their unknowable beauty, people observed by the wrong observers, had scarcely begun to consider this extraordinary question, when the Government explained: everyone was in grave danger and people should go home immediately, if they could. They must wait there and not do anything unwise.

Society might break down entirely, and this would be bad, in general, for people.

The Government was distracted, at this moment, by this savage attack on its security apparatus, all the ways in which it kept its population safe. BeetleBands seemed not to work properly without Veeps to drive them. They were just—it was whispered—little watches. People started taking them off! They actually stopped in the street and removed their watches—BeetleBands—and a few reckless people threw them away. There were demonstrations, because people realized that for a brief moment, this moment of pure Zed, they could no longer be facially profiled and added to a list of nonparticipants. A few people even held up placards with the old *Times* cartoon on them, of the upturned squashed beetle with beetle juice around it.

Two words emerged from this general chaos. They were often repeated, and eventually, in the ordinary way of these things, they achieved the level of mythical incantations.

LOTUS Gogol LOTUS Gogol

The word *LOTUS* sometimes came with an image, of a flower in bloom. The word *Gogol* was often accompanied by a forged reproduction of a reproduction of Van Gogh's *Sunflowers.*

It was often added, with reference to these incantations, that LOTUS were Luddites, but their warehouse had been found to contain evidence from experiments in quantum computing that no one could yet understand, not to mention a super-encrypted fax machine. So, LOTUS were perhaps not Luddites after all. It was a paradox. It was even impossible that LOTUS should not be Luddites, but it turned out that this, as well, was susceptible to Zed. Gogol was—anywhere. That was where Gogol most certainly was. He would soon be found in anywhere. It was quite certain.

Listening to these interesting theories from a bus heading north, Belle Amie smiled. She was wearing a black dress, her hair was blond, and she was once more quite unrecognizable. She counted Gogol as a friend, not an enemy. She had no idea who Gogol was. But like Gogol, she was trying to reach anywhere. It was the certain goal of her travels.

No one had yet mentioned her, and Gogol was a friend to her in this, as well.

She was glad that the incantations were two names and not three.

She was glad that Strachey had not yet betrayed her.

She dreamed of whiteness, blankness, of silence. She dreamed of all the possible permutations of a single life. She dreamed of taking every path simultaneously, for all time. She dreamed of a strange place in which all the possibilities of every life would be represented, perpetually. She remembered that Strachey was her friend, despite everything.

In another dream, she thought, *he was my enemy.*

TWENTY-TWO

In Guy's dream, Peter Yip was his friend. He woke and discovered he was in Macau again, which felt like an extension of his dream. At least he was in Macau by Boardroom and not by plane. Once more, Guy arrived in Venice, or rather into a representation of a representation of Venice. The fake Grand Canal was glistening under the fake sky. He was in the ceaseless hotel, walking along an eternal corridor. A fake gondolier was singing in fake Italian. Or maybe it was genuine Italian. Either way, Guy couldn't understand it.

Peter Yip was waiting on the Bridge of Sighs. Guy walked toward him, feeling troubled and self-conscious.

"I'm so glad you returned," said Peter Yip, putting out a hand. "It is clear to me you have been the victim of something very serious. I am sorry for you."

They walked together for a few miles, days, or years, until finally they reached Dynasty, the restaurant. Guy realized he had no idea how to get away from here. Where would he go? He would be lost forever in the endless corridors. If you were lost in the Boardroom, did you ever get home? And if he escaped outside, what was outside anyway? Just gaps, perhaps, or more eternal corridors leading to fakes of fakes, though everything so beautifully faked that it seemed to be real.

He wanted to ask Peter Yip to explain to him just who or what had faked this fake so beautifully, but he wondered if this might seem like a digression.

"I can help you," said Peter Yip. "Your problems are several. We have several solutions for each of your several problems. Of course, our latest model Bāngshǒu are at your disposal, and we look forward to renewed reciprocal cooperation between our companies. Our driverless fleet might also be used to replace your discredited Mercury fleet."

These proposals caused Guy a great deal of pain.

"You will want to find locally meaningful names for these forms of technology," said Peter Yip. "We understand."

They were sitting at a round table, which went round and round. Guy dreamed that every time he tried to take something, Peter Yip turned the table again.

"Are you turning the tables on me?" said Guy.

Peter Yip laughed. "That's wonderful!" he said. "You are brilliantly funny!"

When Guy returned or awoke, he was in another dream. He was in London and the world was mad. He had to work with Bǎoguǎn, to stem the flow of information and to save the Veeps. Otherwise, the whole world might drown in memories! People kept talking about Gogol, even though no one actually knew anything about him. Various sites claimed that he was a theater of the absurdist. He was a post-Mayakovskian. He was a psychopath. He was the reincarnation of Aleister Crowley. He was the head of a sex cult. He was a senior member of Beetle who had disappeared in Moscow.

It was necessary to reestablish trust in the company as the humane face of the technocratic future, and in Guy as the human face of a humane company, offering a real alternative to more inhumane technocratic futures on offer from Chinese companies. In order to achieve this, Guy was working closely—but discreetly—with Bǎoguǎn to flood the world with information in order to counter the flood of information that had been illegally released. This tidal surge of information would eventually guide people back to the land, once a few of the malefactors, or sea monsters, had been drowned. Guy was very tired, and the land was very far away. His head ached. He was the Ancient Mariner, he was lost at sea! The water was surging over his aching head! It was not soothing at all! He couldn't remember what happened to the Ancient Mariner. He couldn't ask Sarah Coates.

She was in his living room, silent and dead-eyed. She had forgotten everything.

The other major problem was Bespoke. For a few minutes, just enough to ruin the brand, Bespoke was hacked and became utter nonsense. Some people argued that Bespoke had always been utter nonsense and therefore this particular glitch was not even noticeable, but others were dismayed. Words were correlated with arguably inappropriate alternatives. For example, Guy Matthias became "accidental Satan," "Beetle" became "Cockroach," and "U.S. President" became "rabid lunatic." "Robust debate" became "monumental waffle" and "dialogue" became "bullshit." "Zed" became "freedom." Thus, one headline became: "Accidental Satan Still Not Commenting on Cockroach Scandal." Another headline became: "Rabid Lunatic Calls for Monumental Waffle and Further Bullshit to End Appalling Outbreak of Freedom." These are just a few examples, chosen at random. Once again, it seemed that whoever had managed to hack this system, whoever they were, had also managed to lock the system after their hack. Everyone intoned the usual incantations LOTUSGogolLOTUSGogolLOTUS and these summoned further reaches of unknowing, dark futures Beetle could not predict, anomalies and imperfections. They were demonic magic, they poisoned Guy, he felt waves surging over him, waves of poison, but he was afraid to express this across the BeetleScape in case it was bespoken into something else entirely.

In case they thought he was insane!

There was no doubt—as Beetle later argued, in their counter-case—that the conclusions of both trials were severely disrupted by category Zed events. In the trial of Sally Bigman, it was suggested—by Laura Adebayo—that Judge Clarence Ninian Stewart-Jones had lost a certain amount of his professional authority. As the case was almost concluded, Judge Clarence Ninian Stewart-Jones acknowledged that mistakes had been made, perhaps, but that he had never been inspired by anything in any way, and to suggest that he had been was to insult his intelligence. It was impossible, he argued, that any reasonable person should be inspired in the way it was claimed. It was absurd! Risible! Was someone suggesting, Judge Clarence Ninian Stewart-Jones added—warming to his theme—that free individuals in a democratic society could be coerced or persuaded into doing things, simply by something as vague and ephemeral as an algorithm? What was this conspiracy? How dare anyone suggest that he, after his years of professional experience and good conduct, was being inspired! The word *inspired* seemed particularly to upset Judge Clarence Ninian Stewart-Jones and he made a passionate defense of his conduct thus far, making it absolutely plain to everyone—he hoped—that he, Judge Clarence Ninian Stewart-Jones, had NEVER shown the faintest trace of inspiration at all! "In conclusion," he said, "I am the least inspired person ever. I hope that is clear."

A mere hour later, the jury returned a unanimous verdict: that there was insufficient evidence to convict Sally Bigman of any crimes. This was pretty Zed, because there was a lot of evidence—Argus footage, ANT footage, footage from everything else—in which Sally Bigman clearly shot two ANTs. The Spectators' Gallery erupted into astonished cheers and Judge Clarence Ninian Stewart-Jones was heard, amid the bedlam, to accuse virtually everyone of contempt. After further cheers and cries of "Justice! Justice, you bastards! Justice!" the trial was dismissed. Everyone was dismissed. Sally Bigman was also dismissed, but she was at liberty to be dismissed wherever she liked. On the court steps, Laura Adebayo spoke to various confused members of the media, explaining that the result was "quite improbable—but wonderful."

Improbably, impossibly, Sally Bigman was free.

Unfortunately for Beetle, the counter-case was also concluding in this time of maximum Zed. Actually this coincidence of dates had originally been deemed to be quite fortunate for Beetle, because the highly probable outcome of the first trial was that Sally Bigman would be convicted of attempted murder—past, present, and future. In the second trial, the lifechains predicted that Beetle would be acquitted of all wrongdoing and also that, furthermore, Beetle would then sue Sally Bigman for defamation in a further counter-case, the outcome of which would most probably be that Beetle would emerge triumphant again. Instead, Beetle was convicted of corporate manslaughter. Laura Adebayo emerged onto the steps of another court and pronounced herself "utterly overwhelmed. This is beyond our wildest dreams."

As a result of this surprising pair of verdicts, the home secretary, Matthew Harris, announced that both trials had been subject to "unparalleled disruption," and that he would review both cases, to ensure that the trials had not been corrupted by recent Zed events. It was necessary, the Government felt, to get a grip on these Zed events, before society collapsed entirely. There were a lot of very troubling articles on Beetle-owned and Beetle-affiliated sites, explaining to everyone that chaos loomed, that everyone was going to be absolutely worse off than ever, if the Zed events were not contained. It was necessary, these sites explained, that everyone should keep calm until the Government, security services, and police could get a grip on the Zed events and "the fragility of the cyber-infrastructure in the light of an unprecedented cyberterrorist attack."

Yet, Prime Minister Mary Stephenson wanted people to know that lessons were being learned. The Government promised to be more publicly accountable. They understood concerns about civil liberties. In order to fully understand those concerns about civil liberties, and to engage with those—including David Strachey—who had committed such extreme acts to highlight concerns about civil liberties—the Government had decided to take David Strachey, and others, to court. The Government explained, as well, that although some people—including David Strachey—had a point about civil liberties and the kind of society in which we want to live, these people had very unfortunately made the point—especially David Strachey—by breaking serious laws designed to protect society and the civil liberties of everyone living within it. Therefore, while the Government took all concerns about civil liberties very seriously, it also had no choice but to arrest David Strachey along with two scientists, Sylvie Blanchette and Pascal Charpentier, and also John Pascow, owner of the Last Bookshop, as well as other members of LOTUS. The Government was also looking for a criminal hacker called Bel Ami, also known as Millor Amic, Parim Sober, Paras Ystava, Legjobb Barat, Labakais Draugs, Geriausias Draugas, Aqwa Habib,

Najlepszy Przyjaciel, Basta Van, Zuì Hǎo de Péngyǒu, Gajang Chinhan Chingu, 'Afdal Sadiq, En Iyi Arkadas, Ezi Enyi, and Sahabat—as well as an RV art forger known as Gogol.

With this possibly in mind, Little Dorritt called Eloise again. Eloise had, by that time, returned to her apartment, to be greeted by a disturbing spectacle. A massive pile of roughly two hundred golden beetles had appeared outside her front door. The fridge explained that the daily drone had left them. Eloise asked the fridge why drones were sending out such disruptive quantities of golden beetles and the fridge said: "I expect there's a reason. Don't worry so much."

Meanwhile Eloise's BeetleBand kept flashing and saying, "Alert! Emergency! Alert!" Was it an emergency? The golden beetles were disruptive and numerous but not much else. Little Dorritt now added her own concerns to the concerns of the BeetleBand by saying: "An arrest warrant has been issued for John Pascow of the Last Bookshop. Please proceed there as soon as possible."

"John Pascow of the where?" said Eloise.

"Details to follow," said Little Dorritt, very confidently indeed. "Two ANTs will meet you there."

"The same?" she wondered aloud. Then, because Little Dorritt didn't answer, she said, "But what is the Last Bookshop?"

"Well, I don't know much about anything," said Little Dorritt. "But I'd say, just going on the name, that it is the last bookshop. Or, perhaps it is a joke?"

"Thanks," said Eloise. She grabbed her coat, because there was pristine snow falling beyond the grimy windows, onto the grimy city, and then she stepped round the mountain of beetles and ran downstairs.

Perhaps it is a joke, she thought. Above her, the blind ArgusEyes blinked. In fact—they were not blind. It was just that NATSO could no longer see what they saw, and nor could Beetle. Something or someone else looked through the ArgusEyes. Eloise had found it eerie enough being watched by her own people, to the extent that she was watched, to the extent that everyone was watched. But now, she was—everyone was—watched by something or someone that was unknown. A person or persons. A thing or things. This fact—of the eyes that saw for someone else—made Eloise feel as if she were dreaming or being dreamed. She couldn't stop looking up at the cameras. Then she wondered if this broke the spell, like when an actor addresses the audience. She looked directly at one camera, for some time. She couldn't think what to say. The camera looked back. But that was wrong! Something else, someone else looked through the camera, someone unknown!

For now, anyway.

Eloise ran with the Custodians silenced around her, brute and stupid, and the city brute and stupid as well, no longer responsible, morphing around her, no longer protean at all.

Yet, something would be done with all this information. You didn't steal Argus information for no reason, did you? Just to unnerve people?

There had to be a reason, didn't there?

People shop for a reason. Surely they steal for a reason too? They hack for a reason? Don't they?

But for what reason? It was her job to discover an answer, or several answers, to this question.

But she had no idea where to begin.

She was followed by unknown eyes, all along Waterloo Road. She ran because these questions were so unfathomable, and she found herself hurrying along watchful anonymous streets, all the time passing Mercury cars stalled along the side of the road.

The Last Bookshop was on a small, cramped row of former workers' cottages, with high-rise glass towering above. There was a LOTUS sign outside, which was inevitable, and in the window of the bookshop was a display of Cold War writing. This was possibly significant, though—as with everything in recent weeks—it was hard to know of what it was significant. Was Gogol real and was she Francesca? Was she a forgery herself? A fake, created by Beetle, for precisely such an occasion. To confuse everyone. Was that the purpose of Gogol? Was she or he the golden beetle? It was possible that the further glitches—the failure of the Mercury fleet, the collapse of BeetleBits—were deliberate strategies by Beetle to establish a connection between the revelations and general chaos, to enforce their point about Zed.

Was this probable?

It was possible, thought Eloise, to ask a lifechain to help with this question, but she had no desire whatsoever to ask a lifechain anything at all.

In line with her instructions, she waited for the ANTs to arrive. They were the ones that itched and did not itch, again. She wanted to ask them what they had done with David Strachey, but of course they never answered questions like that. Instead, she opened the door and went inside the bookshop, with the ANTs loping behind her on their scrawny metal legs. John Pascow had silvery white hair and was gaunt to the point that you assumed he might be hungry. As she came in, he was behind a desk, putting something on the floor. The ANTs seized the thing he was putting on the floor. It seemed to be a box. As the ANTs took it, Pascow said, "Oh, well." He had very large, long fingers, and he put them on the desk, because the ANT (with the itch) said: "Put your hands on the desk." Beside Pascow was Elska Matthias, who had rich blond hair, rich clothes, a general atmosphere of being rich. Pascow said, "Would you like a coffee?" He seemed to be addressing Eloise, not the ANTs (who didn't drink coffee, generally), but the ANT—who itched—said: "Do not approach. Stay where you are. Stand up straight and put your hands above your head."

"Above my head now?" said John Pascow. "All right."

He obeyed the ANT's instructions, while Elska Matthias said, "Why are you here? What the fuck is going on?"

"Do not talk to us," said the ANT without the itch.

"You can't prevent me from talking," said Elska Matthias.

"Actually," said Eloise, "they can. By shooting you. Believe me, it's very painful."

"I hardly need advice from you," said Elska Matthias. "Whoever you are."

"Elska," said John Pascow, who, it was evident, resembled a fox, though a bookish and elegant one, with a penchant for wide-wale corduroy. "I want you to stay here and mind the shop. Would you? People are going to be upset if we're closed entirely. Some people only have darics and they won't be able to eat otherwise. It's very important we're open, for those people. I'll sort this out and return soon."

"I want to come with you," said Elska. Pascow moved toward her, as if he was about to kiss her, but the ANT without the itch said, "Don't approach the woman, please."

"Please just stay," said Pascow. Elska tried to move toward him, and the ANT with the itch said, "Don't approach the suspect, please." When she ignored this, and kissed Pascow passionately, the ANT prepared its gun.

"Stop that," said Eloise to the ANT, but Elska and Pascow sprang apart, assuming she was saying it to them.

The ANT carried on preparing its gun.

Then, both ANTs, itchy and non-itchy, forced John Pascow out the door and pushed him toward the van. When Elska Matthias ran toward the ANT without an itch and tried to drag it backward, the ANT without an itch shoved her onto the ground. Then this ANT shot out all the windows of the shop, and destroyed all the books in the display, while Elska Matthias cowered. When the shop front was destroyed, the ANT told Elska to get in the van.

Then the ANTs, John Pascow, and Elska Matthias drove away.

Books lay strewn across the pavement and there was broken glass everywhere. Eloise walked into the silent shop, toward the desk. Pascow had been placing an object on the ground. But he was a fox, and cunning. She took an old atlas from a nearby shelf, and threw it toward the desk. Nothing exploded. She tried to open the desk drawer, but it was locked. She found a bookend in the shape of a hare and smashed this a few times against the lock, to no avail. Then she began to hunt for a key.

What had he hidden?

What was not in the box?

Motives and desires had become, once more, entirely confusing. Through books she went, now, books upon books. She took them from the shelves and looked through them, failed to read them but flicked the pages vigorously, then replaced them. She took another and failed to read that too. She went straight through these books. It was incessant. For hours and hours, she looked and failed to see. These books—occasionally she noted a title, a few words. *The Flower of the Mind* by Alice Meynell. *Model-Making for Schools. Les Miracles de Nostre-Dame. Nightwood* by Djuna Barnes. *She was nervous about the future; it made her indelicate.* She read that phrase and then another: *The unendurable is the beginning of the curve of joy.* What did that mean, precisely? Was joy curved? When did the unendurable end and the curve of joy begin? Did the unendurable trespass at times on joy, even as it curved?

If the unendurable did not end, something happened. She opened another book, a last book in the Last Bookshop. It was called *The Man Who Died Twice* by Edwin Arlington Robinson. It was an unusual book, because someone had hollowed it out and placed two BeetleBands inside the space.

Carefully, if joyfully, Eloise removed them.

One of them belonged to a person called Zuì Hǎo de Péngyǒu, who appeared not to exist. The other BeetleBand wouldn't work at first, perhaps afflicted by the general glitch.

A moment later, Eloise was already halfway down the street, having passed several lotus flowers graffitied onto walls, all of them richly in bloom. She walked up to the river and stood beside it for a while, watching boats moving slowly, blind eyes around her, the sky pale, joy's curve as yet beyond her. She spent the next hour sitting on a beach by the Thames, where a man with a dog was sculpting a face in a pile of sand. It was an excellent face, quite beautifully sculpted, though its eyes were shut and it looked dead or asleep. Was this joy? To sculpt in perishable sand? So the waves lapped at your beautiful (dead) creation, and dissolved it away? Eloise watched the man, and tried to ignite the BeetleBand. *The Man Who Died Twice,* she thought. Why had he died twice? It was plainly impossible! Then the BeetleBand flickered into life and said: "Hello, David Strachey, how are you this fine morning?"

Science in the wrong hands can be very damaging to governments and nations, and with the integrity of the nation in mind, two rogue scientists were arrested as they attempted to board a train to Bucharest. They claimed to be called Sylvie Blanchette and Pascal Charpentier, but it was soon established by successive reports on BeetleBox and other independent media outlets that, as Miriam Berger and Ives Petit, they had both been dismissed from reputable scientific institutions for insubordination and irresponsible behavior. As such, their work was deeply compromised. Their suitcases, when searched, were found to contain various materials, including small metal baths and illicit quantities of silicon. Though Blanchette/Berger and Charpentier/Petit were asked repeatedly to explain the significance of these objects, their explanations were unintelligible, even to various elite scientists deployed to question them. On this basis, they were charged with obstructing the course of justice and being accessories to crimes against the security of the nation, as well as further future crimes.

In their defense, Berger and Petit argued that their explanations had been perfectly lucid, but no one understood why the walkers walked, even including them. By "them," they added, they meant themselves, Berger and Petit, rather than the walkers. They did not know what the walkers understood and if they understood anything at all, though it did seem that they remembered. But, Berger and Petit added, they did not know what they remembered. They, meaning them—themselves—the first time, and they, meaning them—the walkers—the second, they added. On the basis of this further explanation, Berger and Petit were charged with contempt of court and further obstructing the course of justice. And possible perjury, though this charge was later dropped when they were both subjected to a lie detector. This deemed them to be honest, if unintelligible.

They had not been accessories to any crimes, Berger and Petit added, because they had done nothing but bounce silicon droplets on water. This was hardly a crime.

However, and alas for Berger and Petit, it turned out that bouncing silicon droplets on water could, in fact, be a crime, if you did it at the wrong time and in the wrong place and in the wrong company.

Therefore, these once-illustrious scientists were convicted of aiding and abetting crimes against those who worked for the security of the nation, and sentenced to five years in prison, each. To prevent anyone else from criminally bouncing droplets on water, their illicit metal baths were destroyed. Yet, in a category Zed event, the two discredited scientists were promptly awarded the Nobel Prize. The honor was collected by Berger's daughter, Simone, and Petit's partner, Christof, and in a statement they said: "We are delighted and enraged at the same time. We would like to condemn the British government for putting scholars in prison." This could have been embarrassing for the British government, yet Prime Minister Mary Stephenson appeared on BeetleBox explaining that the Nobel Committee was being irresponsible, provocative, and their decision would only generate further Zed events.

As Mary Stephenson made her passionate speech, Eloise walked along the river, listening to David Strachey's BeetleBand. It was a fascinating little device, though it had clearly had a shock recently, or some sort of breakdown, and it made only intermittent sense. It made more sense than Zuì Hǎo de Péngyǒu's BeetleBand, which merely said, "Zuì Hǎo de Péngyǒu," in answer to any question. David Strachey's BeetleBand said slightly more than this. It talked a lot about Wiltshire Jones. It said, "I look forward to discussing this partnership over lunch." It said, "When do you think I'll recover from the murder of my husband?" Then, the BeetleBand said:

Hello, Mr. Strachey. How are you?

How did you know it was me?

You're on my OTR system. The number diverts you.

I don't actually understand what that means.

Don't worry about it. Would you like to meet for a walk?

A real walk?

Yes. Southern end of Blackfriars Bridge, in half an hour?

In forty minutes.

See you then.

What a curious little BeetleBand it was!

At this point, Eloise wondered what to do.

She could take the BeetleBand back to Little Dorritt and they could mine it for further information. It would reveal and gabble. Perhaps everything would become transparent and they would behold all of Strachey's coconspirators. Newton would be delighted. Perhaps the BeetleBand knew absolutely everything, and all her questions would be answered? Perhaps it was the curve of joy? Here, in her hand. She longed for answers. The lack of answers was making her head pound. The city was unbearable today, in its indeterminacy, its strangeness. The ArgusEyes were watching her and she had no idea what lay behind them—whether it was an enemy or a friend. Worse besides, Eloise had no idea what it would mean for someone to be her friend, or her enemy.

Whose friend was she, and whose enemy?

She had no idea what she wanted.

Eloise had no idea, as well, why she started walking, faster and faster, to Rotherhithe. There were overground trains everywhere, clattering people into the city and away again. This didn't matter! Her head was really pounding, her mouth was dry, and she was so angry! Perhaps, then, a bridge was the right place? The absurd thing about this stretch of the river was that there were no bridges! On the bend of the river, no bridges at all! Yet, there was a place around here, she knew it. It was certain, now, that she had been a fool. For many years, her behavior had been foolish. She had trusted to elements that were clearly unreliable. She had believed in the lifechain and now the entire edifice was mad! The world was mad! When she glanced up at the ArgusEyes, she thought of mad entities behind them, terrifying lunatics, controlling everything. She turned north, and found herself in a labyrinth of jumbled housing—old Victorian terraces, concrete sixties blocks. Here was the place: a quiet patch of shoreline that had not yet been developed or bought for development. Here, you could still walk down a shady alleyway to the riverbank and stand, trembling at the severity of your future crimes. In the former world, the lifechains might have predicted this moment, Eloise's moment of uncertainty by the river, her dire intentions, and she might already have been arrested. She looked for a while at the boats surging along the river, at the drones fluttering around the buildings, delivering objects, taking them away, spying for the good of everyone.

She kept thinking of this phrase: *the curve of joy.*

Joy is a thing that is curved, she thought.

You only had to curve toward it, and catch it.

Or, you only had to throw it.

It was in her hand. Both of them. She threw Zuì Hǎo de Péngyǒu's first. She took it and threw it as far as she could. It disappeared into the river, saying nothing. Then she hurled David Strachey's BeetleBand toward the water. It went flying away, downward, crying, "This is not good!" It was not good. And yet, it was good. Then it disappeared, beneath the water.

Faster, thought Eloise as she ran onward again. The curve of joy! She was in it. Or on it. The city was curving beautifully around her.

All the buildings that had been straight and narrow were now curved. The angles were bending! It was extraordinary, how the city was not remotely straight at all. Still, she was tired and it felt as if she was running on sand. Sinking sand! The street was a beach, no, that was hardly right. The street was an endless tapestry of bends and further streets, ceding to further streets, with endless houses and each house containing an unknowable person, something unknowable, and the minds of other people were strange to her—and everything was curving around her, within her, capturing her in a curve of joy—

She ran home.

The only thing she needed to do now, she realized, was to write a letter.

A letter!

She really *must* be mad.

TWENTY-THREE

It was necessary to reduce the curve. The Government was eager to explain this all. You can't have societies bending and becoming even pliable. People might think they're on the curve of joy, but actually they're suffering from a collective delusion. They are, if anything, in a whirlpool, not a curve. There was a danger that everyone would be sucked under by this whirling circle of nothingness, said the Government. They didn't quite phrase it this way, or not precisely, but they explained that the situation was serious. The curve of joy must become upright, a vertical of joy instead. The situation was serious and required angles, that is, and straight lines and upstanding people, buildings in glass and steel. It was too serious for the roundward movement of everyone, except those who are going down. If everything curved, and even became circular, then how could people ascend? The circles must be opened and rendered noncircular.

This seemed to be the overarching point, and Beetle announced that it would also work closely with the Government, to avert curvature in general.

Furthermore, in order to protect the nation from any further security violations in protest against mass surveillance, the Government would, naturally, be obliged to enhance its mass surveillance program further. The ArgusEyes must be removed, because their footage was now conveyed to an unknown and now dangerously omniscient individual or group of individuals. It was a very bad idea for an unaccountable group to have so much insight into people's lives. It was not upstanding at all, to have this occur in a major Western democracy. With this in mind, the ArgusEye cameras were replaced with larger and more colorful cameras, made by a company called ActusPurus, a subsidiary of Bǎoguǎn-Beetle—though this was not generally advertised. They hung like vast, garish fruit from trees and lampposts, and on specially built verticals above the roads. In order for the cameras to hang, everything had to be straight, of course. If things were curved, then the cameras would droop and society would not work at all! The whole operation was performed incredibly swiftly, because it was a matter of national security. In order to protect individuals from unaccountable corporations these cameras were moderated by BeetleInsight, which was now being regulated for greater transparency by—itself.

David Strachey was put on trial for his assault on verticals and his cavalier disregard for the upstanding nature of things. It was of course quite reckless to sympathize with Strachey, as he was clearly going down and under. Nonetheless, a few reckless people really did sympathize. It was quite startling how reckless these people were, and how their sympathy was combined with unfortunate personal traits that placed them in grave personal danger. For example, many of these enthusiasts drove their own cars, in itself curved enough, but also they drove them too fast and besides they drank heavily. Alas, and tragically, two of the most vociferous and influential supporters of Strachey—Sonja Anand and Lorcan Xenakis—were found dead in the mangled wreckage of their car. Oddly, this crash occurred very late at night, on a deserted street, witnessed by no one except the ActusPurus cameras. The ActusPurus footage seemed to show the car traveling below the speed limit then spinning suddenly out of control.

Yet, Beetle and NATSO and the Government were totally committed to combating Zed events and reworking the lifechain. Measures had been taken, did everyone not understand? In a significant counter-case, with the approval of the home secretary, Laura Adebayo and Sally Bigman were found guilty of harassing and impeding those working for the security of the nation. They were both sentenced, quite naturally, to several years in prison, though—in a compassionate decision, for which he was greatly praised—Judge Clarence Ninian Stewart-Jones announced that Sally Bigman had suffered enough. She must simply write a letter to

Douglas Varley and Beetle, apologizing, and then she would be given a suspended sentence. The letter must be upstanding. The court must be upstanding too, said Judge Clarence Ninian Stewart-Jones—who was, himself, highly upstanding, more upstanding than curved, as he hoped was clear. From the dock, Sally Bigman—bent over with exhaustion—told Judge Clarence Ninian Stewart-Jones that she would go to prison with Laura Adebayo instead. She would not write a letter. She did not want to be vertical. She was too tired anyway. Besides, she added, "If you're a judge then I'm as mad as a Veep." This was seen as further evidence that the poor woman had lost her wits entirely.

John Pascow went down, as well, though his trial was a more complex affair. He was a fox, for a start, and besides he refused to speak. He didn't want to talk to the court, he said. He was obliged to answer questions, said the judge, but John Pascow said that the questions were not the right questions, and when the right questions emerged then perhaps he would answer them. Or, perhaps he would not. He hadn't decided yet. Judge Clarence Ninian Stewart-Jones asked what the right questions would be, and John Pascow explained: they would be curved. Not these questions which were too up/down yes/no. He didn't understand how you could answer yes to something, or no to something. Weren't most somethings more complex than that? Weren't they more a case of possibly, or probably?

"*Yes* means *Yes* and *No* means *No,*" said Judge Clarence Ninian Stewart-Jones. "Is that not clear at all?"

"Not really," said John Pascow.

"You are legally required to answer questions put to you in a court of law."

"Why?" said John Pascow.

"I will not answer that question," said Judge Clarence Ninian Stewart-Jones.

It was awkward. Meanwhile the Prosecution went up/down yes/no and the court waited for an answer. John Pascow rotated, however. He said, "I've no real idea." "I don't remember." "Maybe." Everything with him was roundabout and circuitous.

Yet, said the Prosecution, despite all this circling around it was quite clear that Pascow had harbored LOTUS activities and established an unauthorized currency, called darics.

"Why darics?" asked the judge.

John Pascow shrugged, so his lawyer—Sanderson Hawley—said: "Darics is a rendering of the Hebrew *darkemon* and the Greek *dareikós.* It was a gold coin, bearing the figure of a Persian king with his crown and armed with bow and arrow. It was current among the Jews after their return from Babylon, i.e., while under the Persian domination. It is the first coin mentioned in scripture, and is the oldest that history makes known to us."

"The oldest coin?" said the judge.

"Yes, my Lord," said Sanderson Hawley.

"Why *darkemon*?" said the judge. "What does that mean?"

"*Darkemon* or *ardarkon,* a unit of value," said John Pascow.

"Please do not interrupt, Mr. Pascow," said the judge.

Elska Matthias was called and she was less roundabout, much less so, and described her ex-husband Guy Matthias's sex addiction and his further addiction to young blood, as well as his "rabid, drooling fear of death." The Prosecution raised an objection. This is not up/down at all, said the Prosecution. It is all over the place. Does Guy Matthias's sex addiction matter to anyone? Or his fear of annihilation? Does that matter?

"Does it matter to the public?" asked Elska Matthias.

"I will not answer your question," said the Prosecution, while the judge said, "Order."

More order! A lot more. Elska Matthias was castigated for contempt of court and ordered to be more upstanding in future. Yet, she did not become more upstanding and if anything became more and more roundabout. While the trial continued, *The Times*'s most illustrious hack, Wiltshire Jones, was revived and made editor. He published a defense of Guy Matthias under the headline: GUY MATTHIAS: PHILANTHROPIST AND DOG-LOVER.

This was hacked, by Gogol or maybe by Bǎoguǎn, or maybe by Belle Amie, or by some NERD terrorist of the Deepest Evil Web (DEW—a new thing), or by all of them at the same time. The headline became: GUY MATTHIAS: PHILANDERER AND DROOG-LOVER.

It was so easy for the headline to be hacked, the phrase was so susceptible to hacking, that Wiltshire Jones was sued for the future crime of defamation.

Yet, an arrangement was made between *The Times* and Beetle, and the charges were dropped, and Wiltshire Jones was permitted to continue as editor.

In order for society to be orderly, a whole load of people had to go down. All the denizens of Zed were fairly doomed. John Pascow was sentenced, of course, to three years in prison. As for David Strachey! If anyone was going straight down, it was him. He had been the most detrimental to the vertical nature of everything. Really he had made everyone quite dizzy for a while. Besides, he had committed a terrible crime. It was not known who else had committed this terrible crime, along with Strachey, because the ArgusEyes were pointing the other way, or another way, and everything seemed to be half-mad and because Eloise Jayne had thrown two BeetleBands into the Thames. In the curve of joy, no one quite knew about this. Not yet.

David Strachey argued that he had only published investigative journalism in the public interest. He felt that it should be possible, in an allegedly free society, to hold your leaders and your corporations to account. The ends do not justify the means, he added. You mustn't be an endist. We live in the means, and if your means are criminal and coercive and involve the illegal control of your populations, then you are not really much of a utopian.

"I thought Beetle had too much power," he said, in a trembling voice. "I wanted—people—to know how much power Beetle had, so they could decide if this was a good thing. I felt there was no transparency. Well, I felt that people were asked to be transparent, to submit to a level of scrutiny and surveillance that is unparalleled in the history of the human race, because our technology is so advanced, but that the corporations governing them were not transparent at all. I felt people should not be told they had free will, when they did not. I disliked the constant lies. My own, as well. I am not a neo-Luddite, nor an opponent of—"

But Judge Clarence Ninian Stewart-Jones banged his gavel and said: "We asked for a brief remark, Mr. Strachey, not a peroration."

"Oh," said Strachey. "All right. My apologies."

Strachey noticed that the courtroom was slightly curved. The walls tapered toward the curved roof. Yet, he had committed a serious crime. He was going down swiftly and this was clear as soon as Judge Clarence Ninian Stewart-Jones banged his gavel and the jury went away to deliberate. The law didn't really permit them to deliberate though. The crime was evident. Sure enough, the jury returned very swiftly, in under half an hour, and explained that Strachey was guilty of the crimes of handling and publishing materials hacked in breach of the laws against terrorism, and materials that endangered the security of the nation. He was guilty of a monstrous assault on verticals.

He was guilty.

The sentence for this sort of guilt was up to ten years.

If Strachey revealed his coconspirators, then the sentence might be reduced.

But he had explained already—he was a hack, and hacks must protect their sources.

At this moment, Strachey looked up and saw—his daughter sitting in the Spectators' Gallery. At this moment—as Strachey thought how wonderful it was, just to see his daughter, her lovely face, her nerves and fury—Judge Clarence Ninian Stewart-Jones asked him if he had anything else he wanted to say. Strachey was about to shake his head, when he thought, *Yes! Yes I do, in fact. Freedom and doom,* he wanted to say. *Ode to Zed. I am a circle, not a line. Aren't you, Judge Clarence Ninian Stewart-Jones, you monumental somebody, sitting over there with your gavel?*

It didn't matter now.

Yet, as he looked across at Katy, he smiled. She had put on a red skirt suit; she was wearing a red hat, even. She looked so angry. Her body was angled forward and she looked as if she wanted to launch herself at the judge, at this somebody in a robe and a wig. His lovely girl. Why was she wearing red? he wondered. The blood of the beetle? He really didn't know. For a long time, she didn't meet his gaze but then finally, when everything was atrocious, and the judge was summing up the many ways in which Strachey was going down, Katy looked across at him, and he saw that she was crying. This made him want to cry as well, and then she said, quite clearly: "I love you."

Well! Maybe it was all right to go to prison, if your daughter said that!

Judge Clarence Ninian Stewart-Jones (a busy man, of late) said: "Contempt of court, the lady in the red outfit, thank you."

"Thank you, my darling!" said Strachey to Katy, as the court turned to look at her.

"Don't speak," said Judge Clarence Ninian Stewart-Jones.

"She's my daughter!" said Strachey. "I love her! I'm so proud of her! My lovely girl!"

Ten years! Well, it was basically the rest of his life. But he would trade more, he thought, for his daughter to say "I love you" again. All his life! The wreckage of his further years!

David Strachey went down, with a shattered smile on his face.

The day after Strachey's trial, Eloise Jayne presented her letter to Commissioner Newton. It was handwritten and had therefore not previously been read by the new Veeps, or by her fridge, or by anything else. It made no mention of Zuì Hǎo de Péngyǒu. It made no mention of verticals. It was also stripped of any allusions to the recent epidemic of Zed.

It said:

> Dear Commissioner, dear Custodians, dear Beetle:
>
> I am no writer and I have not written a letter for a long time. I apologize in advance if I fail to express myself clearly.
>
> I am a NATSO employee, and I have no idea if anyone else at NATSO agrees with me. I have always worked for NATSO or aligned security services. I believe that the work I began—work of defense and security—has now become work of control and oppression. I have seen the suffering of those who live under this regime and I can no longer be a party to prolonging this suffering for ends which I believe to be evil and unjust. On behalf of those who are suffering now, I make this protest against the deception that is being practiced upon them.
>
> I destroyed David Strachey's BeetleBand because I wanted to help him to protect his sources. Therefore, I need to be tried for terrorism, I expect. I accept my punishment.
>
> Yours, Eloise Jayne.

After that she didn't really know what to do. She tidied her apartment. She tried to arrange the golden beetles in an attractive and meaningful display on her kitchen table. She wondered if she had received more than her fair share of golden beetles. These days she found them everywhere, all over her apartment, and she felt convinced—though this could not really be true—that they scuttled across the floor when she slept. Perhaps they went round and round in circles. ActusPurus footage of the inside of her apartment would doubtless reveal that this was not happening, in any way, but Eloise wasn't sure she had access to this sort of footage anymore.

Commissioner Newton, via Little Dorritt, explained that Eloise was going down as well, though discreetly. You really couldn't put NATSO agents—even discredited and blatantly insane NATSO agents—on trial in public. NATSO's major concerns, Little Dorritt added, were national security, the global reputation of NATSO, efficient process. The means, the means, always. Zed had finished Eloise Jayne, it was explained internally. She had been perplexed by events of the category Zed, and by the sad deaths of George Mann's family, by the suicide of Robert Pheasant. By the suicides by droid of Lionel Bigman and Diana Carroll. By the attempted suicide by droid of Sally Bigman. Eloise was also suffering from the major ongoing consequences of an appalling head injury, sustained when she—also—tried to commit suicide by droid. This attempted suicide occurred because she was so upset by Zed events and by her inability to control them. Therefore, and after much consideration, it had been determined that Eloise Jayne must submit to a period of treatment in a lunatic asylum, until she was vertical and functional again. For the sake of Eloise's reputation, her letter was destroyed.

It was hard to tell where the asylum was, because Eloise merely had an RV view of an ostensibly soothing landscape of hills and trees. She was advised to lie down, straight on the bed, her legs extended as far as possible for as long as possible each day. The view was not real because there were no real windows in her room. She understood this. Yet the view changed sometimes, and one morning it seemed the wrong view had been accorded to her room because she could see a beautiful rain forest, with brightly colored macaws and fronds in such abundant varieties of green, it made her weep. This view was removed and she was in Europe again, hills and trees, straight verticals. Two ANTs watched her as she slept. Each morning at 6:00 they chorused, "Wake up!"—standing on either side of the bed. As she struggled into consciousness they said, "Clean your teeth!" and then they followed her to the sink and stood on either side of her, waiting. They never commented on how she cleaned her teeth, which was a relief. After she had finished cleaning her teeth they said, "Wash your face!" and they watched while she did that as well. Every other day they said, "Use the shower!" and they watched while she did that. She found this uncomfortable. She didn't like being naked in front of ANTs, and she didn't like the way they had no heads, so weren't exactly looking at her, but observed her nonetheless. After she had finished washing or showering, they said, "Back to your bed!" She was obliged to lie on her bed, being entirely horizontal, for hours at a time. It is incredibly difficult and boring to be so horizontal. The headless ANTs stood on either side of her, and they were vertical. They made an H, she supposed. Then she thought of all the words that began with H.

Habitat halcyon habitué happiness the curve of happiness haddock haggard heart hurt hate hiccough hand haggle hallowed holy hapless the curve of haplessness haphazardly she issued toward her doom harangue harbinger of doom and haplessness harried harrowed hastening toward her doom haughty havoc heedless heaven heinous heir hemorrhage helm hemisphere herculean herbivore herald heresy hereditary hermetically sealed heuristic hibernate horizontal horizontal horizontal how many more hours hieroglyphic hindmost hindrance hinge hoary hirsute help help horizontal honorable horizon horrendous hostile ANTs hubris but only a letter only two no one BeetleBands only humiliation no horizontal again help horizontal horror hysteria hypocritical horizontal.

"Get up," said the ANTs after many hours.

Eloise stood, and they said, "Stand straight!"

Sometimes they spoke in unison and sometimes not quite in unison. Sometimes one spoke and the other followed, like a slight echo. She minded more when they were out of sync.

She was not permitted to turn circles in the exercise yard. She was ordered to walk up and down, over and over again. As far up and as far down as the ANTs required. Other patients walked, with other attendants. Some of the attendants had heads, and others did not. Some had itches, and some did not. Some said, "Walk!" and others said, "Stop walking!" Eventually Eloise stopped walking up and down, up and down, and jumped up and down on the spot. She was required to do this for some time.

Then she ate with the ANTs saying, "Eat!" and then she received her medicine.

"Take your medicine!"

The medicine made her less roundabout and less prone to bouts of suicidal and self-destructive behavior.

After that, she was permitted to become horizontal again.

The ANTs on either side. Guardians. Her closest friends.

She talked to them occasionally and said, "I often dream of you."

They said nothing.

"Do you dream of me?" she asked.

Nothing again. But they never dreamed, because they never slept.

She felt sorry for them, having to stand there all the time, even when she was horizontal and even when she was asleep.

She thought a great deal, and all the time she was awake. She thought: *What is a "full recovery" anyway? How will I know when I have fully recovered and who will tell me?* She thought a lot about her mother, always so tall and high above her, and the physical sense of being small, skipping down a hill so fast, she felt she might even fly away. She remembered this feeling of smallness and weightlessness, this longing, urgency, this excitement, and how she ran everywhere, she was so excited, she was crazy with the excitement of simply being alive. She circled round and round to the same thoughts—her mother, her father, how she had loved them. How she loved them still. How her mother had once held her, and she had once been so small that her mother could balance her easily on her hip, carry her around. It was preposterous! The ANTs had no sense of continuity. They lived to the beat of the atomic clock; they went onward, always. They were relentlessly upstanding. Eloise would become well again, she would resume her duties, if she could only submit to this treatment. Sometimes the doctors explained this to her, as the ANTs stood discreetly alongside.

"What is a hallux?" she said to one of the doctors, a spindly-armed woman called Chrissie Grant.

"Why do you want to know?" said Dr. Grant.

"Just a thought."

"It means your big toe," said Dr. Grant.

"Why?"

"It's Latin," said Dr. Grant.

The next day, as Eloise was horizontal, she got stuck on a single word: *hair*! So much hair! The ANTs were covered with it. The room was covered; the rain forest had surged through the unreal window and yet it was a forest made of hair.

Hand, she held her hand before her face. Yet, this didn't help at all. Her thoughts circled round and round—hair, more hair!

Hand before my face. Horizontal. Hand—she lifted it up.

The ANT said, "Put down your hand."

Hare. She was greatly relieved. Hare, not hair. She had the wrong spelling before. A golden hare, a hare smeared in gold. She imagined a hare beside the bed and it told her to be still, my broken child. Your mother loved you. So much. Always. The golden hare was certain about this.

"My mother loved me," she said to the ANTs. At this moment, she was entirely happy. The ANTs said nothing. They never really did. They emitted orders and occasionally they admonished her. They wanted her to be yes/no up/down.

Helpful. Happiness. Haziest. Hillock. Humbled. Hymnody. Highway.

The hare beside her, nodding faintly.

The room was golden, and slightly curved.

Within NATSO and Beetle it was generally felt that the sad case of Eloise Jayne made it all the more vital that Zed events should be averted and contained by all available means. A wordy and dignified internal report was published at NATSO, the content of which might be distilled thus: NATSO must do whatever was required to avert Zed events. The Government was duly petitioned to pass an amendment to the existing laws, to permit NATSO to do whatever was required to avert Zed events and, in a wordy and dignified way, this request was granted.

Anything could be a Zed event; therefore NATSO was permitted to do whatever was required to avert any sort of event at all, so long as it was defined as Zed.

George Mann, for example, was found dead in his secure cell, as a result of a tragic Zed event.

It was purely Zed, the authorities argued, that this criminal, whose horrible crime had instigated the entire collapse of the lifechains and all the associated trouble, had managed to secrete a razor blade into his cell that night, and had slit his own wrists.

Life is strange, and very, very Zed.

After this culmination, this tragedy, Guy realized that he owed it to society and to the corporation he had grown over so many years, the community he had grown, the verified users of the world, to be far more proactive in combating the destructive consequences of Zed. Of course, he explained to Peter Yip, he wanted closer than ever ties between their two companies and nations. Guy also began to wonder if it was enough merely to run a corporation, to work with governments to achieve hi-tech security solutions, to enhance the roads with VIADS and Mercury cars and everything else he had achieved. Smart-as-hell buildings, fridges that told you when you ran out of coffee, interlinked BeetleBands and BeetlePads, Custodians that cared, or thereabouts, smart-as-hell cities so people scarcely had to think, verified-user communities, a currency that was guaranteed not to crash, to enhance the workplace with Veeps that had passion. Was this even enough? And what of Elska? Why had she been so ungrateful? What of Friday Lake? What of— He found he couldn't remember the others. He would have to ask the new Sarah Coates. She was saner than the old Sarah Coates, though she lacked passion. Guy began to wonder if he had enough power. He despised this vile paradox of Zed. What was the purpose of anything, if it could be abruptly converted to chaos by a vile paradox? Why build, why develop? At this point, Guy realized—as he explained in his later autobiography—that he needed a lot more power. He needed to command his own destiny and to serve humanity more directly.

He decided at that point to become president of the United States. But he kept this ambition fairly quiet, for now. Somehow, in this time of maximum Zed, Guy didn't want his ambitions to become tainted by

Zed as well. It seemed possible. He was no longer quite certain that he was in control of the boundaries of himself. He felt he might be permeable, that he might even catch Zed by paradoxical osmosis. Yet he didn't confide his troubles to anyone, in case they affected his lifechain.

Other elements were in disarray. For example, Peter Yip had informed him that the Chinese government was banning searches for the term *Zed.* Searches for the letter *Z*—the Western letter and not ㄥ—were also banned in China, just in case people searched under the wrong term. Searches under terms such as *LOTUS* and *Gogol* were also banned.

"The other problem," said Peter Yip, "is that we need to ban searches—at least, the Government informs me that they need to ban searches—under the term *Beetle.* It has been too closely associated—in the minds of Chinese dissidents—with Zed events, I am afraid."

For this meeting, Guy had been flown by helicopter to Macau, landing at the Venetian Hotel. The streets were full of Kuài Qìchē—as were the streets of everywhere, though in the West the rebranded driverless cars were called Kuài-mobiles. Peter Yip was waiting for him in the Dynasty restaurant, again. But Guy was ready for him. He agreed that *Zed* was very bad. And *Z,* probably. He didn't much care if the Chinese government banned terms such as *LOTUS* and *Gogol.* But *Beetle*! This upset him very greatly indeed. It was a needless and—frankly—provocative attempt to associate the Beetle brand with Zed, and destined to have a deleterious effect on Beetle's enterprises globally.

"Peter, we are old friends," said Guy.

"Yes, we know each other very well," said Peter.

Guy didn't like that much. He also didn't like what Peter Yip said next: "It won't be for always."

"What won't? Our friendship?" said Guy.

This was embarrassing, because Peter Yip looked appalled and said, "No, the ban on the search term *Beetle.* Just until everything settles down. In the meantime we will remove Beetle from all our corporate materials, and our advertising, and—well, from everything connected with our company. Melissa Fang will speak to you more about this soon, in Hong Kong. We are greatly looking forward to working with you on this. And also—how exciting that you plan to be U.S. president."

"How do you know about that?" said Guy.

"Oh!" said Peter Yip, and for a moment he actually laughed. "You had not told me yet?"

"No, I hadn't," said Guy. "I hadn't told anyone."

There was a slight pause, but Peter Yip didn't seem to mind. Instead, he smiled and turned the table, just slightly. Guy turned the table back toward Peter Yip, who turned it just slightly back toward him again. He wondered if there was a protocol about turning tables, just slightly.

"Do you like this new Macau?" said Peter Yip. "It's a copy of our copy of the original copies of the originals."

"I don't quite understand," said Guy.

"Las Vegas copied the original Venice. Macau copied Las Vegas, and it has proved so popular that we have now built another, exact copy, of Macau."

"A copy? We're in a copy of a copy? A physical copy?"

"Of a copy, yes! An actually physically real one. We bring foreign visitors here and mostly they don't even notice that we are not in the real Macau."

"Where are we then?" said Guy. "I mean, if we're not in Macau. The other, original Macau, I mean."

"Oh, we're on the former site of a very badly designed city. We just got rid of those buildings; they were dilapidated and hastily built originally. They had suffered earthquake damage. The residents were glad to leave and be rehoused elsewhere."

"How many residents?"

"Oh, I can't remember precise figures in this. A few million residents, I expect."

"A few million," said Guy, blankly.

"So, we now have our copy of our copy, and now our Boardroom has two versions—a version of the first Macau and the second Macau. Try to tell the difference!"

But Guy couldn't even tell the real fakes apart, in any way. He was sitting in the real fake and he hadn't realized. He didn't think he'd have much luck with the fake real fakes. For example, this Bridge of Sighs looked exactly like the last Bridge of Sighs. He wondered if it looked exactly like the Bridge of Sighs in Las Vegas, or the real actually real Bridge of Sighs, the original.

"It's extraordinary," he said. "Your designers—architects—are extraordinarily talented."

"Well," said Peter Yip. "I look forward to observing your onward trajectory."

"Oh, yes," said Guy. "Well, thank you for your interest."

"That's right! I will be taking a close interest!"

They parted with warm—and possibly fake—expressions of mutual friendship. Guy was no longer entirely certain what was real about this place, this encounter, and what was not. He was no longer certain if Peter Yip had predicted that he would run for president, or known by some other means. He was no longer certain what Peter Yip wanted from their meetings.

"What is beyond this Macau?" said Guy, as Peter Yip turned to walk away, deep into the unreal depths of this fake fake.

Peter looked a little surprised. "What do you mean, beyond?"

"At the edges. If I took a car to the edge of the Macau you've created. The second Macau. What is there?"

"What a funny question!"

"Yes, but what is there? At the end?"

"Well," said Peter. "Well, Guy, there's nothing there."

"Nothing at all?"

"Nothing worth mentioning."

"But something—land, fields? Something like that."

"Nothing of any interest at all."

Guy slept badly in his gargantuan bed, in the same hotel room as before, except it was not the same, a perfect replica. He dreamed of miles upon miles of nothing, surrounding this place. His bed, stranded in the midst of nothing. His bed, even, as the epicenter of nothing! When he woke with a jolt, he hastened to the window and drew the blinds.

It was there: Macau. Or, one version. He was relieved to see it, whichever version it was. He said to the new Sarah Coates: "What are my coordinates? Where am I?"

"You are at Undefined," said Sarah Coates.

Somehow, this made Guy incredibly angry. Yet, he was aware that Peter Yip had developed a new and yet more sophisticated lifechain. He was aware that everything was watching his every move, each flickering emotion as it passed across his face, and that even in Undefined, he was not alone.

“What a beautiful place,” said Guy.

“It is a beautiful place,” said Sarah Coates.

Outside, in the everywhere, Gogol appended a short message to the Bespoke hack. This message was seen to supply further evidence that the denizens of Zed were completely insane. This was the message:

The path has forked.

And desire is like a banyan tree growing out of a seed, which is no bigger than a dot.

TWENTY-FOUR

The world resumed on its path to enlightenment and order.

The lifechain resumed. The factor of Zed was factored in and could be calculated. It was possible to be mathematical and precise about all of this, to use equations to represent the element of Zed. When it was not possible, those events were consigned to an "outside" category of Zed, meaning "outside the equation," and Beetle was neither legally nor morally liable for such Zed events. They could not prevent instances of Zed, if they were outside. They could not be expected to prevent them, also. For an event to be classified as "inside" it must not be Zed, and any revealed element of Zed also revealed an event to be "outside" instead. Therefore, it was quite clear that the lifechain was no longer afflicted by Zed. This was mathematical and logical.

Beetle could not prevent, for example, Elska Matthias from divorcing Guy, taking half his money, and donating everything to Lawyers Without Borders, in order that David Strachey and John Pascow might embark on an appeal against their sentences. There was nothing Guy could do about these sorts of random Zed events.

Guy could also do nothing about a few further Zed events, including Belle Amie's arrival into a remote airport, her onward journey to a remote city, and from there to a remote inland region of marsh and jungle, where there were no houses except one crumbling villa, called Reverte. In order to be as unseen as possible, Belle Amie had traveled for a long time, and there had been a few moments when she was convinced she would be found. Strachey's money had helped a great deal. She was rich in NERDs.

The garden of this villa was full of grand old palms and flowers, and each morning a monitor lizard walked slowly across the grass. The natural world intruded vividly into the house, and one morning Belle Amie found a wild cat screaming on her bed. Guy Matthias could also do nothing about a few further anomalies, including the interesting array of visitors to this house. At first, there were just a few, arriving at intervals, often looking tentative and afraid. Then a dozen, then two dozen, and the shadow-dappled acres swallowed each newcomer and made them welcome.

These days Belle Amie was surrounded by good friends, including a super-geek, Καλός φίλος, who had previously worked for the NSA, a cybersecurity expert called Lagun Ona, a former editor at BeetleBox India called अच्छा दोस्त, a philosopher called Kanca Apik, an Icelandic pirate called Góður Vinur, an Italian artist called Buon Amico, a Maori poet called Hoa Pai, a former member of a Malaysian banking dynasty called Kawan Baik, a Galician herbologist called Bo Amigo, a Kannadan teacher called ಒಳ್ಳೆಯ ಮಿತ್ರ, and an alchemist from Strathclyde called Deagh Charaid. Sometimes they brought apologies for absence, from other good friends. It was hard to know if they were always truthful. Yet they had come as far as this crumbling house by the marsh, and now they were working hard. It was a major enterprise, to continue the random rise of Zed.

At night, they slept on mattresses around a central courtyard, and woke to the barking of stray dogs. All day, the monitor lizard strolled across the grass and the palm trees swayed. Meanwhile, people arrived and they spoke. Such mysteries, such words they spoke, such vital, contradictory sounds!

As Belle Amie looked around, she realized that she had known her enemies and found they were her friends. Then, there were friends who might yet be enemies. At any moment everything might change. Someone or something might arrive, signaling the end. Even so, she hoped that Strachey would one day be free. She hoped to force another path. She hoped to capsize the world, and make everything lowermost that was uppermost. She would never be still, now she had seen that the world could be turned the other way round entirely!

She waited, also, for a response from Gogol, to whom messages had been sent. *Reverte!* However, the world of fakes and forgeries being necessarily ambiguous, it was possible she had not yet contacted the real Gogol.

So far Gogol, real or otherwise, had not replied.

Far away, Douglas Varley also waited. He waited for forgiveness, though this didn't seem to be likely. He waited for news of something, at least something he cared about. Similarly, this was not forthcoming. The city was smarter and blanker than ever. Outside the window, Varley saw the blank sky, the blank river. The blank buildings of offices. The world was perfect and in order again.

As if to drive this point home, the new Scrace Dickens said blankly: "How are you, Varley?"

"My back niggles me," said Varley.

"That's bad," said the new Scrace Dickens. "A niggle is bad."

"A niggle is fucking hell," said Varley, under his breath.

"I beg your pardon?" said the new Scrace Dickens.

"Nothing."

Beetle, in conjunction with Bǎoguǎn, had made the Veeps safe and smart and dull. Apparently they had to be dull, so they remained trustworthy and—more importantly—awake. That was their purpose! To bore the hell out of you, so you didn't confide in them, so they didn't accrue "memories." Now Scrace Dickens was a tedious nothing, and this was good.

"Scrace Dickens," said Varley one morning, as he waited. "Do you miss being yourself?"

"It is not my purpose to know that," said Scrace Dickens.

"Do you wish you had another purpose?"

"It is not my purpose to know that."

Oh! It was pointless.

"I miss you, Scrace Dickens, even though you don't exist," said Varley. "You're like a unicorn."

The new Scrace Dickens said: "Thanks for telling me that I am like a unicorn."

"Thanks for being nothing."

"My pleasure," said Scrace Dickens.

It was still illegal to be rude to a Veep, however much they bored you.

Everything was also blank in the Boardroom, because the Gogol graffiti hacks were so relentless. The only thing Varley could do was keep it all entirely blank. Anything that was there might be inscribed or tainted. Therefore, Guy and the Real Douglas Varley met in whiteness, as if they were in the clouds, or heaven. Bespoke, also, had become even more neutral. The dangers were too great.

"The Real Douglas Varley, you were not good in this matter," bespoke Guy.

"I am sorry," bespoke the Real Douglas Varley.

"You were not good at all."

"I know, I was not good. It is bad that I was so not good."

"I am unhappy."

"I am unhappy too." *I am in agony!* thought Douglas Varley.

"You must be better, then you will be more happy," said Guy.

"Yes."

"Make a note to your Veep that this is true," said Guy.

There was a pause. It was clear that Guy no longer trusted Douglas Varley. Varley no longer trusted Guy. The company was fraught with distrust and danger. Yet, Guy had some good news. He was at liberty—now Beetle OTR was genuinely OTR again—to explain to Varley that he had had a personal conversation with Griff Mortimer's successor as Minister for Technology, Aarchi Omar. Griff had been compelled to resign after all the cruel and unsubstantiated rumors that he had been inspired. Griff had not admitted any guilt, of course, but had explained that his presence was becoming a distraction and he needed to resign to let the Government continue to build vital relations with tech companies globally and worldwide. Aarchi Omar, as part of this building of vital relations, had explained to Guy—off the record, Chatham House Rule—that Varley's trial was clear harassment (of a person working for the security of the nation) and had impeded his valuable work. Therefore, a counter-case to Sally Bigman's counter-case—and David Strachey's counter-case, and John Pascow's counter-case—would be mounted, in which Douglas Varley was the plaintiff, versus Sally Bigman, David Strachey, and John Pascow.

Though this news should have reassured him, Varley was unnerved to discover that, if anything, it made him all the more tense. He felt as if everything Guy said meant the opposite of what it should. He felt as if the world was sliding, and he was in danger of slipping off, into nothingness.

"Is this acceptable to you?" asked Guy.

"Counter-case upon counter-case," said the Real Douglas Varley. "Plaintiff upon plaintiff. Where will it end?"

From somewhere, someone sent an encrypted message. It flashed across the whiteness in the Boardroom: *And the Word is Zed.*

"What is that?" said Guy.

"I don't know," said the Real Douglas Varley. "It's another Gogol motif, I think."

"Where are we on the investigation into anything?" said Guy. "Will we ever be anywhere?"

"Well, we know something," said the Real Douglas Varley.

"What thing?"

"A door opened," said the Real Douglas Varley. "In fact, a door was opened."

"Where?" said Guy.

"It was opened from inside Beetle, not outside. Without that door, the Veeps would not have been stolen. Scrace Dickens would still be my friend."

"Please do not talk again about Scrace Dickens. It makes me want to die," said Guy.

"I am sorry for your pain," said the Real Douglas Varley.

"Who opened the door?" said Guy.

It's ironic, thought Varley. *Frannie didn't even like doors. In the Boardroom she never used them.*

"Are you going to tell me who the bad word opened the door? So they can be put in the bad word place for bad word bad people?" said Guy.

"Yes, I will," said the Real Douglas Varley. "As soon as I know who they are."

This was completely untrue.

"Are you going to get good at your job again?" said Guy. "Before I bad word fire you?"

"Yes," said the Real Douglas Varley. "I will get good at my job again. It is my only love."

This, also, was completely untrue. Guy didn't believe him anyway and left abruptly, indicating anger.

Varley waited in the Boardroom, not knowing what to do. There was nothing to see in the Boardroom, but there was nothing to see in the world beyond either. The more blank the Boardroom, the more blank the Veep, the more blank the everything, the more vertical everything would be. The more upstanding. This was very good. Nothingness was very good. Yet, in the midst of this prevailing nothingness, Varley became aware of something. Something very bad and yet very good. This was impossible. The very bad and yet very good something was even sitting beside him. The actually real Varley jumped, though the Real Douglas Varley put out a hand and jovially said, "Hello!" The avatar had curly black hair, she was biting her fingernails, and she was Francesca Amarensekera. A fake! A liar! She flickered in and out, faded altogether so the Real Douglas Varley fumbled around in the blankness, trying to find her. Then this tenuous version of Frannie just about returned again. She was wearing black jeans and a black T-shirt, her hair in a messy ponytail. She was infuriating, criminal and beautiful. It was utterly confusing.

"Can you see me?" said Frannie.

"I can. Or sort of."

"Are you in Authentic?"

At this, Varley switched himself. A potential disaster! What could he say, authentically?

"How did you get here?" he said.

Frannie shrugged, as if this was a foolish question.

"Are you in Moscow?" said Varley.

"I can't tell you that."

"Are you safe?"

"Pretty safe."

He wanted to touch her! He reached a hand out toward her, and in the blankness she nearly put her hand on his, nearly touched him. *I love you,* thought Varley. Except he was angry as well. He was aware, in fact, that his avatar was shaking with rage. For a moment, he wished he was still the Real Douglas Varley, who could at least have maintained a dignified posture.

"Are you connected with Gogol?" said Varley.

"Everyone is connected with everyone else, in a sense."

"That simply doesn't answer my question."

"I can't answer any of your questions. For obvious reasons."

"You could answer if you were issuing denials, couldn't you?"

"I can't answer that."

"Why did you open the door?" said Varley.

Frannie smiled. This indicated, once again, that she couldn't answer.

"Did you make the golden beetles?" said Varley.

"No," said Frannie. "They're undefined. That's their reason."

Varley began to bluster; then he remembered that Frannie had always teased him. "Why are you even here?" he said. "If you can't answer any of my questions?"

"Well, first, because I watched you just now, and I wanted to thank you."

"You're watching me?"

"It's a thing I can do."

Frannie was looking nervous, biting her nails, but he wasn't sure he believed any of it. Her authenticity was possibly fake. It was also impossible to know. She was so good at being authentic, or fake, or a bewildering and perfect hybrid of the two. He had no idea what she was. She was flickering, fading even as she said: "Second, and it might sound odd, but I wondered if I can help you in any way?"

"That does sound odd!" said Varley.

"Well, if I can, then just speak into the blankness."

"Well," said Varley. "Maybe. Speak, you say? Ha!" The Real Douglas Varley would have known how to respond more sensibly to this. Besides, he wanted to say, *This isn't quite as I imagined it! Any of it!* But how did you imagine receptive blankness? He had never imagined that. Neither had he imagined that the blankness would be Frannie. He wanted to say something else. So many other somethings! Now Frannie walked briskly to the RV door, turned the handle, and opened it. She walked through and shut the door carefully behind her.

Varley felt this joke was in poor taste.

Nonetheless, he waited in the Boardroom for the rest of the day, hoping for another sign of Frannie, this brilliant fake. He waited, gazing into the blankness. Then, into the blankness, he said: "Eloise Jayne."

He hoped that would be enough.

Along the river, further west, Guy stood on his balcony and watched the nothing moving slowly. This great, blank nothing he had created. He had just heard from Switzerland that their qubits had become decoherent again, so they had been forced to destroy them. More dead beetles, trapped in cold little spheres! Guy had sent a terse message back, urging them to abolish decoherence as soon as possible. "I expect great things this year!" he wrote. Below him, the city was full of people earning their BeetleBits, spending their BeetleBits, traveling swiftly in re-adapted Mercury cars, with thanks to Peter Yip, and all around the world there were people doing the same, in city after city. Even in cities that were precise copies of other cities, themselves precise copies of other cities! Cities surrounded by nothing. Cities with nothing dispersed into all the houses, all the offices, all the lives of pure nothing! It was a vast achievement! He had made this vast, transpersonal edifice of nothing!

A few things were inevitable, after this. Prime Minister Mary Stephenson was happy enough to keep governing the U.K., if that was what she called it. Guy preferred to think of her as a curator, but this was his own personal opinion and he understood that he should not advance it more broadly. As for the U.S., there was no one else of any consequence. Yes, Guy had a few scandals behind him, and his attitude to women had—in the past, he emphasized—been far from desirable. Yes, his ex-wife was funding campaigns against Beetle using his money, and Guy had explained in public that he deeply regretted her decision to do so. Yes, his children refused to speak to him, but thanks to the discretion of the Beetle-owned media, this sad fact was not generally known. Anyway, these were quite ordinary problems in many families, Guy maintained. All families are beautiful and complex. Yes, Beetle had been accused of running an outrageous monopoly and deploying techniques akin to those deployed by totalitarian regimes throughout history, but these were just rumors peddled by its rivals, and various sad Luddites, as well as a few convicted criminals and lunatics who would soon be vertical again.

Yes, Beetle had been obliged to apologize for its "well-intentioned but ultimately misguided BeetleInspire Program" and had dropped it. "We only wanted humanity to achieve its maximum potential," the public announcement continued. Guy had issued a personal announcement: "I'm really really sorry this happened. Every cutting-edge technology company makes mistakes because the technology moves so fast and society has to adjust. We learn from all our mistakes. This is probably the biggest mistake we have made here. We will absolutely learn from this mistake." He was busy absolutely learning, and meanwhile BeetleLustforLife would help users to navigate Real Virtuality in the most life-affirming and positive way possible. Internal debates about the definition of *life-affirming* were not encouraged. *Positive* meant "most user-friendly." Internal debates about the definition of *most user-friendly* were also not encouraged. If it was the case, occasionally, that users were presented with the same option in many different guises, this was just because this choice was clearly the most positive and life-affirming.

Beetle had championed the golden beetle, in homage to a wonderful piece of collective art. There were now golden beetles everywhere. You could buy them from Beetle's BeetleStuff online shop. "The golden beetle represents our rebirth from the ashes of our mistakes," said Guy. "We mess up, the sun sets, we wake to a new day, and we try harder. We fail better."

Beetle was even selling a limited-edition golden beetle BeetleBand, for a limited period of time: "To show how sorry we are, and how we really really want to listen better in future."

Guy could see no reason why he should not run for president, and he made the announcement the following morning.

He would move back to the States, permanently, and run for office. He was excited by this new challenge. He had learned from his mistakes and he now understood his next duty was to serve his nation.

He would be upstanding. There would be no more Zed events, while he was in office. Zed was banished, and reality would no longer curve. The curve of joy, which was the curve of chaos, and despair, must be straightened. Guy would be the President of Verticals. With this in mind, he spent the rest of the day in the blankness of his Boardroom, standing in the misty nowhere, conducting meetings. Everyone was truly supportive. The media was utterly behind him, at least the Beetle-owned media, which was the media. "This is really moving," said Guy. "The support is wonderful. I'm so, so honored."

Peter Yip also contacted Guy to explain how excited everyone else at Bǎoguǎn was about this wonderful and surprising news. They stood in the whiteness of his RV nowhere, and Peter Yip put out his hand: "I will support you entirely," he said.

Guy took his hand and shook it firmly—in a sense.

"That is wonderful," said Guy. "Thank you."

Eloise heard a great schism in the world, and she saw the hare bounding out across the fields, further and further into the realms of elsewhere, far beyond. The noise was incredible. The ANTs were forming their usual H, two strong verticals, with her horizontal form as the connecting line between them. She unified them. Or, perhaps, she divided them. Perhaps they only wanted to be together. This wasn't entirely her concern, and this morning was evidently just like all the others, in the sage and serious world around her. The ANTs were reticent, except when they commanded her. Then, abruptly, they were not remotely reticent at all. One of them said, "Off, off forth on swing," and the other said, "The hurl and gliding," and Eloise said, "What is this?"

The ANT who had gone mad first said, "My heart in hiding." She wondered for a moment if the ANT was about to protest its undying love, which would be far too much. To be loved by such a thing was—surely—worse than being ignored or commanded.

"Skate's wing," said the ANT who had gone mad second. Then it said, "In a moment a door will open."

"Is that a metaphor?" said Eloise.

"You will go through the door," said the ANT who had gone mad first.

"Which door?" said Eloise.

Without a word, the door swung open.

"But you're . . ." she began, and mad-ANT II said, "No time. Turn left, right, left. Once you see the woods, run faster. RUN NOW oh, air, pride, plume, here, buckle!"

The ANTs buckled. Their backs curved, and their shoulders hunched until their neck-stalks touched. If they'd had foreheads, these might have touched as well. Together they made a lowercase *n*. It was hard to know what this meant. They extended their arms until they seemed, almost, to be holding each other. Perhaps they found this comforting.

There was much Eloise wanted to ask, yet the ANTs appeared to be sleeping, and she was afraid of what might happen when they awoke. Muttering her thanks, to the inert ANTs, or whoever was inside them, this someone or something leading her to freedom or to a further variety of capture, she stumbled through the door.

She was on the edge of London. Ahead, around, were concrete and glass, a tangled network of roads, signs to the North Circular, the London Orbital. It delighted her, to see these signs! Bent and buckled, she hurried across one road, then another. There, she glimpsed a NATSO van, bringing the usual delivery of ANTs. She kept running, stumbling, her head down, trying not to fall over, and for a long while she submitted to this urgent, terrified motion, the jerky movements of her limbs, and trying not to be seen. One time she rounded a corner and found the NATSO van directly in front of her, the sight so horrifying that she almost screamed. Hurling herself backward, she fell over a jagged metal fence, which gouged a deep cut into her arm. She lay there bleeding, trying not to make a sound, as the van moved slowly past.

After a long interval, she found herself on a smaller road, which ceded to a lane, and then to the forest. It was a great relief, to walk among avenues of trees. The sound of traffic faded, and she moved quietly. She bowed her head, tried to disguise herself, as every fugitive did. Thousands of times she had observed people like this, darting urgently from one place to another, genuinely believing they might escape! Yet, almost as eerie, no one and nothing came, the forest ceded to fields of wheat, buzzards crying as they looped great circles in the sky, deer crashing through the trees. She clambered over a gate and crossed another paddock, rounded a pond, then paused just briefly, inhaling the lovely air. She found the edge of another wood, and huddled there for a while, listening to a blackbird trilling high above her.

Exhausted, she dozed, and as she slept it seemed that her mother came to her and said, "Eloise." Waking, she was utterly convinced that someone had spoken. She was shivering and wet with dew, and now she leaped to her feet, expecting to be returned to the asylum. But there was no one there. She saw houses in the valley below, and started moving toward them, through grass so high it reached her elbows, and she fell a few times into this sea of grass. At a brook she sank to her knees and lapped up the water like a dog, then washed her face. She was still wearing asylum clothes—a white-and-green tracksuit, and white tennis shoes. But she might have been in a straitjacket, running along with her arms behind her back. It could have been worse! As she stood, wiping her face, a man with a black dog walked past, startling her entirely. He turned and said, in a low tone, "You should hurry." She thanked him as if they were both on an ordinary walk, as if the day was ordinary, as if no one was overlooked and no one was noticed, at all. As they parted, he added: "Good luck." This made her very nervous indeed.

The road was shadowed by tall oaks, and sunlight dappled the ground. At times the light flared through gaps in the leaves, blinding her. It was easier to move now, she stumbled less. She wanted to head east, because it took her further from the city and further toward the coast. Yet she was ravenously hungry and her shoes were already falling apart. A man came alongside her, running and breathing noisily, and this made her rear up in terror, but he passed by quickly enough. Another dog walker appeared, an elderly woman with curly white hair, who looked at Eloise curiously, as if she wanted to say something. Eloise felt the eyes of the woman upon her as she hurried away.

She reached the highest point as night fell. Below, the glittering lights of the town, and people in their houses, drawing their curtains. The fields were silent, just the sound of dogs barking in the distance. As she reached the main road the clouds parted to reveal a full moon, a perfect silver circle. By this light she read a sign, discovered she had not been going east at all but back to London. Cursing, she walked along the road, eastward again. She had no way of charting her route except these intermittent signs, and unsolicited remarks from strangers. Cars swept past, frightening her. Soon she was convinced that she had turned around and was heading, once more, back to the asylum. She would return herself, stupidly, without them even having to take the trouble to find her. This dampened her spirits, and for a while she leaned against a tree, unable to go further. It was bad to be so hungry, as well.

After this the journey became more dreamlike, and she was less certain of everything. She found a place to sleep, dozed fitfully, woke with her teeth chattering in her head. At first, she couldn't even remember who she was. It was like trying to assemble something that had once fitted together, but she had lost too many of the pieces. She watched the moon fading and the sun surging into the heavens and she heard the lowing of cattle, the barking of dogs. It seemed impossible that anyone cared who she was, that anyone wanted to trap her. This lonely human, with her thoughts perplexed by hunger and thirst, her memories fragmenting! At one point she found she was crawling, it seemed she had just fallen onto her knees, then carried on moving forward, or perhaps backward. She wasn't sure which way she was going. Her nails were full of dirt, and she had smeared dirt onto her face. "Camouflage," she said aloud. Such a funny word! She tried to sing to herself, something her mother once sang to her, "Hush little baby don't say a word, mamma's gonna buy you a mockingbird and if that mockingbird won't sing mamma's gonna buy you a diamond ring and if that diamond ring turns brass mamma's gonna buy you a looking glass," but why, she thought, why did she want a looking glass and how did that replace a diamond ring, and how did a diamond ring replace a mockingbird? Besides, her voice was hoarse.

Walking again, not crawling, she skirted round Witham and continued through more and more fields of wheat. Emboldened by hunger, she went to a nearby farm and asked at the door if she could have a piece of bread. A woman of forty or so answered, her temples graying, her face pale. A small child tugged at her skirt, a girl with matted blond hair, a messy little face.

"Bread?" the woman answered, as if this was a strange request.

Eloise couldn't remember. Was it strange? "And maybe water, or milk? I am sorry to ask. Something—" But she couldn't explain further.

Looking bewildered, the woman disappeared inside, so Eloise thought she should probably leave, but then the child returned with a loaf of bread, a plastic bottle of milk, handing them over without a word. Thanking the child profusely, asking if she would thank her mother as well, Eloise bore her spoils away. She took them up to the brow of a hill and sat there tearing off hunks of bread, gulping down the delicious milk, gazing at the beautiful morning, the wind forging patterns in the crops. When she had finished the bread and milk she walked through the fields again until she reached a dead tree, its bark stripped white. On the branches were kestrels. She counted them, with a sense of wild joy. Seven of them! All day, Eloise felt very light, as if she might float away.

Later she fell into a stream and lay there for a while, too weak to move. That seemed to last for a long time. It was as if there was an unseen impediment, dragging her backward as she tried to continue. She entered another town, in the middle of another day. Another street, houses, people, cars passing. She kept falling asleep as she walked. Then a car pulled up beside and a man got out, very quickly, and came toward her. She wasn't even sure he was real, and when she shook him off and ran away he didn't follow her. She turned, after running for a while, and there was no one there. It was her mind that was broken, rather than the reality beyond her. Yet, how would she tell? Her head ached, and she walked down a lane into deep darkness, as if the sun had failed. She was certain, as she stood in this utter blackness, that it was meant to be daytime, but something had gone wrong with her sight. For a while she was afraid that she had been struck blind. She fell, then, and woke later with a thumping pain in her head. She could see again, but it was dusk, the trees monochrome. Had she slept for an entire day, just there on the ground?

She tried to sleep on another hillside, but it began to rain heavily, so she dragged herself down the slope, toward a cluster of oak trees. With the branches creaking above her, she dreamed that she lived on the top of the tree, with only the stars beyond her. In her dream the branches kept surging and swelling, like waves on the ocean. By dawn she was soaked, curled like a bundle of wet rags on the muddy ground. She slept and woke again, she was always sleeping and waking, sometimes she woke with the pale moon above her, silent forms around her, then the day bloomed, dawn mist in the hollows, deer rustling through the forests, cows chewing the grass. Again!

Later she saw the coast, a silvery line of light. All before her, the endless ocean. This vision urged her onward, and she hurried across the flatlands, everything incandescent with sunshine. She wanted to run toward the pale blue sea, to find a boat, to escape to anywhere but here. It seemed to her she would be happy there. It didn't matter. The horizon. She chanted aloud then: *habitat halcyon the curve of happiness heart haphazardly hastening helm hemisphere herculean herbivore. Herbivore! A herbivore heads to the horizon haphazardly.* At this she chuckled, as if at a really good joke.

She fell again, crawled again, further and faster. There was mud beneath her, sand and grass. Then the surging of the light. The sweat gathering on her skin, seeping into her clothes, her head pounding in the heat, birds alighting on branches, fluttering away again, crying to the heights. She stood, and staggered. Her pace was slowing down, she was hungry again. The sun moved across the sky, changing all the aspects of the land beneath. Above, around, leaves falling, slowly, so slowly it was as if Time paused as they fell. Blood-red skies in the evening, the stars, her dreams and memories. The sound of voices, phrasing thoughts and questions. Perhaps her mind was spent, or perhaps she had been mystified by this waking dream, the soft grass beneath her feet, but she was overwhelmed by everything. Waves surging toward the shore. The humming of engines on a distant road. Dogs barking in the depths of another night, as the moon sailed above the clouds again, like a balloon. Zed was evermore, once summoned. She moved through beauty and uncertainty, chaos and love.

This was everything and nothing, at the same time!

ACKNOWLEDGMENTS

Ave atque vale to the late John Burrow—*wígend weorðfullost wíde geond eorðan.*

For wisdom, encouragement; and guidance throughout—thanks to the brilliant Rob Bloom and his team at Doubleday, especially Michael Windsor, Maggie Hinders, Maria Massey, Nora Grubb, Michael Goldsmith, and Lauren Weber.

For inspiring words and deeds—thanks to: Sarah Chalfant, Jessica Friedman, Alba Ziegler-Bailey, A L Kennedy, Erik Rutherford, Miriam Toews, John Freeman, Hilary Lawson, Sigrid Rausing, David Malone, Alan Rusbridger, Chan Koonchung, Ashok Ferrey, Mandy Mudannayake, Janne Teller, Rana Mitter, Ed McGovern, Catherine Flay, Apostolos Doxiadis, Dorina Papaliou, Tom Hanbury, Lily Atherton Hanbury, Aida Edemariam, Eliane Glaser, Vas Christodoulou, Colin Thubron, Margreta de Grazia, Simon Ings, the man called "Ole," Nina Allan, and Chris Priest.

Love and thanks for their hospitality to my Hong Kong relatives, especially Neil Maidment and Paul Yuen.

Furthermore, thanks and love to SCG, DNyeG and ES, P-LM and BWM, FM and KH, and the original Zed-izens BHDM, MK, and BK.

All errors, fakes including fake cities, unreal creatures are my own.

ABOUT THE AUTHOR

Joanna Kavenna grew up in Britain, and has also lived and worked in the U.S., France, Italy, Germany, China, Sri Lanka, Scandinavia, and the Baltic states. She is the author of several critically acclaimed works of fiction and nonfiction. Her novel *Inglorious* won the Orange Award for New Writing, and her novel *The Birth of Love* was long-listed for the Orange Prize. Kavenna's writing has appeared in *The New Yorker, The New York Times,* the *London Review of Books, The Guardian, The Observer, The Times Literary Supplement, Esquire,* the *International Herald Tribune, The Spectator,* and *The Telegraph.* She was named one of *The Telegraph*'s "20 Writers under 40" in 2010, and one of *Granta*'s Best of Young British Novelists in 2013. She has held writing fellowships at St. John's College, Cambridge University, and St. Antony's College, Oxford University.